UNCONDITIONAL LOSS

ORRIN LIPPOFF
& MLADEN SOLAR

DEDICATION

Twenty-five percent of the authors' net profits from the sale of this book will be donated to the ASPCA, an organization dedicated to the well-being of dogs and other animals.

When the plane began its descent, he saw sparkling lights across the vast dark plain, like fireworks. They were everywhere. "Dog fires."

BIOGRAPHIES

Dr. Orrin Lippoff is an internist living and practicing in Brooklyn, New York. His clinical work and close relationship with his own dachshunds, Alvin and Alice, inspired the main theme for this novel.

***

Dr. Mladen Solar brought his technical and scientific expertise to this book project. He is a cardiologist who also lives and practices in Brooklyn. He and Orrin have collaborated on many and various endeavors.

Prologue

The world suddenly vanished around the team of dogs and their musher, Daniel Gunardson. Blinding snow now hid the distant glacier that had been his only directional, but the dogs would know where to run. Their sense of absolute space remained unbroken, even in a blizzard. Before snowmobiles and GPS and other lifeless gadgets, they had once been the only guides for humans in the arctic. Mutual dependence based on survival is the strongest bond in nature. Gunardson knew this well.

He did not know that all of his dogs had already begun to hemorrhage internally, blood slowly filling their lungs.

He adjusted his goggles, squinted, and tried again to make out the path toward Rohn. The harsh, Alaskan wind fluffed up his parka and drove miniscule pellets of snow through the shroud covering his face. Just a couple of hours into this leg of the 2010 Iditarod Great Sled Race, his beard was already sheathed in ice. His cheeks were crimson. It was negative ten degrees Fahrenheit and the coldest day so far.

All he could see was white, with occasional orange-tipped rail markers and six-foot-high wooden tripods appearing and disappearing like silent ghosts every few hundred yards. At times the blizzard dropped so low to the ground that

Gunardson, perched on the back of his sled, could clearly spot the distant mountains and tall trail tripods but could not see his own dogs. Then, just as quickly, everything would be smothered in a white, swirling blanket.

Kit, his lead dog, surged through the snowdrifts. Just a few hours ago, as the third day of the race had dawned, the wiry Alaskan husky had rousted and ordered his fifteen canine companions, nipping, barking, and nudging to get them all properly in line to be hooked up. He now guided them along an almost invisible trail.

Gunardson and Kit had a special bond. He only had to look at the dog and Kit would respond. The dog's first thought was to serve his master, and he could always be relied upon to sense the proper route through the frozen wilderness, even on a day like this.

Maybe, Gunardson joked to himself, Kit could smell the lamb stew waiting at the next checkpoint. These dogs might burn up to fourteen thousand calories in a single day's run. They needed all the rich, fatty food they could eat. He didn't stint, not for such a marvelous creature like Kit.

They took a long downhill curve soundlessly, and he watched the dogs come in and out of vision. He watched Kit's shoulders, then leaned into the sled and felt the runners tilt.

Bred to run, Kit took to the sled easily. And he was the alpha male of this pack. Kit was serious by nature, and a low growl was often enough to stop some other husky from slacking off. He was also indefatigable. Dogs can run at about twelve miles an hour in a comfortable lope. Kit wanted to go faster, always pulling on the traces. He even objected when it was time to stop. He would obey the command to halt at a checkpoint, but would soon be pacing back and forth, insisting that rest was a waste of time.

Other mushers wanted to buy Kit and had offered a lot of money, but Gunardson never even considered any proposals. He would pet the animal and talk to him, feeling Kit's powerful muscles, and knowing that, someday, Kit would lead him and his sled first across the finish line.

Finally, the storm showed signs of easing. A spot of sun appeared behind the clouds, and the wind swirled in smaller, faster vortexes. Gunardson called out to the dogs, using the brake to control their speed. Once or twice he slowed them to conserve energy. They could run up to twenty-four miles an hour but could never maintain a pace like that. He needed them for at least ten days. To do that, he had to control their speed and not exhaust his animals.

Most of them were eager, fresh, excited, and performing beautifully. But he was a little worried about Tristam, a black-and-white husky near the front on the right. Tristam seemed distracted, almost disinterested. Once or twice he actually looked away. He would have to be dropped. It was still early in the Iditarod dog race, but Gunardson knew he could continue with a few less dogs. Maybe he could leave Randi, the smaller bitch toward the back, behind as well. She was struggling to match the other dogs.

A couple of the other dogs had seemed strangely hyper before the start of the third day's run. They had growled at him when he attached the lines, and Tristam had even snapped. Gunardson was surprised by the odd behavior but had projected himself into the problem and decided the dogs felt as anxious and nervous as he did.

The initial few miles on the flat, the open tundra of Ptarmigan Pass, had been easy, a straight run to Pass Creek. The snow was not deep, so the sled's runners slid smoothly along. The dogs' paws were protected with booties and suffered no problems. Then the trail dropped steeply before it became tight and twisting. Scrub willows appeared as black images in the blinding snow. One or two caribou appeared and then vanished, exciting Kit momentarily as he strained to chase them and then disciplined himself.

Gunardson urged his team on. They made it through Rainy Pass, which, at 3,500 feet, was the highest point of the race. The dogs struggled noticeably in the thinner, colder air. Their heated breathing turned to white vapor, instantly blown apart by the wind. At least the temperature was bearable, nothing like the –130° recorded one miserable year.

The land leveled, and Gunardson relaxed a little. The dogs seemed strong, although they had slowed considerably. The increased elevation must have taken a lot out of them. He, too, could feel the effects of the thinner air. He remembered his recent vaccination. There had been talk of canceling the Iditarod this year because of the Rohn flu, but the collective urge to run was too strong. Many mushers planned their year around the event, proud to compete in the hardest race on Earth. Everyone had gotten their vaccinations weeks ago, long before the rest of the population, and no one was sick as far as he knew. Maybe a musher or two had dropped out before the start due to illness, but Gunardson didn't know anything about that. He only knew that he felt unstoppable. His dogs were racing at adequate speed, pulling the four-hundred-pound sled as though it were a toy.

Gunardson took another turn with the dogs. He needed all his strength just to keep a hold on the handle bar. This is what he trained for, he told himself. He kept his knees loose as they shot over a field of bumps. He felt the urge to clear the ice from his face with a hand, but waited. He leaned again, slightly against the dogs' trajectory to level the sled.

He squinted. Just ahead someone had posted a "Watch Your Ass" sign just before the steep two-hundred-foot hill down into Dalzell Gorge. Gunardson prayed the storm had frozen over the lake at the bottom. One year when the air was surprisingly warm, the glare off the ice and open water had blinded him and he had crashed. Mushers had even had to build makeshift stone bridges to get across the two-foot deep stream.

Dismissing any dark thoughts, Gunardson sped into the gorge and began running alongside the sled, pushing it. Then he jumped back on, held fast, and applied the brake. Almost at once the sled tipped, and he leaned fast toward the opposite side. For a sickening couple of seconds, the sled teetered. Several dogs got tangled in the effort to keep upright. Finally, Kit got the team going forward. Even Tristam was obeying. Randi, however, was barely moving. Gunardson finally stopped the team, unhooked her, and put her on top of the supplies in the sled. The dog lay there, barely breathing. When she did breathe, it came in short bursts, and her tongue simply hung through slack jaws. Flecks of blood had darkened her muzzle. Gunardson gave her head a quick pat, got back in position, and started up the team again.

Only five miles more to the Rohn Roadhouse and the checkpoint, Gunardson told himself. The river surface was icy and slippery. Once or twice he barely skirted a rough patch and veered away from open water. Kit led the sled across the river ice, onto the left bank, and into the trees. The checkpoint was no more than a mile away.

Gunardson could feel the cold bite into his wrist, briefly exposed as he shifted his grip on the handlebar. He watched Kit pull the sled to the right, following the path. With the snow stopped, everything was clearly visible, including the checkpoint cabin sheltered among spruce trees at the far southern end of the runway. Even though the run was short, maybe thirty-two miles, Rohn was a good place to get some quality rest. Other competitors could make this a lengthy stop, but Gunardson wouldn't wait here long.

His sled glided into Rohn, hurtling past the sign which read: "Iditarod Trail Checkpoint. Slow Down." Gunardson obeyed.

All that was here was the cabin and a few tents, and a landing strip made of gravel for the Iditarod Air Force to fly in food and supplies. People who volunteered to help Iditarod competitors flew in on bush planes or drove over on snowmobiles to the remote spot. Rohn really didn't deserve a name, but there was a spot on the map. That was it. The few folks who made the annual trek to greet the mushers lined the entry, standing behind orange fencing. They cheered as Gunardson and his team appeared, happily welcoming them as they would all the competitors who came this far.

The clock stopped once the sled crossed the line into the village, and Gunardson felt a sense of relief. He really wasn't concerned about his time yet. He hadn't even made it this far the previous year when his sled had tipped over. So far so good.

He guided the dogs toward the wooden cabin where he would need to check in. Kit stumbled, and Gunardson was startled. The dog actually appeared to be laboring. Huskies could run six or seven hours without a break, yet Kit seemed winded after only three hours.

He put the brake on a few yards from the Rohn Roadhouse, a one-story log cabin with moose antlers over the front door and a pile of fresh-chopped wood that sat waiting on the left side of the entrance.

He carefully unhooked the dogs from the gang line. They would not wander off, and volunteers were there to help him. The dogs were normally thrilled to see so many new people. Now most of them lay on the ground panting. A few glanced around and rolled their eyes lethargically, while the rest just put their heads down. Concerned, Gunardson got out their food and left them to their feast while volunteers watched. He then went over to get Randi.

The dog was dead. She lay crumpled in a pool of blood that was already half frozen. Gunardson stood stock still. He had never has a dog die before on the trail. Has Randi stepped on something? Had she eaten something poisonous? How? And what kind of poison could invoke this level of carnage?

He glanced over at the other dogs. Tristam was listless. He was nestled in a snow bank, his head resting on his paws. A couple of the dogs were gulping at the chunks of food, but most could barely move. He was stunned by their listless behavior. What had happened? Could they go on?

"Worked 'em too hard?" a gruff voice said in his ear.

Gunardson glanced up at an old, kindly face. "Dr. Jespar," the man said, extending a hand. "Walt Jespar."

"Look at my time," Gunardson pleaded. Dr. Jespar would see his team had been slower than normal. Gunardson knew that. He hadn't driven the dogs too hard. Some mushers ran their teams hard, trying to set records, but he just wanted to finish this year, to prove to himself he could accomplish such an arduous feat. Winning could come later.

Dr. Jespar looked skeptical, but Gunardson didn't argue. The veterinarians were there to check on the dogs again. They had all been examined in Fairbanks before the race started. The vets had looked at everything: teeth, eyes, heart, lungs, joints, and even tonsils. They had taken tests for evidence of illegal drugs and searched for wounds. Females were examined to make sure they weren't pregnant. Then, at each checkpoint, vets did it all over again, this time checking for exhaustion, injuries, weight, hydration, appetite, and attitude.

Dogs have died on the trail—six in 2009. That was the worst total since 1985 when nine didn't reach the finish line. Sometimes the dogs froze to death. That's what happened to two dogs on a team caught in negative-forty-five-degree temperatures and howling winds for more than twenty-four hours. Others simply died at times for no apparent reason.

"I don't know what happened," Gunardson finally said. He felt utterly hopeless. He knew dogs would have to be dropped. Most mushers ended up with about ten dogs by the time the race ended. Still he had never had one die before. He had raised these dogs as puppies, taught them the commands: gee, haw, and whoa. He had cared for them as if they were his children.

"Got another one," Dr. Jespar said, turning toward him.

Gunardson followed his gesture. Tristam was rigid in a crimson pool, his light fur slowly wicking up the cooling blood.

Gunardson heard his boots crunch on the snow like a distant echo as he walked to the dog. This couldn't be poison. And it couldn't be an accident—two dogs? The amount of blood... God, it looked like they'd had their throats slit like hogs in a slaughterhouse, but he could see no other wound. What was going on?

"Daniel," Dr. Jespar said. He had moved and was standing by Kit.

For a few seconds Gunardson could not move, could not breathe. *This can't be happening,* he thought. He dropped to his knees next to the once strong, vibrant dog. Kit looked momentarily happy to be greeted, but there was a deep sadness in his blue-gray eyes. Gunardson patted him again and again. He studied the familiar face and was appalled to see blood begin to drip through Kit's teeth onto the snow.

"Kit!" he cried out. He watched and then screamed out the name again. He raised his arms to the sky, and his powerful voice echoed through the small village. The sound seemed to reach the Alaska Range behind Rohn and shatter it.

Gunardson walked around in a circle, and then he felt the man's hand tapping his shoulder.

"Dan...Daniel!" Jespar's voice broke in the middle of the name. "They're all dying!"

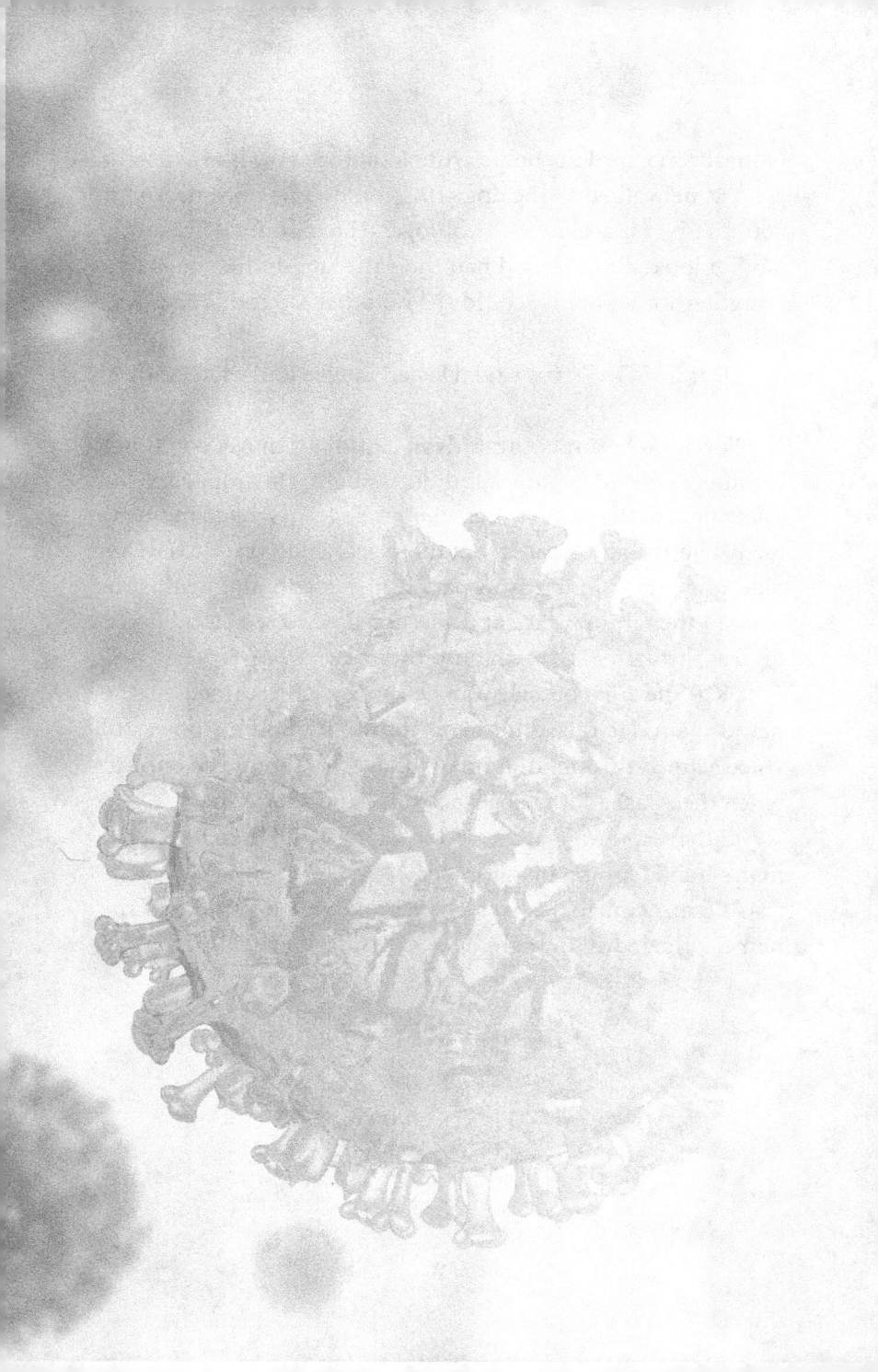

Chapter 1

Dr. Preston McBride removed his white lab coat from the closet, put it on and sat at his desk. His workspace inside Novilis Pharmaceuticals was perfectly organized. All the items on his desktop were either organized in rows or aligned at 90 degrees: pens, slides, flash drives, samples and an MP3 player. His degree from the University of San Francisco School of Medicine had been carefully aligned so it hung parallel to the edge of his computer monitor. McBride knew it was annoying—Kendra had suggested more than once that he may want relax just a tiny bit—but order was like gravity in Pres's universe: without it, everything just flew apart. Even Ethan Willis, another virologist who worked nearby and was also something of a neat freak, couldn't compare.

McBride turned on his MP3 player, chose a Dvorjak concerto, and took several deep breaths. The music filled him and lifted his spirit, and he smiled. He had been so relieved to make it out of grad school, where even some of most promising students listened to blaring rock 'n' roll or even hip hop while they were working. Even as a teenager, youth culture had struck him as vapid and hollow, and he had been more than happy to put it behind him.

He felt good: relaxed, ready to focus, and confident that through his ongoing experiments he would eventually identify the various genetic strains comprising the new and virulent flu virus. In medical research the first or five-hundredth try could yield the desired result; the task was to be forever diligent, to keep going and remain alert. This was what it would take to clearly identify the genetic makeup of this new flu that had already reached the status of a pandemic last year.

The morning's auspicious beginning lasted only until McBride slid his key into the locked drawer on the right side of his desk and discovered his printouts were missing. He could always print another copy, but it was immediately unsettling that someone had been in his desk. He knew some other staff members had keys, but he had never found his papers disturbed before. He shook his head, trying to dismiss it, and entered his login into his PC.

His computer buzzed, and up popped a flashing notification: "Access Denied." McBride froze. His right hand remained extended toward the keys. He leaned forward to reread the message as if it would miraculously change. It didn't. "Access Denied."

Perhaps he had mistyped his password. It was early; maybe his coffee hadn't kicked in yet. He rubbed his fingers together like a magician preparing for a trick. Slowly and carefully, he typed in his password.

"Access Denied."

Taking a deep breath, he fell back into his chair, trying to recall his actions of the day before. He recalled putting the latest printouts away and locking his desk drawer, just as he had done at the end of work for the last three months. He was absolutely sure of that. He performed the same "closing up shop" routine at the end of each workday since he was always the last one out. He always kept his lab coat in the same place. Even pens on his desk were carefully arranged for easy access and coding. What had happened in the night?

"Ethan?" he called.

Willis was reading some research printouts and didn't seem to hear him.

"Ethan," McBride called again. His voice echoed around the large room and rattled notes stuck on walls like little flags.

Willis looked up.

"The printouts of my research on the flu virus are missing. Do you know what happened?" McBride asked. He knew better than to expect much help from Willis, but there was no one else to ask.

Willis stood up, placing the papers on his bench. "They're missing?" he asked. McBride watched as the older man strode over to the cold room with his graying ponytail wagging behind his head. It was hard to read the man's expression because of his scruffy beard. Willis was a generation older than McBride, but from their conflicting demeanors, one would have thought that McBride was the older scientist with a cresting career and Willis a flashy young upstart, bragging about his sexual conquests and blasting Cream and The Allman Brothers loud enough through his headphones that it could be heard across the lab. Even physically, they were at odds. McBride was short and stocky with dark brown hair, short and stiff as a scrub brush, his body as methodical and purely functional as his brain. Willis was taller and much thinner. He swayed when he walked, almost as if he were dancing. He was known for constant innuendoes and the occasional filthy joke, but McBride knew a lot of bitterness lurked underneath.

Looking up at the computer screen quizzically, Willis paused. "Interesting," he said softly. He didn't smile, which was unusual, as Willis almost always wore a nervous smile. Now McBride felt his coffee kick in and felt shaky. He wished he had Willis's practiced veneer. Nothing seemed to ruffle him; everything slid off that greasy exterior.

"Denied access?" Willis mused. "Maybe it's your computer's time of the month." He leaned over and typed in his own code. The computer welcomed it and quickly responded. "Nope," Willis said, logging out. "She seems to like me just fine." And there it was, that oily smile of his.

This was a sensitive project with a high security rating. McBride couldn't hide his disappointment that Willis didn't have any insight into either his missing printouts or his expired login. McBride rarely enjoyed working with Willis, but today he found him deeply unnerving, repugnant even. The man was a staff veteran and had worked at Novilis for more than fifteen years. He had been the first to greet McBride upon his arrival five years ago and had charitably offered his own warped guide to the intricacies of office politics. The company's social environment had been a novel experience for McBride, fresh out of his self-imposed quarantine at California State's microbiology lab in Fullerton. There he'd had the luxury of only communicating with his professors. Here, he had to ask about everyone's weekend, mother, grandmother, child, and dog.

Willis knew precisely what McBride was working on. The flu vaccine was the biggest thing Novilis had developed in the last ten years easily, and it couldn't have come at a better time.

The company had stumbled recently, and there were rumors of cutbacks, even layoffs. With government funding being poured into the search, this vaccine would resuscitate the company's bottom line and maybe even be the dawn of a new era for Novilis. Vaccines rarely made any money, but propelled by public unrest, this one was going to be the exception. As a result, all company resources had been devoted to the work.

Company President Alvin DiAngelo had even held a video conference with the Elmira, New York staff to emphasize the importance of the project. Lang Hofferman, the department director who usually kept accounts of such minor items as the stained interior of the break room microwave and vacation scheduling, now reminded them of the importance of this project daily.

"The data is gone, too, huh?" Willis said. He carefully checked the other shelves. Then he walked over to the micro-fridge and then the aspirator, half-heartedly poking and peering, and then finally returned to his papers without another word. McBride watched him anxiously, knowing that Willis was just trying to get him off his back, yet still hoping the research would turn up. It was no secret that Willis was selfish and lazy, but he was also a sycophant and usually made a big show of trying to be the most unselfish and helpful researcher in the lab. Yet somehow today he couldn't be bothered. McBride shook his head in disgust.

"Maybe you should talk to Hofferman," Willis finally offered without looking up.

McBride blanched. No one wanted to discuss anything with Hofferman, who was not a doctor but a bureaucrat with a useless MBA at best. He could chat about paper clip inventory and the price of emollients, but the man had absolutely no understanding of research. He only grudgingly approved needed purchases and constantly harped about costs. Everyone knew that money was tight at Novilis, especially now. Hofferman, however, had a death grip on the laboratory budget and was grimly determined to squeeze every penny out of it.

"It'll be all right, man," Willis assured McBride. He chortled to himself. "It's not like you're asking him to smoke a joint in the break room with you."

"I just want access back. I can print new copies of the damn data," McBride said, his voice rising despite his best intentions to remain calm. This was important, and all Willis could do was make jokes about illegal drugs? He was almost trembling. Why now? He was so close to determining which virus was causing the new round of a possibly deadly flu. He couldn't sit around until someone fixed what was obviously just a dumb computer error.

That someone was definitely not Hofferman. He barely knew how to use email. Still, whom else could he talk to? IT? Those guys didn't even understand English, much less speak it. And then there were the missing printouts... McBride grimaced sourly. He checked the clock. It was eight a.m.; Hofferman would be at his desk, calculating nonstop. He arrived every day at precisely 7:58. Some of the researchers seriously debated whether or not he had a metronome built into his body.

McBride returned his coat to the rack and headed up the stairs to Hofferman's second-floor office. He had no idea how to broach the subject. How could he explain the loss of such vital research and his inexplicable inability to access his computer?

Hofferman had placed him in charge of the research, overseeing an eight-person team. This was his first major assignment. He recognized both the importance of the work and the significance of his position.

"The company has big plans for you," Hofferman had told him.

Now what? McBride reflected. If a duffer like Willis could hang on for fifteen years, well, they weren't going to fire him. Still, he shuddered to think about the consequences of this inexplicable gaffe.

Susan Johnson, the secretary, grinned at him as he knocked on the office door. A tall, thin blonde with a few sun-kissed freckles and a gap between her front teeth, she was infallibly genial while seemingly harried beyond human endurance. Her desk already resembled the interior of a home flattened by a tornado.

"Hiya, McBride, how goes it?" she said, flashing him a quick smile while hunting through a stack of papers for a lost invoice or something.

"I gotta talk to Hofferman."

"I'm sorry to hear that! Well, you're in luck. 'The doctor is in,' as it were."

"Thanks, Susan, I…I'm sorry, how are you?"

Susan looked at her desk, shrugged with a sad grin and flipped her hair, indicating that McBride was to follow her.

She led him to the gaudy inner office with its lengthy rosewood desk, pine siding, and plush leather visitor chairs. Hofferman had decorated the wall with his framed diplomas, pictures of his family and their two dogs, and what looked like a bad copy of a Dali. The watches weren't so much melted as squished.

Hofferman looked up and smiled broadly at McBride. "Come in, come in," he said cheerfully. McBride walked slowly forward, feeling like a doomed man greeted jovially by his executioner. Hofferman indicated a chair. McBride slumped into it. His stomach bubbled, and he felt the awful taste of bile in his mouth.

"Good news, I'm assuming?" Hofferman said. "You know the company sure could use some. That Rohn flu looks like it could turn out to be a killer, and there's lots of pressure to come up with a vaccine. I'm getting calls all the time from top government officials. The Feds are really pouring money into this."

"Yes, sir, I understand," McBride managed. Hofferman's arms strained the fabric of his suit when he flexed, and McBride found himself staring as his boss rambled on. Hofferman flexed unnecessarily several times while retrieving a single piece of paper. McBride remembered when the man had talked about starting a workout routine, and it now seemed that Hofferman had stumbled onto the secret of manufacturing muscle. He appeared grimly intent on getting the most out of it. Hofferman struck another pose and this time his chest stretched his white shirt. When he twisted his neck to look at his monitor, McBride noticed how thick his neck had become; his head seemed disproportionately small. Human beings were such a vain and inefficient species, McBride thought, and then glanced down at his own stomach, pressing against his white button down. Jesus, was Kendra getting him fat now?

"Did you see the latest press conference on the flu?" Hofferman continued. McBride shook his head. He had never had an appetite for TV. "You should take a minute to keep up," Hofferman counseled. "You spend far too much time staring into computer screens and reading printouts. You're the ultimate 'lab rat,' you know that, McBride?"

"Yes, sir." He'd heard that before and knew better than to protest it now.

"Look at this," Hofferman said. He swung his computer screen around so McBride could see it. After several agonizing seconds struggling with his computer mouse, Hofferman finally clicked on a video clip on CNN.com. Apparently his computer skills were progressing.

US Surgeon General Dr. Charles Witherspoon was standing in front of a group of reporters. "He's one of ours," Hofferman said excitedly. "He was once a medical researcher at the company like you and eventually became Chief of Operations before being tapped by the Federal government."

McBride nodded, still unable to address the problem that had brought him to Hofferman's office. McBride thought Witherspoon was unprofessional, and more than one colleague shared his opinion. Witherspoon was given to overwrought responses to seemingly trivial situations. Just a few months ago, he had fired off an alert about some nasal spray that reportedly could alter the sense of smell. Later tests indicated that the nasal spray actually did alter the patients' senses of smell—by opening their nasal passageways, which is what the product was advertised to do. McBride couldn't believe that a man that shortsighted had ascended to such a prominent position in medicine.

However, Witherspoon had been out front on the Rohn flu. Initial reports on the disease hadn't caused any particular alarm. The flu was not immediately deadly; that seemed clear. Then, as the number of people who got sick increased, the media accounts grew shriller. Americans had become jaded after neither the supposedly dangerous avian flu nor the much-heralded H1N1 delivered the full-on plague the media had promised. As a result, despite the news stories, the Rohn flu initially evoked merely a few yawns. However, medical findings showed that it affected the body's organs and weakened them. At least a dozen people who had come down with the flu and recovered soon experienced fatal pancreatic and/or liver failures. That connection had begun to get people's attention.

"We realize the public wants answers," Witherspoon was saying. "We are proud that people have so far handled this disease in stride. We've had epidemics before in this country. Americans know their government is doing everything possible to combat this disease."

At the press conference, the director of the Centers for Disease Control, Dr. Lauren Jessence, accompanied Dr. Witherspoon. They had become a daily fixture in the news, making simple, common-sense declarations about hand-washing and giving homely advice for care almost as if they were publicists for the disease. Chicken soup sales tripled. However, as the number of reported illnesses and related lost work hours mushroomed, both of them began to look tired and at their wits' end. Jessence's sallow features, in particular, began to sag badly as she tried to reassure viewers and weathered the badgering of reporters. Standing side-by-side in an American Gothic pose, the two white-haired old people seemed to illustrate the ominous nature of the disease and the ineffectiveness of the government agency they represented.

"We expect to have a vaccine shortly," Witherspoon was saying. "Researchers have isolated the virus and have developed the first vaccines. Animal testing should begin this week."

"He's referring to your work," Hofferman interjected, nodding at McBride. McBride felt adrenaline dump into his bloodstream like someone had slid a long cold needle deep into his spinal cord. This morning couldn't get worse.

"We expect results within the next month," Jessence added.

"Mass inoculations were not our first choice," Witherspoon continued, "but became the solution that evolved. We need to stop this dreadful disease in its tracks."

Jessence then launched into a brief discussion of how the international medical community had once isolated and defeated smallpox. "That's our hope with Rohn flu," she said in a monotone. "We can quarantine those who get the disease and we can inoculate the rest of the population. In a very short time, no human hosts will be available. All we need is a safe vaccine."

Hofferman muted the computer. "That's what's important, the vaccine," he noted. "You can't believe what people are saying about this flu. Some people think the government is covering up deaths! The bloggers are up in arms about it; it's all over Facebook and, you know, Twitter."

Despite his mounting concern, McBride struggled not to roll his eyes. Hofferman didn't know the first thing about any of the social networking sites he'd mentioned—he was just parroting what he'd heard on the news.

"Do you know a bunch of Pentecostal ministers announced that the Rohn flu was one of the riders of the Apocalypse, the pale rider signifying death? Crazy. A couple of nights ago, I saw a news story that a Cardinal predicted the disease marked the beginning of Armageddon."

He picked up some printed sheets on his desk, flexing several times for emphasis. "Headquarters is shifting all the bizarre emails to me." He read quotes. "Could Rohn flu turn into Ebola or one of those other horrific diseases usually confined to Africa? Didn't the CIA start AIDS? Is the Rohn flu the latest effort to wipe out the Third World?" He shook his head.

"Sounds like we've got our own intellectual Third World right here," McBride commented dryly.

Hofferman grunted. "Sad," he said. "Now the flu is a right-wing conspiracy. Or is it a left-wing effort to force universal health care? This flu started in Canada. Everyone had nice thoughts about Canada. How could a deadly flu start there? Isn't it too cold up there?"

"The French," McBride said. "Blame the French." He was glad the conversation hadn't gotten around to him. In fact, Hofferman seemed to be avoiding it. Still, he couldn't bullshit like this forever.

Hofferman laughed. "You'd better hurry up before the whole world goes crazy," he said. "This company is counting on your team to identify the virus so we can get that vaccine in place."

Before some other company develops one first, you mean, McBride thought to himself. He felt a cold chill. This was not going to be very easy. "We're working as fast as we can," he said.

"Good, good," Hofferman said. He settled back into his chair expectantly.

That was the invitation to explain why he was here. In a flash, McBride knew how to slip the news to Hofferman. He launched into the densest technical labspeak he could muster. "Sir," he began, "as you know, after isolation, the DNA of the virus appears as a negative supertwist or as an open circle with at least one single-strand scission. Under the denaturation conditions usually applied, such as heating in the presence of formaldehyde or application of alkali, Form I molecules could appear as 'relaxed' circles without single-strand scissions. On the other hand, Form II molecules show partial or complete strand separations. With that knowledge, my team and I have started the process of isolating and identifying the pathogen."

He could see Hofferman's eyes start to glaze over. A little more, he decided, and Hofferman would be numb. Then he could tell him the printouts were missing. "Maintaining the molecules with denaturation solution finally transformed them into partially denatured circles exhibiting strand separations easily measurable on electron micrographs. Denaturation maps of Form I molecules are being constructed by computer and compared with denaturation maps derived from partially denatured Form II molecules," McBride recited prolixly.

"Amazing," Hofferman gurgled. He glanced at his computer as if hoping to find some relief there.

"Unfortunately," McBride continued, "when I came in this morning, all the research was gone."

Hofferman blinked. He tried to say something, but only his lips moved. Finally, he turned around to get a glass of water. This was bad. Incredibly bad. The sound of the water being poured from the pitcher sounded like a cascade. He turned back, clearing his throat. "Gone?" His voice rose in pitch, stretching the tiny word out to two, almost three syllables.

"Yes, sir." McBride waited for the blast to follow. Hofferman was able to work himself into quite a lather. He seemed to have a switch: one minute, he was placid; the next, he was red with rage. Last week, he had fumed for three days after being informed that a researcher had "borrowed" findings from a colleague and added them to her own work.

"Now, I could easily reprint the missing data, sir," McBride continued, "but I seem to have lost access to my computer."

Hofferman's mouth ratcheted open by degrees, and McBride braced for the onslaught. At that moment, Hofferman's computer beeped, indicating a message of highest importance. Hofferman, huffing and puffing, turned to his keyboard while McBride waited with growing anxiety. As Hofferman read the message, his eyebrows went up, and he seemed flustered. He glanced sideways at McBride, then reread the message very carefully. Finally, he turned back to McBride, a strange expression on his face. "Anything else?"

"No, sir."

"Then we're done. Thank you," Hofferman said abruptly. He looked down at the printed copies of emails, showing the bald top of his head to McBride.

McBride was stunned. "What do you want me to do?" he said.

"Go back to work," Hofferman said without looking up. His voice was cold and flat and caromed off the desk.

McBride stared at him. "On what?"

Hofferman glared at him with his dark, narrow eyes. "You are the virologist," he said fiercely. "You find something to do."

McBride was stunned. He could not move. Hofferman began shuffling the papers, ignoring him. Finally, McBride eased out of the chair. He was overwhelmed. He fairly staggered down the hallway and back into the laboratory. Mindlessly, he put on his coat and sat down on the stool next to his work area. He felt so helpless. Months of work were gone. He had been so close.

"Are you all right?" someone said softly. He glanced up. It was Kendra Mayfield, a nurse who had become a lab technician. She had also become his girlfriend. Straight, dark hair framed her plain but open face. Today, it clearly showed concern. "You look sick."

He murmured what had transpired, including Hofferman's strange reaction.

She thought about it. "Did you see what he read on the computer?" she asked.

"No."

"Maybe I can find out," she said.

"How?"

She smiled at him. "Women have ways of getting things done, Pres."

"Thanks."

"Have you told anyone about your lost data and lack of access?"

"Just Hofferman. And Willis knows."

Kendra made a face. "You trust him?"

McBride rolled his eyes. There was no answer to that. How could he trust Willis? How could he trust anyone here? From the day he entered Novilis, he always had to keep one eye on his research and another on his coworkers, any of whom would steal an idea without a second thought and would report any supposed anomaly to Hofferman. McBride glanced around.

Everyone seemed to be watching him. Was he just worked up, or was there really tension in the air?

"Kendra," Willis called, "if your Romeo can spare you a moment, I require your assistance."

They both winced. Willis could be unbearable.

"Later," Kendra spit out under her breath and walked stiffly across the hard tile floor to Willis's work area. The one person he could count on was walking away. McBride watched her as Willis smiled broadly and put his arm around her shoulders. Kendra flinched. Was she putting on weight, too? He hated himself for even thinking that.

He sat up. Moping was not going to help. He had been abruptly shunted off the project. Why? What had he done? Was he going too slowly? He was working as hard as he could, poring over computerized virus models late into the nights, pushing his team accompany him. What could he do? He rapidly organized his thoughts as the music sifted around him and calmed him. He was off the project. He felt as though he had been kicked in the stomach. Everything on his desk seemed so far away. As it turned out, even his ruthless organization couldn't keep chaos at bay.

Of course, he thought, he could have reported something, chosen a virus from among as many as twenty options, and freed up animal tests on the vaccine. That would be Willis's approach. He often cut corners. McBride had rejected that direction out of hand. He already knew very well what happened with such methods.

He recalled sitting in court about two years ago. DiAngelo was trying to explain his opposition to the placement of a warning label on a radiation gel created to treat the effects of cancer treatments. The gel had been developed in the lab, but had not been properly tested. Instead, one brave employee tested it and reported back that it had worked. That was enough for Novilis.

Three people died before Novilis was hauled into court and sales of the product were frozen. McBride was subpoenaed as a witness about the product's development but was never called to testify. He came away particularly upset that no one else seemed concerned about the ensuing judgment against the company.

"The cost of doing business," Willis told him with a shrug. "Collateral damage."

McBride knew that term and didn't like it. It meant civilian deaths caused by military action against the enemy. It sounded better than murder but meant the same thing.

Finally, not wanting to simply sit in the lab, McBride began to clean around his desk, moving pens and equipment as if reshuffling would provide the magic answer. *Three months*, McBride thought grimly. All that work gone. And Witherspoon? He was saying the vaccine was almost ready for human use.

Idly, McBride retrieved a slide. The heavy metal compounds were already in place. He would have to mold the negative stain around the virus particle to create a negative image. That would allow him to clearly see the virus interact with the animal tissue's cells. It was something to do. Lab technicians were filing in. He needed to do something.

His phone rang. "Hey, Pres," a voice said cheerfully. "I have completed initial animal testing with the Rohn vaccine per your request. Can you come down to review the data?" It was Rob Connelly, the portly man who managed the animal research facility. McBride suspected he may be an alcoholic, but at least he was easy enough to work with.

"Completed? We're not ready to commence animal testing," McBride said, puzzled. "It will be weeks."

He heard Connelly pause. "But I got batches of the test vaccine two weeks ago and was told to get started."

"You're kidding."

"No, sir." Connelly said. "When Willis brought them down, he told me this was a priority and to get to work as soon as possible."

"Connelly, I… let me call you right back." McBride closed his eyes and put the phone down while Connelly was still speaking. What the hell was going on? He looked over at Willis. The older man was innocently peering through his microscope.

As calmly as possible, McBride stood up. He took a deep breath and tried to control his pulse rate. Kendra asked him if he trusted Willis. He hadn't answered. Now that it was too late; the answer was clear. How could Willis have submitted vaccine samples if he didn't know the composition of the virus? He must have stolen the research. It was as simple as that.

McBride stared at the older man. He had been in one fight in his life, in high school, in algebra class. A freshman, he had been in the same class with graduating seniors and was the constant target of Jeff Fisher, the school's soccer and basketball star, for answering their professor's queries correctly. That was the point of going to class, right, to learn something? Finally, one day Pres's rage boiled over. The professor wrote out a lengthy algebraic equation on the chalkboard and asked if anyone wanted to give it a try. "I nominate The Prez," Fisher said, grinning broadly. "As everyone knows, he likes 'em long and hard." The class tittered. Pres stood, his face flushing, and walked over to Jeff Fisher. Fisher was out of his chair in a second, towering over Pres. With no hope of winning a fight, Pres swung wildly for Jeff's face but came up short when Jeff leaned back, and the punch landed on his throat. Jeff immediately grabbed Pres and started wailing away, but he quickly fell off, clutching his closing windpipe. Pres sustained a black eye and a few bruises, but Jeff Fisher never said boo to him again.

His veins coursing with rage and fury, McBride strode toward Willis. He could hear the pounding in his ears. The thump of his heart created a drum roll that accompanied him as he walked slowly across the floor. His hard heels cracked against the tile, adding to the staccato sound. What was he going to do? He didn't know.

Someone was using the ultracentrifugation, but the whirring noise was muffled by McBride's own heartbeat. Even the music emanating from various desks faded away. McBride's world grew silent, save for the rushing of his own hot blood.

Willis must have caught a hint of his looming presence. He leaned back, staring straight ahead, and then slowly turned. For a moment, the two men looked at each other.

"I was told not to tell you," Willis said.

"I don't believe you," McBride replied coldly.

"It doesn't matter what you believe," Willis said and smiled. It struck McBride that this was the first genuine smile he had seen from Willis, and it was not a pretty thing, like watching a shark smile with a dead seal pup dangling from its toothy mouth.

"What the hell is going on?" McBride shouted, knowing that he should remain professional but unable to contain his anger.

"It doesn't affect you," Willis said calmly.

"That's ridiculous! Who could it affect more?"

"The company," Willis fairly hissed. He turned back to his research.

The company? McBride wanted to scream. What did the company have to do with this? Willis had taken the research and had initiated tests without doing a shred of research on them. He was not even on the team developing the vaccine. He had simply out-and-out stolen everything.

"The needs of the many…" Willis began.

"Dwindle to nothing when there's one man's fortune to be made!" McBride finished in fury.

Willis shrugged. "Then you understand," he said quietly, and returned to his work.

Surrounded by silence, McBride spun and walked out the door. He threw his coat onto the closet floor and marched up the stairs. He hoped the staff heard him leave the lab, and Hofferman heard him coming.

Johnson was sitting at her desk. She did not try to exchange pleasantries this time—McBride was clearly past that.

"I'm going home," McBride told her flatly. "I'm sick of this shit." He didn't wait for an answer but marched away. Already he felt the sweat on his brow cooling—it wasn't Susan's fault, why was he swearing at her?

"Um… feel better?" she called after him.

Less than twenty minutes later, he was pulling into the driveway of his apartment. The short drive had done little to diffuse his temper. Outside, the wintry weather in upstate New York brought him a chill. What now? Had he blown a big problem into a full-on catastrophe? He still had no idea what was going on. He wished he were back home in Pomona, on the other side of the continent. He wouldn't have even made the trek if his family doctor, Abe Crossland, hadn't called his brother, a vice president at Novilis, and recommended him for this job. McBride hadn't really wanted to work so far away, but Abe Crossland had been encouraging.

"Do you really want to hold someone's sweaty hand? You prefer research to patients," Crossland reminded him. "You can do important work. Maybe you'll discover a cure for cancer or something really significant."

Maybe, McBride thought, *I'll have all my work stolen out from under me.*

He slammed the door behind him, knocking icicles off the eaves. The apartment was cool and empty. He filled it with his frustration, pacing from room to room. What was he supposed to do? Go back to work? Supervise the animal experiments? Why? So Willis or someone else could pilfer the results again? He was deeply unhappy in New York State, and his research was one of the few things that brought him any comfort or relief. You could spend your whole life studying one person and never figure that person out, but the laboratory held a sterile kind of hope. True, it took diligence and patience and great care, but Pres honestly felt that given enough time, any problem could be solved in a laboratory. Well, any scientific problem, that was. Human beings, he would never understand. He surveyed his mostly empty apartment where he only slept and showered with its cheap particleboard furniture and unused couch. He felt his gut through his cheap cotton shirt—he was getting fat! Who was he, living in this anonymous apartment, grinding away in the lab just to have his research stolen by a sloppy coworker? His life felt pointless; he felt like a stranger, even to himself.

His cell phone rang. Kendra came across clear, but muffled. She must have been standing outside, trying to talk in the cold air. "You went home?" she asked.

"Yeah," he snapped. "What did you expect me to do?"

"Well, I don't know," she countered. "I mean...yes, Willis is a creep, but maybe try to look at it positively? Does it really matter who got credit, just so long as the vaccine worked? No one cares about whose name is on the bottle. There were 300 million Americans hoping for a cure, and billions more worldwide."

McBride began to cringe. Maybe he had overreacted.

"You're paid to do a job. You were doing it. Nobody's looking over my shoulder to see what I'm doing because, well, my work isn't half as important as the work you're doing. You must have been on the right track. Pres, if there's recognition to be had, you'll get some," Kendra continued. "Was that what you were upset about? Who gets credit?"

McBride's shoulders sagged but he made no answer.

"Who won last year's Nobel Prize for Medicine?" Kendra asked him.

"Well, actually it was split between two parties, actually a total of three scientists, there was the French team—"

Kendra cut him off. "Okay, Pres, who other than you knows that?"

"No one," he admitted. He felt like an idiot. He was an adult. He needed to act like one. "I'll be back to Novilis tomorrow," he said wearily, "and I'll make sure the vaccine tests are done properly."

"I think you're doing the right thing," she told him. "I think it'll pay off down the line."

"Thank you," he said.

"Well, I'm not done, Pres. I got a copy of the memo Hofferman received when you were in his office. Would you like to hear it?"

McBride smiled grimly. He could hear in Kendra's voice both that she was cold and that she was smiling. "Now how on earth did you get that?"

"Well...maybe you've noticed that Hofferman is pretty clueless about his computer? And that Susan doesn't much care for her boss?"

"Yes, of course, but..."

"As his assistant, she reads all of his work email. You know, we talk every day, just to keep up with each other. I asked her what the email said, and she just printed off a copy for me. She was more than happy to do it!"

Pres rolled his eyes. How he would function in society without Kendra, he didn't know. "Can you read it to me?"

"Sure."

"It's from Charles Crossland. Who's he?"

"Vice president," McBride said. "He oversees the research wing."

"Here's what he wrote: 'Expedite testing. Willis is doing most of the work, anyway. If McBride comes by, *do not* address the subject with him. We don't want to lose someone of his caliber, but we can't sleep on this opportunity. He wouldn't accept the use of an attenuated vaccine, anyway. It's an imperfect solution, but our cost-benefit analysis shows it to clearly be the best path.'"

McBride gasped aloud.

"He didn't say anything bad about you."

"Attenuated viruses?" McBride repeated. "No, they can't be serious about that."

"What's an attenuated virus?" Kendra asked.

McBride took a deep breath. "An attenuated virus means it's still alive. You put it in a foreign culture or an egg or even animal tissue, and then inject it. That's what was done with polio, yellow fever, chicken pox. The MMR vaccine uses that approach. You can create a vaccine a lot faster that way. The viruses are generally dying or altered in some way through laboratory cultivation, but there's still a significant risk that they could reproduce or mutate."

"Don't the vaccines all have live viruses?"

"Not anymore," McBride told her. "These days, most vaccines use recombinant DNA sequencing. Some have harmless toxins produced by the virus or components of viruses, but they can't reproduce. Injections for influenza typically use recombinant DNA. The whole idea is to activate the immune system. That's what's wrong with attenuated viruses. They work, of course, but no one wants the virus to mutate and produce a more virulent form. With attenuated viruses, you need booster shots. There's always the danger someone with a low immune system will get the disease or pass it on. That's not what I was working on. I wouldn't have consented to it!"

He suddenly could see what was happening: Willis knew how to play the political game. Willis was the white knight, charging ahead to lead the company to success. McBride would be the small figure in the background, waving his arms as he slowly vanished in the distance.

Attenuated viruses? McBride shook his head. Yes, it could be a safe vaccine. People still got polio shots. But in this instance, the risk far outweighed the reward. Viruses were like every living thing: they evolved constantly to survive. There's no way to guarantee that another polio epidemic wouldn't occur when the virus mutated. That was also true with the Rohn flu. He was not going to be party to that.

"Jesus. This is a huge deception. They are lying to me and to the American public. Am I going crazy?" McBride sputtered. "Kendra, I can't go back to work."

"Pres," Kendra said in exasperation. "I thought we just went through that."

"You don't understand," he said. "I can't be associated with an attenuated virus vaccine when I'm not even sure the vaccine contains the correct weakened virus. It's too soon. It's too dangerous."

"You said that other vaccines used it. Besides, the company has to move fast or lose their opportunity. You just said it's easier to use an attenuated virus."

"Unless we know specifically which virus it is, which is what I had been working so long and hard on, it's a hit or miss proposition to use any attenuated virus. There are worse things at stake than Novilis going belly up," he said.

It was true, but it just sounded like a lame excuse to his ears. The real reason he wanted to leave, he finally admitted to himself, was because he wanted to leave. He just wanted to do research, important research, without having to guard his research from jealous coworkers, or flatter his vain, incompetent boss, or get beers and watch the Giants with the guys in Animal Testing. He could see himself in the mirror on the back of the closet door. Stress was already adding lines in his forehead. Was that the beginning of a jowl hanging down under his chin? He could feel weariness flood over him. He had to leave, had to flee this wintry gulag and get home to California and regroup. He had to get as far away from Novilis as possible. He told Kendra. She listened without speaking and he could hear hurt in her silence.

"Do you want to go with me?" he asked hesitantly. She was his one source of comfort in New York, and he knew he would miss her horribly.

"I've got a good job. I was born and raised here. My family is here," Kendra said.

"I understand," McBride said. He had never felt so sad in his life. Still, he knew his East Coast misadventure was over.

"Pres, I...I've got to go back inside. My break is over, and I'm freezing," Kendra said. She hung up the phone.

McBride flipped shut his cell phone. This disastrous day was complete. He was alone. What a mess he had made of everything. An attenuated virus? That was something the public would need to know. Maybe he should call Witherspoon or Jessence. As if they'd listen. He felt helpless.

He went upstairs and began to pack. His suitcase wasn't big enough for everything, but he didn't feel the need to bring more than was absolutely necessary. He didn't want any souvenirs of this place.

He called his mother. "I'm coming back home," he told her.

"Good!" she said. "Just in time for the Winter Solstice ceremony!"

"Mom, I…we may have to forgo my participation this year."

"Oh, you will be there," she said cheerfully. "We dance at midnight with candles and incense. I think twenty-five or thirty women are coming. No men, of course, but we'll make an exception for you! Who knows, maybe you'll meet a nice girl…"

McBride was about to protest that he had a girlfriend and then recalled that he no longer did. "You're too kind," he said wearily. His mother the twenty-first-century hippie. She had enjoyed the 1960s so much that she had never left.

By four p.m. he was ready to go. His leased car had been returned to the dealer. He hadn't even thought about buying a plane ticket. He'd just take a shuttle to Corning Regional Airport and catch a commuter to LaGuardia or Kennedy. None of it mattered. He just wanted to get as far away from there as possible.

The cell phone rang again. He flipped it open and looked at the number: Kendra.

"When are we leaving?" she asked.

"You're going with me?"

"Pres, if you think I'm going to stay here with Willis, then you really are going crazy."

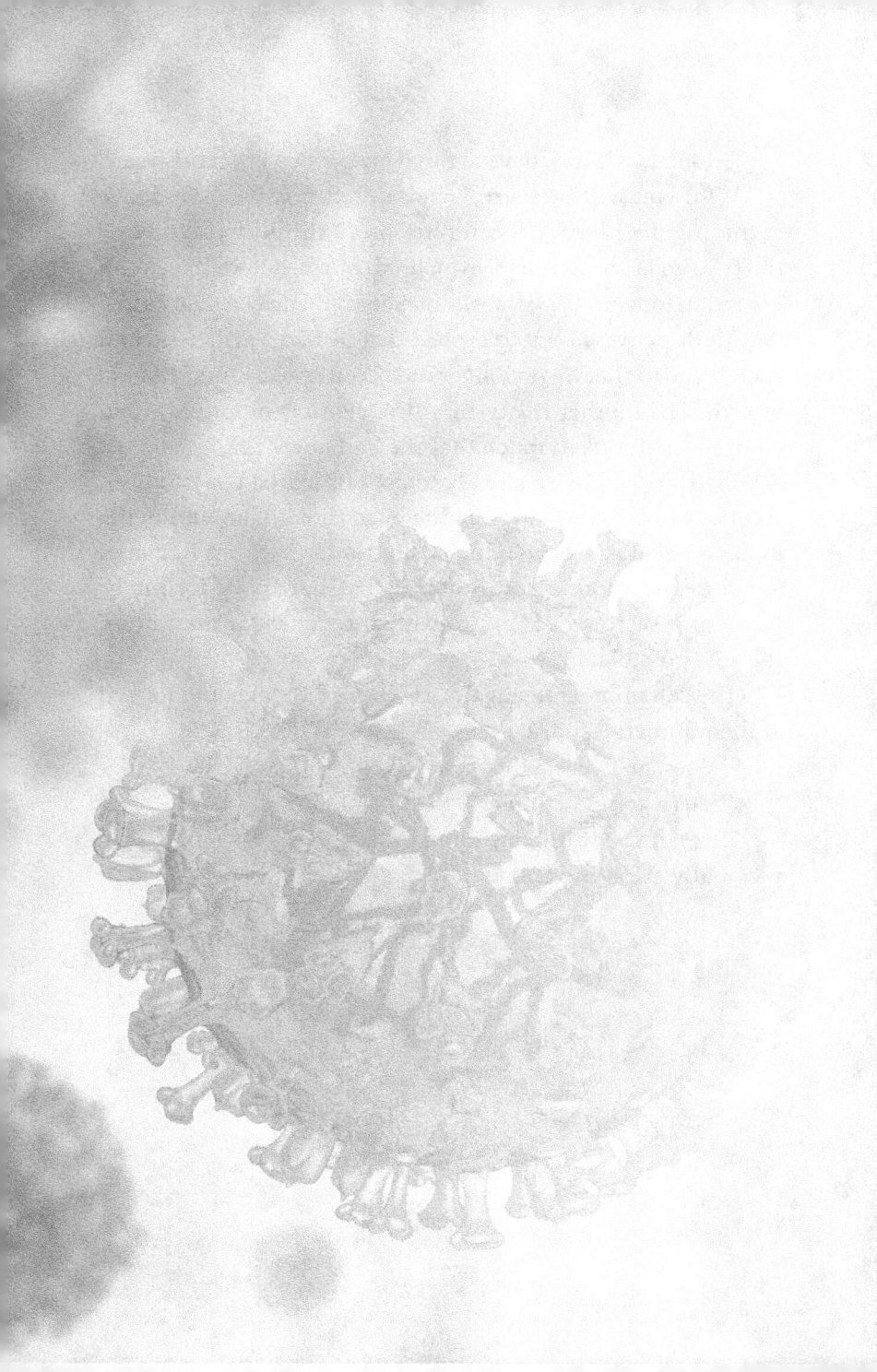

Chapter 2

"**D**o I look all right?" Kendra asked nervously. She smoothed her beige cotton skirt with a hand as McBride steered their Civic through Southern California traffic during evening twilight, heading toward the San Gabriel Mountains, which loomed before them.

"You're fine," McBride assured her. "Mom doesn't stand on ceremony."

"I think there's a spot on my blouse," Kendra continued. She scrubbed at it vigorously with a handkerchief. He didn't notice any difference, especially since the blouse was multicolored.

"Tell Mom it's tie-dyed. She's a '60s chick, remember," McBride reminded her. He had suggested she wear something casual, even jeans, but Kendra insisted on getting dressed up. No perfume, he said. Mom hated that stuff, as well as make up, eyeliner, and even lipstick. He put on a plain tan shirt and brown slacks with tennis shoes. His mom wouldn't have tolerated anything else.

"We should have visited her sooner," Kendra continued her litany of concerns.

McBride sighed. He could hear the tension in her voice. Meeting a boyfriend's parent was a momentous occasion, a step forward in the relationship. As a result, Kendra had been anxious from the moment they agreed to join his mother for dinner. He knew Kendra missed her life in New York, and it was beginning to manifest as fussiness with their lives there. Her angst had continued unabated since they left their rented home near Frank R. Bocelli Park in Pomona to head down Foothill Boulevard toward Rancho Cucamonga. His mother had moved to an apartment complex there years ago because Rancho Cucamonga straddled what used to used to be famed Route 66. She said living there was good Karma.

"How's my hair?" Kendra tried. "I can't do a thing with it." She ran a brush through her hair, tossing her head to shake up the strands.

McBride took a quick glance. Kendra's hair was wavy and dark brown. It had been cut short in a style that still framed her face beautifully. "Stop it," he said. "You look great!"

"You think?" she said.

"Of course," he said. "I thought you were beautiful the first day I saw you, and nothing has changed since." He wondered if it sounded insincere and glanced at her, hoping she did not come at him. The sad truth was that if Pres found her beautiful, he would have never had the courage to talk to her. He thought she was cute verging on pretty. But she seemed to accept the compliment and smiled.

Kendra began to relax and talked about her new job, assisting doctors in radiology at the hospital. His unwillingness to seek a job didn't enter the conversation. Far from curing his funk, their move to California had deepened it. Instead of spending long hours at the lab, he now wasted his days in the air-conditioned womb of their living room, marooned on the couch staring at the TV, his new best friend. Rather than losing weight, he had continued to pack it on. More than a month after quitting his position in New York, he still felt upset and burned out. Kendra talked her way around the subject of his sloth, carefully avoiding it.

Soon they had something to focus on—just how to get to their destination. McBride had managed to get lost in Rancho Cucamonga. His mother had said he was to turn left off Foothill when the actual turn was right.

"My mother doesn't have a conservative bone in her body," he noted calmly. "A right turn must have been an anathema." Kendra didn't smile.

They finally found her apartment complex, which featured a large parking area and a series of identical buildings, all with rustic wood siding and gray shingles. Maggie Henderson-McBride lived on the seventh floor of the seventh building. Even in a staid apartment building, she had found a way to be the cosmic freak.

When McBride pressed the button, the doorbell sounded with a gritty, low quality recording of Bobby Troup singing the familiar, "Get Your Kicks on Route 66." Seconds later, the massive head of a dog appeared in the front door's lone window, which had to be six feet off the ground, then quickly disappeared. The dog's face flashed in and out of the window as it leapt for a look at the strangers, but the barking continued nonstop.

"That's Canada," McBride said as Kendra drew back. "He's a keeshond. My mom's had him four or five years now."

"The guy can really jump," Kendra noticed.

"He's friendly. A little too friendly," McBride said and winced.

"Pres," Kendra said hesitantly. "I'm allergic to dogs."

McBride straightened. "I didn't know that," he said. "I'm sorry." He did know—she had told him that back in New York—but he had forgotten. Since he didn't have a pet, he hadn't recalled. She didn't grill him about it now, though, just dug in her purse for tissues. McBride pushed the button again, restarting the short loop of the annoying song and increasing Canada's frenzy. Where was that flaky mother of his?

"It's all right," Kendra said. "I just start sneezing. There was no way to avoid it anyway. I'll be all right for a little while." She sounded doubtful. "If I start feeling sick, I'll let you know."

"Just don't mention the allergy to Mom," McBride warned. "She loves that dog."

"Hello, hello, hellloooooo!" Maggie, a short, stocky woman, opened the door, ending the song and singing out a greeting of her own. She had to block the dog with her legs so they could enter. The bottom of her flowing lilac purple muumuu Hawaiian dress covered Canada, who kept poking his snout through whichever opening he could find. McBride kissed his mother on the cheek and then knelt down to acknowledge Canada. The gray-black dog had thick fur and a bushy tail curled over his back. He wagged his body and licked McBride's face.

"He remembers me," McBride said happily. He had never had a dog as a child but somehow he was good with them. *At least animals I understand,* he thought to himself.

"Down, Canada," Maggie tried. "Oh, that dog. He never listens to me." She cheerfully welcomed Kendra with open arms and a warm embrace. "Kendra, right?" Kendra nodded. "It's so hard to keep them straight," Maggie said.

McBride's rolled his eyes. "You knew I was bringing Kendra. And there isn't anyone else," he added, for Kendra's benefit.

Maggie tossed her head, sending her short brown curls shot through with gray bouncing. "Oh come on, Don Juan, I'm old and you know my memory isn't what it used to be," she said. "Come in, come in."

She led them to the small living room, which featured three brightly colored beanbags. The walls were white, highlighted by several sunflower decals stuck on at odd angles. A crystal mobile dangled from a ceiling on a hook, sending shards of light throughout the room. A thick incense candle was burning by the open side window. The pungent scent added to the aroma of several small containers of potpourri placed on the top of a small bookcase and the television. *That is Mom,* Pres thought, *tacky, fruity, and totally over-the-top.* For the millionth time, he wondered if he was adopted.

"I got a tattoo," Maggie announced without any preliminary comment.

McBride stared at her. "Really? Why?" He hesitated. "Where?'

"You are so gullible," Maggie nudged him with an elbow. She winked at Kendra. "You can tell him anything."

"Mom!"

"But I did get a tattoo. A darling cupid with a red rose," Maggie said.

"How nice, Mrs. McBride," Kendra offered politely. The dog started to sniff her legs. She tried to shoo it away, but with no success. "Where is it?"

"I can show you, but not him," Maggie whispered. "And call me by my first name. I'm not 'Mrs.' Anything. Given how rarely my sons come by, I'm hardly 'Mom' either."

"That's not fair," McBride protested, aware that Kendra was giving him a familiar I-told-you-so look. "It takes time to find a place to live, get acclimated and all that. Kendra got a job at Pomona Valley Hospital Medical Center on North Garey, up the road from Abe Crossland's clinic."

"And all you are doing is lying around and gaining weight," his mother said. McBride stiffened. He knew he was adding a few pounds. In fact, he was beginning to fear he would look like his father.

"Just like his father," said Maggie, with seeming telepathy, "who went from having a beautiful athletic build in his twenties," she said and reached for McBride's growing midsection, "to having a belly the Buddha would envy in his thirties."

Pres shrank away from his mother's incriminating touch. Once again, she was embarrassing him in front of company. And she wondered why he never came to visit.

Pastries filled a plate on the table and McBride eyed them. What was wrong with him—even with his mother taunting him about his weight in front of a girlfriend, he was thinking about food. Canada seemed to see McBride looking and sauntered over and began sniffing the plate, as if he had first right of refusal. Maggie chastised the dog and proffered the cakes to her visitors.

"Here, Pres," she said. "It's a low-calorie one with no fat."

"Really?" he said. Relieved, he reached out and took a gooey cherry tart.

Maggie laughed. "Do you believe everything people tell you?" she chortled. "Hang on to this one, Kendra," she advised, rolling her eyes dramatically. "This absent-minded scientist may be too slow on the uptake to run around on you!"

Kendra laughed nervously. Shaking his head, McBride settled awkwardly into a beanbag chair. He could tell his mother was making her uncomfortable. He made up his mind that they would get out of there as soon as he could manage it without offending his mom. He put the tart on his lap, trying not to give in. He thought about slipping it to Canada but imagined the dog gagging on it. His mother would have a fit—that dog ate more expensive cuisine than most people he knew. Sighing, he left it. Kendra ate hers. Boy, they were both packing it on.

"Are you still gainfully unemployed?" Maggie asked her son, instinctively honing in on the subject he most wished to avoid. He sighed and nodded.

"I'm planning to start looking in a week or two," he explained lamely.

"I bet you never thought you'd end up with such a mover and a shaker, did you?" Maggie asked Kendra.

"Stop it," McBride grunted. He knew she was just trying to be funny for Kendra, but he also knew that she was upset by his failure to visit sooner, and that bitterness was giving her jokes teeth. He did call her, after all. Twice. That was a lot. She didn't have a computer so he couldn't email. If she had a computer, McBride told himself, that would make it easier for him to be a better son.

"Do you do yoga?" Maggie asked Kendra, who was trying to sit in her beanbag gracefully but having little success. Canada had apparently taken a liking to her. The level of the beanbag meant Kendra and the dog were eye-to-eye.

"No," Kendra said, smiling and trying to be friendly. "I like to walk," she said, struggling to find common ground between them.

"You should do yoga before and after walking," Maggie announced, and Kendra's smile faltered a degree. Maggie stood up, raised her arms above her head and leaned back. "This is called Salutation." She held it a few seconds. She then dropped to the carpet, put her legs out straight behind her and raised up on her hands, bending her back while keeping her neck straight. "Bhujangasana," she announced. Canada came over to investigate. He sniffed her. "Get away from me," Maggie ordered. The dog simply dropped down next to her.

"He's doing a Bhujangasana," Kendra whispered to McBride. They shared a smile.

Maggie was not through. Several more poses followed. McBride thought she looked like a small whale attempting to perform ballet moves. Finally, breathing heavily, Maggie plopped back into the beanbag, which gasped under her weight. "I feel great," she announced.

"You certainly make it seem so easy," Kendra said.

"Dinner," Maggie announced abruptly, as if she hadn't heard. She hurried to the door. "I hope you like Adzuki bean mango stir fry with cilantro, lime, and coconut sauce."

"Yummy," Kendra said. Maggie vanished into the kitchen with Canada trotting along behind her.

Only Pres caught her slight sarcasm and grinned. "Whew," McBride said. Kendra feigned mopping her forehead. His mother had become pretty pushy and entrenched in her own world in the last few years. He recognized she was upset that he hadn't been over sooner, but what sort of impression was she making on Kendra? He was glad she seemed unconcerned about his mother's behavior. He was grateful for her patience. His mother could be overwhelming. At least one girlfriend broke things off after a similar evening with his mother years ago. He didn't want that to happen again.

"How did you turn out so different? You must have taken after your dad," Kendra said.

He had heard that question before. And he had heard that answer, too. "I like to think I'm a foundling."

"I've never heard you talk about your father. Are your parents divorced?" Kendra asked.

McBride flushed and shook his head. The only thing to do here was tell the truth. "My parents were never married," he said quietly.

"I'm sorry," Kendra said quickly, "we can talk about it some other time."

Pres noted with sadness that she didn't say, "We don't have to talk about it." How was he going to explain to his conservative, mild-mannered girlfriend that he was the love child of a flower girl and a renegade chemist who had been jailed before Pres was born for producing LSD in a lab in Laurel Canyon? It was McBride's darkest, most shameful secret, and he feared, even at this late stage in their relationship, that it would send Kendra running.

For a moment, there was silence. They could hear the quiet footsteps of people in neighboring apartments and the gentle "yip" of some frightened dog not far away. The quiet didn't last.

"Yoo hoo," Maggie called. "Dinner is served." Canada came running in, jumping up on McBride.

"We're coming, boy," he assured the dog.

Dinner was served Japanese style in the dining room with pillows on the floor and a short wooden table. Maggie offered everyone chopsticks; Pres quickly reassured himself that there was silverware available.

"You should make this," Maggie told Kendra, placing a wok filled with a noodle stir fry in the middle of the table. She added a pot full of whole-grained rice next to it. "You just need a few things like coconut milk, chopped fresh cilantro, some garlic, sliced ginger, and agave nectar. I stir fry it, adding mung beans, carrots, and mango slices." As she filled plates, Canada prowled around, trying to get close enough to sample something. Maggie kept shooing him away. He would just try someone else.

"It's good," Kendra announced after a tentative bite. She tried to use the chopsticks, but could only manage a mango slice once or twice before giving up and taking a fork. Pres didn't even try.

"Noni juice?" Maggie offered. "It's from Tahiti and is an antioxidant."

McBride declined. He didn't like the flavor. Kendra, however, took a glass of the dark liquid and sipped it. Then she put it aside.

"So, tell me. How did you lovebirds meet?" Maggie asked. She was demonstrating tremendous dexterity with the chopsticks, more than a little self-consciously.

"At work," McBride said. He glanced at Kendra.

"Love at first sight?" Maggie probed. "The ladies seem to love Pres!"

McBride flushed. Not only was it not true, his mother was embarrassing him in front of his girlfriend.

"No," Kendra said. "He was doing the research. I was just an assistant. He was always the last one to leave, and so we ended up spending a lot of late nights alone together."

"Love in the laboratory! I love it!" Maggie crowed.

Kendra glanced at Pres. "Maggie, you may not know your son as well as you think you do. Pres hardly spoke to me at all the first three weeks we worked together. Even when it was just the two of us alone together, he wouldn't talk to me! At first, I just admired him for his work ethic, but after a while, I was like c'mon, you know, wake up. I'm right here."

Pres couldn't help but smile. It was true that he had noticed Kendra right away, but he felt it would be unprofessional to start a relationship with someone at work. So because he had been attracted to her, he had remained distant—thereby giving her the impression that he didn't like her at all, which was the exact opposite of how he felt. Maggie grinned at him.

"Pres, you always were such a little nerd! After he'd read all the other books in the house, he started reading the encyclopedia! So how did you trap him?"

Here Pres picked up the story. "Actually, it was just coincidental. One night when we came out of the lab, Kendra had a flat tire. It was the middle of winter, so I wasn't going to let her wait for Triple A. So I drove her home…and she made some dinner for us, to thank me for driving her. We drank some wine, played some Scrabble, and Kendra beat me the first game so…well, I'm not going to tell all of it, Mom." Pres looked down, smiling despite himself.

Maggie clapped her hands together, hooting. "Scrabble? Nerds of a feather flock together!"

Pres noticed that Kendra was giggling so hard she had her hand over her mouth.

"Pres," she said, "I never told you this."

"What?" he said. He didn't like surprises, especially not in front of his mother.

"A month later, Susan fessed up that she had given me the flat tire! I guess she saw us mooning around each other and figured we would never get together without a little help."

Susan Johnson, Hofferman's overworked secretary…he had barely acknowledged her, and she had both gone out of her way to bring Kendra into his life and then gotten them a copy of the memo that explained what was really happening at Novilis. Pres felt a flash of guilt and swore to himself that he would stop taking people for granted. He had only ever spoken to Susan out of a sense of obligation, and she had gone out of her way to help him not once but twice.

"What a lovely story," Maggie said. She spied Canada carrying something. "Oh, you bad dog," she cried, running after the animal, which apparently thought they were playing a game. Canada sped around the small apartment with the tart McBride had left in the living room. After a few minutes, Maggie came back. "I couldn't catch him," she wheezed. "I'm afraid he ate the pastry."

She sat down on the floor and folded her legs across her lap. With the purple dress, she resembled a large eggplant. She looked ruefully at the wok and pan in front of her.

"More?' she asked.

"No, I'm stuffed," Kendra said. She patted her stomach.

"Pres, I know you have room for more," Maggie said. McBride declined, too. There was no way was he going to overindulge after having had his mother call attention to his weight in front of Kendra.

"Did you do all your eating in New York? That was so far away." Maggie grew somber. "Your brother Nathan running off to San Francisco and you running off to New York...I miss my boys! Pres, I have missed you so much. I know that it wasn't me that brought you back here, but I am glad to have you closer to me no matter the reason. With your father gone, well...thank goodness, I have Canada, that's all. He's great company."

Maggie looked like she was going to tear up or, even worse, start telling stories about his father. For all his shortcomings as a father, Alexander McBride was no criminal. He was an intelligent and sensitive man and a brilliant chemist who had, unfortunately, turned his skill to making an illegal drug. In prison, he had been forced to live among real criminals, and it had been incredibly hard on him.

"Mom, why don't we help you clean up? It's not fair to stick you with all the dishes when you've cooked for us," Pres said as a means of changing the subject. Somehow, it worked. He was always surprised when that happened. They carried the plates into the kitchen, which was really just a narrow hallway with room for one person walking essentially sideways between the sink and the refrigerator. Canada stayed nearby in case anything edible fell as the three washed, dried, and put away the dishes in a quiet, efficient assembly line. The dog was not heavy yet, but definitely thickening around the middle.

"Oh, the news," Maggie cried as the sink was draining. "I never miss Katie Couric."

She turned on the television. There was an ad on for some new herpes medication. Pres scoffed. The many side effects—headache, nausea, diarrhea, cottonmouth, and so on—overshadowed the fact that the drug "may diminish frequency or severity of outbreaks." But what did he know, he didn't have herpes and never would—he had only been with four women before he met Kendra. He would marry Kendra eventually, he imagined, and that would be that.

"I hope we didn't miss anything," Maggie said, and Pres perked up—she seemed to be addressing what he had just been thinking. "There's so much happening these days. My psychic thinks something really great is just around the corner."

The second item in the newscast concerned the Rohn flu. Couric said the United States Surgeon General had made a major announcement regarding the vaccine.

"Oh no," McBride seethed.

"Shhh," his mother whispered. "You may not care, but I do. I have two friends who got very sick with this flu."

Witherspoon appeared on the screen, talking to reporters. "We will announce when the mandatory shots will be required. Our friends in Canada have requested to be involved so, in a gesture of international diplomacy, we have gifted the initial batches of the vaccine to the Canadian government. Plans are for the initial vaccine testing to commence in Canada where this flu first started. Very soon thereafter, will be testing the vaccine in the area of Oakland, California, which has endured first outbreaks of Rohn flu in the United States."

"I can't believe it," McBride almost shouted.

"Pres!" Maggie and Kendra said together.

"Testing on animals has concluded with very encouraging results," Witherspoon said. "There were no side effects. Human tests will start shortly. The president believes that a mandatory vaccine will be required to insure the health and safety of the American people. The test will be conducted on healthy adults between the ages of eighteen to sixty-four. Participants will receive two shots three weeks apart and will undergo blood tests to determine if they are generating an appropriate immune response to the virus. Because the Rohn flu is a new strain of a previous existing influenza, participants might require higher dosing and two injections rather than one to provoke the desired level of immune response."

"Oh my God," McBride said. "They're using a weaker dose and giving it twice to increase potency! They're really courting disaster with this."

"Is that bad?" Maggie asked.

"Doubling anything in medicine is rarely a good thing," Kendra told her.

Couric reported that though the World Health Organization had only recorded a few deaths directly from the Rohn virus, thousands and thousands of people were enduring serious, long-term illness, and a big leap in mortality was expected. "The Rohn flu has sped around the world at unprecedented speed," the WHO said. "Symptoms are mild, including a fever and cough, but the long-term effects, such as liver and pancreatic failure, could prove to be devastating."

"So can a vaccine using an attenuated virus," McBride said sharply. "They're gambling with the health of the public."

"Be quiet," Maggie told him.

"Mom," McBride replied loudly, "you don't understand."

"I understand you're talking so loudly I can't hear anything," she said. "Yelling at a television set isn't going to change anything."

"It makes me feel better," Pres grumbled.

There was a knock on the door. McBride answered it. An old woman smiled at him. Her white hair highlighted her dark face. "I'm sorry," she quavered, "but could you keep your voices down? My dog has an upset tummy, and you are disturbing him."

"I apologize," McBride said. He gave her a quick smile. "I hope your dog feels better."

She nodded. "He ate something he shouldn't have. Naughty dog," she murmured as she tottered away. Pres rolled his eyes.

"One of my neighbors," Maggie said. "She's always complaining. I don't know her name. I call her Terrier Lady. She has one of those little dogs that yip all the time. That noise doesn't bother her, but if my Canada gets a little loud, she's over here in a flash. Her terrier is always eating something it shouldn't anyway."

"I don't think this announcement should cause a panic." Witherspoon was answering a reporter's question. "We are treating this disease in a straightforward manner. Once the testing is finished, I know Americans will visit their family doctors for vaccinations. This was done with polio back in the nineteen fifties, and we can do it again."

"I hope so," Maggie said. She clutched her hands to her chest. "This is such a horrible disease."

Couric came back to introduce the next story. McBride was not listening.

"How can they know what the long-term effects are?" he raged as quietly as possible. "A vaccine used to counter a Fort Dix flu in nineteen seventy-six ended up causing Guillain-Barre Syndrome and temporary paralysis in some recipients."

His mother and Kendra looked at him like he was speaking in tongues. "Come on," he said, "you remember drugs with disastrous side effects like thalidomide and Vioxx."

"Pres," Kendra said calmly, "they aren't even giving the shots yet. Can't you wait till then to go ballistic?"

"It'll be too late then," McBride answered coldly.

A chill swept through the room. His mother finally flopped down on a beanbag again. Canada cuddled next to her. "Why are you so upset?" she asked.

"Because he was working on the vaccine and isn't getting credit," Kendra said.

"No, that's not true," McBride responded. "I don't think the vaccine is safe." Still, he felt doubt seeping into his mind. Was Kendra right? No, he told himself, he was only thinking about the public good. He didn't say that aloud. It sounded like a weak excuse, even to himself.

"You deserve credit for any work you do," his mother said fiercely. She smiled. "Of course, it would help if you were working."

"I'll get a job," he told her wearily.

"You'd better. You are supposed to support me in my old age. Nathan certainly won't make enough money, not teaching high school biology," Maggie said. "You know, if the government wants everyone vaccinated, Dr. Crossland will need help at the clinic."

"I don't want to inoculate people," McBride said. "I went into research because I don't like working with patients."

"Beggars can't be choosers," Maggie told him.

Kendra sneezed. Though he shot her a concerned look, secretly Pres was grateful for the distraction. Maggie jumped up, grabbed Canada, and made the sign of the cross with her two index fingers. "You aren't sick, are you?' she demanded.

"Allergies," Kendra said hesitantly.

"It's those incense candles," Maggie sighed. "I like them, but they make lots of people sneeze. Come on. Let's get out of here and go for a walk."

Canada was so excited by hearing the word "walk" that for several moments, he refused to calm down enough that the leash could be attached to his collar, thereby forestalling the walk he anticipated so greedily. Eventually, after much chiding, Maggie succeeded. Canada towed her to the door. They left the television still blaring.

Canada rarely paused to explore the scents along the route which eventually took them through the complex and out onto Vineland on a cool, very pleasant California evening. Kendra, despite the occasional sneezing fit, had no trouble keeping up. McBride matched his mother at first, and then quickly began to lag. His leg muscles protested against the unexpected exertion. His stomach bobbed up and down, creating the sensation that he was carrying something under his shirt. When he had occasionally strolled in the park, he moved more leisurely. His thoughts may have raced ahead toward his uncertain future, but his legs made no effort to keep pace. Now they had barely walked a couple of hundred yards, and he was looking for a place to rest.

"Oh," he puffed, "look." A man had emerged from his house with a small dog on a leash. It looked like a bundle of hair with no defined face or legs.

"That's Aristotle," Maggie said. "I know all the dogs around here."

The dog stopped to stare at them as they approached. Then, its rear end—or, at least, one furry end—started wiggling in overt happiness. Maggie knelt down and started petting the dog. A red tongue emerged from the living mound of fur to lick her hand. Canada hung back, looking bored.

"Hi," McBride said weakly to the owner, who was middle-aged with short white hair on the sides of his otherwise bald head. He had a pleasant smile and nodded a greeting back. "Nice dog," McBride added.

"He very smart," the man said with a thick European accent. Italian, Mc Bride thought. "He a Yorky-Maltese mix," the man continued.

"Ari," Kendra told the dog, "you are so cute." Though she clutched a tissue in one hand, she was kneeling down to get closer to the animal, which now had rolled over for a tummy rub. She gestured toward McBride to join her. He knelt down and patted the dog. It had thick fur that completely encased its face, but he could see two dark eyes looking up at him with gratitude for the attention. Such simple creatures, Pres though, envying the dog its bliss. When they stopped petting to continue their journey, Ari barked at them.

"He hates it when I leave," Maggie whispered. She laughed and waved. "Bye, Ari," she called.

"What's the guy's name?" McBride asked.

"I don't know," Maggie admitted. "I usually only know the names of the dogs."

Across the street was a beagle named MooMoo. He had a fondness for rolling in whatever disgusting thing he could find, Maggie announced with a mixture of sadness and pride. On the next block was Gabby, an elderly shih tzu, who was blind and almost totally inert. Gabby's owner could not bear to part with her and often had to carry the dog outside. His only son lived in Kansas, Maggie reported, and the dog had kept him company for 16 years.

Then there was Max, a 100-pound German shepherd puppy whose live-in companion was a 13-pound bichon frise that the wife had named Chianti and the husband nicknamed Snack. If Max ever got hungry, Kendra explained, that's all Chianti was. Chianti lived to chase rubber balls, but Max was curious and much more intelligent. He once managed to retrieve a bottle of bourbon from a liquor cabinet, but thankfully had not succeeded in removing the cap. Pres almost made a "party animal" joke but resisted at the last second. It made him realize that he was actually feeling good for the first time in a long time.

"No allergies?" he asked as Kendra gleefully ran her fingers through the thick fur of another dog overjoyed to see her.

"I can't have the dogs in the house," she said, "but I can pet them out here without any problems. I'll just wash my hands when I get home."

McBride found the stories the owners told amusing. He even forgot about the distance he walked. His attention was consumed by one dog after another, each of whom Maggie would describe in loving detail. He despised the anonymity of generic apartment buildings, but through the dogs and dog owners, Pres was surprised to find a real community. There was a thin, waif-like woman who walked a greyhound whose body type mimicked her own. A rescued dog, Maggie said. It was too old to race, and the breeder was going to euthanize it. Another woman had two fluffy, tan Pomeranians that kept entwining their leashes as if that was their goal. At a house beyond the apartment complex, two malamutes came charging at a wire fence as they walked by. Frick and Frack, Maggie called them, from the Car Talk radio show she occasionally listened to on National Public Radio. Canada had to be restrained from joyfully frolicking with them. The three dogs howled together for a moment before Maggie tugged Canada away.

Near the end of Vineland, McBride heard something barking fiercely. It was a tiny black-brown Chihuahua, only a little taller than the grass it came charging through, fiercely defending its yard. Its owner, a chunky woman waving a cigarette, ran after it from the house.

"Manga, Manga," she yelled. "Stop that."

That dog, intent on guard duty, did not listen. Maggie knelt down and extended a hand while passing Canada's leash to Kendra. Timidly, Manga came forward to sniff, taking two steps forward, then one back. When Pres inched closer, it backed away again and started barking.

"I'm sorry," the woman said. "He forgets he's only three pounds." She scooped up the dog. Maggie extended a hand to pet it. The Chihuahua pulled back. Its big, brown eyes glared at her as worry lines creased its tiny forehead. The owner had to struggle to hold it.

"He needs a while to get used to people," the woman said.

"He's so cute," Maggie cooed. Manga clearly was not impressed with compliments.

There was no way to say anything like that to the last dog they saw: a small, dark creature with a tuft of white hair on its head and, bizarrely, its tongue hanging out the left side of its mouth. A Chinese crested, the owner said. He proudly announced that the dog, Muchapoopa, was an annual entry in the Ugliest Dog Contest held annually in Petaluma. The darn thing couldn't see itself in a mirror and was as friendly as any of the dogs were, despite its strange appearance.

"You have a regular route," Pres observed aloud to his mother after returning to her apartment.

"I don't have to wash 'em, take 'em to the vet, or buy 'em chew toys," she said. "I just get to love them."

"They're only dogs," he said. Even as the words passed his lips, he knew that he was missing the point.

"You don't understand," Maggie replied perhaps a little sharply. She hugged Canada. "This is my life now. My son is gone. My husband is gone. I have my dog."

Pres absorbed her rebuke without responding. The walk that Canada had taken them on had showed him that, well, dogs weren't only dogs. In fact, noticing several children playing with dogs, Pres felt bad that the cramped apartments he and Maggie had shared growing up hadn't permitted him to ever have a dog. He had had a turtle and a hermit crab. *Both animals who live in their shells,* Pres thought, *just like me.*

Later, in the car, Pres took a deep breath. "I hope that wasn't too overwhelming. My mother is a little wild."

Kendra patted McBride's shoulder. "Don't be too hard on your mom," she said. "I think she's scared of getting old and people seeing her as old."

"We're all scared of something," Pres answered. "We're just not necessarily scared of the same things."

"What are you scared of, Pres?" Kendra asked.

Pres couldn't respond, not because he couldn't think of anything, but because he thought of too many things.

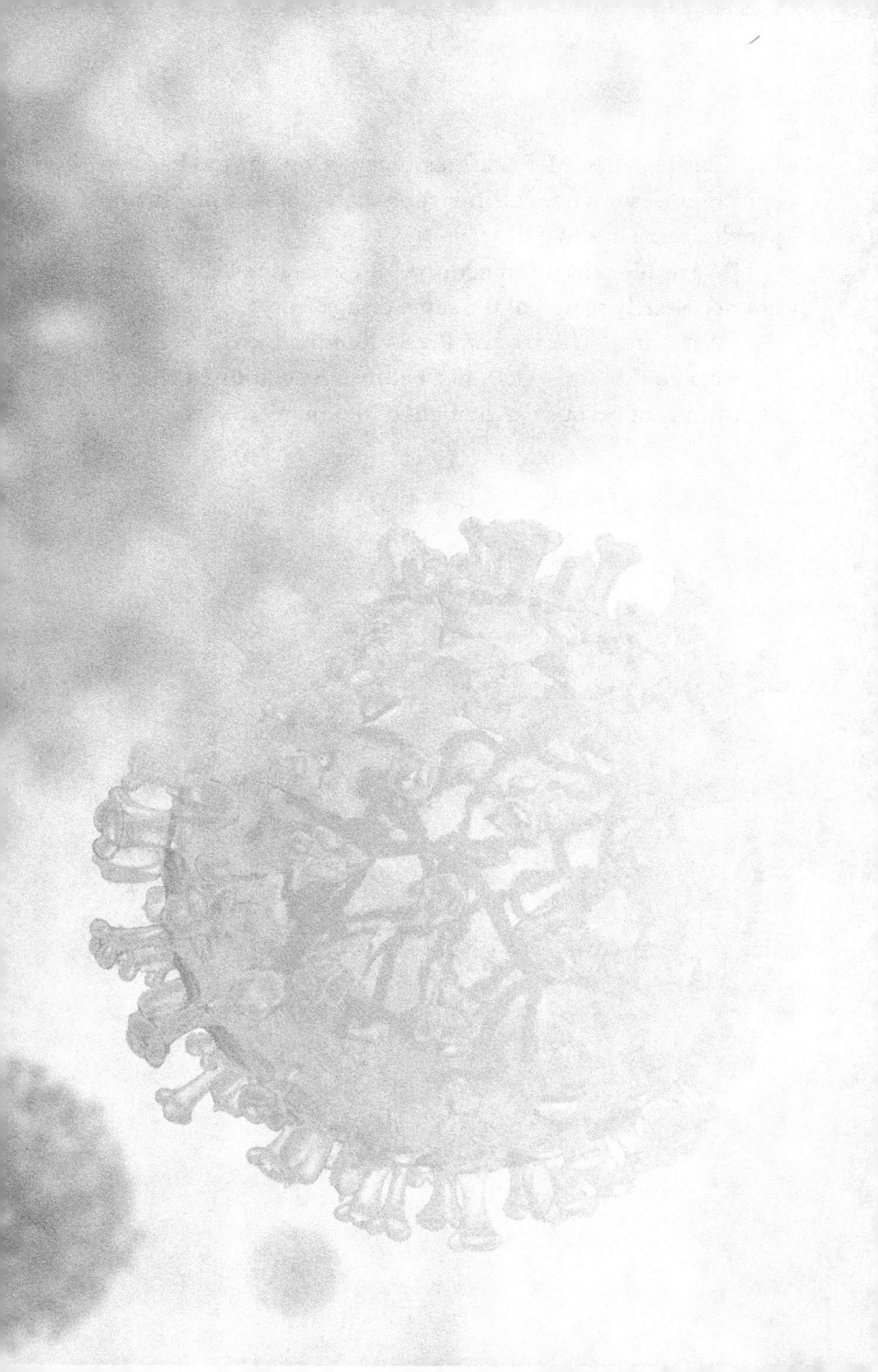

Chapter 3

The first person to greet McBride as he entered the small, crowded waiting room in Dr. Crossland's clinic was a cheerful older man holding a squirming little dog under his arm. He was standing by the door, as all the seats were taken.

"Hello," McBride said, stepping by him.

The man smiled. He was stocky with a rounded red face and thinning white hair, "Allo," he answered in a strong Spanish accent. The animal struggled to get closer to McBride, licking the air frantically with kisses well short of their mark.

McBride reached out a tentative hand. The dog contentedly licked his fingers. "Nice dog," he said.

"He's a stunning mutt," the man said proudly, setting the dog on the floor. "I call him a stun-mutt."

McBride nodded slowly. He made a guess. "Part poodle, part...what?"

"Part bichon, part Maltese, part something else," the man replied.

"What's his name?" McBride continued. Kendra had beseeched him to improve his manners with patients and people. He would try, now that he had agreed to help Dr. Crossland at the clinic.

"Amante," the man replied. "Lover." The dog was making every effort to live up to the name as he mounted McBride's knee.

"Marvelous, but, you know," McBride said, trying to discreetly shake the dog off his leg, "Lover should probably not be in here."

The old man listened, but just smiled. No one else seemed concerned. In fact, at least two other people in the waiting room gave up their seats to come over and pet Amante, much to the dog's delight. McBride gave up and walked over to the reception desk.

"Dr. McBride," Rosa Mendales exclaimed as she looked up. She was short, with dark features and black hair neatly tucked into a bun. Her eyes maintained a steady, practical gaze. "You didn't have to wait in line to get a shot."

"I'm here to help Dr. Crossland," McBride explained.

"Oh," Rosa blushed. "I didn't know. He'll welcome your help. There are so many inoculations."

McBride smiled at her. "I'm glad to be working here now."

She smiled apologetically and buzzed him through the door. In New York, McBride would have had to pass through two levels of security just to reach the lab. No ID was necessary here. One button in this place and he was in. Rosa, like two other clinic nurses, Laura Silverstein and Janette Rosen, was a long-time employee. McBride had met the nurses several times while visiting Crossland. They all remembered him.

McBride opened Crossland's office door, found a white coat left for him, and headed to the nearby treatment area. The office, once a private home, had six small rooms for patients and true to form, Crossland was having patients ushered into each room one by one, giving them shots, talking to them and making sure records were accurate before heading to the next patient. The result inevitably was a very slow-moving procession.

A door swung open, and Crossland emerged from a treatment room trailed by Rosen. He glanced around and got his bearings. McBride could see the weariness: the old man's cheeks had sunken in; his eyes were bloodshot. After originally having misgivings about getting involved with patients instead of test tubes, McBride now was really glad he had agreed to provide assistance. He had seen Crossland while on vacation six months earlier when they had even talked about his future. Then, Crossland had been vibrant, even youthful looking. Now, his white hair was disappearing rapidly; his back was bent a bit more, and he shuffled rather than strode. Old age had made a fast claim on him.

For a moment, Crossland stared at McBride. "About time," he finally rasped at him before walking briskly as possible to the next room.

He glanced at Rosen. "Where's my next file?" he snapped. She produced it quickly. He didn't smile.

McBride shrugged. Crossland had the grumpy old man routine down pat and wasn't likely to change. McBride glanced at the clock. It was only 8:55. The clinic supposedly didn't open until nine o'clock, but Crossland had seen patients waiting and hadn't hesitated to usher them in. McBride prided himself on being early. Now he felt late.

"He's been awful," Rosen whispered as Crossland marched away. "Ever since his wife died, he's been snooping through files, peering over our shoulders. Two new nurses quit. You know I feel sorry for him. I know he's suffering. But maybe you can you talk to him?"

"I'll try," McBride said, a bit stunned. Caught up in his own turmoil, he had no idea what had happened to Crossland's wife. "Lucy was his rock. What happened?"

"One day, she was fine, as energetic as ever," Rosen answered softly. Tears welled in her eyes. "The next, she was lying on the office floor. Pancreatic cancer. She must have felt it every time she ate, but didn't say a word. We had no idea anything was wrong. She would occasionally lean against the wall or something, but we all get tired. We did all we could for her, but that wasn't much. She went quickly. Dr. Crossland didn't say anything. You know he doesn't show emotions."

McBride nodded. The man rumbled and grumbled, but disguised his real feelings behind that gruff facade. McBride knew the rough exterior wasn't real. So did his patients. He had been running this clinic successfully for at least thirty years because everyone knew he cared. He listened intently and was extremely thorough. Most people rarely had to sit in his waiting room past the appointment time, but they might watch the wall clock for a while in one of the simple treatment rooms while Crossland meticulously examined another patient.

"He only took a few days off," Rosen marveled. "But now he's obviously getting tired sooner, staying longer in the office than he needs to, speaking endlessly to patients, and growing obsessive over even minor symptoms." Her voice lowered further. "I'm afraid his mind is drifting away at times. Rosa and Laura are upset, too."

"Janette," Crossland yelled, poking his head out the door. "Stop the yapping and get in here."

She rolled her eyes and turned away.

"Distract him," McBride suggested. She nodded, more in resignation than in agreement. An idea crept into his mind. There might be a way to redirect Crossland's attention. McBride smiled. He might have enough time at lunch to take care of a little errand.

Before the door closed, McBride heard Crossland rumble, "Back again, Mr. Francisco? Stop your damn drinking and you wouldn't have to crawl in here so often."

If she thinks I'm bad, Kendra should see how the old man handles his patients, McBride thought. Now close to seventy, Crossland was the epitome of the old-time family doctor who found himself tortured by ultramodern technology. The new instrumentation and methods that quickly diagnosed his patients' ailments challenged his feelings of self worth and simultaneously limited his social contact. From a gradual, mounting resentment of the new ways, he no longer cared what he said or who he offended.

"If they want better bedside manners," Crossland said frequently, "let them read a fairy tale."

Silverstein led McBride to the rear three rooms. All were full. He took the file from the door and walked into the closest room. A young woman perched on the treatment table with a small girl twined around her leg. The girl held a stuffed dog clenched in her pale hand. Both patients looked up at him. McBride introduced himself.

"Soy Maria Fernandez con mi niña Andrea," the woman said.

So far, so good, McBride thought. He understood that. The few years of high school Spanish had stuck. He hoped she didn't start an in-depth conversation.

"¿Dónde está Doctor Crossland?" Maria continued.

McBride tried to reply. "No aquí. Soy doctor y aquí." She nodded. "Está bien?" he asked.

She shrugged.

"¿Quéquieres?" he tried, instantly realizing that was the wrong question. It led to a torrent of Spanish, which left him mystified. When he lived in Pomona as a child, Spanish was not a necessity. Now it was. He looked over at a potted plant by the door and then back at her.

"It's OK," Silverstein quickly assured him. "I speak Spanish."

It turned out that Maria just wanted a Rohn flu inoculation for her daughter and herself. The Friday before, the government had ordered mandatory Rohn flu vaccines. That's when Crossland had called and invited him to help out. There were bound to be many people flocking into the familiar clinic after the weekend. McBride couldn't say no, since he owed the old man so much. Crossland was the one who had slapped his bare bottom thirty-five years ago at Pomona Valley Hospital Medical Center to help him take his first breath. He also got McBride the research job in New York.

I've spent the last two months ranting about the damn vaccine, and now I'm going to inoculate patients with it, McBride thought when he got the call. Still, he felt he couldn't tell Crossland no.

The treatment room was well stocked with a line of sealed hypodermic needles and vaccines. He picked up a small vial of the vaccine. It contained five mml, good for ten doses. The liquid inside was clear, giving no hint of whether it would be dangerous or not. McBride wished he knew. In the past, adverse reactions to attenuated flu vaccines had extended from convulsions and seizures to fevers. Maybe this one would not be so bad. He hoped his fears were unjustified.

Practice in the lab helped him fill the hypodermic, but he felt awkward plunging it into the little girl's arm. It had been years since medical school and his internship. His fingers felt thick. Silverstein watched him with something like mild contempt. Nurses should be doing this, but the government had mandated that doctors must apply the shots because of the serious nature of the disease. Silverstein cleaned the spot with alcohol and waited with a Band-Aid. He had to do the rest.

The vaccine went into the muscle, which was much easier than finding a vein. The little girl didn't cry, although she clutched her dog tighter. Her mother sat stoically, too. Both thanked him.

"Adiós," Andrea piped. She waved the stuffed dog as a goodbye as she got up to leave.

McBride's eyes lingered on Maria's trim waist and muscular legs as she swayed out the door, glancing at McBride over her shoulder. He shook his head—what was he doing, checking out another woman, and a patient, no less? He had to pull his head together and quick.

More patients followed rapidly. McBride must have fumbled with one needle for a good ten seconds, to the amusement of the nurse and the consternation of an old woman waiting to get pricked. Part of his ineptitude laid in the constant thought, each time he jabbed someone, that the risk-reward ratio was in favor of hurting them with this live vaccine. It had the ability to grow and multiply and would shed from the body for a few weeks after, through feces and skin pores and hair follicles. Until the injected person built immunity to it, it was absolutely contagious.

"I hold the record for juggling needles in medical school," he told the old woman.

"Practice somewhere else," she snapped.

He saw the old man with the dog again. Crossland treated him. No one mentioned the dog even though Crossland and the old man stepped aside and chatted for several minutes in the corridor as the animal went berserk around them. McBride watched them pensively for a moment and then he had yet another patient to vaccinate.

"The hospital's swamped, too," Kendra reported during the lunch break, over the phone. "It shouldn't be a surprise."

McBride agreed. Just like everyone else, he had watched the virus move from level four to five to six via the Centers for Disease Control and World Health Organization's declarations.

"I just wish they had tested the vaccine for more than two months," he said.

"No side effects so far," Kendra noted, cautiously optimistic.

"So far," McBride emphasized. He had seen the reports from Oakland, where the first Rohn Flu vaccine tests were conducted on human volunteers. Not one had gotten sick or keeled over. Still, he told her, similar mandated Swine flu shots back in the 1970s eventually killed thousands. President Ford had ordered the vaccinations and had then reversed it himself and stopped them. "It was months before the real impact was felt," he cautioned Kendra.

"Think how many lives were saved," she said.

"I doubt that was much consolation for those who died from getting a flu shot," he countered. He quickly excused himself from the call with Kendra; he had another pressing phone call to make.

By late afternoon he was very tired, but McBride had learned two new words: "la gripe" mean flu; "la vacunación" meant vaccination. By the end of the day, he was able to ask, "Are you here for a flu vaccination?" in Spanish. He even found out how to provide the standard inaccurate but reassuring "this won't hurt a bit"—"Esto no va a doler un poco."

That phrase had been especially useful as the patients kept trooping in. Everyone in Pomona, maybe even nearby Ontario, Rancho Cucamonga, and Chino seemed to have headed to this familiar office. From the looks of it, McBride decided, most of them had rushed in immediately after the announcement.

Finally, the last patient bared his arm, grimaced as the needle darted into the skin, then smiled and left. McBride let Silverstein clean up the treatment room while he walked stiffly down the corridor to Crossland's office. Clearly, the occasional scotch and a leisurely stroll around a park hadn't boosted his conditioning. His back ached. His arm hurt. Kendra had teased him about getting out of shape. He was beginning to agree with her on that subject anyway. The long hiatus after leaving his New York job had definitely added to his waistline. This was it, though; now that he was again gainfully employed, though humbly so, he swore he would get back in shape.

Crossland was already in his office, lying back in his over-stuffed chair. Its leather, like his face, was worn and wrinkled with experience. His eyes were actually closed when McBride came in to say hello and compare notes. The computer screen behind the old man was on, displaying a CNN news article.

The younger man almost didn't say anything, not wanting to wake Crossland. He started to walk away quietly.

"I don't bite," Crossland said in his raspy voice, adding with a growl, "much."

McBride turned around, pulled a nearby chair close to the old man, and sat. "Long day," he noted wearily, rotating his head to ease the dull throb in his neck.

"They all are," Crossland replied sourly.

"I just needed to relax a minute," McBride said. "You're a workhorse. I feel whipped, Abe. I hope I have your energy when I'm older."

Crossland's eyes narrowed in pretense, as if upset at the hint about his age. McBride was not concerned. The old man liked compliments. He wanted people to think he was younger than his years. Crossland stood up, shoulders straight. Even if he were tired, there was no way he was going to let a younger colleague know anyway.

"You don't eat right," Crossland recited. "And you don't exercise enough." He paused. "You should get a dog. Then, at least, you'd go for an occasional walk."

McBride couldn't even muster a reply. Maybe, he thought cheerily, all that raising and lowering his arm to give shots burned off some of the ten pounds he had added recently.

"You want your shot now?" Crossland asked.

McBride shook his head. "I'll get it later," he decided. He didn't explain. Until he was sure of its safety, he was not going to get an injection. He'd take his chances with the flu.

"Give me mine now," Crossland ordered. He stood up and took off his jacket, hanging it on a clothes rack by the side of his desk. He was wearing long sleeves and calmly rolled up the one covering his right arm. "Come on," he said, gesturing at a needle and vial placed on a small table behind the desk with a bottle of rubbing alcohol and cotton balls.

McBride used the alcohol and cotton swab to clean Crossland's arm. The skin was wrinkled, dry, and sagging. He picked up the familiar vial. He carefully inserted the needle and drew out the required amount of vaccine. He worked slowly, both because he was tired and to avoid any mistakes. That would have been very embarrassing.

"By the time you finish, the damn virus will have mutated three times," Crossland snarled. He used his left hand to hold his body steady. "I must see five patients in the time it takes you to see one."

"I don't talk as much," McBride said.

The needle slid easily into his arm. Crosland did not flinch. McBride slowly pressed the plunger, sending the vaccine deep into the muscle tissue. A small red drop appeared when he removed the needle. He started to place a tiny bandage over it.

"Don't bother," Crosland said. "I need something to remind me I'm still alive."

He rolled back his sleeve and straightened his bowtie. "Get some rest," he ordered. "Tomorrow will be just like today." He marched around his desk to the door. "Turn the light off when you go," he continued, then paused by the door. "Try not to fall asleep here."

There was a knock on the door. Crossland stopped. He smoothed his white coat and ran his fingers through his hair.

The three nurses trooped in. Silverstein was in front; Rosen and Mendales hung behind. They were all smiling coyly. Mendales had her hands behind her back.

"More complaints?" Crossland asked with a harsh tone. He went back to his cushioned office chair and plopped down. His shoulders slumped. He didn't bother to straighten up this time. With his elbow on his desk and his head resting on his knuckles, the old doctor appeared the picture of indifference.

"No, sir," Silverstein said in a calm, professional voice. A thin woman with curly brown hair, she seemed full of energy despite the many patients she had seen. "This marks the thirtieth anniversary of the clinic, and we thought a celebration was in order!"

Crossland frowned. "That was two months ago," he noted. "I set this place up in April, not now." He looked at them curiously. "Do you know I was born in Massachusetts?"

"Yes, sir," Rosen said quickly. "We've been too busy to celebrate earlier," she offered. Rosen was thickset, sturdy, and definitely the most enthusiastic of the trio. She looked like she was ready to climb an alp.

"Now is a good time," Mendales added.

"Fine," Crossland said. "Put the cake on the table. Throw confetti in the air. Then start filing."

The nurses looked at each other and tried not to react to his callousness. Silverstein gestured at Mendales, who came forward and placed a square, brown, plastic carrier on the desk. For a moment, everyone looked at it. McBride could hear some shuffling and whimpering from behind its wire mesh door. He tried to hold back a smile—how would Crossland respond?

"Not cake," Mendales said. She opened the door, and a small dachshund with a collar on its small neck edged out nose first. The puppy sniffed the desk and looked up at Crossland, then at the others.

"What is going on?" Crossland grumped. He was still trying to sound tough, but his tone was already softer. He reached out a big hand and began to pet the dog. It licked his fingers. "Hello there, little man." For a few moments, the room was very still. A small smile flickered across Crossland's face and then, just as quickly, it was gone. "I hope he's housebroken," he growled.

The nurses quickly cleared the desk.

"I...we thought you could use a friend," McBride said. Wide-eyed, Crossland looked at him.

"He's mine?"

The nurses nodded in unison.

"I hope you like him," Silverstein said.

Crossland picked up the dog. His big hands engulfed it. He pulled the dog to his chest. It didn't squirm, but nestled close. It looked sleepy. "I love dachshunds," he said, almost accusatorily, staring at his staff as if they had caught him in a secret.

"We know, sir," Rosen said. Everyone laughed. There were at least five pictures of a dachshund on Crossland's shelving behind his desk. A large framed painting of a dachshund hung next to his diploma on the wall.

"What should we call him?" Rosen asked.

"Al," Crossland said. "Good boy," he cooed at the puppy. "Al was the name of a dachshund I had as a child. This one would be Al, Junior. But we will call him Al." He petted the dog. "Do you like that name, Al?" The dog licked at him.

"I guess that's yes," McBride noted, grinning. It was amazing the magic a dog could work, even on a hardened, overworked, lonely old curmudgeon like Crossland.

"Did anyone get him some food?" Crossland darkened.

The nurses quickly darted outside the office. Mendales produced a bag of dog food and a box of snacks. Silverstein brought in a leash, a dog bowl, and a chew toy. Rosen showed up with a pile of newspapers. Crossland opened the carton of snacks and offered the dog a bit of a biscuit. It nibbled at it, then wolfed it down, smacking its lips.

"I don't want Al in the office during the day," Crossland noted harshly. "He'll get stepped on. Dogs shouldn't be in a doctor's office anyway. Allergies, you know."

McBride started to say something about the dog that the old man had brought earlier, but didn't want to spoil the mood. Besides, Kendra had already told him that lots of doctors in the area brought pets to work.

"I already spoke to your neighbor," Silverstein said calmly. "She'll be happy to keep an eye on Al while you are in the clinic."

Crossland sat up. His lips moved, but no words came out. He put Al on the desk. One by one, the nurses hugged him.

"I should be getting home," he said, trying not to meet anyone's eyes.

"Yes," Silverstein said. "It's late."

Crossland placed the dog on the floor and attached the leash. "Turn the light off when you go," he ordered. He straightened his shoulders, his head held high. "Try not to fall asleep here." Then proudly, the little dog held his own head high and led the much bigger man out of the office. Rosa followed with the rest of the supplies.

The remaining two nurses waited a few moments until they heard the front door thud as it closed. Then hugged each other and laughed.

"Did you see the two of them strutting out of here?" McBride said, smiling so hard his cheeks hurt. Man, he had forgotten what that felt like.

"Thank you so much, Dr. McBride," Rosen said. "That's the first time he's left the office before eight p.m. in months."

"I don't think he'll be much of a problem again," McBride said.

"I agree. His neighbor is a widow and very eager to get closer to Dr. Crossland," Silverstein chortled. "She couldn't wait to take care of the dog for him."

They cheerfully walked out, talking to each other. McBride watched them go. This had been a very good day. Seeing that old man with the overly affectionate mutt had given him the idea. Rosen supplied the car, and a pet store on South Garey had the perfect dog.

He sat down in Crossland's worn office chair and glanced at his computer. Crossland had been looking at a strange story from Canada, something about some kind of disease that was killing dogs in the Iditarod. *Odd*, he thought. He didn't see any signs of illnesses in dogs around here. He hoped the illness stayed north of the border, but was realistic. Rohn flu had spread quickly. Was the Great White North becoming a hotbed for diseases? It didn't seem likely. Even if there were some kind of mammalian flu that was affecting dogs, it was unlikely it would affect him or Kendra. She was allergic to fur, which ruled out everything from a hamster on up to an alpaca, and he wasn't about to run out to get a monitor lizard. His childhood experiences with the turtle and the hermit crab had taught him that it's hard to care for any creature incapable of loving you back. The love Amante had for the old man—even the love Al showed for Crossland upon just meeting him—was open and unconditional, and humans seemed to respond in kind. Still, Pres wasn't about to choose a dog over Kendra.

McBride flipped his cell phone from his pocket and hit her number on the speed dial. "Hi. Everything okay?" He listened for a moment. "I'm done. When can you pick me up?"

"My shift just ended," she replied sweetly. "See you in fifteen or so minutes. Bye. Love you."

He hung up.

He shut down the PC, hit the light switch, and left the office. It was amazingly empty. This was like when he left the Novilis lab in New York late at night. He would check to see the doors were locked and the lights were off. He liked that moment of solitude and would even stay late to revel in it, alone.

He still felt cheerful as Kendra drove into the empty parking lot a few minutes later. She pretended to stop and then pulled away from him, laughing at him through the window. This happened three times before he finally got in the car.

"Give me a break, will you?" he said. "It's been a long day."

Once she let him into the car, he told her about the dachshund and the thought that had nagged at him all day. "I was just thinking about some of the people I saw," McBride said. "They have no idea what I was putting in them. Even I don't know what I was putting in them. But the government ordered flu shots, and they all lined up."

"It's a panacea," she said. "People need their illusions."

"There was one old guy who brought his dog to the clinic," McBride continued.

"Did you give the dog a shot, too?" Kendra teased.

He laughed lightly. "I told him that he shouldn't bring the dog inside. But I guess this isn't a lab."

"He got angry, didn't he?" Kendra said.

"No, not really," McBride replied. "I don't think he understood English very well."

"So much for improving your bedside manner," Kendra noted. "You can't take dogs away from their owners. That's like taking their children. Especially the old people. Their kids don't call. They hardly talk to their neighbors. There aren't many activities for them. Their dogs are their lives."

"Dogs shouldn't be in a medical facility," McBride said gently.

"Aw, don't be such a grump," she chided him gently, smiling. "There are dentists here that have cats living in their offices. I heard about a financial planner with a large dog. There must be two or three doctors around here who have dogs," she said.

McBride sat up. "Really?"

"Sure. Now that you've gotten out of intensive care yourself, maybe you'll learn some of these things," she teased.

Kendra gunned the motor, and the Honda responded as best it could. All the way down West McKinley and then north to their rented home near Mountain Meadows Golf Course, McBride peered through his window and could see people walking their dogs. Around Arbor Circle and onto Savannah, he counted at least eight to ten dogs. Maybe a dog in the office wasn't that unusual, he decided. Thank goodness he could concentrate on people, he thought. They sat still, most of them, took their shots, and understood what was happening. Treating dogs would be a nightmare.

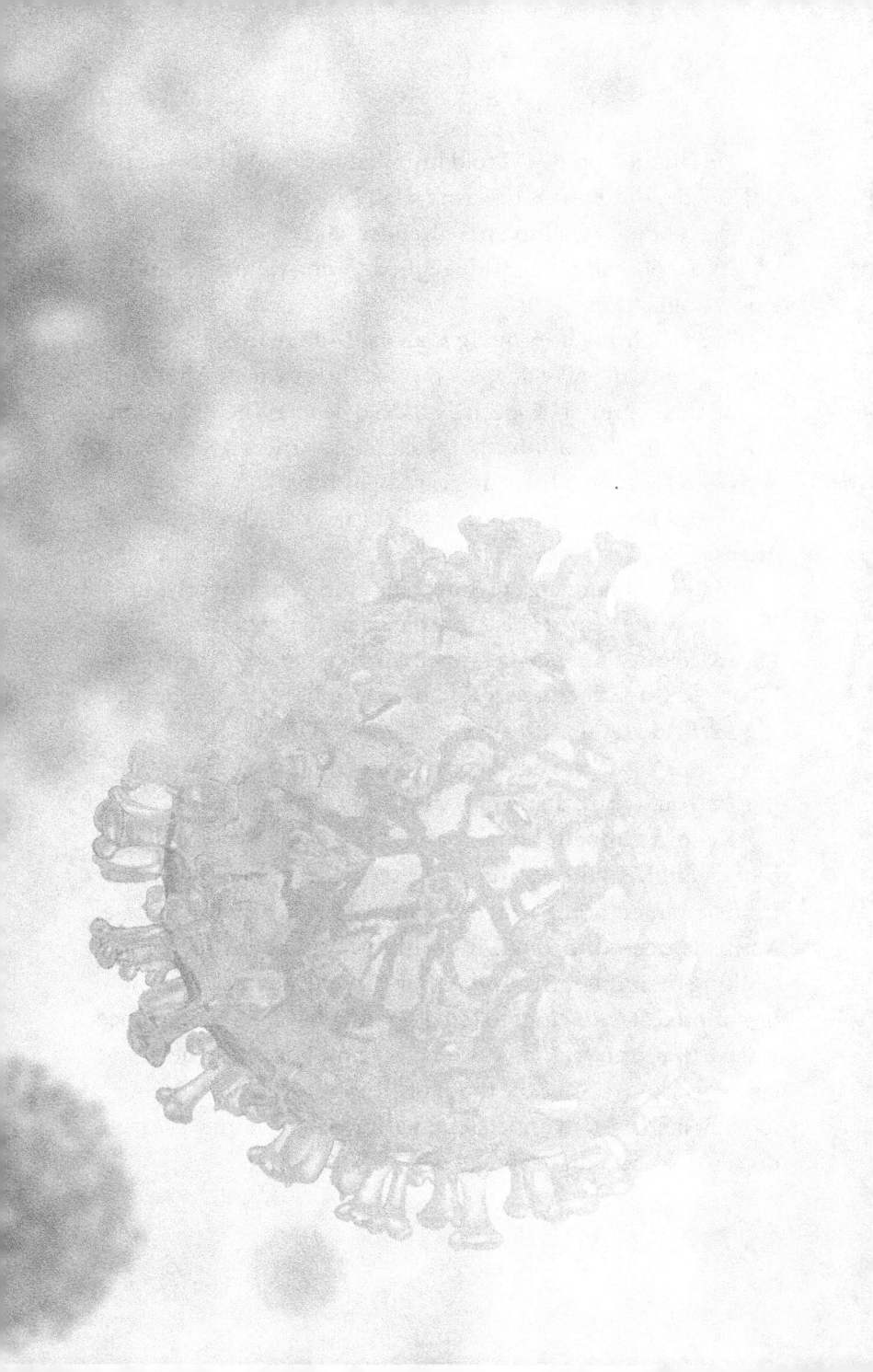

Chapter 4

"Each day is pretty much the same at the clinic," McBride told Kendra as he joined her for the first time on her regular evening walk. The Santa Ana winds had blown for a few days but had stopped. This evening was calm and unusually clear. The light, dry air and the blue-orange horizon reminded him that this part of California was still a desert. "People get shots and leave satisfied that they are now safe from the Rohn flu. Once in awhile," he said, "someone comes in for a different reason, but nothing serious." After a pause, he said, "I don't want to get used to the routine. I still want to return to research."

"Novilis has a facility out here. Do you think they'd hire you back?"

He shrugged. "I do good work."

"God, Pres, I was kidding. Would you really go and work for that slime ball?"

"That slime ball" was Ethan Willis, who had been named vice president over at Novilis research labs. McBride had laughed out loud when he read that on CNN. The same guy who had stolen credit for his work had gotten a sweet deal. A deal that might have been his. Then he could have fired Willis. Still, Willis knew him and knew the kind of research he did.

Something might work out. *Forget the past; concentrate on the future.* At this juncture, he couldn't afford to rule it out.

"Of course not. The clinic's a workable situation, I guess."

Things were easier now at the clinic, in any case. In just a few weeks with Al, Crossland had relaxed. All someone had to do was ask, "How's the dog?" and his craggy face would break into a smile. "Good, good," he'd say and relate one of the endearing, silly things the dachshund puppy had done lately. Al had dug up the flower garden! Al had scared the pants off the neighbor's cat! Al had gotten big enough that he could now jump into bed all by himself! He spoke emotionally and without embarrassment. As each day drew to a close, Crossland would stand up. "I should be getting home," he would announce, "Al will be waiting for me," with all seriousness and head out the door. The worry lines around his eyes even seemed to fade. He would still say some very odd things at times, particularly when he was tired, but his gait was surer, his energy level solid.

"He hasn't snapped at me all week," Rosen whispered to McBride on Friday. "Maybe I should get a dog, too!"

McBride had noticed how many people did have dogs. Just about every other household in the neighborhood included one. The owners put sweaters on them, bought fancy food for them, and at times, treated their pets better than they did their kids.

On one evening walk with Kendra, McBride saw a man slowly trudge toward them. He was old with heavy jowls and long circles under his eyes. A wide nose extended almost to his mouth, which made chewing motions that indicated a lack of teeth. His back was bent so that the slight breeze failed to ruffle the remaining tufts of gray hair on the top of his head.

He was the kind of person McBride usually avoided. Kendra walked right up to him.

"Jay!" she exclaimed. "How is Bruno?"

The man beamed. His gray eyes filled with light, and his back straightened a notch. "I didn't think he was going to make it," he drawled, "but that old dog has guts."

"Bruno," Kendra explained, "had heart surgery."

"An aneurism," Jay added cheerily. "Right near the heart. It was about to bust, the doctor said."

"But he pulled through?" Kendra asked.

"He's still a bit weak," Jay reported. "I got him a puppy to keep him company. They romp around a little, and then Bruno lies down." Jay checked his watch. "I'd better get back. Bruno needs his medicine." He waved goodbye and trundled off.

McBride tilted his head and watched Kendra watch the old man leave.

"Some purebred dog?" McBride wanted to know.

"No," Kendra said, "just a mutt."

"Kendra," McBride said, gently ribbing her, "you're turning into my mother. What's next, some patchouli stir fry?"

Kendra swatted at him, but Pres dodged quickly. They walked back quietly, at ease with one another. It grew dark, and McBride became aware of the sound of his own footsteps. He let his mind empty for a change.

"Those dogs are more than pets, aren't they?" McBride said over dinner. Kendra had cooked up a thick steak with mashed potatoes, with pudding for desert to celebrate his first month at the clinic.

"Have you just come to that hypothesis now?" Kendra asked. "Have you concluded you research? Open your eyes,

Pres! Dogs hold a neighborhood together. Do you think any-one would talk to Jay unless he had a dog? People ask about Bruno. They talk to him. He looks strange, but he has a dog, which I guess in some ways means that he's a human being, a participating member of society. You can't walk a cat, you know? They're usually annoyed you're around unless you have a bag of food in your hand."

She put down her knife and fork. "Look at society today," she said. "We're all being forced into isolation. You are on a computer alone. You can drive a car alone, watch TV, chat, Facebook or whatever by yourself. If you don't want to talk on the phone, you don't have to. With these online communities, well, I think they encourage isolation—they only work when you're far apart. Dogs physically bring people together. I think that's good."

He sat back. "I hadn't thought about it that way," McBride said. "Remember, I never had a dog."

"Your mother did," Kendra noted.

"She got Canada not long after Dad died. Nathan and I wanted her to have a companion but not necessarily a man, you know? But something that required a little maintenance. Of course, we were totally clueless about it, but she found Canada on her own one day at a pet shelter."

"That must have been a hard time for you."

It had been. When his father had been paroled from prison, Pres had been almost ten. He had only ever known his father as a distant entity in a dark green jumpsuit surrounded by stern guards with badges and guns, rather terrifying for a small kid. Pres remembered his father before he had gone to prison, but only slightly. First he moved to a halfway house, which was okay; Pres got to see his father more often and received his first chemistry kit and microscope. But when his father graduated from the halfway house and moved in with them, well, that was too bizarre for all of them. Pres had thought about him and heard about him so much that it was almost as if Batman had come to live with them. And his parents fought, quietly at first, behind the thin door of their bedroom, then with the door open, then in the living room, in the tired old Volkswagen van his mother drove, everywhere. It was a relief when his father moved out.

But after Alexander failed to successfully rejoin the family he had tried to stay connected to while in prison, he slowly, in the minutest of increments gave up hope for a fulfilling life, day by day. He bounced around California, working a series of humdrum laboratory jobs, doing his best to distance himself from his former life as first the producer of some of the most potent hallucinogens in modern chemistry and then as Inmate #8754492. But he drank and he ate, looking a little rounder and less healthy with each visit, the visits themselves becoming less and less frequent. Still, he wrote to Maggie frequently, and when he called, they talked for hours. Maggie never took another lover, at least not that Pres had seen. Finally, his father had suffered a stroke and lingered on in a painful state of half-being at a managed care clinic near Maggie's apartment complex before finally expiring. It was not that he had died as much as he had slowly erased himself, and all because he had become enamored with rock 'n' roll and LSD and vapid youth culture.

Pres's cell phone rang. He pulled it out and looked at the number. His mother. He hadn't seen her since she came to the clinic for her flu shot three weeks ago. Since then, they had only talked on the phone occasionally.

"Hello?"

"Pres," his mother wailed. It took a few second for Pres to calm her down and find out what was wrong.

"Canada is sick," his mother said tearfully. "You need to look at him. He just lies on his blanket. He's not eating anything, and he can barely stand up!"

"Mom," McBride explained slowly. "Better to take him to a vet. I'm a people doctor."

"A doctor is a doctor," his mother insisted.

Pres sighed. This was not the first time this discussion had taken place. Canada had been limping maybe a week after the dinner at his mother's house. Burrs had gotten caught in his front right paw. McBride hoped nothing was more serious this time. He had repeatedly pointed out to his mother that dogs had a different biology than humans.

"Hurry up," Maggie insisted.

"I'll come over," McBride said. He told Kendra what was happening. She didn't complain about the half-eaten dinner. There wasn't much she could say or do, and she felt sympathetic to Maggie.

McBride drove off into the gloom of evening, taking the Foothill Boulevard to Rancho Cucamonga. His mother had moved there years ago to be close to his father's group home, but the smoggy air had deterred McBride from following after returning from New York. The San Gabriel Mountains served as a barrier to block the pollution generated by the city from leaving. His mother, however, loved the ethnically mixed population and never failed to tell everyone she lived on Route

66. The famed road no longer actually existed, but his mother was undeterred.

He pulled into the parking lot less than thirty minutes after her emergency call. The elevator to the seventh floor rose quickly, but he found himself behind a small wedge of people crowded around his mother's apartment's open front door.

He worked his way through the curious gathering into the apartment. Canada lay quietly in the corner of the living room. Several years ago, Maggie had purchased a wicker basket with a plaid blanket treated with flea powder for the dog's bed. Canada was still curled up there, but his eyes were closed. He looked sunken into the bed, not like he was sleeping but like he had slumped there in defeat.

The room hushed as McBride knelt by the dog, who tried to wag his tail but gave up quickly. His mother leaned over his shoulder, her hand covering her mouth. He could hear her short, agonizing breaths. The apartment, usually filled with incense and bright lights, seemed muted, almost dark. A single sage-scented candle burned on a window sill. Instead of her traditional multi-colored muumuu, Maggie was wearing a gray frock that matched her somber expression.

McBride touched the dog's nose. It was warm and dry. He knew that couldn't be a good sign. He pulled up an eyelid. Canada did not respond. The one brown eye tried to focus but then stared vacantly, as if lost in another world. He could see the dog's chest rise and fall with shallow gasps, but not a muscle stirred.

"What do you think?" his mother whispered in his ear.

"This dog is really sick," he replied.

"He's sick," Maggie announced to the crowd as though issuing a revelation. That word was repeated by those in the doorway and circulated quickly. Heads nodded in agreement.

"Yesterday," she told her son, "he was so out of sorts. He wouldn't eat and growled at me. He never growls at me. I used to growl at him. He slept most of the day away."

McBride bent over the dog and saw blood on the mouth. *Think of Canada as a human patient,* he told himself. He ran a hand over the dog's paws, looking for maybe a puncture wound, bite, or sting. Nothing. No burrs. No hint of a scratch. The blood had to be coming completely from Canada's mouth. He pried open his jaws. Canada's teeth were tinted light pink. Had he eaten something poisonous? McBride didn't know. Then the dog gurgled, and Pres saw red before Canada sleepily shook his jaws from Pres's grip and swallowed roughly. That was blood, Canada's blood. Was the dog bleeding to death?

"Listen to his heart," his mother suggested.

He glanced back. "Mom, I don't carry a stethoscope around with me."

"He doesn't have a stethoscope," Maggie called to those by the door.

"No stethoscope," he heard the crowd whisper shamefully.

"Why not?' she asked.

"Why not?" the crowd murmured.

McBride looked at his mother. Her face was sallow with shadows formed in the deep lines around her eyes and down her cheeks. Her lips quivered.

"It wouldn't help," he whispered to her. The dog was dying. He gave it hours, or even minutes.

He heard the word 'help' echo through the crowd: "We need to get help." "He can't help."

"What can you do?" his mother pressed anxiously. He could feel her leaning against him, seeking assurance.

"I'm going to take Canada to the vet," McBride decided. He scooped up the dog. It was just dead weight, possibly fifty pounds. Canada's tongue fell out the side of his mouth and more blood dripped off the end as though it were saliva, landing on one of Pres's clean white shirts. It spread out quickly, bright red like a bad omen.

Neighbors gasped at the sight. One woman crossed herself. There was complete silence.

McBride turned around. There must have been eight people now in the apartment doorway. "Mom," he said, "please ask your friends to move."

"I don't know them," she whispered.

"Talk to them," he said to her sideways, "I need a path now."

"Shoo, shoo," Maggie cried, waving her arms. People edged away from the doorway.

"I'm sorry," McBride called, "but I need room. This dog is very sick." Onlookers quickly moved aside as he carried the dog into the corridor.

"Doctor," an old woman tugged at his right sleeve. "Could you look at my dog next?" McBride could see her plaintive eyes staring up at him. "He's very sick, too."

"Sure," he gasped, struggling under Canada's limp weight. "When I come back."

Her aged face immediately broke open in a grateful smile, and then a moment later she started crying.

The dog did not resist when McBride placed him gently in the backseat. If anything, the animal now was barely breathing. McBride remembered how his mother had said Canada enjoyed nothing more than a ride in the car. He was eager to get in, stared, slobbered, and bounced around while they drove, and then was just as eager to exit. Now not even his tail moved as he lay on a towel.

McBride noticed that Canada's fur seemed shiny and healthy. Whatever had sickened the dog was not reflected in its appearance and had come on quickly. McBride crossed mange off the list of possible causes since tufts of hair would be falling out. He had familiarized himself with dog diseases the time his mother's first dog was ill. McBride was pretty certain the dog was not suffering from malnutrition. He had needed to know about possible symptoms. Canada did not have any that were familiar. Other than his lethargy and sour mood, the only other noticeable symptom was the blood in his mouth.

McBride slid behind the steering wheel. Where was the animal hospital? He tried to remember. He knew it was off Foothill Boulevard. His mother's apartment was on Vineland, so the hospital was not far way. He headed north and then turned onto the freeway. A moment later, he saw the Spruce Avenue exit. An image clicked. He had been there with Canada not that long ago because of the burrs. One had really embedded itself and required some delicate surgery to remove. Canada had limped for several weeks. This was far more serious. McBride anxiously scanned the darkened shopping center before spotting the small animal hospital. Yes, he told himself with relief, there it was.

He pulled into the parking lot. On the southern corner was the Waverly Animal Hospital. It was the only storefront with lights on. He could see the familiar sign in the window: twenty-four-hour emergency service.

Two other cars were parked in front. He pulled as close to the front door as possible, retrieved the dog from the back seat of the Civic, and walked to the entrance. Canada was really heavy, and Pres labored to carry the animal. The dog's face touched his cheek, and he just barely detected the presence of a spirit, as if the dog were almost gone. Could it be? He had been such a vibrant animal.

After groping at the door a moment, someone inside opened it for him. It was a man maybe ten years old than him with sad smile. There was something automatic in the greeting. McBride stepped inside the waiting room. Most of the chairs were empty, but McBride hadn't expected anyone else there this time of night. He could feel the oppressive silence as he carried Canada to a vacant chair and placed him gently on it. The other man returned to his seat alone in the corner without a word. A large sheepdog lay at his feet, on its side, almost more like an animal skin rug than a living dog. McBride hadn't even fully absorbed the grim scene when a distressed woman entered. Following awkwardly behind her was a long-faced teenager laboring under the weight of a Labrador retriever, completely limp in his arms.

"Join the crowd," the man said to the mother and her son. He held his hands out in a mute appeal.

Oh, God, thought McBride as he petted Canada. Something ominous was happening. All that was audible was the hum of air conditioning. No one moved or said anything. McBride wondered if it was appropriate to speak, but he couldn't resist the opportunity to do some research.

He patted Canada idly and walked over to the owner of the sheepdog. "Do you mind if I look at your dog?" he asked the man softly. "I'm a doctor."

"A vet?"

"No," McBride replied, "but medicine is medicine." His response surprised him—he had always protested to his mother that his training didn't qualify him to care for Canada.

He knelt down. The same symptoms: the dog was barely breathing and unresponsive. When he gently peeled back one of the dog's lips, the teeth were also pink with blood. Something dark was definitely happening.

"It started this evening," the man said helpfully. "The last few days, he was a bit cranky. Yesterday he didn't want to play with the kids, which wasn't like him at all. He is a very pleasant fellow."

The man might have gone on, but the side door opened and an elderly man crept out. He wore a red shirt with a white collar under a black cardigan. He could barely walk and leaned heavily on a cane. He paused in the doorway and looked behind him. His lips moved, but nothing came out. He tottered toward the door. For a split second, his shirt appeared to glisten in the fluorescent light of the waiting room as he passed Pres. He pulled on the handle with a trembling hand, but lacked the strength. The teen jumped up to help him but by the time he reached him, the old man was gone. Wait, had that been blood on his shirt? Was that even possible?

"He had a golden retriever," said the man in the waiting room, watching McBride who still stared at the closed door.

In his mind's eye, McBride suddenly saw his mother in the old, dejected man.

He was opening his mouth to question what he had seen when a nurse appeared, holding a folder. "Mr. Chandler," she called. The man scooped up the sheepdog with ease and carried it through the open door. McBride watched him. The guy was thin, almost scrawny, but clearly very strong.

He glanced over at the teen and woman with the black retriever. The woman's eyes were pleading. He understood. He walked over and knelt down by the dog. The signs were all too familiar: the teeth pink with blood, the lack of movement, the dull eyes. Something similar to what had laid Canada low had attacked this dog, too.

"I'm sorry," he whispered. Tears welled and dribbled down the woman's cheeks. Her son put his arm around her shoulders.

"Do you know what's happening?" she asked haltingly.

McBride shook his head. "I wish I did," he said.

He sat down next to Canada and idly ran his hand over the dog's head. His mind began to sift through clues. It had to be some kind of infection. A bacteria or fungus, maybe even a virus. It was being passed from dog to dog. They sniffed each other. Maybe there was something in their urine or fecal material. Dogs used that as territorial markers, and a virus shed through fecal matter and hair follicles and skin pores. Other dogs might stop to check out any visitors and inadvertently pick up a virus. Or it could be some kind of virulent parasite. That was possible. Were the animals linked in some way? Maybe the retriever was from the same neighborhood as Canada. Or maybe they had eaten the same brand of tainted dog food? There were just too many variables.

McBride wasn't sure he should bother the woman to find out. Her son was doing his best to comfort her. Still, McBride had no idea when the opportunity for assessing clues would occur again. He took a deep breath to steel himself. He disliked the doctor-patient conversations, but this situation with the dogs was forcing him to change.

"Ma'am," he called, "if you don't mind, could you tell me where you live?" She hesitated, not sure why he was asking. "I..I'm trying to figure out how and why this is happening. It might help," McBride suggested.

"Off Haven Avenue, near Chaffey Community College," she replied uneasily, clearly unwilling to give him her exact address.

"Thank you," he said thoughtfully. That was nowhere near his mother's apartment house. Could they have visited the same dog park?

"Is there a dog park near there?" he asked.

"No," she said. "The closest is off highway sixty or near Upland. We were there once or twice, but that was a long time ago."

McBride waited a moment, trying to find some connection. "Did you know the man with the sheepdog?" he probed.

"Yes," she said. "He lives a block or so away from me. We see him on walks occasionally." She smiled. "We talk about our dogs. His dog's name is Sammy. But I really don't know him. I don't think I even know his name."

That was something. The two dogs could well have had some contact. How did Canada fit into that equation? His mother wouldn't take him several miles away from the apartment just to walk in a strange neighborhood. Maybe she had friends there? That was possible. She had friends everywhere. She might have taken Canada with her and then walked him.

The man finally came back out without his sheepdog. He seemed to be barely holding himself together as he marched through the office without looking at McBride or the other couple. His lips looked blue, his face pale. Then he, too, was gone into the night.

Canada had still barely stirred. McBride tried not to think of Maggie and how she would react if… but he couldn't bear to consider that end. It was just a dog, he told himself, but he knew that it wasn't just a dog to his mother. And so it was not just a dog to him. If anything happened to Canada, the fallout for his mother and consequently for him would be massive. And what about someone like Dr. Crossland, who now appeared to depend on his dachshund Al not just for companionship? Al's need for Dr. Crossland at times appeared to be one of the few things that kept Crossland tethered to reality.

An ashen-faced nurse finally came for McBride, who carried Canada inside to the examining room trying not to hit the dog's legs on the door or narrow hallway walls. The dog felt like an anchor. She ushered him into a treatment room. A frazzled orderly was mopping the floor. That was unusual. The room stank of disinfectant.

"Put him on the table, Dr. McBride," he heard a woman's voice say. "It is a he, isn't it?"

"Yes. His name is Canada," Pres said and laid Canada carefully on the hard table covered in fresh white paper. "Dr. Maria Santiago," she introduced herself, closing a file folder and tucking it into a tray on the back of the door. She was a petite Latina with light brown hair and dark, observant eyes. She seemed at once slight and sturdy and, concerned as he was about Canada, McBride marveled that someone so physically diminutive could still have such a powerful presence. Her face expressed intense concentration tinged with sorrow, even horror. Pres could tell both that she had considerable intelligence and emotional strength and that she was nearing the end of her rope. She wore no lab coat, just somewhat ill-fitting scrubs, Pres noted with growing alarm. She appeared very professional—had her lab coat and normal scrubs already been retired because they had been tainted in some manner? With a sigh, she bent over Canada and listened to his heart with her stethoscope. Her slim, tapered fingers pried open his mouth. Canada's mouth now seemed almost sticky with blood, and the dog struggled to swallow. The veterinarian's shoulders sagged as she turned to face him.

"Your dog is going to die, Dr. McBride. I can continue with a complete examination if that will make you feel better, but I can say with utmost certainty that Canada will not be with us for much longer," she said with real sadness in her voice. "This dog is the same as the others."

"Dr. Santiago, I…I trust your medical opinion. Thank you. I…what in the hell is going on? What's wrong with my dog?"

"I don't know," she said wearily. She took off her plastic gloves. "I'm heartbroken. There's nothing in the literature. Your dog is the fifth one tonight."

"Can't you do anything about it?" he said. But then he caught himself and stopped there. He was acting no differently than the family of a mortally ill patient who insists a doctor perform a miracle.

"No," she said. She looked ready to burst into tears. "He will be dead in a few minutes."

"There has to be something. Tainted food? A parasite? I'm a virologist and…well, I couldn't help but notice a pattern in the waiting room and start working on the problem," he said with a sad smile.

She paused and straightened. "Let me show you something," she said, and turning her back on Canada, she strode over to the plastic tray for patient folders on the back of the examination room door.

McBride glanced over his shoulder at Canada, reluctant to follow her. Santiago caught his glance. "It's okay, he won't be going anywhere. He's past worry, Dr. McBride. In fact, it's best that we give him a little room right now."

Pres was reluctant to leave Canada, but the dog was unresponsive, and he already knew that he trusted Santiago, both as a person and as a medical professional. Before he knew what he knew what he was doing, he had leaned over and put his face in the shaggy hair on Canada's neck just to say goodbye. That familiar wild smell of the dog was already fading. Then he stood, embarrassed by the true emotion he felt for the dog and embarrassed that he had possibly allowed himself to be contaminated by whatever was poisoning the dying dog in full view of another doctor. Santiago already had a folder open and began speaking as Pres hurried over.

"I've been trying to gather any information I think is relevant. I received something yesterday that seems connected."

She handed him a printout of an email. "Some doctor in Oakland started seeing dogs as ill as your keeshond and did some inquiries," she explained. "I got this from a doctor in L.A. who was trying to alert everyone."

McBride quickly scanned the printout:

As you may recall, veterinarians received word of a new flu about five years ago. Called H3N8, it was not considered particularly lethal. It apparently jumped from horses to dogs. Humans are not susceptible. Then, it was thought to be dangerous only to dogs with limited air passages such as a Pekingese, a pug or a shih tzu. The flu has been largely confined to Florida, New York City's northern suburbs, Philadelphia, and Denver.

Recently, however, I treated several dogs with a new condition caused by an unknown agent with similar but dramatically heightened symptoms.

Initial symptoms may include coughing, listlessness, and irritability. It is probably easily passed by dogs that rub against each other or use the same water bowl. Humans may enable the disease by carrying it on their clothing.

Between 5 to 8 percent of this country's seventy million dogs that catch this disease could die. To prevent the disease, the United States Department of Agriculture has announced approval of a vaccine.

Because of its dangerous nature, I am urging all DVMs to encourage owners to get their dogs vaccinated. Supplies are available through the USDA.

McBride straightened. That would make sense. A flu. Influenza once killed millions of people in 1918. This one simply attacked dogs. Knowing that did not provide a cure or, for that matter, much hope, but owners would have some solace. At least, they would know what was happening.

"I have tried to get some of the vaccine," Santiago said, somewhat bitterly. There was no point going further. She was not like Crossland, who knew whom to ask and how to get supplies. From her appearance, McBride guessed she was a recent graduate of a veterinary school. Besides, the clinic had only been open for a couple of years, hence the twenty-four-hour service. Once the facility had enough regular customers, Santiago and her partners would likely initiate regular hours.

McBride jumped when he heard a screeching sound behind him. He whipped around—miraculously, Canada was awake and trying to stand, his claws tearing easily through the paper on the examination table and sliding on the metal. McBride dropped the folder to rush to the dog when Santiago's arm clamped on his bicep.

"Stay back," she hissed in his ear. Her grip was strong, and the cold dread in her voice froze McBride in his tracks.

Canada had barely made it upright. His paws were set in a wide stance, as if bracing for an onslaught. His eyes were open but they were both panicked and groggy and he seemed to take in neither the veterinarian nor Pres, who he had dearly loved. His abdomen heaved, and a fine mist of blood shot out of his nostrils onto the white paper like an accusation.

"He's choking!" Pres cried out. Santiago was silent and grim, and her grip got tighter.

Canada's eyes grew ever wider, as if he had observed Death enter the room. He drew in a series of short, terrified breaths. Then he opened his mouth, and with a wet, painful heave that sounded like his soul tearing from his body, he coughed what appeared to be all the blood in his body onto the examination table.

It made an audible slapping sound when it hit the table, quickly covering the surface and cascading onto the floor. The keeshond's white fur drew the blood up like straws, and the dog's paws, tail, and underbelly were red with gore. Canada's head and jaws looked like he had just emerged from gnawing on the entrails of a huge and still living beast, his green eyes blazing through the red blood like one of the Devil's own hellhounds. And still he coughed and choked and spit blood, spraying it all over himself, the table, and the examination room.

After what seemed like an eternity, Canada's convulsions lessened until the dog lay still, only occasionally twitching and shivering as he was finally released from his suffering. McBride stood, rooted to the ground, stunned by the fountain of blood that had preceded the agonizing death of his mother's beloved dog.

"A shot would have been too late for Canada," Santiago said, attempting to console him. Her voice sounded very far away.

"This is awful," McBride said, barely audible. "I want to stop this virus from killing so many more dogs. This is…god, this is just not right."

McBride thought for a moment. Santiago watched him, wondering perhaps at what he was contemplating.

"When did this start?" he asked.

"Three days ago here. Lord knows what's happening in other parts of the country," Santiago replied.

"Have you autopsied any of the dogs?" he said.

"As you may have guessed, the dogs bled to death internally, the blood gathering in their lungs. It was like their veins and arteries simply dissolved," Santiago reported somberly.

"Like Ebola," said McBride, referring to a dread African virus that destroyed the walls of blood vessels, causing its victims to drown in their own blood.

"Like Ebola," Santiago agreed. She started to lead him back to the waiting room. He understood; there were bound to be other patients coming into the hospital. They would have to get this room cleaned up and ready for the next victim. "It might have begun in Canada. The Iditarod had to be called off because so many dogs died. The symptoms seem similar."

"H3N8 attacks lungs," McBride thought aloud. "Would that create all that internal bleeding?"

She paused. "Ebola is a hemorrhagic fever. If this is similar, I guess the pulmonary artery could break down," she said.

"I guess," he agreed, but wasn't sure. Wouldn't there be blood coming from the anus, ears, nose and other orifices? That's what happened with Ebola. These dogs only had blood in their mouths.

"It's all guesswork right now," Santiago said.

McBride nodded. There was nothing more to say. He glanced back at Canada before leaving, then quickly looked away. He wanted to say goodbye properly, even though the dog was not his. Somehow it seemed wrong just to walk away. But what remained on the examination table appeared in essence distant from the dog his mother had dearly loved. The bloody red mess already appeared to be stiffening, the blood congealing around it. There was no sign of life. There was nothing else he could do. Like the others before him, he opened the side door walked into the waiting room.

The mother and teen with the Labrador retriever had not been as fortunate as he had been, to at least have his dog die under the watchful eye of a veterinarian who knew what to expect. The waiting room floor was a sea of blood, the woman was bent over, sobbing. The teen appeared catatonic. Both of them were drenched in blood.

McBride tried not to look at them as he strode out of the animal hospital and into the night. He felt like he should stop and try to help, but he knew he had to just get out of there. And what could he do for them, anyway? He felt a deep, abiding sadness coupled with growing fear, as if he had been dropped into a war zone. *Dogs bring people together*, he thought, remembering the walk through the neighborhood with Kendra that night. *And their impending deaths divide us again.*

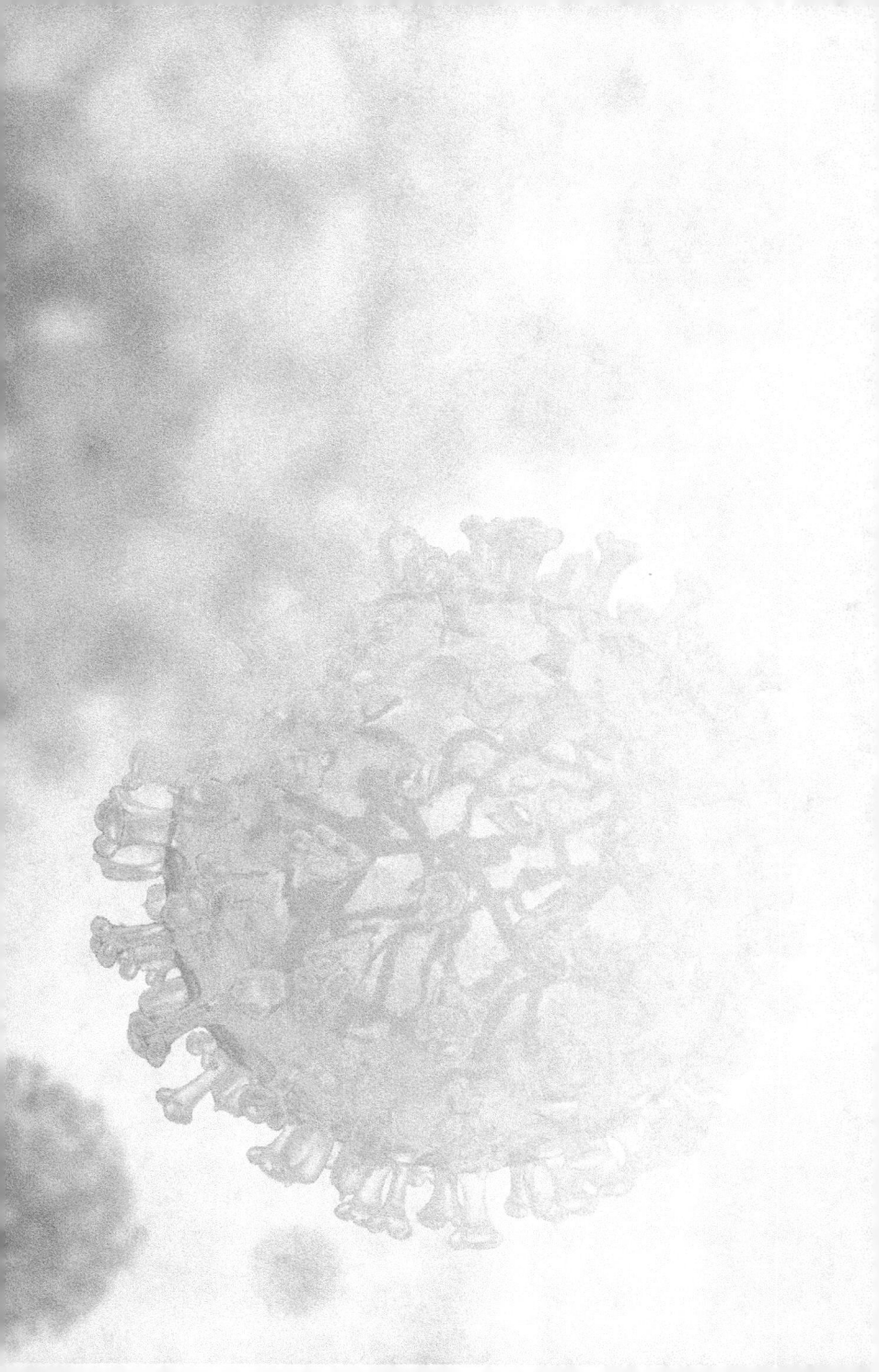

Chapter 5

Driving slowly, Fran Maribeau kept trying to see street numbers on the weathered homes lining Burgundy. This area of New Orleans, the Ninth Ward, had been inundated by the Mississippi River in the aftermath of Hurricane Katrina in 2004. The surge had reached such heights that high-water marks weren't left on the remaining structures.

Maribeau checked her appointment sheet. A veteran city social worker, she had been given three places to stop this morning. The one on Burgundy Street headed her list. She could see FEMA trailers in front yards, but most of the homes were still standing. Signs pleading with the city not to bulldoze the debris marked telephone poles.

She knew this Holy Cross area well, having been in and out of here for more than fifteen years. The front section—toward the river—had been a thriving, blue-collar community until the hurricane slammed ashore and undermined the levees. The waters saturated every home, but most endured. Maribeau had been among the many volunteers who picked through the rubble and helped survivors cope with the internal and external damage.

Few people actually came back. However, according to her assignment, a family living in one of the battered homes between Lizardi and Egania needed help. The father was unemployed; the children hadn't been in school for days. Phone and power had been cut off for nonpayment. Mirabeau continued to look for any sign of life in the area. There was very little.

One old man was slowly pushing a rusted shopping cart down the sidewalk. She pulled up next to him. He ignored her. An aging, hefty woman walked slowly on another block.

"Excuse me," Mirabeau called. The woman stopped and stared at her. "I'm looking for 5246 Burgundy Street," she said.

"I don't know," the woman told her. She trudged away.

Finally, Maribeau parked her car. She walked up to the first home and couldn't see a number. There was none on the second home either. Finally, she knocked on the closest door. No one answered. She was not surprised. Many people had simply left. An impoverished, desperate family wouldn't hesitate to go somewhere else. She ached inside, wanting to help, but knew her resources were limited. She noted her failure to find the home on the report and started the car.

The next stop was on Chartres near Reynes. Mirabeau drove down Burgundy and then turned left at Forstall. She seemed to be the only person on the road. In the distance, however, she could see that some people had gathered on the banks of the Mississippi only three blocks ahead where Forstall turned into Douglas.

Mirabeau drove toward them. There weren't many of them, maybe six or seven, but they were the only people out on the street. They were standing along the stone walkway that ran alongside the river. No one was talking or shouting, nor did she hear any music. They were just standing there. As she watched, another two people joined the small congregation. No one showed any reaction as her car drove up.

She got out and walked quietly to the riverside. Another man joined the group from Douglas. They were all silent as if gathering to witness something. Mirabeau had no trouble walking to the front of the right flank. She stared at the river, unsure of what she was looking for.

She followed the gaze of those around her. In the gray, turgid river, she saw the stiff body of a dog floating by like some gruesome marionette. Its fur, once white, was now the color of silt, but its muzzle, head, shoulders and forelimbs were stained the horrid red-brown of old blood. The crowd watched it progress in the swift current. It approached rather close to the shore and Mirabeau was subjected to grim, graphic details: the dog's lips, still a fleshy pink, curled back from the teeth in a death's head grin, the eyes dead and staring in a caricature of life, a collar, once bright green, encircling the dog's neck with dog tags—she could see one bone-shaped and one clearly heart-shaped. This wasn't a stray; this had been someone's beloved pet. The scene reminded her of the real-life video footage of drunk driving accidents she and another students had been forced to watch in her high school driver's education course. The images had been horrific and yet somehow distant. This was very real. Too real. No one said anything. People stared.

Mirabeau watched, transfixed, as the dog passed them and then was swept downstream. She knew about the dog flu. Some of her grief counseling dealt with that. Children were traumatized. Parents were grieving. Still, she was focused on rebuilding the community. It was sad that dogs were dying, but the SPCA or the CDC would do something about it. There were still thousands and thousands of people in New Orleans who desperately needed help.

An old black man, shrunken with age, gestured at the river with a gnarled right hand. "See? Here come 'notha one. Soon come more."

A large collie was now approaching them—she could tell by the long, narrow nose and the long fur, so beautiful in life, that now hung off it like dirty seaweed. This was a fancy dog, a rich folks' animal—in the river? Its face, too, was tainted with blood and lots of it. Soon followed a smaller dog, what looked to be an Airedale or a terrier of some kind from its stiff, coarse fur, then a poodle, its curls thick with detritus, and finally a raft of several dogs that had clotted together as if clinging to each other for comfort in death. It was horrifying. She thought of slaughterhouses, muddy deltas in Vietnam, and the bloody secret slaughter of dolphins in secluded coves in Japan. This, in America, in public, and nothing being done about it?

Finally, she tore herself away. She had two more homes to visit this morning, but no longer felt any energy. Walking on wobbly legs, she retreated to her car. This could not be happening, she told herself.

Somehow, she had made it through Katrina, helping, consoling, soothing, guiding, and doing anything she could to provide solace to so many devastated families. At least 1,500 people had died in this ward alone as the result the hurricane. This river was no stranger to destruction, debris, and bodies—human bodies—but somehow this mounting stream of dead dogs seemed to foretell something worse.

The river bore the corpses with calm indifference. Mirabeau could not fathom how. But it had been there long before human beings had lived there and would be there long after. She sat in her car simply staring into the overcast horizon. It looked like rain was on its way. She felt a growing sense of dread and thought again, in detail, about what the river would look like when dogs, people, and all trace of human life as she knew it was gone. Then, from deep inside, Mirabeau felt her own storm forming. It quickly overwhelmed her. Tears began to flow. She rested her head on the steering wheel and cried.

Chapter 6

It was a quiet, intense ride back to his mother's apartment. McBride was not sure what he would say to her. The dog was his mother's confidante. Many times, she preferred to stay home just to be with Canada. Kendra liked going to movies or to the theater, and they always called Maggie, inviting her to join them, and she always said no. She didn't want to leave Canada alone for hours lest he do something mischievous.

McBride shook his head and smiled. "To be alive is to be related," a wise man had once told him, and mothers had a hard time relinquishing their motherhood as their kids grew and moved on. They always stood ready to renew that role. Pets were a way to perpetuate it very easily and directly, without complexity. Without a single argument. And the love they gave was unconditional.

"That dog is running your life," McBride would often tease Maggie.

"Isn't that great?" Maggie would reply. "Canada shows so much more sense than many people I know."

There was no question that Canada was different. Maggie had made a complete and lengthy survey of dogs, spent hours at pet stores and animal shelters, McBride said, searching for the perfect companion. When she saw Canada, the bonding was quick and permanent. Canada had been in good health, still filled with the promise of long-term affection. Worse, McBride thought, she probably shouldn't get another dog right now, not with the threat that the virus still lingered in the house. She probably wouldn't want to anyway. Her grief would not permit it this time, he felt. How could she chance going through something like this again?

He tried to sort out what few facts he knew about the disease that killed Canada: it caused severe internal bleeding, apparently from the lungs. It spread easily and quickly. It had a brief incubation period. Dogs began to show changes in behavior a day or two at most before the worse symptoms appeared.

That Oakland doctor had recognized it and concluded it was something new and menacing, even if he had failed to recognize how serious it was. Or perhaps it hadn't manifested so severely in the cases he saw? It was frustrating: there was more unknown about this disease than there was known. McBride wondered if there were any reports about this illness from the East Coast. That's where H3N8 started and had the most impact initially. Some of the dogs infected with that flu must have died. Did they show signs of bleeding, he wondered?

He parked right in front and walked up the steps. It appeared that all the lights were out in her home. But when he knocked, he soon heard her footsteps. She held a candle and its small light cast their distorted shadows onto the walls of the foyer. "Mom…"

She put a finger to her lips and hushed him. He could see that her eyes were swollen. She took his hand.

They went into her bedroom, where she kneeled and resumed her meditation. "Om, om, om," she repeated, vibrating with the sound, drawing her breath through pursed lips.

McBride simply watched her. It was a long time before she turned around and faced him.

"Hello, my captain," she said. She looked at him expectantly, but when she realized he didn't have a dog, her gaze turned to the ground.

McBride told her about Canada's passing, carefully leaving out the worst details of his gory, painful demise. Each word he spoke seemed to administer pain, and her body shook when he had finished.

"The Lord giveth; the Lord taketh away," his mother announced. McBride found it bizarre that her hippie attitude co-existed peacefully with religious fervor, but at this point, he wasn't going to deny her anything that provided her with comfort.

The old woman who had wanted McBride to check her dog had gone to bed. His mother said she'd inform the woman about the illness to ensure that she wouldn't have to endure such a loss.

"Mother...you'd better throw out everything Canada touched," he said. "If it's a virus, well, you want to get any vectors for contagion out of the house. Then maybe next week or sometime soon, we can start looking for another dog for you. I will help."

His mother turned a stricken face toward him. "Oh, Lord," Maggie said, and she slowly slipped back down to the floor. For the first time, he saw the full impact of Canada's death in her eyes. "No," she admitted. "I could not endure it."

He checked the refrigerator and made sure she had food and bottled water, and he left soon after. He was not sure that she even noticed his departure.

The ride home gave him time to focus his thoughts on this disease. Clearly, it was like Ebola. Could it have started from the same virus and mutated? How did it get to California? Were there reports coming out? He hurried, speeding down Foothill. The car was a manual transmission and he revved the engine between gears as his thoughts churned. He made the corner on his street at a thirty-degree angle and slammed on the brakes. He parked the car outside, not bothering to open the garage, and burst inside. Kendra was reading quietly in the living room, an old battered copy of *Wuthering Heights*. She glanced at him for a split second and waved him on with a dismissive flourish from one hand. She had sensed his mood from afar and did not wish to be interrupted. Fine. He wasn't quite ready to socialize, anyway.

He quickly hurried to the computer in the bedroom. It sat on a plywood desk, the only piece of furniture in the room except for the bed, both purchased at a second-hand store. Most of the house was bare, too. Kendra saw no reason to fill a rented home with furniture that would have to be moved someday. McBride didn't care. He was used to spending most of his time in the lab—for a long time, home had been just a place to sleep and shower.

Fifteen minutes passed in silence. "What happened?" Kendra finally called out, when he had not spoken to her at all. He didn't answer. He didn't even hear her.

Kendra quickly realized he was completely preoccupied. He would simply cut off the world whenever he conducted research. There had been many days when she'd had to call him at the lab to remind him to come home. She hoped that wasn't happening again. It was hard to have a fulfilling relationship with a workaholic. She readjusted herself in her chair and returned to Kathy and Heathcliff on the moor.

McBride had no problem finding a lot of material about Ebola. It was transmitted directly though blood, secretions, or other body fluids. That could make dogs very susceptible, since they marked territory with urine. Incubation could be as short as two days. That fit, too. Everyone he had spoken to about the disease noticed a change in their dog's behavior a day or two before the internal bleeding started.

What were the symptoms? He read through the material. There it was: "Ebola is characterized by the sudden onset of fever, intense weakness, muscle pain, headache, and sore throat. This is often followed by vomiting, diarrhea, rash, impaired kidney and liver function, and in some cases, both internal and external bleeding. Laboratory findings show low counts of white blood cells and platelets, as well as elevated liver enzymes."

That was helpful. He needed to examine some blood to see if there were low blood counts and the elevated liver enzymes. Where could he find the equipment? Did Dr. Crossland have a facility attached to the clinic? He didn't know. Maybe Ethan would let him conduct some research at the Novilis lab. Ugh, that wasn't a relationship he was eager to renew.

There was also a lot of data on the H3N8 flu that had been first discovered in some Florida racing greyhounds in January 2004. Symptoms were "low-grade fever, purulent nasal discharge, and cough for ten to twenty-one days." McBride read that twice. How different that flu seemed from the torrent of internal bleeding that killed Canada and the other dogs. He read on. Some dogs died "with extensive hemorrhage in the lungs, mediastinum, and pleural cavity." According to the report, autopsies showed the virus had infiltrated the breathing tubes and eroded the cells. Now he was getting somewhere.

Still, McBride thought, the volume of blood that he saw couldn't have been created by eroding cells. Bleeding then would be limited and internal. Canada was gushing blood as if a major artery had been cut. Blood seemed to leap out of him. God, what a horrible way for such a sweet dog to die. Pres put his head down. Was he about to cry? How long had it been since he had cried? He pulled himself together.

He had to get into a lab and isolate the virus. It could be a mutation, a much more virulent form of H3N8. Or it could be a totally different disease. There was just so much work ahead of him.

McBride checked his watch: ten fifteen. Would Crossland still be awake? As he recalled, the doctor liked the Tonight Show. Still, it had been a very long and hard day, and the man might have gone to sleep early. McBride didn't want to rouse him, but was too impatient to wait until morning. He picked up his cell phone and called.

Crossland answered gruffly. McBride apologized for bothering him, but explained he needed to conduct some research on the disease affecting dogs, leaving out Canada's death as he didn't want to distress the older man. Crossland offered him use of the hospital lab. It really didn't have all the necessary equipment, but was accessible.

"By the way," McBride asked hesitantly. "How's Al?'

Crossland was silent for a moment. "Funny you should ask," he said. "He's out of sorts. I think he's mad because I haven't been with him much. He's not quite as cantankerous as I am, but, you know, I'm pretty sure the little guy's angry with me." There was a sound over the phone of Crossland chewing on his lip.

McBride's heart sank. "Did you get him a flu shot?"

"Now why the hell would I do something stupid like that?"

"Not for Rohn flu. I think there may be a dog flu going around," McBride explained.

"Dog flu?" Crossland barked. "He'll be fine. Damn dog's too ornery to get sick."

McBride couldn't argue. If the dog had Crossland's personality, no virus stood a chance. He promised to be early to work the next day and said goodbye. He quickly began to scour the Internet for information about this new dog-killing disease. He could not find a thing. He did locate the LA doctor's letter. The AVMA also had a brief note on its website about possible mutations of the H3N8, but said "reports so far are inconclusive."

The concern was still for the Rohn flu. The virulence of the Rohn flu was still up in the air. It had not yet delivered the pan-epidemic feared earlier with both SARS and the bird flu, but anxiety was still high. Thousands had died worldwide, and hundreds of thousands had fallen ill with the disease. Countries worldwide were inoculating everyone they could with the vaccine, while, in third-world nations, desperate villagers in smaller communities were besieging medical facilities in large cities. The atmosphere was calmer in the United States, but media reports on the Internet still spoke of desperation, particularly if a family member became ill. Mask hoarding was commonplace; online sales boomed as the truly frightened never ventured outdoors. McBride read those accounts, too. They were chilling. He realized how, as a relatively well-informed doctor, he hadn't experienced the full effect of the media's fear mongering. He had carefully read the statistics buried deep in the articles—though thousands were ill, few had died after the first wave of infections, and now the vaccine appeared to be doing its job well by halting the disease's spread. Sure, he had seen more than one person wearing a mask at the grocery store and scoffed, wondering if those same people bothered to wash their hands and avoid touching their eyes or nose. But now, reading the same news that other people were reading, he understood how a small rural community could be devastated by paranoia. If anything, the disease appearing to stall out now only made their anxiety worse: they were waiting for the other shoe to drop.

Finally, near midnight, McBride began to relax. Despite people's mounting anxiety, the Rohn flu appeared to be leveling out, if not tapering off. Kendra had gone to bed, but his mind was still too active to sleep. This could be an isolated event, he thought. Perhaps a few dogs or several hundred dogs would sicken and die in California and that would be it. It would still be tragic, but at the end of the day, it was manageable. He would have to get some sample tissue from Dr. Santiago and isolate the contagion. After work, he thought. The clinic would be too busy. He couldn't leave Crossland alone for the long hours necessary for research.

He turned off the computer and started for the bathroom. His cell phone rang. He flipped it open. Crossland.

"You're on your own tomorrow," the old doctor said without any preliminaries.

"What? Why?" McBride gasped. He felt like he'd been blindsided.

"Al's sick," Crossland reported tersely and hung up.

McBride stared at the phone. There was something terrible happening. Suddenly, he was sure of it. He stared out the window. The stars swarmed in the heavens above, impervious to diseases down below on this planet. Venus was in Aquarius, the morning star. He'd had a telescope as a kid, and Maggie had once said that Venus, so positioned, was an omen. But he could not remember what the omen portended— whether it was good fortune or bad. He sat there on the windowsill in silence, staring up for a long, long time until a reef of clouds passed by and blocked his view of space. Then many more clouds appeared until it was as if, one by one, all the stars were going out.

He went to bed and curled around Kendra. After a minute she felt him, rolled over, and whispered in his ear, "Don't feel like you have to be the one to solve it all, Pres. Okay?" He nodded his chin into the soft part of her shoulder a few times. She had just enough energy to roll back over and begin snoring again.

McBride staggered into work the next day. Patients were dealing with it as best they could and let him examine them, but each one wanted to know where Dr. Crossland was. The nurses picked up on the tension and did their best to diffuse it. That evening, McBride finally got a chance to check out the clinic's lab. It wasn't much. Crossland had simply converted what had been a bathroom in the old building, adding a small refrigerator, some glass slides and a microscope, and a few other instruments. There was no way to conduct any research there. McBride wasn't sure where to turn. A day or two later an answer came to him. Maybe the veterinarian Maria Santiago knew of a lab that would be available. She wanted to find a solution, too. He wanted to visit her office as quickly as possible after work, but Kendra insisted he eat a sandwich first. They fought, but with little energy—it was a fight they had had many times before and both sides were getting worn down.

Still, by eight p.m. that night, he was pulling into the parking lot at his mother's apartment house. He intended to make a quick stop and give her some emotional support, then head over to the veterinary hospital.

He knocked on her door but didn't get a response. *Maybe she's out,* he thought. He could call her later. As he turned away, the door opened. The old woman who had wanted him to check her dog the previous day looked up at him. Her weathered face was framed by her white hair.

"Shh," she said, putting a quivering finger to her thin lips.

She only held the door open a crack, but he could see a little of the interior. The room was dark with just some flickering lights.

"Madge is trying to talk to her dog," the old woman continued in a low voice.

"Her name is Maggie," McBride whispered.

The old woman blanched. "I really don't know her well. We just walked our dogs together."

"How is your dog?" McBride asked.

"Gone," she said, patting his arm. "I know you did your best." She opened the door wider.

"Come on in." He stepped inside. "Having our dogs die has been very rough on some of us," the old woman said under her breath. "I know Madge took it very hard." She inched back to the end of the living room.

His mother had pushed the furniture back to one side and was seated on a large pillow in front of Canada's wicker basket with her legs crossed under her muumuu in yoga fashion. Three other women were perched on pillows in a circle around the basket. The old woman filled in one open area with the last vacant pillow and gestured at McBride to sit next to her. He did so, too confused to question her. The wood floor was hard.

A lone candle had been placed in a glass holder and set inside the wicker basket. Two other lit candles were on the dining room table a few feet behind the women. Shadows created by the spare light played against the back wall.

Maggie's eyes were closed. Her thumb was pinched against her fingers in each hand, and she held both arms straight out from her body. "Sit," she said in a commanding voice. "Speak. No. Heel. Stop." She grew more excited with each word. "Supper. Walk." Each word was spoken sharply, like a clarion call.

McBride sighed. He had seen this once before. When Dudley, a neighbor girl's parakeet had died, his mother had held a similar séance, only with just her son and the neighbor girl, no other adults. She had tried to evoke the spirit of the bird by using the vocabulary she was sure the bird understood. What was the point of saying something Dudley wouldn't recognize? The dead parakeet didn't manifest itself. And at the moment, Canada was not acknowledging his ghostly presence either.

"Sit. Speak. No. Heel. Stop. Come. Supper. Walk," the women in the group repeated in unison.

Complete silence followed. The woman reached out and took each other's hands. McBride reluctantly followed suit. As he grew up, he had recalled Dudley's séance and understood that his mother had undertaken it just for the benefit of the children. Did she really think something was going to happen? The old woman's hand was small; she was trembling. The woman on his other side gripped McBride's hand as if she feared to let go.

"Sit," they intoned. "Speak. Heel. Stop. Come. Supper. Walk. No."

More silence.

"I think I heard a bark," Maggie McBride finally said. "Did anyone else hear a bark?"

"There might have been," a woman on McBride's left said. She was black with a wide, somber face. "It was more like a yip."

It was the squeal of a tire from nearby Foothill, McBride wanted to say. At least, that's what it sounded like to him.

"Canada didn't yip much," Mrs. McBride replied thoughtfully. "That must have been another dog."

"My dog yipped," the old woman who met McBride at the door reported. "He yipped a lot."

"Maybe we reached Agnes's dog," Maggie said happily.

"Audrey," the old woman corrected.

"Poppin's owner," Maggie amended. Everyone nodded. She began to hum. Everyone joined in. After several seconds of humming, she repeated the mantra, "Sit. Speak. No. Heel. Stop. Come. Supper. Walk."

She stopped talking. The room grew completely still. Even breaths were muffled. Everyone strained to hear even the slightest sound. Nothing. McBride mused to himself that Canada was busy romping with his other dead pals and was not interested in obeying human commands anymore.

Finally, his mother stood up. She stretched. "Bad position for my hip," she said. "Still, I am encouraged. We may have heard a bark. Or a yip," she added, glancing at Aubrey. "It doesn't matter. We made contact."

"Yes, yes," the others enthused. They crowded around her to take her hand before saying goodbye. Maggie saw them to the door, then turned on the overhead light before blowing out the candles.

"I'm glad you came, Pres," she said. "I am sure Canada appreciated it."

He kissed her trembling cheek and could see how distant her eyes looked. She seemed focused on some spot very far away. "Are you all right?" he asked.

"I sometimes see him," she said dreamily. "I walk around the corner and expect to find him. I may see the end of his tail before he disappears around the corner, or hear the dog bowl being pushed around." She nodded to herself.

He hugged her. He wanted to say, "Mom, I know you loved him very much, but you'll have to let him go." But the look on her face silenced him.

She cried a little, softly. "He was a grown dog, but you know, still so young, so alive. " She looked up at him. "He used to wake me every morning by licking my face. I woke this morning and was sure I felt his tongue on my face."

"You'll just have to get another dog," he suggested. "Come on, Mom, let's clean the house out together tonight."

"No," she said. "No more. I told you I can't go through this again." She left him to sit back down near the wicker basket. She began her chanting again. He touched her gently on the shoulder, squeezed and then slipped out quietly a few minutes later, when it was clear that she had already retreated very deeply into her own mind.

He drove on to the veterinary hospital, realizing for the first time how much impact the dog had had on his mother's life. He had known it would be bad, but not like this. They had talked a few times since Canada died. She had sounded sad, but lucid. Now, he wasn't so sure. How many such séances had she held? What else was she doing? The loss had clearly devastated her to a degree beyond what he had imagined possible.

A panicked crowd had congregated outside the veterinary clinic with dogs on leashes, in metal cages, and in hastily made kennels of wood and wire. One was entirely wrapped in plastic wrap with only two duct tape snorkels extending from the front and back, each of those covered with an air filtration mask. McBride only made it to the door without getting shoved by pulling out his ID to demonstrate he was a doctor. Every seat was taken in the Waverly waiting room when McBride made it inside. People spoke quickly in raised voices and several children cried unabated, their parents too preoccupied to comfort them. The scene made McBride think of ill-funded clinics in Africa, the Middle East, and Central America, and also immigration offices in Poland in 1939. These people were terrified; they had no idea what lay ahead. Neither, McBride realized, did he.

A little boy played with a dirty popsicle stick at his mother's feet. Their dog, a schnauzer, lay limply on the chair in an all-too-familiar pose. Too soon, the dog would be gushing blood. McBride felt that seeing a dog he knew was very close to death shouldn't disturb him so much, but the sight still stunned and saddened him. Another person, an older man, had a cat. Somehow that was a relief, although McBride did wonder if the disease could jump from one pet to another of a different species.

AIDS went from chimps to humans, he thought. Ebola came from animals, too. So did malaria, swine flu, avian flu, H1N1, and so many other diseases. On the other hand, those viruses had not left humans for other animals. That could mean domestic cats were safe.

He took a quick glance at the cat. It was sitting up on its owner's lap. McBride could see no sign of bleeding around its mouth. Nor did it look lethargic. The owner had to keep a firm hold because the animal kept trying to jump off. The schnauzer had no such energy.

The harried receptionist dutifully took his name and asked him to wait. She explained that his wait may be up to six hours. He explained he wasn't here with a pet, but had to talk to the doctor. The receptionist nodded—obviously he wasn't the only one who "had" to talk to the doctor—but she scrawled a quick note with his name. From the handwriting, McBride guessed she was training to write illegible prescriptions. She went back into the office. He leaned against the wall, trying to appear nonchalant. That schnauzer would be perfect for testing. He was itching to get some blood samples and get started before the scene turned even grimmer. He forced himself to relax.

The side door opened. "Dr. McBride," the nurse called. He hurried after her while the other people in the waiting room stared at him with rage and disbelief. Santiago was in a recently vacated treatment room. He walked along the worn linoleum flooring and could hear some animal noises coming from a separate room. Some creature was trying unsuccessfully to claw through steel mesh. The clinic smelled somewhere between a zoo and a field hospital in Vietnam.

"Yes, Doctor," Santiago said. "How can I help you?" She looked exhausted. Her dark hair hung limply to her shoulders, and shadows had collected under her eyes.

McBride explained quickly how he wanted to start conducting tests, but lacked an adequate facility. "I can't find anything suitable," he said. "Do you know of a decent lab I may be able to get access to?"

"No," she said. She seemed to look him over again, almost as if they had just met. He saw intelligence in her eyes, and confusion and fatigue. Still, she was a long way from whipped. He identified with her immediately. They were two people with a common interest. And a common enemy.

She continued to watch him for a moment in silence, as if she were making a decision about him. "Look, I know someone at Novilis. That company might want to help. I'm really busy right now," she looked down at the floor and up again. "But I'll call my contact and let him know I have someone, a friend, who needs a lab. Okay?" She nodded sympathetically, and then somehow, a brief but genuine smile broke out on her face. Then she turned back to the animal on the table before her.

At Crossland's clinic, too, McBride and his nurses once again dealt with a torrent of humanity. The flu pandemic and the ensuing paranoia had everyone on edge. The deaths, though hovering in the thousands now, were still not that far beyond a normal flu. But the disease was turning up everywhere on the globe. The East Coast of the United States had been hit harder than California, which somehow increased the local anxiety. There was an urgency that they had to do something before it hit. McBride knew from experience that anticipation of a pandemic in recent years had often proved overblown—avian flu, SARS, and swine flu had all proved to be relatively minor events—but that was almost impossible to communicate to his patients.

Several days after dropping in on Santiago, Rosen brought McBride a message from her. In it, Santiago said Novilis was not interested. The company was doing its own research and was far too preoccupied with its Rohn flu vaccine to devote any time or resources to a disease that was only affecting "a non-food, non-essential domestic animal."

McBride wondered if the disdain that radiated in the note reflected Novilis's response or Santiago's reaction to the rejection. She had also asked him to call after he saw his last patient. At the end of the day, he retreated to the private office and sat in Crossland's empty chair and suddenly thought of the old man and his dog. How long would Al live? What would be the consequences? He shook his head as he punched Santiago's number on his cell.

She had changed her mind about the lab at her clinic. "My lab is small," she said, "but it does have enough equipment to begin the research."

He debated the idea. He really didn't want to get part way on the work and discover an inability to progress any further. That would be incredibly frustrating. Still, the invitation to start work was too tempting to turn down. As grim a subject as it was and as serious and professional as their conversation had been, he was sure he could hear Santiago grin on the other end of the phone.

He called Kendra next. "Will you be gone every night?" she asked.

"I don't know," he replied. "This is basic research. It could save thousands of dogs' lives."

She shook her head. "Dogs. I mean, I understand trying to cure human diseases, and I don't want dogs to die. But Pres, you're only one man. Aren't you busy enough with the clinic? I hardly see you as it is."

"I will get it done as quickly as possible," he said. It was a lame line, not necessarily a lie, but definitely in bad faith. He really couldn't predict anything as far as time commitments and progress. Some research took years. He knew he didn't have much time, but had no idea how much work was necessary.

***

That night, after dropping off Kendra at home, he headed directly to Waverly. He would explain to his mother later. He just didn't have the time to waste any time in some magical rite, even if it made his mother feel better. A sense of urgency had totally overtaken him now.

He passed some gang bangers along the way, and they pulled even with him in their low, souped-up Honda Civic—a kid's BMW, shaped basically like a 3-series. Two of them turned to look at McBride carefully. They wore their baseball caps backwards, double ice-cubes on their ears. Just because he had a Civic, too, they were checking him out. He was tired and frustrated and glared right back without thinking. When they saw that he had not made a single change to his car—no fat tail pipe, no bigger air-intake, no nitro—they scoffed and shot him a look of mild contempt. Not even worth a bullet.

He was getting tired of the damn car and the weird kind of attention it attracted. He pulled in the Waverly lot a little too fast, parked, and walked to the entrance. The nurse saw him and immediately buzzed the side door open so he could enter the back area. The lab was little more than a sink, empty slides and a high-powered optical microscope with two metallic cabinets painted white to hold supplies for the hospital. He looked around helplessly. This wasn't going to help much. Still, he was going to try.

Santiago had put several test tubes with blood in them by the microscope. He created a slide and placed the smear under the microscope. He could see red blood corpuscles, looking like flattened circular discs floating in the liquid. They appeared normal: the center was darker than the rim, the result of light refracting from the disc's double concave form. They were frozen in a moment of time; stationary after the stain had frozen them, piled up along each other's edges. The images were familiar: dog blood is no different from pig or human blood.

Here and there, McBride spotted smaller, white corpuscles. Not many, but this could well be the case. He looked closely, and no bacteria seemed to be present. He looked up at the ceiling and exhaled hard. Damn! The slide showed a Wright

Stain, used to determine this. No bacteria meant it probably was a virus. He felt numb. His perception of the danger at hand ratcheted up a notch.

An optical microscope would not be able to locate and identify a virus. No way at all. This one used light—refracted, diffused, or reflected to study the cells. But viruses were a hundred times smaller than a bacteria. He would need an electron microscope to shoot electron beams through very differently prepared tissue to confirm the virus and study it. Microscopically speaking, a virus existed on another level beyond normal optics and the human eye.

Santiago came in while he was re-examining the slides to confirm the total absence of any bacteria. Twice he found none, zero.

She placed some tissue samples in the nearby small refrigerator. He thanked her and retrieved one. It was a thin section cut from the liver of a dead golden retriever. It had been fixed to the glass and stained. He slid it under the microscope for a quick, superficial look. Based on his study of pigs, the tissue appeared healthy. He saw no evidence of lesions or infection. The dog's liver had not been busily fighting off the virus.

He then examined feces for evidence of parasite eggs or pieces of tapeworms that might have broken off. All of that was standard procedure in any laboratory, and all he could do without better equipment. The virus was too small and could be lurking anywhere.

He glanced up at the clock. Somehow, he had spent two hours examining the slides. It had not seemed that long. For the first time, he felt tired. His back was stiff from leaning over the microscope for so long, and his eyes were sore from straining to see.

"Anything?" Santiago asked.

McBride shook his head. "Nothing out of the ordinary." He washed his hands in the nearby sink after cataloging the slides. "I need a stronger microscope," he said.

"We'll have to get one," she said.

"I hope something turns up." McBride looked at her curiously. There was something about this woman that intrigued him. He always felt like she had more resources at her disposal than she was letting on.

"The vaccine hasn't been working," Santiago said. "I've read reports from various places that have been using the vaccine much longer than I have. Dogs are still dying."

She handed him a printout of an online story published that day. The New York Times was reporting that veterinarians in the Northeast were warning patients about a deadly disease that was decimating dog populations there. Sanitation departments were already scrambling to deal with the dramatic increase in dead animals to deal with.

"It's spreading," he said somberly. She nodded and sighed. "This is just a small hospital," she said. "Yet, I must have seen fifty to sixty dogs today alone, all of them dying. The corpses are out back—I need to keep calling the waste removal company. Every day there are more. Lord." She slumped onto a stool. "This is bad…I mean, it's overwhelming me."

McBride walked over to her and put his hand on her shoulder. Just touching her moved him to feel more of her being, her pain, and he withdrew his hand. "We'll find the answer," he vowed. She gave him a wan smile. Her dark hair shone.

Her brown eyes, tinged with melancholy, seemed to radiate an inner light. He pulled back. It continually caught him off guard how pretty she was.

"I'm exhausted," she admitted. "I usually come in around eight p.m. and stay until Dr. Jamison arrives at seven a.m. Lately, I've been here as early as four p.m. I can't stand to see so many dogs dying."

He didn't reply; there was nothing to say. "I see patients going crazy," she said. "They watch their pets bleeding to death, and there is nothing they can do."

McBride nodded fiercely, thinking of his mother. And Crossland—what was up with him? "I want find the answer," he told her. "I will find it. I just need time. And damn it, I need the right equipment." He stood poised for a moment, like a fighter poised to deliver a stunning blow.

"But there is no time," they both said in unison. They smiled at each other in exasperation.

He walked into the waiting room. There was one man waiting there. He struck McBride as strangely familiar as they eyed each other. Then McBride saw the white poodle lying limply on the neighboring chair. The man had been carrying the dog in his arms at Crossland's clinic two weeks ago, while waiting in line to get his shot. The dog was almost gone. Amante. He remembered the dog's name. The man looked up at McBride with a vacant, listless expression. All the life had been drained out of him, too.

For a moment they just stood there, gazing at each other silently. Then the man stood up. He took his dying dog in both arms, raised its head, and kissed it. Solemnly, he walked over to McBride, and they faced each other, and the man extended the dog toward McBride.

Not sure what to do at first, McBride took the dog in his arms.

"He is dying," the man said hoarsely. He stared at the dog for a moment and petted its limp head. Tears coursed down his cheeks.

"Yes," McBride said, "he is going to die." There was nothing else to say.

Amante's owner gazed at the dog a moment longer, then turned and walked out the front door.

McBride watched him, feeling the dog barely breathing in his arms. He shook his head. Too much sadness all around him. He did not feel personally responsible, he decided. "Not yet," his conscience replied.

But, my God, what if the man was right? What if it was too late and the entire dog population was going down, he thought. Every last one of them. He thought of Crossland and Al. The dog was probably gone, maybe soon Crossland would be gone with it. He walked quickly back to the examination room as he knew Amante wouldn't last long.

Chapter 7

"Are you going to call Novilis?" Kendra asked at dinner the next day. McBride had just told her about his research problems and need for the right instruments. She affected a casual tone, but both knew it wasn't a casual question. Canada's death and the rash of deaths of other dogs that followed it had cast a pallor over Pres and Kendra's life together. Every moment he could spare, he worked towards finding identifying the cause of the illness; moments he couldn't spare, he found himself obsessing about it, mentally exhausting himself.

He hadn't eaten since breakfast, and when he opened his mouth, he found himself dumbstruck by the rump roast on the table, a dish McBride particularly enjoyed because his mother had eschewed red meat since the 1970s, and he'd never gotten enough of it as a kid. A favorite family story was about the time when he was seven or eight and had returned from a sleepover and told his mother about the wonderful, strange food he had enjoyed for supper. "What was it called?" she had asked. "Steak," he'd replied.

Kendra was sympathetic about his need for a decent lab. Her hospital had some of the proper tools, but would not allow access to a doctor who did not have visiting privileges. McBride still had his license to practice in California, but without visiting rights. Novilis was the only other obvious choice, but he really didn't want to think about that.

"I'm torn," he finally admitted between bites. "I really need an electron microscope, but I'd rather eat sand than talk to Ethan. As vice president, he's going to have to approve anything I do."

"Maybe he won't remember you," Kendra said.

"I doubt that," he scoffed. "I made quite a stink."

"All he can say is no," she replied. "Besides, what are you looking for anyway? There's already a dog flu vaccine."

"It's not working," he said. "The vaccine for the Rohn flu is. Fewer people are getting sick from it. And they were Christian Scientists or Amish who refused to get shots. The dog flu vaccine has been out for at least a month now, and dogs are still dying. If anything, they seem to by dying faster."

"So," Kendra asked, "what can you do?" She stood up and started to gather the dirty dishes on the table. McBride began to help.

"Maybe identify the actual virus causing the deaths," he said. If he could look at the virus itself, then he could help create a better, more accurate vaccine. He'd have to start on his own. There wasn't as much money devoted to research in pet diseases when compared to human pathology. Maybe he could stumble on something that would lead to a cure. After he picked up the used silverware, he rummaged through his pockets for a piece of gum. He found none, instead fishing out a folded up piece of paper : Crossland's address on a note with Rosen's cell phone number.

He had been so busy at the clinic and obsessed with finding a facility for his research that he had completely forgotten.

Rosen had stopped him around four p.m. earlier that day. She seemed upset at the time. Crossland hadn't answered her phone calls. He'd called her back when Lucy had passed away, she said, but he hadn't been to the office in a week, and there had been only silence. Something must be seriously wrong. Maybe he was angry with her over something. To ease her concern, McBride had promised to drive over and talk to him. But then he'd had his attention and energy consumed by one needy patient after another until the day had been over and, like a robot, he'd driven home and put the clinic out of his mind.

"I'm sure he's still upset about the dog being under the weather," he had assured her. He was sure Al was only sick and hadn't died, as he was sure that Crossland would have told them about it.

"There's more than that," Rosen said. "His brother, Charles, committed suicide. He was raising a stink about some ethical issue at Novilis, and it ended up with him getting forced out of his job."

McBride reconsidered this now. Charles had hired him at Novilis. He had agreed to call Abe, had put the note in his pocket, but had forgotten about it amid all patients freaking out about their dogs dying.

He glanced at his watch. Kendra and he had lingered over dinner; it was already eight thirty p.m.

"I'm going to see Abe," he finally said.

Kendra straightened and looked at him coldly. "Are you ever staying home?" she asked.

"Janette—Nurse Rosen—is worried about him," McBride explained. "I promised I'd stop in and check on him. Somehow,

I totally spaced out until just now. I'm so sorry, K, but I have to go."

"Why don't you just call him?"

"He hates cell phones and hasn't been answering the land line," McBride explained.

"Can't the nurse go?"

"She asked me. I mean…look, his brother lost his job at Novilis and killed himself."

"Oh my God."

He hadn't wanted to drop that on her, but it just slipped out, and now he'd upset her. Crossland would just have to wait till the morning. He came into the kitchen to help load the dishwasher, but Kendra stopped him.

"You'd better go," she said. She touched a breast with one hand, and she looked down at the floor, trying to hide her disappointment.

He turned to walk away. He could sense her growing isolation and wanted to say something. The one thing she had feared in moving to California was being alone. Her family and friends were all back in New York. But there was nothing he could do tonight. Crossland was alone, too, and more than likely in need of help. He would have to make it up to her. He thought of buying her a gift of some kind, but it would mean little. He knew she wanted time together with him and nothing more, and that was the one thing he couldn't give her right now. She had talked happily about joining the clinic staff so she could be with him during the day. McBride had not encouraged this at all. The veteran nurses would never say anything in front of her, fearful that any negative comments would get back to him, and this was no way to work. So far he had temporized by suggesting that Kendra wait until he was more familiar with the clinic. That was another reason to talk to Crossland. He was the owner. Hiring Kendra would be his decision. McBride promised himself that he would bring it up with Crossland tonight, no matter the situation there.

"Gotta dash," he said and walked out the front door, grabbing his keys off a side table as he went. He felt relieved the minute he walked out of the house, and he hated himself for that.

The car was parked in front of the house, and he acknowledged to himself that it looked like shit—a battered Civic like every other in a hood. It almost got him shot the other night at the vet clinic. He finally voiced his frustration with the car and the people who judged him for it. "Doctors drive Benzes, Beamers, right?" he said out loud. "People just do not fucking understand that the good things come later, after the long, slow climb upwards!" He crawled in and slammed the door shut, fired the ignition and peeled out. He could feel Kendra's eyes on him from the window. Keep abusing this car, he thought, and he wouldn't even have this piece of crap to get around in.

The old doctor lived on East Third Street near South Garey in a fancy brick complex called the Metropolitan. After Lucy died, he'd sold the house and rented a two-bedroom apartment overlooking the building's large pool. The area was well lit. McBride pulled in like Dale Earnhart, Jr. and found a visitor's spot near Crossland's aged Plymouth Valiant. The old red car must have been twenty-five years old, but didn't look it. Crossland enjoyed keeping it polished. He rarely went anywhere in it anyway, just to the clinic, the grocery store, and home. McBride wondered if the car had fifty thousand miles on it yet.

Crossland lived in a ground-floor apartment. McBride found the door, checked the number, and rang the bell. He heard the chimes gonging inside but no one responded. He finally rapped on the door with the gold knocker attached to it. He listened for a response. There wasn't any. He hit the door harder several times with the palm of his hand. The sound echoed down the corridor.

A head covered in curls poked out from apartment on the left. A young man, probably seventeen or eighteen, gazed at him. He had a wispy mustache and half-lidded eyes. "Yo, man, is that totally necessary?" the teen asked.

"Sorry," McBride said.

"Dude's deaf anyway," the young man said.

"Do you know if he's home?" McBride tried.

"The real question is, 'Do I care?' And the answer is, 'No, I don't,'" the teen replied and shut his door.

"Useless little prick," McBride said under his breath. I mean, you expected lip from kids in New York City, but for some kid to have that much arrogance out here in the promised land of the California suburbs? Did video game addiction just breed ill manners? He looked again at the closed door in front of him. What could he do? Get the super? McBride wasn't family so the building manager didn't have to let him in. The police? Crossland would be enraged if he were merely sleeping and McBride called the cops. He knocked again.

"He doesn't answer the door," a woman called over her shoulder as she trundled by carrying a bag of groceries.

McBride glanced at her. She seemed middle-aged with a firm walk and broad shoulders. She must be the neighbor who agreed to look after the dog, he decided. "Madam," he called, realizing this was too formal, "uh, when was the last time you saw him?"

"This morning. You don't see a newspaper in front of the door, do you?" she replied sourly. *Crossland must be the cheeriest soul living in this building*, Pres thought. She freed up a hand to knock on the apartment door next to Crossland's. "Open this damn door up," she yelled. There was no reply. Finally, she put the bag down and found her key in her purse. "The goddamn kid," she snorted. As she put the key in the lock, the door opened. The young man looked at her.

"What took so long?" she snapped.

"I was busy," the teen said.

"Busy!" the woman cried angrily. "You lay on the couch, plugged in to the TV all day, and you're busy! You should try actually doing something for a change." She swatted him on the side of his head, grabbed her groceries, and stormed into the apartment. The door slammed violently behind her. Her yelling continued inside the apartment for several minutes. McBride couldn't believe the kid had had the nerve to tell him to keep it down—the whole complex must be able to hear the battle raging inside the house. Then the door swung open again and the teen reappeared.

"I didn't kill the fucking dog, okay, Mom? So don't fucking take it out on me!" He smashed the door closed behind him and sprinted furiously down the hallway. His combat boots pounded on the hard flooring before he disappeared out the front door.

McBride stood there, silent. Another household that had been rent apart by the disease that was destroying dogs. He felt fate closing in.

Suddenly, just as Pres was about to head home with his tail between his legs, Crossland's door creaked ajar. A single bony arm reached out toward the floor. Fascinated, McBride watched it. Crossland was feeling around for something. Finally, he opened the door wider.

"Hi," McBride said, looking down at Crossland, who was on his knees. The foyer behind him was dark.

"Did you see the newspaper?" Crossland asked wearily. "I thought I heard the paperboy throw it."

"No," McBride said. "It wasn't here."

Crossland glanced up at him. "Maybe later," Crossland muttered. He struggled awkwardly to his feet and started to close the door.

McBride blocked it with his foot. "Can I come in?" he asked.

"No salesmen," Crossland said sharply, not making eye contact. He was dressed in old gray slacks and a white, short-sleeve undershirt. Yellow stains on the front of the shirt glistened in the light from a single living room touchier.

"Abe, it's me, Preston," McBride said. He spoke more forcefully.

The old man turned around and studied him. For a moment he seemed to recognize McBride, and then a shadow fell across his face again. "I don't know any Preston," he said. He shuffled across the pale blue carpeting in a pair of old slippers, his feet barely leaving the floor.

McBride slipped inside and gently closed the door behind him. The apartment had a musty odor. It had not been cleaned for some time. A pile of newspapers, still in their plastic casing, lay unread on the carpeting next to the far wall. A tray had been placed in front of the living room couch. An old

TV dinner rested atop it. From the appearance of the dinner, it had been there awhile. The television was on, but not the sound. Unfamiliar black and white images flickered across the screen. Crossland apparently had found a station that played old movies.

McBride tried to calm himself. This was worse than he could have imagined. Crossland really appeared to have gone off the rails.

"Abe," he tried, "we are worried about you at the clinic."

Crossland turned. "Have you seen Al?' he asked.

"No," McBride answered. "Um…did something happen to him?"

"Oh, no," Crossland said. "He's just a puppy." He attempted to whistle, but the sound was more of a sodden blat. "Al," he called. "He's small. He's probably under something. Here, Al. Come here, boy."

"I'll look for him," McBride said. "Why don't you sit down?" He guided Crossland to the only chair and gently eased him into it. The chair smelled sour. Was that just sweat or was it urine?

"Here, Al," Crossland whispered. "He likes to chew on my slippers." He held up his feet so McBride could inspect the worn slippers. They were a pale green and definitely showed signs of abuse.

McBride went into the kitchen. "Have you eaten anything lately?' he called. Crossland did not answer. McBride opened the refrigerator. It was almost empty and stank of rotten food. There were some eggs in a carton, a bottle of catsup, an open can of dog food, an empty container of orange juice, and a partially eaten loaf of bread. The remaining pieces were dotted with a blue-gray mold. The freezer contained ice cubes and one frozen dinner. The only sign of food in the kitchen was a Burger King wrapping that lay crumpled on the floor.

He opened a cupboard. No dishes. He pulled out utensil drawers. They had been emptied, too. There were no pots, no small appliances. Someone had taken the microwave. It had been pulled out of its spot above the stove. The only thing left was a small glass vase with a couple flowers in it. It was filled with water, but the flowers were old and drooping. McBride glanced at it oddly. The vase seemed so out of place in a room where stains marred the countertops. Was it a holdover from when Lucy had still been alive?

Swallowing hard, McBride leaned against the kitchen sink. The room was spinning. The space was psychologically oppressive, even overwhelming. He could hear Crossland still calling meekly for his dog. The sound seemed amplified, adding to the confusion. He took a deep breath and focused. Crossland needed help. McBride straightened and gave himself a pep talk. He had to get Crossland to a hospital. A real hospital. There was no medicine that would help him in the clinic. He needed to be examined by a psychiatrist and probably medicated if not institutionalized with round the clock nursing care. A few more days here alone and he'd have starved to death.

Resolved to act, McBride marched back into the living room. "Maybe we should go out and grab a bite," he suggested.

"I've eaten," Crossland replied.

"When?"

"I'm not hungry."

"I am," McBride said. "Why don't we go out together?"

"Who are you?" Crossland said. His eyes narrowed, and he looked genuinely puzzled.

McBride sat down on the couch. "Abe, do you have any relatives around here?"

"I have a brother," he said.

Yikes, that would be Charles, who had just offed himself. "Anyone else?"

A sister," the old doctor said. "She died." Tears came slowly down his cheek. "She was younger than me. I told her she should get a dog. They keep you young."

"Who brought you flowers?" McBride wondered.

"Flowers?"

"Do you get visitors?" McBride tried.

"Sometimes."

McBride felt a chill slice through him. Someone had come in the apartment and stripped it clean. He thought of the kid next door.

"I'm seventy years old," Crossland said with a faraway tone in his voice. "My parents are long gone. You're too young to know them. They lived in Boston. I was born in Newton. Maine, New Hampshire, Vermont, Massachusetts, Rhode Island, and Connecticut. Those are the New England states. Some people think New York is in New England, but no, not at all."

McBride looked around the living room. There had been pictures on the wall, he could see by the outlines that remained. There was only the chair and a couch with that one lamp to illuminate the room. While Crossland continued to call for his dog, McBride slipped into the bedroom. The drawers were all open. He didn't spend too much time in there: if Crossland owned any jewelry or anything of value, it was gone now. The clothes were, too. The bed contained an uncovered pillow and a single rumpled sheet. There wasn't even an alarm clock or a lamp. He tried to flick on the overhead light but the overhead light was missing the bulb.

On the floor of the empty closet was a gray shoebox, and next to it a small blanket covering something. As he got closer, he stopped, he stood stock still, and his heart went cold. It was the smell of death, an unmistakable stench that every doctor knows too well. He leaned over and took a corner of the blanket between two fingers. He turned it back and saw the hind paws and legs first. He pulled the blanket away entirely. Al lay on his side, his face locked in a mask of pain. His final expression was something like bewilderment and intense pain. That struck McBride as odd, that a dog would appear to have been puzzled by suffering. McBride touched the dog. He was cold and stiff, but to McBride's surprise, his fingers came away clean. Had Al died in a much less bloody manner than Canada and the other dogs he had seen? He smelled his fingertips for blood and smelled only lilacs. Al had been washed and his fur shampooed, like a human corpse washed and made up for a funeral.

He replaced the blanket and then cautiously opened the shoebox next to the pup. It had some tissue paper covering something dark inside, a gun. McBride didn't touch it, but recognized it: a Lorcin L 380, a .380 caliber handgun. A Saturday Night Special, a gun known for its shoddy construction and its use in many low-rent armed robberies and drunken killings. A friend at medical school got one after several break-ins in nearby apartments. McBride was not afraid of guns, but wondered if whoever stripped the house might have been. He thought of the alienated teen again. Would the kid have passed up the chance at owning a real gun, as obsessed with violence as he probably was? He closed up the box, shoved it into the closet corner. As he was walking out, he glimpsed something on the far side of the dingy mattress—a discolored patch of carpet the size of a throw rug. It was dark brown, but McBride knew after an instant that it had once been bright red. So Al had exploded in blood, just like the other dogs. God, that must have been hard for the old man to take.

McBride went back in the other room and sat on the couch across from the old doctor. His eyes had finally adjusted to the weak light, and he could see Crossland clearly as if for the first time. His white hair, thin and stained, lay across his forehead. He had not shaved in at least a week. The grizzle combined with the shadows to make the lower part of his face black. His eyes had sunken deeply into his face. The old man had pulled himself out of the abyss before when Lucy died. Now, the abyss seemed insurmountable.

"Al," Crossland continued to call plaintively. "Come on, Al."

"You know," McBride said, "Al might have gotten out when you got the newspaper."

"Did he get out?" Crossland said. "He might get lost."

"We should look for him," McBride suggested.

"Maine, New Hampshire, Vermont, Massachusetts, Rhode Island, and Connecticut," Crossland intoned. "Those are the New England states. Some people think New York is in New England, but no, not at all."

"That's so important," McBride said. He walked over to Crossland and took the old man's right arm, helping him stand. Crossland seemed so frail. His halting voice added to the overwhelming sense of age and weakness. "Let's go look for Al," McBride said.

"Oh, is Al missing?" Crossland said. He tried to pull his arm away, but lacked the strength. McBride steered him toward the door.

"I think he's outside," McBride said.

"Who are you?" Crossland asked.

McBride introduced himself again.

"Do you know there are six states in New England: Maine, New Hampshire, Vermont, Massachusetts, Rhode Island and Connecticut," Crossland said. "Some people think New York is in New England, but no, not at all." He nodded vehemently. "I was born in Newton."

"That's nice," McBride said. He was beginning to breathe hard. This was going badly. Crossland had lost a lot of weight, but he was still a substantial man. He was also having trouble walking. He would list to one side. McBride had to push to straighten him up. Then he would tilt in the other direction. He never seemed in danger of toppling over, but they barely made any progress towards the door.

"Where are your keys?" McBride asked.

Crossland shook his head. "I've lost my keys," he whimpered. "I know I had them." He felt his pockets. "I don't know. Maybe Janette has them. Or Lynne."

"Lynne?"

"I don't have any keys," Crossland moaned. He was crying. He turned to look at McBride. His brown eyes stared out plaintively. They looked glazed with emotion. Gone was the spark of energy. It had been replaced with a sad mournful plea: help me. McBride realized he had seen that look once before, in Canada's eyes.

Crossland straightened and smoothed the front of his shirt. Somehow, McBride thought, some sense had seeped through the haze. For maybe an instant, Crossland recognized what was happening to him. They made it through the apartment door, but that split-second of awareness did not seem to last.

"We'll take my car," McBride said. He left the apartment door unlocked, pulling it shut with his left hand while keeping a firm hold on Crossland with the other. He was suddenly grateful Crossland's apartment was on the first floor.

"I need to get my coat," Crossland said. He emphatically jerked his arm away from McBride.

"Where's your coat?" McBride asked.

"In the bedroom," Crossland said. "I can get it." His voice sounded firmer, as though his personality had once again slid back into his body. He gave McBride a wan smile, "It's all right, Pres. I can handle this."

Coat in the bedroom? There had not been anything in there. But Crossland had recognized him and even called him by his name. McBride almost said something, but instead just watched the old man totter slowly back into the bedroom.

"Al," he heard Crossland say, "I knew I'd find you."

McBride ran for the bedroom. He didn't want Crossland to be forced to deal with Al's death again.

"Hold still, boy," Crossland was saying. "I just need to do this."

"Abe?" McBride called. He was almost to the door of the bedroom.

"Bye," Crossland replied. His voice was small and frail.

There was a sudden bang. It echoed through the apartment like a firecracker. McBride recognized the sound and was trying to place it when he heard Crossland's body hit the floor. A bullet. They never sounded like they did in the movies. He sped into the bedroom. The old man was lying on his side, his head resting on his right arm. It was extended with the gun pointed toward the closet. The box sat behind Crossland's body, open, with the tissue paper pulled up. Ironically, blood and brain tissue covered pictures on the dresser of Al and Crossland's wife, the only ones the thief had left. The frames must not have been worth anything.

"Damn it!" McBride yelled. He grabbed his temples and pulled his hair and screamed. Then he got a hold of himself and fell to his knees beside Crossland. The old man was still breathing. The hair on the remaining side of his head was matted and soaked with blood. A stream of blood flowed down his neck. McBride felt his pulse. It was faint, but still there. From his knees, he called 911 on his cell phone.

"911, what is your emergency?" the operator said and then, before McBride could respond, "we do not handle animal emergencies." Damn it, he had never heard that before—had it already come to that?

He detailed for the operator the nature of Abe Crossland's injury and the severity of the situation. When the dispatcher asked for an address, he had to fumble in his pockets to find Silverstein's note. His hand shook. Tears interfered with his ability to read. He choked out the address and answered questions. He returned to Crossland, but there was little he could do. The bleeding was profuse, life ebbing away. Within a few minutes, he could hear sirens.

He waited there with Crossland, hearing the faltering breath rasping into the quiet room. Had the realization of senility been too much? He wondered. The death of his dog? The loss of his brother? There would be no answers.

He heard a knock and the static from walkie talkies and went and opened the door, hanging onto it to stay upright. The EMTs looked at him and he gestured with his eyes to the back room. They rushed in and he felt them going by. A policeman started talking to him. He would have to get a test on his hands, the cop said. McBride looked at him blankly.

"He shot himself," McBride mumbled. "I knew him well; we worked together. He…was there when I was born…" He stared down. "I'm a doctor, too" To expedite, McBride showed him his medical ID card.

The cop looked at it and took down the information. "Thank you, doctor," the cop said. "But I still need to ask a few questions, and I need for you to answer me. Do you know where he got the gun?"

McBride told him about the shoebox.

"Was it his?"

"I don't know," McBride admitted. "I had never been to his house before." Briefly, he outlined the situation. The cop nodded and took notes on a thick spiral pad he pulled from his pocket. He seemed to write incredibly slowly. But then, after everything had happened so fast in the bedroom, time seemed to stretch like molasses.

A few minutes later, a stretcher came rolling by them in the opposite direction. McBride barely glimpsed an image of a thick form covered in a sheet. His mind began to clear, and he pulled himself together. He took a deep breath. There were things to do.

The cop finished taking his personal information and asked him if he planned on going anywhere out of town. McBride said no. They walked outside together and the cop suddenly said, "I saw the dog in the bedroom. That was his animal, I take it?"

"Yes."

The cop stopped and shook his head, and then shook it yet again. "This is becoming a problem… You know, doc, this is the fifth older person we've found dead with their dog this week."

McBride stared at him and nodded. "Are you kidding?"

The cop shook his head. "This dog disease, whatever it is, is hitting very hard now, and the older people don't seem to be able to handle it so well."

"He'd lost his wife last year," McBride added, as if that were meaningful, more substantial, more explanatory. Was a dog really enough to put someone over the edge? God, there were just too many parallels between Crossland and his mother. Pres forded himself not to think about it. "This was too much, the added pain."

The cop nodded and touched the rim of his cap. "I wish you well. We appreciate you guys—you take care of us when we come into the ERs…so I wish you well." He turned away.

"Thanks," McBride said after him.

The night was so clear that he could see all the stars shining, unaffected, untouched by the grief that had formed beneath them. He collected himself and forced his mind to go quiet. It was only then, in that silence, that he realized he had loved Crossland. The man had had a fundamental kindness that

McBride had counted on in his life. It was only now that that light had been extinguished that Pres realized how he had flourished under it.

He walked in a circle and then looked back at the open door. He retrieved his cell phone from his pocket and called Rosen. Two rings and she answered. "Meet me at Pomona Valley," he told her softly.

"Dr. Crossland?" she asked hesitantly. McBride could hear the catch in her voice.

"Yes," he said. He hesitated. "Well, yeah...I...don't know what to say. I'd like to speak to you in person, if I could." He became aware of his own awkwardness as he spoke.

But she didn't ask for details. Mercifully, she seemed to understand with almost no explanation. He got inside his Civic and sat behind the wheel for a few minutes. He turned on the radio and tried for something soothing, but kept getting blaring hip-hop or oversexed rock 'n' roll, so he turned it off. He could not shake the sight of Crossland lying on the bedroom floor. It appeared in his mind like the after-image of a gunshot, on and off like a strobe light. It took a few minutes for this to go away.

He turned his key and fired the engine. The lot was not busy, and McBride was able to turn the car around quickly. Only then did he realize the Crossland's Valiant was no longer in its parking spot. McBride had an instant flash of anger. It had to be the teen-age neighbor. That's who had the keys. The neighbor needed them to take care of Al. Was Lynne the woman with the groceries? No wonder they both wanted McBride to disappear. If Crossland hadn't answered the door, McBride would have never known what was going on inside.

McBride looked in his rear view mirror, back at the apartments. He was filled with anger. The neighbors would have let Crossland die without a second thought. Could they have been the ones who supplied him with the gun? He would have to call the police and clue them in. But first, he had to get to the hospital.

Rosen arrived at Pomona Valley about ten minutes after he did. At least fifteen other people were also there, sitting in the black chairs in various states of illness. One young man had an arm injury of some kind; a woman nearby was coughing steadily into a handkerchief, seemingly timing her coughs to the start and stop of the air conditioning. Most of the people were idly watching television on an overhead monitor. One little girl was playing with toys in the back.

One older man had been placed by himself in the corner. Everyone else was giving him as much room as possible. He was leaning back, obviously very weak. "Rohn flu," someone whispered, gesturing at him.

With tears streaming down her eyes, Rosen looked at McBride. Without a word, she knew that Crossland was gone. They hugged. Finally, she sat down in one of the chairs, staring at the wall. McBride sat next to her.

"You went to his apartment, didn't you?' she said without look at him.

"Yes," he replied.

She didn't answer immediately. "Thank you," she finally said.

After a few moments, McBride went outside and phoned the police and they said they would meet him. An officer came by about fifteen minutes later and wrote down the description of the car and the teen. He called in the information. "Shouldn't be hard to find," he said. "There aren't a lot of cars like that around."

"Only one I know of," McBride assured the cop.

"Can you identify any of the household stuff," the cop asked.

"No," McBride admitted, "but I'd recognize some of the clothes."

"That stuff will be gone," the cop said. "Probably sold or pawned." He folded up his notebook. "People wouldn't treat a dog like that," he said, looking right at McBride.

"Damn right." McBride said. He thanked the cop and went back inside. Rosen was leaning back in her chair, staring at the ceiling. He sat next to her.

"What happened?" she finally asked.

McBride told her.

"I was afraid of something like that," she said softly. "He was okay when I talked to him, but I could feel him slipping away."

He stared at her. "He was more than slipping," he finally said.

"He went fast," Rosen said.

"He was still seeing patients not that long ago," McBride said. He kept his voice low. There was no reason to share what had happened with anyone else even though no one in the room was showing any interest.

"That's why I was always with him," Rosen replied.

McBride had a sudden realization. "There was no government rule that only doctors could give the flu shots, was there?" he asked.

Rosen shrugged innocently. "That was the clinic rule," she explained.

"You didn't bring him flowers by any chance, did you?" McBride asked.

She nodded. "A week ago," she said. "He really wasn't too bad." The dog really pushed him over the edge.

"Couldn't you get him out of that apartment?" he asked, unable to restrain himself. She had to have seen that Crossland was losing his mind.

"What was I supposed to do? I'm not family," Rosen said, her voice laced with anguish. "I didn't want police to take him. That would have been humiliating. A man of Dr. Crossland's stature. I couldn't bear it. I tried to get him to leave, but he refused."

"You didn't want me to go," he noted.

"I thought he just needed time to find himself," Rosen said. "That little dog's dying really unhinged him, I guess."

"Did you know he had a gun?" McBride asked.

Rosen nodded. "I got it for him a while ago. He'd been upset, worried. Something about a neighborhood boy," she said.

They sat there quietly as McBride digested that information. Another thought intruded: what about the clinic? He didn't own it, Crossland did. It could close tomorrow. Abe's lifetime of work could evaporate in mere hours.

Rosen was still dabbing at her eyes. McBride didn't know how to approach the issue. Crossland clearly was no longer capable of running the clinic, but had he sold it? That seemed very unlikely. He had been still seeing patients not that long ago and, soon after, would not have understood any legal documents.

"Tomorrow ..." McBride started.

"We'll open the clinic like normal," Rosen intercepted him.

"Dr. Crossland is ill. That's all we have to tell anyone," Rosen said firmly. She straightened. "The clinic will not close."

McBride nodded. "I'm glad to hear it. We'll figure out a way to handle the legalities. I can be the licensed practitioner."

"Hey, Pres," someone called.

McBride turned to see a doctor in a white coat, stethoscope around his neck, coming toward him. He was familiar, but McBride couldn't place him immediately. He stood up, and they shook hands. The name suddenly popped into his mind: Phil Baretta. They had been in medical school together.

"I thought you'd moved east," Baretta said.

"I'm back," McBride told him. "My mom's here. She's getting older."

Baretta glanced at Rosen.

"No," McBride said quickly. "This is Janette Rosen. We work together."

Baretta shook her hand. Rosen gave him a frozen smile. Baretta waved a hand around. "Like it? I'm in charge of the ER."

"Good for you," McBride said. Baretta had always been ambitious.

"I expect to be chief of staff in a little bit, too," Baretta bragged. "Still doing research?"

McBride winced. Baretta had always played the big man who liked to needle everyone. He had grown a beard and looked professional. He was also older, having gone into medicine later in life. "No, I joined a clinic," McBride admitted.

Baretta surveyed him. "Really? I don't recall you liked working with people that much." He nodded at Rosen. "This guy used mess up floor work like you wouldn't believe. Have you figured out which end of a hypodermic to use?"

"I still like research," McBride said, reddening.

"You should talk to a friend of mine at Novilis. They always need good people," Baretta suggested.

McBride perked up. "Who's your friend?"

"Ethan Willis," Baretta said. "You'll like him. Expects to be head of the company some day. Good man to know."

McBride nodded grimly. All roads seemed to lead to Willis. "I may take you up on that," he said, but added nothing about knowing Willis better than Baretta possibly could.

"So what brings you to our fine facility here at Pomona Valley?" Baretta asked.

McBride told him about Crossland's death. Baretta nodded gravely. "I'm sorry. Does he have family?"

"No, no one."

"I'm sorry about that, Pres." Baretta looked genuinely sympathetic for a calculated moment, then gave a hurried goodbye and rushed off without talking to anyone else.

McBride sat down next to Rosen and tentatively placed an arm on her shoulder. She was sobbing. He resolved to call Willis at Novilis. With Charles Crossland dead, Willis was his only meaningful contact there. It was a significant blow to his ego, but he had to work harder get to the bottom of this disease. Dogs were no longer the only ones dying from it. Because of the deep bond between people and dogs, they were taking their masters with them when they went. Who would be next?

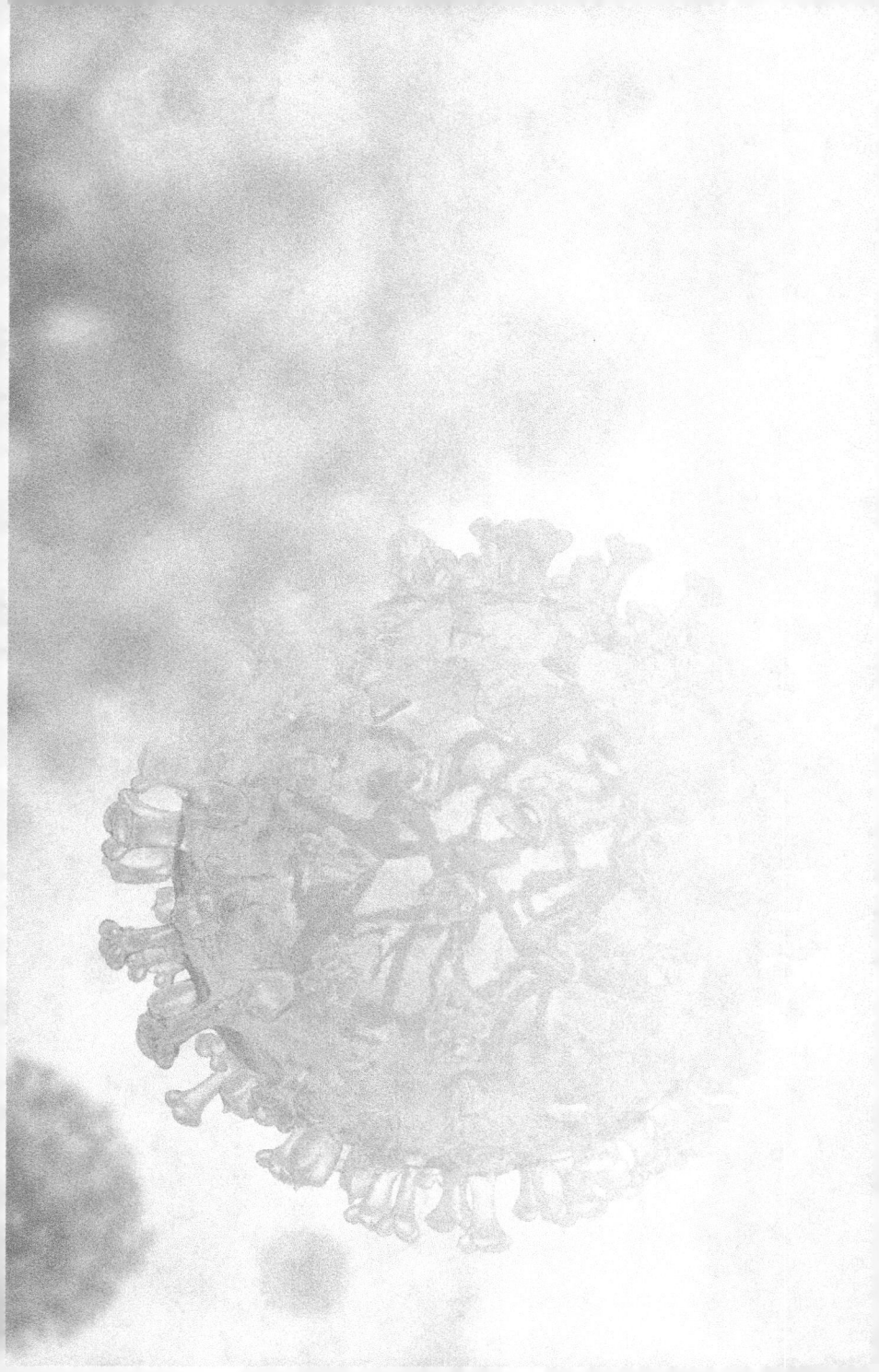

Chapter 8

Shotzi placed his nose in the grass and stared straight ahead at a man wearing heavily padded protection over his left arm and standing maybe twenty yards away in an open field. Every couple of seconds, the dog would look up at his trainer, Max Leibert, who did not say a word. He stood beside the dog, no more than a few inches from his right leg.

For several seconds, the air was still. The wind slipped softly across the open field and glided toward the mountains in the near distance. Leibert enjoyed these rare seconds of peace. The wind broke around his thick, stolid frame. The overhead sun created deep shadows as though Leibert and Shotzi were rooted in the soil.

The rest of the week, they were in the training area with the obstacle course and grim-faced police officers watching every move the dogs made. Today, however, was for fun, a chance to get out and play, to enjoy the summer in northwest Germany.

Then, somewhere, a dog in the kennel coughed and snorted. Several others barked. Quiet followed. Shotzi did not stir. Neither did Leibert.

Finally, Leibert held up a thumb. The man in the protective gear, Wilhelm, nodded. Leibert looked down at his dog, tense and eager. "Go," he urged Shotzi in German. "Go."

Shotzi did not hesitate, already moving by the second time the command left Liebert's lips. He sped through the grass like a black and brown shark moving towards a hapless seal pup. Leibert's second utterance had not yet dissipated by the time Shotzi had begun to bite at the white protective wrap on Wilhelm's arm. He tried to pull away, but the dog was too strong. He kept snapping, digging its teeth further and further into the cloth, shaking his head like a crocodile that had caught a meal and was thrashing it to death. Wilhelm lost his balance and fell. The dog growled and snapped as the man tried to wriggle away. The dog was ferocious, almost feral. He dug into the ground with its hind legs sending up clots of dirt and grass.

"Halt!" Leibert shouted.

The dog instantly obeyed, racing back and kneeling at his feet. He continued to stare with dark brown eyes at Wilhelm as he struggled to stand and catch his breath.

"Wilhelm, are you all right?" Leibert called.

"Yes, yes," Wilhelm replied between gasps. He pulled off the thick sleeve. "That's some strong dog."

"It was your idea," Leibert teased. Wilhelm had just joined the company and had watched the dogs attack during training and in demonstrations. He wanted to try it. Now, panting and sweating, he may be having second thoughts.

Leibert leaned over and patted Shotzi. The dog was breathing hard. His brown sides heaved. Yet he was focused, ready to launch itself again. He acknowledged the caresses by rubbing his muzzle against Leibert's hand, but never took his eyes off its target.

"Whew," Wilhelm said, wiping off his pants and walking toward them. "I don't want to do that again." Leibert gave a short laugh. Wilhelm offered an embarrassed grin and reached down to pet Shotzi, but Leibert stopped him. The dog could get very confused when a man he had been told to attack suddenly became friendly.

Shotzi was in no mood for any hint of kindness. His lips curled back, and a low growl emerged from deep down behind his tongue. The dog had been out of sorts recently, anyway.

Wilhelm drew his hand back. "I'm a friend," he told the dog, who clearly didn't believe him.

"You can't reason with an attack dog," Leibert noted. "You can't intimidate him or scare him. The only hope you have is if the handler calls off the dog."

Wilhelm stepped back. "I guess he's ready to go," he commented.

Leibert did not reply. He knew when one of his dogs was ready for police work. Maybe in a few months, Shotzi would join a long line of dogs trained at his school in North Rhine-Westphalia. Until then, he would continue to work with him to improve his ability to follow commands and attack a suspect, one who did not wear thick cotton padding on his arm.

"What kind of dog is he?" Wilhelm asked.

"Belgian malinois," Leibert answered after a moment. For years, the only dog he worked with had been German shepherds. His grandfather had started training the dogs just after World War I. German Shepherds had been the dog of choice because of their fierce loyalty and intelligence. Now, he thought sadly, breeding had made the dogs gentler, kinder animals.

His grandfather had seen the change coming. "They're going to turn this soldier into a lapdog," he had snarled. Now, thirty years after he died, that was exactly what was happening. Mixed breeds were hardier, but Leibert preferred the malinois, which reminded him of his shepherds. Shotzi was about the size of a medium shepherd with similar black and tan coloring, but the dog's black ears stood straight up. He also seemed more erect, not slinking the way Shepherds had been bred to do.

Wilhelm didn't know anything about the dogs yet. The usual trainer, Reinhold, had called in sick with the bug that seemed to be going around. Leibert had warned everyone to get a shot, but Reinhold had objected. He didn't like needles, and now he was ill. Leibert shook his head at that. He hoped Reinhold recovered quickly. He really didn't want to train Wilhelm. He was just getting too old to break in a new man.

"Come," Leibert ordered the dog.

Shotzi heeled beautifully and trotted along as they headed back toward the large house. It nestled on the edge of the Teutoburg Forest, an ideal landscape for the dogs. They loved to romp through the tall grass, rolling around in the rich dirt. This had been a farm long ago. But for nearly ninety years, the Leibert family had raised dogs instead of crops.

Leibert walked proudly beside his dog. He never felt more at peace than when with one of these magnificent creatures. He was with them when they were whelped, checked them carefully during the first few hours of life, and lovingly raised them. Some were only fit to be pets, but the smart ones, the ones who learned obedience and understood orders quickly, became the chosen few that were placed in the training school. Leibert dogs were respected worldwide, and Leibert knew the names and locations of all of them. With great pride, he read of their successes in drug busts and airport security; with sadness, he learned of their deaths, often in the line of duty. His dogs were both weapons and companions, and when they selflessly laid their lives down to protect their handlers, they were often mourned as equal to those they served.

His wife, Bronwyn, had left some report on the back porch. Leibert picked it up. More deaths had been reported from some kind of disease sweeping through dogs worldwide. Thank God his dogs were safe, Leibert thought. Out here in the eastern part of the state, far from big cities like Düsseldorf and Cologne, a contagious disease had little chance of spreading.

"Everything all right?" Wilhelm asked.

"Couldn't be better," Leibert replied. He felt good. The arthritis in his hip seemed to have eased. Without the tension of a demonstration, where even a well-trained dog might get distracted, he was relaxed and content.

Several dogs in the kennels behind the house began to get excited as they smelled Leibert nearing. They rose up in their wire enclosure and barked madly. Others remained behind, lying down, watching. Leibert only had ten dogs now, part of his decision to cut back as age bore down on his shoulders. Without a son to follow him, Leibert had no idea who would take over the training. The demand for dogs remained steady, but fewer people wanted to enter the field his grandfather had pioneered.

He called for Gunter, a mix-lab and malinois, who had more of a yellowish coat. Brandolph, the young man who minded the kennels, opened the wire door. Several of the other dogs clamored to leave, too, but Brandolph expertly held them back. They complained loudly and then gathered to sniff Shotzi as he returned. At least three dogs, heads on paws, looked as if they had little interest.

Brandolph seemed distracted.

"Party too much last night?" Leibert asked with a laugh. Brandolph had a well-deserved developing reputation of enjoying an excess of schnapps whenever he went into nearby Minden.

Brandolph shook his head. "The dogs are acting odd," he said.

Leibert didn't press him. Brandolph was laconic, not given to long explanations. He was probably hung over and was looking at the dogs through bleary eyes, Leibert assessed.

Gunter eagerly slipped through the chain door, hurried over to Leibert, and looked up expectantly. Dogs had keen senses of smell, but Gunter seemed exceptional based on earlier tests. He might have a career sniffing for contraband at airports, if he could focus. Too often, the dog seemed distracted. That's why he had failed yesterday's test. Today, he would have another chance without any distractions.

He led the dog to the back concrete steps leading into the house. "Stay," he ordered the dog. Gunter crouched on all fours and waited.

"Did you hide the marijuana?" Leibert called to Wilhelm. The young man nodded as Gunter's ears pricked up.

"Find," Leibert ordered the dog.

They watched as Gunter hustled into the nearby barn and from there to the shed filled with garden tools and the riding mower. With his nose to the ground, he twisted and turned. To Leibert's surprise and consternation, Gunter actually slowed a few times, resting, and then hurried on. Leibert did not know where the drugs were to avoid giving the dog any subtle hints. He watched it move, sniff, move on, sniff, stop, move on. He glanced at Wilhelm, who shrugged. Shotzi wouldn't do that, Leibert reminded himself. That dog never paused. Gunter seemed to have a lazy streak. It had better find the drugs this time. He had no time for any dog that couldn't be trained.

Suddenly, the dog stopped by a ceramic flower bed on the sill outside the kitchen window. He was whining and showing. Leibert walked slowly to the box. Wilhelm was beaming, so that must have been the hiding spot. Leibert sighed. Bronwyn was not going to approve the choice, not with her petunias disturbed.

He removed the box, which was heavier than it looked, and placed it on the ground. The dog tried to paw the dirt. "Sit," Leibert commanded. The dog obeyed.

Leibert dug his thick fingers into the soft soil. Within seconds, he felt something hard. He pulled it out: a small amount of marijuana in a bag.

"That's it," Wilhelm said excitedly. The dog cocked its head to look at him as if the find was nothing. "What a great dog," the youngster exclaimed.

"You are too easily impressed," Leibert replied. "When Gunter can smell drugs in a wrap soaked in perfume or in heat-sealed Mylar bags, inside plastic-lined crates coated with foam sealant, inside a closed storage garage, then you can applaud."

He flipped the marijuana toward Wilhelm, who dropped it. "Bury it again tomorrow," he ordered. "This time, stay away from the house and hide it in something plastic."

"Mr. Leibert," Brandolph called. His voice was high-pitched, almost like a siren. Leibert looked toward the kennel to see the young man running toward him, calling his name. "Mr. Leibert."

Leibert waited. While Brandolph rarely got worked up, he would sometimes react in strange ways to something completely innocuous. A small mouse that somehow sneaked into the pens several weeks ago had evoked a similar outburst. The mouse was dead and eaten by the time they had returned, just a small smear of blood remaining inside one of the kennels.

"Come. Come quick," Brandolph called. He was breathing hard. His eyes were red. He looked as if he had been crying.

"What's the matter?" Leibert asked. He hoped his calm manner would quiet the young man, who was gasping for air.

"I don't know," Brandolph admitted. "You must come." He grabbed Leibert's arm.

"Easy, son," Leibert said. "Don't pull so hard. I'm getting fragile."

"It's Schnell," Brandolph sobbed. Leibert began to pick up the pace. Schnell was only a puppy, forever running pell-mell everywhere. That's how he got his name.

They entered the kennel. Two dogs greeted them. Others were lying down. Leibert glanced around. It had only been a few minutes. These dogs looked exhausted. Schnell was on his side, paws extended. His dark chest rose and fell slowly. Brandolph knelt next to the dog. "He's sick," he said.

Leibert could see that. The dog simply didn't move. His tail lay stiffly. There wasn't even a feeble twitch. He knelt down by the dog. It could have eaten something in the field this morning, although it had already seemed lethargic then. Puppies could be groggy in the morning, though, like many children, so Leibert hadn't thought his behavior was particular unusual. Antifreeze could poison a dog quickly, but he kept none on the farm, and besides, antifreeze made the dogs sleepy and slightly euphoric. Schnell looked distinctly unhappy. Leibert glanced around, hoping some plague of distemper or some similar disease wasn't sweeping through the kennel. That had happened once in the past. But all these dogs had been properly vaccinated.

The dog was drooling. That wasn't saliva. Leibert bent closer. It was blood. He gently lifted a lip. Blood filled the dog's mouth. Leibert glanced around helplessly. He had never seen anything like this. Brandolph was checking on a dog on the far side by the entrance to the dogs' quarters. Wilhelm was simply looking around like a sapling caught in a stiff breeze, staring stoically at nothing. Suddenly, Schnell coughed hard, spraying Leibert's face with blood, filling his open eyes and mouth.

He gagged and stumbled backwards, frantically wiping at his face and gagging. When he opened his eyes, he could see Schnell struggling to get to his feet. Perhaps the dog had swallowed thorns or something and had just vomited them up in a clot of blood?

Leibert could see Franz lying against the side of the concrete wall behind him. He hurried to the dog. It, too, was stretched out. When he peeled back a lip—carefully, with a loose twig, so as not to taint it with any of the blood on his hands—he could see that the saliva was pink, indicating the presence of blood.

"There are two more down over here," Brandolph called.

"Get the dogs that seem healthy out of here," Leibert shouted. "Move it. Get them away." Wilhelm stood there, not responding. Leibert angrily grabbed his arm. "Didn't you hear me?" he shouted.

"They're all sick," Wilhelm squeaked in a small, weak voice.

Leibert whirled. The only dog on its feet was Schnell, who wobbled like a punch-drunk prizefighter. Then, in a series of wet, hacking coughs, the puppy's head appeared to disappear in an explosion of blood. Moments later, its lifeless corpse toppled over as if it had taken a sniper's bullet to the skull.

For a moment, the old man stood there. The sun blazed against the top of his balding head, and the sharp wind nipped at his face. Suddenly, with a horrifying clarity, he realized that he had just watched the harbinger of destruction that would bring his world to an end.

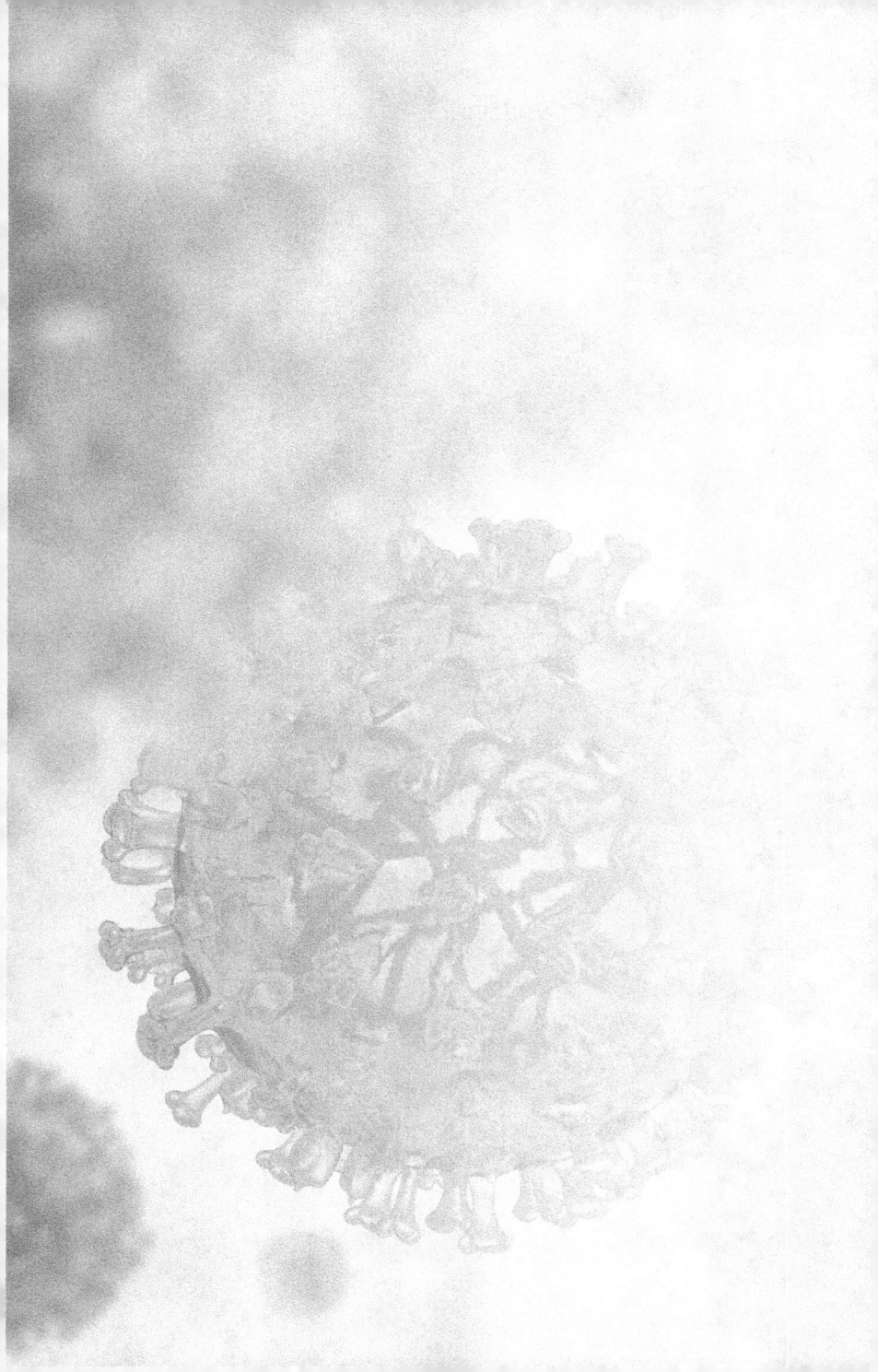

Chapter 9

A lmost overnight, the dog flu crisis descended on humanity. Like a stray bomb dropped into a crystal clear lake,
the ripples shot outward with lightning speed, colliding with
one another, whipping each other into froth. First scientific
journals ran small pieces on the unexpected deaths of a team
of sled dogs in Alaska, then pop science web sites picked it up,
then CNN, ABC, NBC, FOX, and then suddenly it was the only
thing everyone was talking about while filling up at the gas
station, eating dinner, at the water cooler, everywhere. Right
wing bloggers blamed liberal immigration policies, left wing
bloggers struggled to relate the dog flu to the health care debate,
religious conservatives called it a judgment on a society that
valued their pets over their unborn children, and animal rights
activists were ready to go to war. Across the board, however,
was a great sense of loss. It seemed everyone, regardless of their
creed, color or financial status, had been emotionally wounded
by the sudden onset of the dog flu. Instead of this universal
grief bringing people together, it was quickly spun into anger
and fear, and then xenophobia, paranoia, and outright panic.

Much in the same way that violence follows traumatic
human events like a foreclosure or the discovery of infidel-
ity, violence followed the mass death of dogs. There were

innumerable fights between children and teenagers about who was to blame for the death of a favorite pet. In Florida, a fourteen-year-old was beaten unconscious by a group of his former friends and stuffed into the doghouse that had belonged to an ex-friend's dead dog. In rural Michigan, a boy who was "defending" his dog by killing neighbors' dogs with a rifle was attacked, shot, and killed by one of his neighbors. Gang violence had exploded in southern Los Angeles one day when many of the pit bulls belonging to the Latin Kings suddenly sickened and died. They retaliated with a strike on a rival gang that was already armed and angry due to the death of *their* pit bulls. Both sides suffered heavy casualties. For the first time in the history of many animal shelters, all their dogs were gone: those that had not been adopted to replace dead pets had themselves died. Sanitation departments were overwhelmed disposing of the bodies of dogs; police departments were overwhelmed dealing with the violence borne of despair.

Just as looting and other evidence of the worst of human nature often follows natural disasters, all manner of scams arose around the mass dying of dogs. Unscrupulous men and women solicited donations for victims of the mysterious dog illness and pet-death related violence and pocketed what they made. Overnight, "dog quarantine" services popped up—of course, there was no guarantee your dog would survive, and, as one new program showed, most dog quarantines were the best way to ensure that your dog would sicken and die. Of course, disposal charges of your dog's corpse were extra. The pet cemetery business boomed. Many opportunistic physicians offered "dog checkups" though they were not licensed veterinarians; psychotherapists suddenly specialized in "pet grief counseling." Where spam email seemed to have been devoted exclusively to the subjects of penis enlargement, the sale of Vicotin and Viagra, and the recovery of "found" money in Lagos or Nigeria, suddenly scams sprung up for dog vitamins, dog vaccines, disease resistant puppies—nearly anything to take advantage of grieving dog owners everywhere.

For some other doctor, McBride thought ruefully, Wednesday afternoon would be spent on the links or at a spa. Instead, he was driving to the Novilis Co. research facility in the stuffy town of Fontana. He didn't know the area well, but found Sierra Avenue easy enough to locate. The four-lane street ran through the heart of downtown. He could see the Spanish influence in the structures with squared roofs and stucco walls, but the details were off. A small poem came back to him, one that he had never forgotten after reading it in an obscure book one day: "In all my travels, I still have not seen those Spanish Castles in my dreams." He smiled at the remembrance.

One odd house caught his attention: a large white mansion sitting by itself on a hillside off Sierra, bravely fighting off the winds from the Cajun Pass. He wondered who might live there. Zorro?

He drove on, and the San Gabriel and Jurupa mountain ranges soon towered on the horizon, glistening in the late morning sunlight. McBride enjoyed the scenery and tried to just let his mind wander, as he knew he had been too tightly wound. Then he saw a sign on side of the road: "Puppies—$10,000 each." Yes, dogs everywhere were dying, and he was so powerless in the face of this plague that he was about to confront his least favorite person alive. Even phoning his office had been difficult for him. He had tried the day before.

"Phil Baretta suggested I call," he had told the receptionist, who had been noticeably unimpressed. "One moment, sir, I'll transfer you to Personnel," she had announced.

After finally convincing the woman in Personnel that he wasn't looking for a job, she agreed to take a message, but insisted there was no guarantee Vice President Willis would call back. She'd emphasized the words "vice president."

To McBride's surprise, Willis had the receptionist call the clinic later that afternoon. When McBride was able to take the phone, Willis then came on. "Willis here," he'd said gruffly, as if he were deigning to answer McBride's call and not returning a call.

"Hi, Ethan, thanks for returning my call. Isn't it odd we both ended up in California?" McBride said, trying to strike a friendly, conversational tone, emphasizing their commonalities.

"There's nothing odd about it. This is a way station, not a final destination," Willis corrected him immediately. McBride got the message: the company's headquarters were in Elmira, and Willis had his eye on the top prize. He was also in no mood to chitchat. "What do you want?" he asked abruptly.

McBride had explained he had a project in mind that would be mutually beneficial. He'd done his best to make it sound important but avoided details. Willis in turn had pressed him for a moment before agreeing to talk to him in person. The secretary had worked it out for Wednesday. Her manner was coldly efficient, but her voice had sounded familiar. Still, Pres couldn't place it.

After hanging up, McBride had immediately called Santiago. He was still using her lab for basic studies of canine blood and tissue. He was beginning to understand the impact of the disease, but not what was causing it. He knew she'd be excited to hear he might be able to gain access to more sophisticated equipment.

"Do you think he'll let you?" she'd asked eagerly.

"I don't know," he admitted. "I'll turn on the charm," he said sarcastically. That would get him nowhere with Willis.

"That won't work," Santiago said firmly. "A man like that needs hard facts. I will pray to St. Jude. I am sure he will intervene."

She was a piece of work. A scientist who was going to pray to God for hard facts? Santiago always had one saint or another on her to-call list. He admired her religious enthusiasm and envied the comfort and confidence it brought her but didn't share her faith for a minute. Instead, he mentally ran through scenarios of how the meeting would go. In the end of each visualization, Willis always gave him permission.

Running through imaginary conversations was the easy part. Actually visiting the research plant was not. McBride felt his throat tighten as he now neared it. He didn't know why, but had a premonition of something dreadful happening. No, it wasn't that something dreadful was going to happen, it had already happened, and he was just going to discover it. Some of the stress he had often felt going to work in New York filtered through his mind. He remembered the enormous sense of relief he felt the day he walked out. Now, like a dark shadow blotting out the sun, he felt anxiety lurking over him.

He slowed a block or two from the facility. A car honked behind him, the driver irritated with how slow he was going, but McBride ignored it. He could see the brick entrance with the guard and the wooden gate. It looked so familiar. He drove by twice before finally turning in, and his dilapidated car immediately attracted the guard's attention.

In New York, the security guys all knew him, but would still peer into the car before waving him on. Here, the guard was a small black woman with a clipboard who wrote down his name and license plate number. She checked his driver's license and recorded that number, too. She then called to Willis's office to confirm the meeting.

"Tight security," McBride said lightly. "Good thing I'm just a mild-mannered virologist." He had trouble smiling.

"I'm just following orders, sir," the woman answered without a hint of humor. She looked the car up and down again. Then she gave him directions as to where to park and raised the gate. He drove through and couldn't resist giving her a short wave, just to mock her unfriendliness.

The facility had an austere white appearance, rigid and uncompromising. It was divided into three tall buildings, all at least five stories high. A small, manmade lake shimmered in front of the largest structure. McBride wondered if anything deigned to live in such a sterile pond. The third building was incomplete and under construction, with just the outer metal shell in place. Men in hard hats were working on it. A giant crane towered above the structure. That part of the lot was closed and filled with equipment and cement trucks. The second building in the middle was complete. Its lower floors had the conventional array of windows, but the top two floors had been cantilevered so they lay at an angle, as if somebody made a tall cake and misaligned the top two layers.

Behind these front buildings was a two-story structure that that stretched like a straight line with walkways attaching to the three main structures. From the air, McBride surmised, it probably looked like the letter E or a W on its side. He was sure Willis saw it as a *W*.

McBride pulled into a lot to the left of the first building. The first spots had been set aside for administration and were filled with expensive cars, including a Jaguar, BMW, and a Cadillac. Willis's sign carried his title and name in larger letters than the other signs. A silver Mercedes-Benz SL 65 "Black Series" rested regally in the oversized space. McBride took a moment to look inside. It featured a gray leather interior with synthetic suede across the ceiling. *The seats probably massage you while you drive,* he thought. For a moment, he wondered what a new one cost. Probably $150,000. It didn't really matter. The car advertised that Willis obviously was doing well, and McBride wondered whether this was wise of Willis—for the man to put himself on display.

After a moment used to adjust his tie and smooth his suit coat in the car's driver-side mirror, McBride approached the ominous office building.

The first building held the administration offices. It featured a high-arching, all-glass front with two towers on each side. Walking between them on the concrete sidewalk shielded by shadows was intimidating. The side towers stood like sentinels guarding the center. Overall, the place seemed very pompous. It was intimidating for sure, but not in the way he suspected the architect had intended. Instead of awe-inspiring, it just seemed sinister.

He sidled up to the front door, which was all glass with no knob. A uniformed guard opened it for him. He nodded at McBride, who felt oddly obligated to salute. He felt his right hand start to rise, but fought the impulse. He felt like he had walked into the movie *Dr. Strangelove*.

The receptionist sat in the central atrium, which rose majestically the full three stories. A plaque by the door announced that Novilis-California was "one of the largest and most complex high-containment medical research facilities in the world." McBride gave a sly smile. Willis was probably galled he wasn't heading the largest such facility.

He found himself walking carefully, slowly, but his shoes still echoed with each step. The sound cascaded around the large room like gunfire. Every time his heel made contact with the gleaming marble flooring, McBride felt as though he had stepped on a snare drum. There were no other sounds, not from the air conditioning or the receptionist who was watching him approach. McBride knew that he was supposed to feel intimidated, and it was working. It didn't diminish his intimidation, just added embarrassment and resentment to the negative feelings accruing inside him.

The receptionist looked up at him expectantly, and McBride immediately identified himself and explained the reason for his visit. He signed in as the young woman took notes on an electronic device. She seemed almost inhumanly efficient, calmly answering calls via the computer and shunting the calls to various offices while still seeming to pay attention to him. Occasionally, she would talk into a headset, wait for a response, and then route the call. He wondered if she were a robot, a perfect replicant.

"Please wait a moment," she told him. "I will contact Vice President Willis's secretary for you."

While standing by the desk, McBride glanced up the full length of the glass wall at the back of the building. On the top, he saw a tall, thin figure looking down at him. The person stayed only a moment, then walked away. McBride stared for a few seconds. *This is just like the old lab*, he thought. *Everyone watches everyone else; everyone wants to know what's going on.* He felt a chill like a cold stone next to his heart.

He stood by the front desk for several minutes. There were no chairs in the entry. He suspected both that he was being made to wait and made to stand just to unsettle him, but knowing his faceless opponent's design somehow didn't diminish its effectiveness. McBride finally wandered over to one corner where there was a large display with a report on the Rohn flu vaccine and a series of framed and laminated letters from government officials lauding the company. They all mentioned Willis by name. All by thieving his work. And now he reigned in the ivory tower while McBride rotted in a dingy, barely furnished townhouse.

"Dr. McBride," the receptionist called. Her voice easily carried around the room. "You may take the elevator to the third floor now. Vice President Willis will see you now."

McBride glanced around to find the elevator. He finally spotted two of them side-by-side along the wall to his right. They also had solid doors, allowing them to blend into the side of the building. They were distinguished only by a gold border. He did not press the button—there was no button. The door on the right instantly slid open, silently, eerily. He stepped inside. There was no control panel, but the back wall contained a schematic drawing of the facility. "Based on a design for the US Army Research lab," it noted. Eventually, it would include more than ten thousand square feet of "modern, high-technology laboratories."

Next to it was an office roster. He saw two familiar names: Susan Johnson and Lang Hofferman. Apparently Willis had brought some of the old staff here, although he was not sure why, especially their old boss. Poor Hofferman, McBride sighed to himself. He now had to report to Willis. How galling that must be.

Although there never had been any overt arguments, the two had not gotten along in New York. Willis had rarely said anything about Hofferman, other than once to complain that the wrong man was in charge. On the other hand, everyone had understood not to talk to Hofferman after he'd had a meeting with Willis. The older man had been out of sorts for hours after even a brief discussion.

McBride wondered why Hofferman had moved west to work for someone he detested so much. Willis must have wanted someone familiar in an important position. The prospect of controlling someone who had had power over him must also have been appealing. And enough money would make anyone forget his animosities.

The elevator stopped smoothly on the third floor. McBride stepped out to find himself in a glittering waiting room with a glass chandelier reflecting the sun so gloriously that for a moment he thought it was the sun. Marble floors glistened as light flooded through the lofty rear window; two black plush visitor chairs contrasted with the silver-painted walls. Two oil paintings faced each other across the room: one was of the founder of the company, Rodolfo Novilis, and the other was company President Alvin DiAngelo. DiAngelo seemed to have a wary look as if concerned about someone approaching him. McBride wanted to scoff at it, but found he didn't have it in him.

A lone receptionist sat at a long, Brazilian cherry wood desk and smiled at McBride. He immediately recognized her. "Susan!" he burst out.

"Good morning, sir," Johnson said efficiently and coolly without a hint of recognition. A handful of papers lay to her right. A computer and printer sat directly in front of her along with a telephone. Otherwise, the desk was clear, including the empty in-basket. Behind her, wooden paneling reflected the interior glow, adding to the bright light coming through the window. The impact was almost overwhelming. Where was the charismatic, brassy woman with the disaster-area desk he remembered? "Vice President Willis has been delayed by some pressing issues," she droned. "He will be with you shortly. Please have a seat."

Stunned for a moment, McBride stood still. "What?" he asked. "Is he brushing his long, beautiful hair?" he said and smiled at her.

"Sir," Johnson said with emphasis, "please take a seat. Vice President Willis will be with you as soon as he can. He is very busy."

He was astounded. This office felt like a bad dream with the familiar face gone hollow and sinister. Then, almost imperceptivity, Johnson winked at him. He sat down in one of the black chairs. It was made of soft leather and was extremely comfortable. He felt a little better.

After a moment, Johnson rose elegantly and walked across the room. Her heels rapped in a steady beat on the hard flooring. "Can I offer you some coffee, sir?' she asked. The tall, thin woman appeared to have aged a lot in half a year. Still trim, her hair was now laced with gray strands, and the lines in her face seemed more ingrained. Had she lost weight? In Elmira, she'd dressed somewhat casually—business-like but hardly expensive. Here, she was clad in an almost-formal gown, akin to something worn to a major cultural affair—maybe in Thailand. She seemed alien.

"No, thank you," McBride said. He was feeling nervous now and feared spilling some on his clothes.

"Are you sure, sir?" she asked. She leaned over. "Everything is taped," she whispered. She nodded to her left. "He's watching us on close circuit. Ditch the wisecracks."

McBride winced. This wasn't a good way to start, with Willis eavesdropping on McBride making jokes about his hair. Still, it was good to know that Johnson hadn't completely lost her soul. He owed her a lot, he realized again, and wondered why she had gone out of her way to help him.

"Is Willis paranoid?" McBride said out of the side of his mouth.

"That, too," she murmured. "Not even some tea or some cold water?" she said in a normal volume. "We only use Perrier and Evian."

"You convinced me," McBride said, warily looking for a camera. He thought he saw one possibly camouflaged in a portrait of a dignified-looking Novilian. Perhaps inside an eye; or, maybe, hidden in a dark lapel. "Evian's fine." He rolled his eyes slightly.

'Very good, sir," Johnson said. She clicked and clacked across the floor to a door to the left of her desk. Moments later, she returned with a gold-rimmed glass of water. "We have it on tap," she said.

Good God—Evian on tap? He supposed she had been instructed to let people know that it was on tap. He took a sip. It did taste refreshing. He took another sip, trying to forget that a camera was recording every moment.

"Do you like it here?" he asked.

Johnson sat behind her desk, keeping her back straight. "Yes, I certainly do like it," she said with overwrought enthusiasm. "This is so much better than New York. Just look at the view. I am inspired to work here."

"I can understand," McBride said. She sounded unbalanced in her delivery, like a person who smiles too often precisely because she is miserable. "And working for a man like Ethan Willis. He was the researcher I admired most back at the lab. I was doing something I thought was cutting edge and little did I know, Ethan was miles ahead of me. Unbelievable! And now he is vice president. Imagine that!" Whoops, maybe he shouldn't have let that slip.

"A wonder," Johnson echoed. She smiled gratefully at McBride. He wondered if she needed a few more cues or if Willis had heard enough.

He didn't have to ask. Her phone buzzed. "Yes, sir," she answered and looked up at McBride. "Vice President Willis will see you now," she reported. "Please follow me." She walked to her left and pressed a button on the side wall. The wood panel slid easily to the right. A large office came into view. McBride stood, leaving his water on the small end-table next to the chair.

Willis was sitting behind the desk with a small electronic device in his right hand and a large computer in front of him. All that was immediately visible was the top of his head and a small cell phone attached to his ear. He straightened. McBride could see he was holding a sheet of paper in his left hand. There was a small stack on the edge of the desk in a metallic holder. He glanced up and then continued commenting on the paper. "Have Wilson check the duo stat," he ordered. He put down the paper, but continued to hold the tiny recorder.

"Good luck," Johnson whispered. McBride straightened and took several quick breaths to calm himself and put all of this in perspective. "He's in a good mood," she continued and stepped back. McBride walked further into the office. The door closed silently and efficiently behind him. It was like being in Star Trek.

For a moment, McBride looked around. The office featured crossbeams overhead, dark paneling, wooden flooring, two lush visitors' chairs, a fake fireplace in back, and walls laden with oil paintings. "Nice place," he noted. It seemed better suited for a hunting lodge than the main office of a giant research lab.

"This doesn't look like the lab," McBride said before he could catch himself. He and Willis had always spoken directly to one another, in the past.

Willis stood up. "That's the idea," he replied laconically. He walked around his large desk with an extended hand and McBride shook it. Willis's hand was hard, and his grip was strong. The ponytail was gone. So was the scruffy beard. He looked good, too, with his dark hair neatly trimmed and realistically colored. A hint of gray remained around the temples, but that was all. If anything, he seemed younger than McBride remembered him and more vigorous, if not outright younger than McBride himself. His broad shoulders strained against the rich dark fabric of his suit, so sheer and flexible that McBride wondered if it was silk. Silk seemed to be the fabric of choice for a cult leader.

"That's an original Alfred Gockel," Willis said, waving a hand airily toward one abstract oil painting. "Over there," he pointed, "is an original Peter Max. I have a Leroy Neiman, too, on the back wall. I also have a Miro lithograph, a Chagall print, and several more. You probably don't recognize them?" Willis simpered, smiling.

"No," McBride said. "I'm not really into art." In fact, McBride felt and appreciated excellence in many fields of life, and though he was no student of art, he could tell that the paintings were done by masterful hands—he could have stared at them for a long time, just digesting them. But he was hardly into Willis and wasn't going to give him any undue satisfaction.

"Most scientists aren't," Willis droned on. "Left brain, right brain—I've never been that limited." He paused. "I also play electric guitar now. I practice at home. I have one that was owned by Eric Clapton—I'm not sure if that name would mean much to a philistine like yourself?" He let that information linger in the air. "These paintings are worth a lot of money. You see, Pres, art appreciates. When an artist dies, the price of his work really takes off. I would estimate this collection is probably worth one million dollars, but easily could top four or five million in a few years. That Chagall is probably over two million now, give or take a hundred thou. Gockel is up and coming, although he's an old man. When he kicks off, his works could be worth an awful lot."

"Amazing," McBride said. "Maybe he'll get the flu and your painting will go through the roof. Too bad he's not a dog; we could almost count on it!"

Willis arched an eyebrow and smiled, as if he had under-estimated McBride's predatory sense. He then sat down in his chair behind the desk and turned the computer table to the side. McBride saw two monitors. Willis then clasped his hands so that the large green emerald ring on his left hand pointed directly at his visitor. "I don't imagine you came here for a lesson in modern art," he said and gestured at the closest chair.

"True," McBride said, sitting down. "I came here because I have an idea that could be mutually beneficial." He heard his voice echo around the room.

"I am always interested in that," Willis replied casually. He had already started looking at another piece of paper on his desk. The door opened, and McBride turned to see Hofferman shuffle in. He had lost the presence from his days in New York. Instead of standing ramrod straight, he now had bent shoulders. He looked down, not forward, and he seemed to have shrunk. He had gone completely bald with bare fringes of hair around his ears. *A rapid deterioration*, thought McBride.

"The latest report on the V…" Hofferman started to say, and then stopped, realizing that Willis wasn't alone.

"No matter," Willis growled. "You are not interrupting anything important."

"Thank you, Ethan," Hofferman said. He walked across the room to hand the sheaf of papers to Willis. "I'm sorry," Hofferman continued. "I should have attached it to an e-mail."

"I'll discuss it with Mrs. Johnson," Willis said. "It is not your fault. She knew I was in a meeting."

McBride sat there, watching this. "Lang," he finally said, quietly, "it's nice to see you."

Hofferman nodded firmly at McBride and smiled. But the man seemed lost. "Do you need anything else, sir?" he asked Willis.

"Coffee," Willis said. "No sugar."

"Sure, I remember," Hofferman said. He scuttled out.

"He is such an idiot," Willis murmured. "I really dislike that man. He can't even figure out how to use a computer." He smiled as if suddenly realizing what he'd said. "I'm sorry," he added quickly. "Would you like some coffee?"

"No, no thank you," McBride said. It was becoming harder and harder to suppress the contempt growing within. "I know you are busy," he began again.

"What mutually beneficially plan do you have?" Willis asked sharply.

McBride told him about his obsession with the disease that was killing dogs. Willis didn't seem to be paying attention, but this was a poker game of sorts. McBride didn't let himself get distracted. "With a proper vaccine," he continued, "we can help a lot of people."

"You're still on the white-knight kick, aren't you?" Willis snorted.

"I got into research because I wanted to help people," McBride said. "And because it interests me." He kept his voice low.

Willis gave him a pained looked. "I did, too, before I grew up," he said. "I started out like you, all wide-eyed and innocent. Save the world! Cure diseases! Then I realized that I had to watch out for myself. I spent fifteen years in that goddamn lab before I figured that out. Once I did, I was on my way." He stood up. "Unless you've got something better than a crusade against evil, I've got more important things to do. I'm sorry about the dogs. I've got one, too. But I'm more concerned with Novilis's bottom line than canine flu."

"All right," McBride said. "Think about this: you are making a ton of money from the Rohn flu vaccine. An estimated 65 percent of all Americans have pets. More than half own dogs. It's a sixty-four-billion-dollar industry. They'll do anything for Rover. Not everyone will get a Rohn flu vaccine, even if it's mandatory. You can bet dog owners will get one for their dogs. Every last one of them. You'll have another grand slam on your hands. And this one will be more meaningful as it will be your second consecutive winner."

Willis rubbed his hands together thoughtfully. Without a word, he picked up his electronic recorder. "Item. Can we produce a dog flu vaccine?"

"There's one now," McBride added. "It doesn't work."

"It would have to be a replacement," Willis mused. "Why doesn't the current one work?"

"I don't know. That's why I need to use your lab," McBride answered.

"What have you done so far?"

"As much as I can with the limited equipment available," McBride told him. "I have specimens of infected tissue and blood. I need an electron microscope to isolate and identify the virus."

"For the dog flu, correct?" Willis added. His eyes narrowed.

"I left the Rohn flu to you a long time ago," said McBride.

Willis smiled, and for some reason, it made McBride think of the way a shark's eyes roll back into its head before it strikes. "Is there any link between the two—the sick dogs and the Rohn? I don't know what you know so far about this dog virus….but I'm curious." Willis sat up straight, his eyes suddenly burning with curiosity.

"No. I mean, I've yet to establish a link…why do you ask?" McBride said.

"Nothing, no reason. Look, if you use our equipment, we own all rights," Willis told him, getting back to the point. It wasn't a suggestion. "We would own everything you do."

"Fine," McBride told him. "You can do the same thing you did with the Rohn vaccine. Take all the credit, I don't care." He managed a smile in the interests of making this work. "Just let me do the work."

Willis sat back in his chair and looked thoughtful. He seemed to be calculating the costs and comparing them to the possible rewards. Behind him, the imitation log in the fireplace made crackling noises as the flywheel spun slowly in circles to simulate flames.

McBride waited.

Willis finally said a name aloud. After a pause, he asked, "What is Vetter working on?"

McBride was baffled—was he supposed to know the answer to this question? He opened his mouth but no sound came out. Willis cocked his head as if he was listening, and then continued.

"Vester. Don't correct me." Another pause. Jesus, Willis had activated the earpiece he was wearing without giving any indication he was doing so; he was on the phone with someone else.

"Are you shitting me?" he continued. "We don't need that. I thought he was working on an anti- flatulence pill. Retter is doing that? Damn it. Tell him to clean up and go home. Vester, not Retter. Listen to me, goddamnit. You can leave, too. I don't care what excuse you give Vester. I need his lab space." There was a long pause. "Stop arguing," Willis shouted. "This isn't a discussion. I don't care if we promised him a promotion. I didn't promise him a damn thing; you did! We don't need him. Maybe next year he can come back, but not now. I need that lab space more." Another pause. "That's better."

His face was red when he looked at McBride. "You got yourself a place."

"Hey, I don't want to cost someone a job," McBride said, putting both hands in the stop position.

"If you weren't sitting here," Willis told him, "you wouldn't know. You wanted access to the lab; you got it. Don't start getting noble on me. I think you understand how I operate by now."

McBride stiffened. Whatever Vester was working on could not have been as important as curing the dog flu, he told himself. "I can only use it at night. I have to be at the clinic during the day," he said.

"That's no problem. Security remains the same. You used to do a lot of work at night anyway," Willis replied. "No one else was around to see what you did," he added slyly.

"I used magic incantations."

"You'll need them now," Willis said. "Look, you figure out this dog virus and we'll make it a platform for getting you in here in a very comfortable capacity. You make us some money, McBride! Then we have a way to relate to each other. This is my show now, and the bottom line is the only line. Otherwise we get derailed. I know it sounds crude to someone like you, but meditate on it. You know and love biology." He picked up another sheet of paper and spun the computer around to face him. "Biology says that nature is a battlefield." He stared into McBride's eyes. "You with me?"

McBride nodded.

Willis started reading his paper again.

McBride recognized the dismissal and stood up. "Thank you," he said, extending a hand.

"I hope you get quick results," Willis said. "I'm not usually very generous, and when I am, the mood passes quickly. Don't make me regret this." He shook hands perfunctorily.

"I'll keep you informed," McBride said.

"You won't need to," Willis said, his head already in his paper. "You won't do anything I don't know about. I'll assign you a computer on my network, and I'll control your password and your access." He sat back down and picked up the phone. "Mrs. Johnson, the usual," he said. He looked up at McBride. "She'll get your paperwork ready. You'll need to get a badge from the receptionist. She'll have your ID ready by the time you get downstairs."

"Thanks, Ethan," McBride said again. He backed toward the entrance. He suddenly thought of Santiago. He thought of her at odd times now. She was his comrade in arms. She would be pleased. He told himself that now he was finally going to find some answers.

Willis kept on reading his papers and talking into his portable recorder. He had never touched his coffee.

The door opened automatically. McBride exited. The last view he had of Willis was the one-time researcher turned corporate demigod sitting at his desk, completely isolated in a large office where the artwork continually watched him.

Johnson was at her desk, typing on the computer. "I thought he'd have your balls nailed to the wall by now," she murmured.

"Someone else's are already there," he replied under his breath. "What does he have on Hofferman? It was bizarre watching him serve coffee."

"I don't know," Johnson whispered. "Almost ready, sir," she added loudly. "You'll get your badge from the receptionist." The printer produced a few pages. She collected them and handed him the sheaf. "Please fill these out."

"I'll need some help," he said. He sat down in the chair. She came over and stood by him. He pointed at something. She knelt beside him, making a point to peer at the paper.

"I wish to God I knew what was going on," she said under her breath. "He's making the company so much money, no one at headquarters cares. I think DiAngelo is scared shitless."

"I got it," McBride said loudly, writing in the requested information.

"I just know there's something going on," Johnson continued. "There have been a lot of meetings recently. At least two US Senators have been here, and then a week later the Vice President of the United States."

McBride stared at her. His eyes glazed over, and he was lost in concentration for a moment. "Do you think it has something to do with the vaccine?" he asked.

"I don't know," she said. "But what else could it be?"

"Let me know when you find out," he asked.

"What are you going to do?" she asked.

"Try to answer some questions," he said. He stopped and looked at the floor and then up again. "Actually, one critical question. I need just one answer."

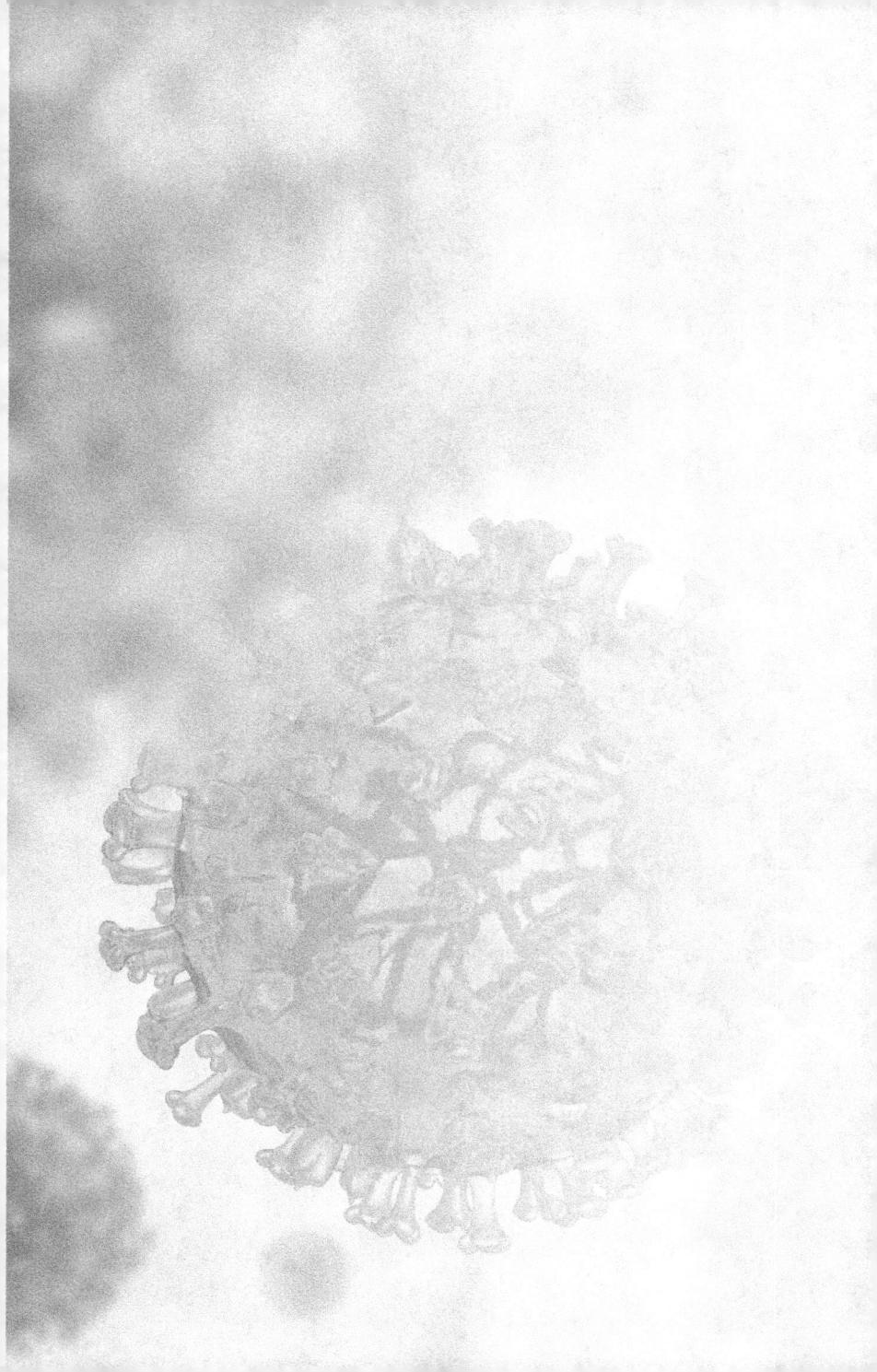

Chapter 10

Lisette labored under the weight of her shopping bags. She was sure she had sweat through her clean work blouse, but she was past caring. She'd had to stay late doing inventory at her job at H&M as two of the other girls had called in "distressed" that day. As if everyone wasn't distressed by the death of their dogs! There was still a job to be done, damn it. By the time she'd stopped at Associated for some groceries and made it onto the notoriously late J train, the sky was already growing dim. When she stepped out of the train at the Myrtle stop in Brooklyn, it felt like the middle of the night. At least no one would notice the dark stains under her armpits as she struggled the ten blocks home, laden down with heavy plastic bags stuffed with food for her children. At any rate, she didn't have to rush to walk Beulah before she messed in the house. But Lord, Beulah had been a good dog, paid back all the mothering Lisette had given her as a puppy and then some by looking after the kids. Even if they could have found another dog, it would have been impossible to replace the thick, protective Rottweiler.

A strong, unexpected wind gusted down the street, and Lisette felt a chill and imagined the salt leaching out of her body, crystallizing against her dark skin like frost on a window pane. Even the wind was hot—why did she feel cold for a second? The streets were black, lit with orange from the overhead streetlights. The bulbs in the lights weren't all smashed as they had been when she was a child growing up in Brooklyn. Still, between those lights, the street gave over to a thick, oily darkness in which anything could hide. Oftentimes she'd been walking home and had seen a lone pit bull emerge from that unguent darkness, followed quickly by three, four, a dozen others—all dogs that had been abandoned by local hoods and gang members who had abused them, fought their dogs for sport, and used them as weapons. The dogs had been discarded just like the tiny empty plastic bags that had once held coke and heroin, glass vials that had held crack.

But they weren't bad dogs, necessarily. In fact, many were probably abandoned for being too soft, lacking the killer instinct necessary to survive in Bed-Stuy. They had scared the beejesus out of her as a child, but now that she was a mother with kids of her own, she'd gotten a lot tougher. Scary as they seemed, there were worse things in the hot night than a pack of lonely dogs looking for garbage to eat. *Move, legs, move,* she thought. *No use standing around dwelling on the past. Them kids will be starving by now.* She hurried down Stuyvesant Avenue.

Of course, those loose packs of flea-bitten strays were gone now, dead as Beulah and sent up in flames by the city. There had been all kinds of outcry when the mayor proposed sending all the corpses to Freshkills to be incinerated. It made sense to him—isn't that where they had sent all the debris from 9/11? But there, that was the point—no one wanted the unclaimed ashes of their lost loved ones mingling with the tainted corpses of dogs dead from some strange bloody plague. Mr. Lopez, her old super who had worked in Manhattan as a janitor, was the only person Lisette had known who had died when the towers came down, thank God. She had loved Beulah dearly, more than lots of people in her life, but still she understood how objectionable the proposition was. Poor Mr. Lopez, such a hard-working man.

So the city had reclaimed the tip of Randall's Island that had once housed a tuberculosis hospital and, almost overnight, installed a giant incinerator there. The collection trucks went around and each day, thousands of 'em went up in flames. But New Yorkers, for better and for worse, were bootstrap people, doing for themselves when they felt others couldn't do for them. There was many a day when she caught a whiff of fuel and burning hair and flesh mixed with superheated steel and concrete from some of the locals burning dead dogs in dumpsters or cinder block fire pits. It never failed to remind her of that severely clear September day when the world had turned on its head, and her hometown had come under attack with death hurtling out of the skies. The worst thing you could imagine, then something worse, then something worse. It felt like there had been no safe place.

Lisette put her bags down for a second, shook her hands until some feeling came back to them, then grasped the clammy plastic handles and rounded the corner on to Greene Street. Best not to stop on Greene Street, even in the daytime. The few foolish white kids who had braved the hood got out quick after the downturn, and the street had given way to crack houses and shooting alleys. One house had burned down that winter; some bum who had nodded out over a trash fire sent it up in flames. They were lucky the whole block hadn't gone up, a white fireman with a thick gray mustache had told her as if he was scolding her, Shawn clinging tightly to her neck and Roxanne holding on to her leg. No, she said, they would have been lucky if it had.

There was light and activity in the back of the burned out lot, Lisette noticed as she approached. *Too late to turn back now*, she thought, and pressed on, trying not to look, just keep her mind on her own business. But the scene in that vacant lot was impossible to ignore.

The local toughs—she recognized a few of them, in sweatpants, undershirts, and skullys—had gathered in a loose circle. Inside the circle, two young men, neither of them even out of their teens, beat each other bloody. Blood already streaming down their faces, they closed in, battered fists flailing, until one of them fell. Each time, a man dressed all in black sweats stepped in to pull them apart so they could start anew. Each time one of them fell, she noticed, voices rose around the circle—the spectators called out names and numbers. Finally, one of the young men—James, she thought his name was, his mother had been yelling at him outside the liquor store—fell flat on his back and did not stir. His face was swollen and pulped almost beyond recognition. She heard the assembled crowd boo and cheer and watched money change hands. Her eyes widened.

During better days, these young men had fought their dogs to near death. Now, their dogs dead, they made their friends their animals for entertainment. It was human blood that was spilled for sport and profit now.

She wouldn't run, she refused to run, her mother didn't raise her to run. But against her will, Lisette broke into a low trot until the vacant lot was several blocks behind her. Sweat coursed down her face as she ran up the steps to their building. Home, safety, her tiny fortress in this war zone. She rifled in her purse for her keys; then, her heart rising in her chest, she pushed the front door open. The lock had been smashed in.

Lisette dropped her bags of groceries and ran up the stairs, calling out frantically "Shawn? Shawnee? Roxanne? You there, baby? Mama's home! Roxie, baby, answer me!" The door to her apartment had been roughly kicked in, and splinters hung askew from the doorframe. This never would have happened when Beulah was around! That bark shook the roof; no one would have messed with them! The kitchen was destroyed, every shelf pulled out and trashed by shaky hands searching for just enough scratch to buy one more rock, just enough not to feel bad…and then maybe a little to feel good.

"Mama?" She heard Roxanne's voice, scared and trembling.

"Baby, where are you? Mama's home. It's safe now," Lisette said, tears of relief coursing down her cheeks as she heard Shawn begin to cry. She pulled her terrified children out from under their bed. The TV was gone, the Playstation was gone, and she didn't know what else, but her children, her babies were safe.

"It's okay, my babies, Mama's here, Mama's gonna protect you." Even as the words left her mouth, they sounded hollow to her, and fear finally came for her. She would not be able to protect them when she wasn't around, and she had to work to feed them. And, with the locks kicked in and the world gone crazy, who would protect her? The nightmare had finally come true—there was no safe place.

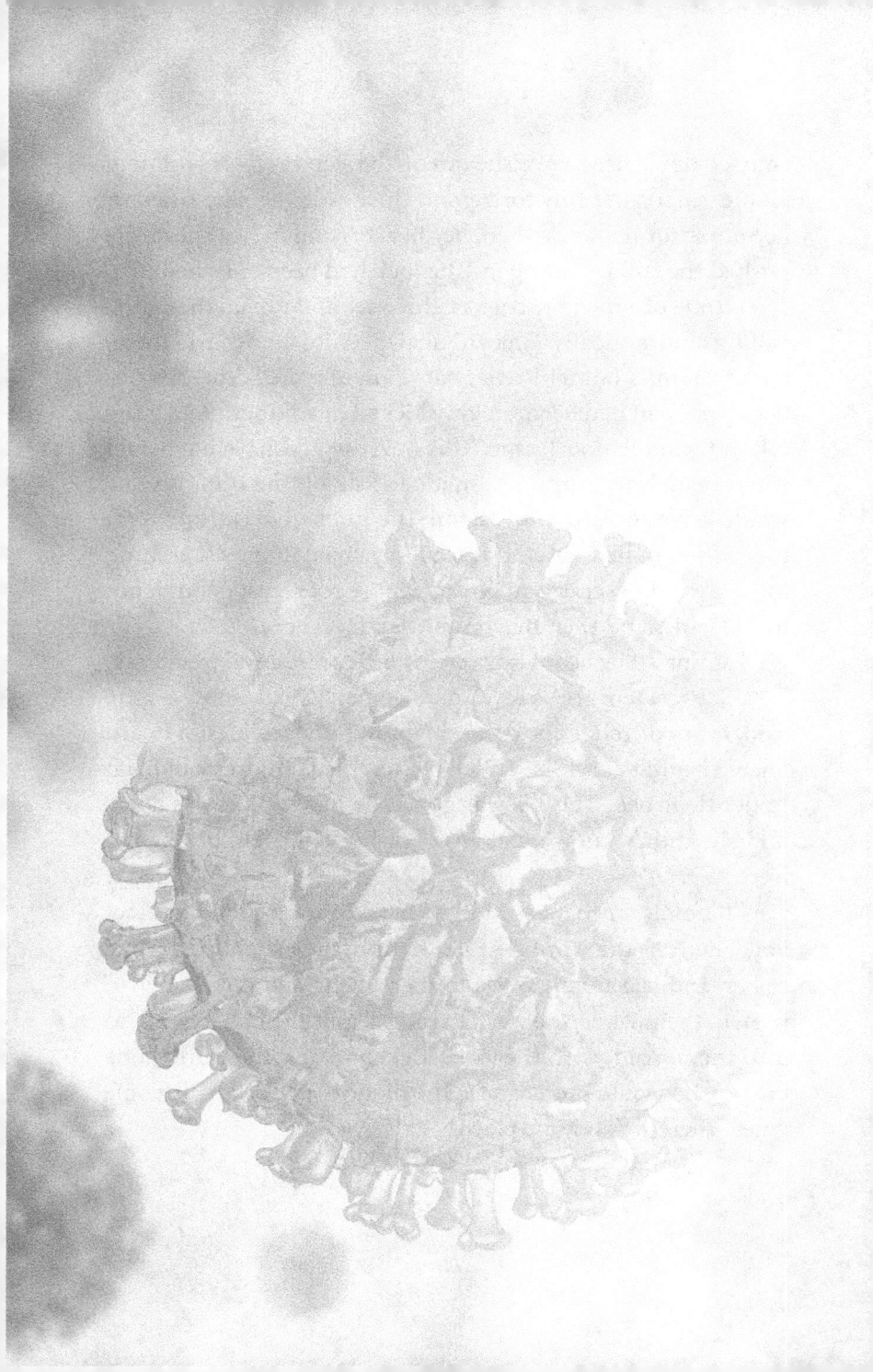

Chapter 11

McBride spent his first week at the Novilis lab avoiding Willis but still coming and going freely. His security clearance provided ease of access and got him into the better of the two cafeterias. He even had his own parking space near the entrance, though his weather-beaten car looked sorely out of place. The lab room he occupied was shared by only one other researcher and had a divider. It was a better setup than he had hoped for.

He was left to himself, but he had to log in to his computer through an account Willis had set up for him, one that only the two of them could access. All of his modeling and files were accessible to only Willis and him, as far as he knew. It wasn't ideal, of course, but it was a big step over the inadequate spaces he'd been struggling to work in.

The first night, he'd stood awed in front of a magnificent TEM electronic microscope. For a moment, he even hesitated to touch it. That damn thing was so impressive with its orange and green stripes, Novilis's colors. He felt like he was in heaven. Novilis was an evil corporation, that was for sure, but at least they knew how to spend their ill-gotten gains. The microscope was deeply cool. Finally, he turned it on and slid the first slide into place.

Initially, McBride saw only squiggly lines. In his first lab back in college, his high school biology teacher had told him to look hard at those lines. That's what early scientists saw in rudimentary microscopes centuries ago while trying to understand what caused the Black Death. It was as if someone was drawing a line inside a cell. Only this line shifted positions and squirmed.

Night after night, he pressed forward. Slowly, a pattern began to form; the information began to take shape. *It's not possible*, he told himself. He didn't say anything aloud. Back in New York, other researchers would have run to him, hoping to share in the discovery. This was all his, something beyond anything he could have imagined. When the importance of what he had discovered hit him, he felt like he was having an attack of vertigo and actually had to sit down on the cold floor of the lab before he fell over.

Using embryonic hens' eggs, he had been able to cultivate samples of the virus found in the dog tissue. The images were startling clear: H3N8 had a round structure with tiny tendrils extending from the main body in all directions. The virus he saw was more like a series of round building blocks that had been stuck together. The disease that was killing dogs was not caused by the H3N8 virus. He did not have to guess what it was; he knew its structure well. It was the same virus he had worked on in New York—H1N1.

It just wasn't possible, he told himself over and over. He ran more slides through. He checked for contamination. Maybe the H3N8 virus had mutated into something similar to H1N1? Even as he conjured alternate hypotheses, he knew they were false, and he was just trying to avoid accepting what his research kept proving and what he knew intuitively to be true. The Rohn flu vaccine, the vaccine that Willis had stolen from him in its unfinished phase and that Novilis had forced on the public with inadequate testing was somehow jumping from humans to kill their pets.

His eyes grew suddenly large, wide open. "Oh, my God," he whispered. "Collateral damage." Feeling like a spy who had stumbled on a nefarious secret, McBride hastily collected all the slides and copied all the data onto his jump drive. He would need a day or two to digest this, to go back over everything once again, to double check what he had already double checked. That night, when he drove through the guard gate, he kept looking back. What would Willis do? McBride shuddered at that thought.

***

The next Friday, he and Kendra decided to visit Maggie. Kendra had received a strange phone call from her the day before. Kendra said Maggie had insisted Canada had returned. They had looked at each other. "She must have somehow gotten a new dog," Kendra decided, "I mean, she still has some weird underground connections, right?" Even if that were true, McBride couldn't imagine that his mother would sign up to have her heart broken again. He wasn't an alarmist by nature, but as insane as the world had been lately, it was impossible not to be concerned about his mother.

He and Kendra walked to the Civic, and McBride did a lap around it, as if suspicious. He kicked each tire hard and then put his full weight on the rear to test the suspension. The Civic went down hard and came up slowly, flopping not just up and down but also side to side. The shocks were shot to the point that the car was hazardous to drive. What if things really went in the toilet and they had to flee to the countryside until things cooled down? Nothing he could do about the car right now. And besides, where would they go? People were going nuts everywhere. McBride polished a spot on the rear fender with his shirttail, then walked around and got in the driver's seat.

He inched out of his driveway, made the right turn and then pulled up to the corner stoplight. He nodded while Kendra talked about Maggie's recent irrational calls. As he drove, he noticed several of his neighbors convening in the street and in front yards—something that normally happened earlier or later in the day. He watched a man consoling a woman, holding her by the shoulders as the woman sobbed into her open hands. McBride squinted at them through the sunlight and recognized the woman. He had often seen her walking her dog, a golden lab, which was absent from the scene. McBride realized that he couldn't remember the last time he had seen the dog. He wondered if it had been transformed by the flu into one of the bloody anguished corpses barely resembling a beloved pet that Environmental Services had picked up in their white vans with hazmat markings that were making daily rounds now.

A mile and a half ahead, the neighborhood changed to a poor section, and here and there he could see a few large plastic bags laid out with the garbage cans, in some cases with bricks holding them down. The edges of one of these dark plastic bags flapped in the wind and revealed a dog's head and shoulders, a red mask of pain, its lips frozen in a howl of agony. He remembered Santiago's clinic and the blood on the floor. Careful as he had tried to be, he had been in a hurry to get out of there after Canada's death. He recalled the sick sensation of the soles of his shoes slipping on the bloody linoleum tile floor. He had had the presence of mind to wipe them off before he had gotten in the car and to scrub them with alcohol before he brought them in the house, but he could have still been a good vector for transferring the disease. And what of the other people who had no idea what was going on? They could have tracked blood all over the state, all over the country, even. Had one of those people gotten on a plane? Good God.

Rounding another corner, he saw an old black man dragging the corpse of a dog, a red-haired mutt, in a small wagon. He struggled because the corpse was too large for the wagon. The dog must have just died as blood was soaking through the dingy white blanket he had throw over its head out of respect for the dead. Or maybe it was just to shield others from the horror the man had experienced; it looked like he was barely holding himself together. Kendra stopped talking, and they pulled over and watched the man's slow, sad toil. It was like a vision from the Black Plague. What was next—mass graves? Flaming pyres of the contorted bodies of man's best friends?

"Jesus, it's all over the place," McBride said, nodding to himself and then at her. "If this thing picks up, it could wipe out every last dog."

"Oh my God, " Kendra said, cupping her mouth with a hand, vividly imagining this horrible extrapolation for a moment—a world without dogs. "I'm so glad we never got a dog! I couldn't bear it."

They passed through a few more neighborhoods, taking a back route to Maggie's just to see what exactly was happening at the street level. McBride opened a window, and the smell of fresh blood and stale decay rose till they both felt physically ill. There was an air of quiet desperation when compared to just a few weeks ago. People whose dogs had died didn't want to go anywhere; still, they had to do something to dispose of the bodies. Though the Rohn flu appeared to be in decline, the rise of the dog flu had re-activated the public's waning anxiety. Even those people without pets were reluctant to leave their homes unless forced to. Many neighborhoods looked virtually deserted. The few people they encountered hurried quickly on their way, often wearing a face mask or covering their mouth and nose with a handkerchief. Wherever there were homes, there seemed to be dead dogs lying in the street, wrapped in plastic, wrapped in blankets or just rudely deposited next to the trash like another object that had been used up and discarded, at least one per block, often more. They did not see a single live dog the entire drive. Kendra and Pres drove in silence, dumbstruck.

McBride parked the Civic on the side of Maggie's building and walked to her door, dread swelling in the back of his skull. As he walked, McBride looked back at the car. It now appeared lopsided for some reason, and one door appeared to be coming off its hinges. But it had shut. He made a mental note not to slam it again.

Maggie's front door had a framed picture of Jimi Hendrix on stage, dressed in buckskin, with his white Stratocaster. Next to this was another framed picture, of Canada, swathed in a buckskin blanket. Was she going off the deep end in the flakiest way possible? Kendra and Pres knocked together, two hands rapping at once.

"Hi, Mom," McBride said as her front door opened slightly. Maggie peered at them through the sliver of an opening. She left the chain in place.

"I have to be careful," she said. "Canada wants to get out."

"He's not jumping as much," McBride noted dolefully as Maggie unlatched the door. The keeshond definitely was not leaping to look out the window or the door. He wasn't barking either.

"He's older now," said Maggie, who was wearing a red loose-fitting wrap with a band of black fabric around her right arm. She kissed her son. "Samantha!" she cried and hugged Kendra.

"No. Kendra," McBride said, awkwardly.

"Of course, she is," Maggie said, winking at Pres. "Of course your name is Kendra!"

"Mom, I don't know any Samantha," McBride said, cringing. She had really worn this line of humor into the ground.

"You didn't know a Kendra before either," she replied and smiled mysteriously.

Oh Lord, McBride thought.

"Come on in and close the door."

The living room was well lit now, with multiple candles blazing. There was the persistent smell of flowers along with something oily sweet but indefinable filling the apartment. They could hear dissonant, rhythmic sounds of Indian music sweeping from the bedroom. The beanbags had remained in place despite McBride's admonitions to sterilize the apartment. McBride also could see Canada's bed in the corner of the living room, apparently unmoved. Maggie hadn't even discarded his blanket.

"Canada," Maggie called. No dog appeared. "That dog has gotten very timid," Maggie said. Kendra and McBride exchanged worried glances. It seemed that one of the only ways they connected these days was through worry over his mother.

"I'll get him," Maggie said. She walked off.

"This does not look good," McBride whispered.

"Shhh," Kendra said under her breath. "Maybe there is a new dog. Or heck, even a cat she's calling Canada? That could be great for her." They waited quietly. Maggie started rummaging around in her bedroom. Then they saw her walk into the spare bedroom, which she used for storage. There was no sign of Canada, nor any other dog or living being of any kind.

As always, the television was on. CNN Headline News was reporting on the epidemic of dog deaths nationwide.

"While the Rohn flu seems to have eased due to the success of the Novilis vaccine," the male announcer said, "the death of dogs around the world continues unabated. Congressional leaders are now calling for a thorough investigation into the dog flu and the inability, so far, of medical authorities to halt the death toll. The President is personally concerned and has moved his own dog, Beau, into isolation inside the White House."

That sanitized understatement was followed by sound bites from Witherspoon and Jessence, both assuring the public that everything was being done to find a cure. "I want everyone to know," Witherspoon said, staring in the camera, "there is no known connection between the Rohn flu and the dog flu whatsoever."

"We continue to encourage the development of a working vaccine to confront this problem," Jessence said.

"Neither Dr. Witherspoon or Dr. Jessence own dogs, but they do both own cats," the CNN announcer concluded. Pres snorted. Who cared about these bureaucrats' cats? With all the dogs dying, cats seemed to be safer than ever.

The broadcast moved on to a story about legendary actress Brigitte Bardot staging a hunger strike in France to protest government apparent inaction there against the dog flu. An image of the famed beauty appeared on the screen. She already looked emaciated, McBride thought.

"She cannot afford to lose more weight," Kendra noted, pointing at her.

The program cut to a commercial. Maggie hadn't come back.

"I don't think there's a dog," McBride said softly.

Something crashed. Both of them jumped. If that was a dog, it must have been as big and as powerful as a horse. The noise came from outside the apartment and echoed like thunder down the hallway. Maggie ran past them and threw open the door.

"I hope they got you this time, Sonia," she shouted. Her face was red, and she was breathing hard when she closed the door.

"Sonia?" McBride asked.

"The lady who lives down the hall," Maggie said. She was clearly upset.

"What did she do?"

Maggie's eyes grew very wide. "Everything," she snapped. "She is poison! She was taking care of people's dogs while they worked. A dog-sitting business. Ha! They all died, and her schnauzer never even got sick. Typhoid Mary, that's what she is!"

"Typhoid Mary?" Kendra asked McBride quietly.

"She was a cook in New York a hundred years or so ago who made everyone else sick, while she stayed healthy," McBride explained.

"She was a real person?"

McBride smiled. "Yes. She ended up quarantined so she couldn't affect anyone else. Didn't you read about her in nursing school? My mom cites her all the time. As kids, if we didn't wash our hands enough, she'd call us Mary."

Maggie opened the door again. "You are the devil, Sonia. You know that? The devil!" she shouted.

There was another bang, then a series of them. McBride ran after his mother into the hallway. A crowd of about half a dozen people stood outside an apartment halfway down the corridor. They were pounding on the apartment door with their fists. One was holding a dark green bottle, broken at the neck. Bits of glass littered the tile flooring, and a red splotch oozed down the wall. The scent of sweet, cheap wine was heavy in the hallway.

McBride recognized Audrey in the small group as well as several women who had been at Maggie's séance. The lone man among them looked familiar, too. He was the man who had pushed his dying poodle into McBride's arms. Now he was pounding on the door and kicking at it with dull fury.

"Sonia!" one of them shouted.

"Get your sorry ass out here!" the old man threatened loudly. He swung at the air hard with both fists, in a slow motion flurry. It struck McBride as comical, but he realized the old man still had quite a bit of power behind his punches. This could get ugly. They were all past the edge of reason.

"Call nine one one," McBride told Kendra as he moved down the hall.

"Pres," Maggie called after him. "Do you want the baseball bat? That'll teach her."

Maggie moved quickly, scurrying into her apartment and then back out, forcing an ancient Louisville Slugger into Pres's hand. McBride shook his head—had she just gone off the deep end? Still, better for him to have it than her, he thought.

Moving quickly, he had to use force in order to make his way through the gathering. Still, he held the bat low, embarrassed by its presence in his hands. "Please, please," he told the crowd. He quickly got between them and the apartment door and tucked the bat in the doorframe behind him. "It's not Sonia's fault. It's a disease. Not every dog gets it."

There was a moment of silence. The old man glared at him.

"That's easy for you to say. Your dog didn't die," he snarled. Instead of the round happy face McBride remembered, the man appeared hideous, transformed by grief. He hadn't shaved in days, and his eyes burned with undiluted hatred.

"Look," McBride said, holding up his empty hands defensively. "I'm sorry about your dogs. Everyone is."

"Who the hell cares what you think?" Aubrey snapped.

"Listen…I'm a doctor," McBride said. "I'm working really hard to find out what's killing the dogs."

"We already know," another woman said. McBride remembered her as quiet, almost shy, repeating the mantra that day in his mother's living room. She now seemed like a fury bent on seeking vengeance. Her eyes were red, exhausted. Her chin jutted out defiantly and she held the broken bottle in a firm grip.

"He couldn't save my dog," Aubrey told the small crowd, which was growing larger. "I asked him to see my dog, and he didn't even come by. Some doctor."

"You can't blame one person," McBride pleaded. He strained to hear police sirens, but could only hear doors opening down the corridor and the sounds of feet marching toward him. This was moving quickly from disturbing to genuinely frightening.

"One person?" the old man snorted. "She is part of a conspiracy. People are killing dogs for food and shipping them to China. I have proof." He wore a Disneyland sweatshirt, Snow White and the Seven Dwarves, and his whole body shook with anger.

"No, no." McBride shook his head emphatically. "You've seen the corpses—they aren't being eaten." He could feel the anger and violence escalating in them all, and began to worry for the woman behind the door he stood in front of. How many people were there? His head spun. He counted seven now. What was taking Kendra so long? He saw her worried face at the back of the crowd, her cell phone pressed desperately to her ear. "Kendra?" he called. He needed the cops *now*.

"It's a CIA experiment," someone in front of him sneered. "They were testing some kind of drug. Once they know it works, they'll use it on us!"

"I can't get through!" Kendra cried out, almost bursting into tears, "I'm just getting a busy signal!"

So it was true, what he'd read: 911 was so overburdened with calls that their network couldn't take it and was shunting calls. He could not believe that things had gotten so bad so fast.

"It's the government," someone else in the crowd growled. "Next, they'll be using it on old people. It's the beginning of euthanasia, I tell you. This is all part of the socialist healthcare scam!"

The crowd inched forward, pushing against McBride. Though he held up his hands to ward them off, they pressed him back against the hard wooden door. He stepped back and kicked something behind him—the baseball bat. He had almost forgotten about it. Really, a bat, against a bunch of senior citizens? True, they were older people, but crazed and now totally threatening.

"Stop it," Kendra shouted from behind the group, her cell phone still hopelessly glued to her ear. "What's the matter with you people?" The pressure on McBride eased minutely. "He's doing the research to find out what's wrong," Kendra continued breathlessly. "You've got to give him time."

"Time?" the old man said. "My dog is dead! I can't get another one. The animal shelters are empty! They've been taken over by Environmental Services for animal morgues! Soon there won't be any dogs left!"

"That can't be Sonia's fault," McBride tried.

"We can start with her," the old man bellowed. "She'll tell us who else is involved."

"Someone is behind this," Audrey yelled. Her eyes bulged now, and her voice had the ring of insanity. The old woman was completely unhinged.

A moment of quiet followed her shrill outburst. McBride seized his chance. "It's not that simple," he said. "There are twenty recognized families of viruses that can affect humans and animals. Each one is identified differently."

They paused, confused by the academic nature of his words, so he got even more technical. "An arbovirus, for example, is a single-stranded enveloped RNA virus with haemagglutinating properties. I would have to isolate the virus and IgM and IgG antibodies by haemagglutination-inhibition, a lengthy, delicate process—and even then, it might be the wrong virus."

"What the fuck?" yelled the old man in the seven dwarves sweatshirt.

"You're right," McBride responded quickly, thinking on his feet. Could he confuse them into dissipating? "H3N8 jumped from horses to dogs directly, but that doesn't mean, however, it's the virus killing dogs now. H3N8 is what was used in the current vaccine, and it's not been effective."

Shit, that was a misstep. The crowd moved sideways, reacting like one organism now. They were dangerously close to him and easily within striking distance. He sensed that he had saved Sonia by becoming their new target. He looked to the back of the crowd for reassurance from Kendra, but she was suddenly nowhere to be found.

"That's why I've had to start from scratch," McBride said. If he could just keep them engaged in a dialogue...

"How long is it going to take? How many more of our babies need to die?"

"It may take a while," he conceded. *With a team*, he thought, *it would go much faster*. But he was alone. "All research takes time. We need the real answer. The real cause. Scapegoating your neighbors isn't going to bring your pets back, and it's not going to prevent other pets from dying."

"That's not good enough," the old man said. "If we can get Sonia to talk..." He surged forward.

"She doesn't know anything!" McBride shouted. "No one does."

The crowd howled. It was what, fifteen people now? McBride swallowed sour bile and one of his hands fumbled nervously for the bat by his right leg.

"Get him out of the way," a familiar voice shouted from the back. "Whatever you have to do to kill the witch!"

"Mom?" McBride sputtered. Jesus, was that his hippie mother calling for him to be attacked so they could spill a neighbor's blood? What the hell was going on?

"Stop protecting Sonia!" the old man said. The woman next to him raised the broken bottle. McBride was taller than anyone there and could see some of the other people were also armed. One had a metal flashlight, another held a metal rod—was that a jack handle? It would have been pathetic—an octogenarian brawl—had not their rage become so acute.

He tensed up. He was bigger than the people in the crowd and younger, too, but they had multiplied. They could overwhelm him easily. He wanted to pick out a leader, make an example of him, and force the others to back off. But no one seemed in charge. They were just waving arms and shouting. Suddenly, he was exhausted. He was working at the Novilis lab in the mornings and nights, and was simultaneously working the clinic during the day. Would he ever be able to sleep a full night again?

"Please," he pleaded but he could see no one was listening.

Finally, thank God, a police siren. He could hear it blaring, getting louder. Kendra, she must have finally gotten through to someone. The sound stirred the crowd. A few people in the back slipped away. The rest grew agitated and began to jostle each other.

"Move your ass, youngun!'" the old man screamed, sensing that their cause had grown more urgent with the police on their way. His clenched fists were white at the knuckles.

"Shut the hell up!" McBride said, tired of the man now. He felt his face get hot.

The old man moved for him, and McBride swatted him hard on the side of the head with an open hand. McBride watched him almost fall sideways and then catch himself. His eyes shifted fast between the old man and the crowd.

"Break it up!" someone yelled. McBride could see two uniformed police officers running down the corridor.

"Damn," Maggie said loudly. "I thought we had her this time!" She sounded sorely disappointed.

The crowd began to break up, and McBride let his guard down for a second. The old man flashed a bitter smile and took another swipe at McBride. McBride noticed it and ducked away, but the old man still caught him in the mouth. McBride tasted his own blood. He gripped the bat firmly with both hands and rammed the butt end hard into the center of the old man's chest, knocking him off his feet. Instantly he felt foolish, and ashamed, like a child caught bullying someone much younger than himself. But Jesus, what had they been planning to do to him? And to Sonia?

The police were busy dispersing the others. "What's going on?" one of the officers demanded, seeing the old man on the ground, rubbing his sternum. The cop was a big man with blond sideburns and a wide, red face marked by tiny broken veins. He held his black nightstick high. The other cop, a small woman with alert eyes, got on her radio out and began calling in a report.

"We were going to beat the crap out of someone who was killing dogs," Maggie told the closest officer, "but that killjoy stopped us."

"Maggie!" Kendra grabbed her and steered her away.

McBride identified himself first and then managed to give the police a clearer explanation. "These people are upset," he added wearily. "I'm sure they wouldn't have done anything," he said, blotting carefully at his fat lip.

"Really?" said the policeman, whose badge read Rick Stickney. "At least five people were beaten this week, some almost to death, all over dogs. The same thing is happening all over the county—damn, all over the country! We've been breaking up this kind of bullshit all week. This is the third time we've been to this complex."

McBride was stunned. He wished he had more time to follow the news, but he'd been living like a hermit, from bed to lab to clinic to lab to bed to lab again. Santiago had been filling him in when they spoke, but he was like a zombie when not in the lab.

"You protected your neighbor, and I wish other folks had that impulse," Stickney continued, "but you gotta be real careful. You could wind up in the hospital next time. Or worse. The only reason we were able to make it here is we were in the neighborhood answering another call. A dog-related suicide."

McBride thought instantly of Crossland. "Yeah, this disease has been incredibly hard on seniors, you know. They don't have a lot else in their lives. How old was the poor guy?"

Stickney gave him a sad, cold look. McBride had never seen such a look of wounded pain on a cop's face. "She was sixteen," Stickney said, his eyes shining. He quickly looked away.

The female officer knocked on the apartment door. "Police," she called.

After a few moments, the door was opened maybe an inch. A frightened face looked out. She saw the uniforms and opened the door wider. McBride recognized the rather kind African-American woman who had sat next to him in the séance. Her face was grayer now, the pale color of ashes, and her dark eyes were filled with pain.

"Are you all right, ma'am?" the female cop asked.

Sonia nodded. "This is the fourth time they done that," she said hoarsely, "and every time, there's more of 'em." She saw McBride and seemed to withdraw.

"It's all right, ma'am," the cop said. "He just did you a big favor. He stood down the crowd till we could get here. Pretty brave for just one guy."

"Thank you," Sonia said. "It's his mother I'm scared of, not him."

"Maggie just makes a lot of noise," McBride said, his face reddening.

"With a baseball bat?" Sonia replied. "She damn well hit my door three or four times last week." She pointed at deep dents in the metal door. The door was badly battered. So that's why the Louisville Slugger had been so close at hand. What had gotten into his mother?

"People are really upset," Stickney said. "They seem to be taking it out on anyone who hasn't suffered the loss that they have."

"But my dog is dead," Sonia protested. "She died, just like all of theirs."

McBride looked at her. "When?"

"Not right away," Sonia said. "And that's why they're so upset. She was fine for maybe three weeks after everything started. I got a flu shot to protect her, but then she died right after, anyways."

"Try that again?" the cop said, confused.

"Wait," McBride said, cutting in. "Did you get the flu?"

"No," Sonia said.

McBride was suddenly lost in thought. What did this mean?

"Maggie said you're a doctor. Did my dog die from the same flu?"

McBride looked at her and shook his head. "No."

Sonia thought the dog might have died from Rohn flu, but that was not possible, he realized. Humans and animals got Type A influenza. The canine influenza virus was a Type A H3N8 influenza virus, and the feline version was Type A H5N1 influenza virus. But human influenza didn't affect animals and vice versa. Just what exactly was going on?

The female cop looked at him curiously. "You're a doctor?' she asked.

"Yeah," he said. "So I am."

She told him the police were always grateful to the doctors who patched them up in the ERs. There was a bond there, and McBride thanked her for saving his skin this time.

The officers went door to door to warn people that any more demonstrations or shows of force would result in arrests. They demanded the old man they were now calling Snow White to clean up the broken glass and wipe down the wall or face assault charges. He did so, shamefaced.

McBride rejoined Kendra and his mother in Maggie's apartment. She was sitting in one of the beanbag chairs, still steaming. They dropped down next to her and McBride discreetly tucked the baseball bat under one of the chairs. His mother didn't need to have access to it, and it didn't appear the beanbags tainted with whatever killed Canada would be going anywhere anytime soon.

"Why did you have to interfere?' Maggie demanded.

"Mom," Pres said, "the woman's dog is dead, too."

"Sure," Maggie said, "after she killed everyone else's! She did that to throw us off. She's evil. Evil!"

"Cut it out! Just stop it," McBride told her. "I don't want to have to bail you out of jail. I do not have the time or the desire, goddammit!" His fear for his mother seemed to well up around him. He realized that, in some ways, she still was his world.

"I've been there before," Maggie said, sticking out her chin.

McBride rolled his eyes. She was so spunky, it was almost impossible to stay mad at her. "Mom, trespassing on the White House lawn is different. This would be destruction of property, assault and battery... They wouldn't just be holding you till you cooled off."

"I was arrested," Maggie said defiantly in Kendra's direction. "I have a record. I'm a con."

"She was trying to interfere with the annual Easter egg hunt," McBride explained to Kendra.

"Separation of church and state," Maggie said. She looked vehement.

"C'mon, Mom," McBride said and his voice got quiet. "Don't you think one inmate in the family is enough?" His voice cracked. He hadn't realized how painful it was going to be to think of his father when he was at this low ebb.

"Canada!" Maggie shouted. She seemed to follow the movement of a dog into the room, but no animal was visible. She began to move her hand as if petting a dog.

"Mom," McBride said gently. This was too much.

"Don't you recognize him?" Maggie asked.

McBride started to argue with her, but Kendra pulled his sleeve.

"We'd better go," she said. "You know, my allergies?"

"Right, I forgot," Maggie cried. "I shouldn't have lit the incense candles. It's hard for an old lady like me to keep it straight—Preston's girlfriends all have something wrong with them. He's a doctor; I think he's drawn to cripples."

"Mom," McBride said again. He had to get them out of there.

"Sorry, wrong word," Maggie corrected herself. "*Disabled*."

"Exactly," Kendra said, heading for the door with a disheartened Pres in tow. "Just staying here proves I'm mentally disabled."

McBride followed her outside, dejected.

"Say goodbye to Canada for us," Kendra said, waving sarcastically.

Maggie gave her a broad smile. "You're such a good girl, Kendra," she said. "I hope you can get this guy I brought into the world here to warm up."

The door closed behind them with a sinister noise.

"Jesus." McBride breathed. "What the hell is going on?"

2/3

Kendra took his hand. "Lots of very sad people, and lots of dead dogs." She kissed his cheek. "Don't worry about your mom. It's a harmless delusion. I'm sure she's going to calm down in a couple of days. Besides, it appears that invisible dogs don't make me sneeze. I had a neighbor who was sure her dead husband joined her for breakfast every day. She cooked him scrambled eggs. She didn't seem to mind that he didn't eat any of it."

"It's not so much the dog illusion," McBride said. "I don't think her neighbor Sonia would agree with you that she's harmless." His mother had been at the helm just now, calling for blood as much as anyone there. More. He shook his head, unsure what to think. He remembered Twain's words: "Everyone is like a moon and has a dark side that he never shows to anybody."

"Well," Kendra said, trying to cap it on a positive note, "there's no danger Canada will bite anyone now."

They got into the car. McBride gave the keys to Kendra. She arched her eyebrows in surprise. "I don't think I should drive right now," he explained.

"What's wrong?"

"Just an exhausting day."

"Pres, you've been pushing yourself too hard! Up at the crack of dawn and then I don't see you again until the middle of the night... I mean, it's nice to see you energized and that you've lost some weight, but Pres, I...I feel like I hardly know you anymore."

It was true, he thought, glancing at his face in the passenger's side mirror as Kendra pulled onto the freeway, choosing now to spare them the sight of all the neighborhoods mourning the loss of their pets. Worry had slimmed him right down. He hadn't been exercising, just rarely eating and never sitting down.

"Just cause I'm not chubby anymore? Come on," he said, forcing a grin and grabbing at her leg. "I bet you like the slimmer me better. Didn't you hear it when that cop mentioned how brave I was?"

"Yes, I heard her stop short of calling you 'stupid.'" Kendra gave a tired little smile that blossomed into something genuine. So there was that, at least. Lately, she had become brooding and cold. She understood what he was doing, but resented the hours away. Loneliness was slicing into her. She really had met only a couple of people in Pomona, despite trying. She didn't like to socialize with nurses, which spoiled that avenue for meeting new friends. She had tried different churches, but hadn't found one that reminded her of home. Once upon a time she had talked to the neighbors, but the rising toll of dog deaths meant fewer people ventured out. For McBride, isolation was not a problem. It was his personality—researchers were used to long, lonely hours. Kendra wasn't.

"Kendra, you know I've got to keep working long hours so I stay skinny and look good when I'm on the news for my breakthrough discovery on the dog flu."

"Are you making progress?"

Pres sighed. "Slowly. I'm figuring out what's not working. The current vaccine for the dog flu is useless."

"What's in the vaccine?"

"Attenuated H3N8," McBride said. "I ran that through the tests immediately. That's why the vaccine isn't working. It's designed for the wrong virus."

"Are you sure?" Kendra asked.

Although he would have preferred quiet on the way home, he was really glad she was interested and talking to him for a change. They hadn't been connecting at all lately.

"Positive," he answered. "H3N8 has a round structure with dangling tendrils. The virus I saw was different, block-like."

She looked at him for a long moment as the car continued down the highway. He nodded. She understood.

"Yes, I think it's the same virus we worked on in New York, H1N1," he told her.

"That's not possible," she said.

"I know. That's why there's more work to do," he said. "Maybe the sample was contaminated. Maybe the H1N1 mutated."

"Maybe the dog flu is a vector," Kendra said thoughtfully as they neared their home.

McBride nodded. Interesting idea, that the H3N8 could be a vector for transmitting a different, lethal disease from one host to another. The H3N8 wouldn't be killing the dogs itself; it would be another virus that the H3N8 carried with it.

His cell phone rang inside the car. He had left it in the tray. Santiago—Pres immediately answered it.

"Hola." He greeted her in Spanish—with no idea why.

"Qué tal?" she laughed. "How is it going?"

"I'm not at the lab tonight," he said.

"Oh," she replied, slightly disdainfully. "A lot of people are depending on you."

"I had to see my mother," he explained.

"Is she all right?"

"Mas o menos."

Kendra heard his Spanish again and threw him a glance. "Hey, will you be at the lab tomorrow?"

McBride paused. "Maria, even if I find what is killing dogs doesn't mean anything can be done about it," he said.

"Yo se," she replied. "But at least we'll all know. Everyone thinks it is the dog flu, but the vaccine is not working. Not even close."

"I'll be there. And you know I will do what I can," McBride promised.

"So will I," Santiago said. "I'll pray for you. Good luck. I mean, I know you will get it right."

She sounded disconsolate, a little depressed. He realized, again, that she was in the trenches every day with this—just a stunning amount of death to deal with. They said their good-byes and hung up.

"Who was that?" Kendra asked.

McBride told her. "She's the vet I took Canada to," he added.

"I don't remember you saying anything about her before," Kendra said quietly. "What's with the Spanish—she doesn't speak English well?" She pulled into their parking spot and quickly got out of the car. He followed, wearily.

"Just practicing. No big deal," he said.

"I guess not," she said.

They walked quietly into the house.

"Why do you think Sonia's dog didn't get sick right away?" McBride asked, thinking aloud.

"How the hell do I know?" Kendra said.

Okay, so she was mad; he hadn't been sure. Still, Santiago needed this information about Sonia's dog as soon as possible;

he couldn't believe he hadn't mentioned it to her before. He pulled out his phone and punched Santiago's number.

"We need more information," he told her without any introduction.

"Por supuesto," Santiago said. "We always need more."

"Can you contact the Veterinarians' Association?" he asked.

"Yeah," she replied. "I do not know if they will answer."

"See if you can get a letter sent out asking for any information from vets who know about dogs that didn't get sick, at least right away," he said. "There have to be a lot of anecdotal reports."

"Porque?"

"I have an idea," he said. "Not everyone died from the Black Death, and there turned out to be an important reason for that. It's possible that we'll see a pattern in the dogs that survived longer."

"What kind of a pattern?" Santiago asked.

"I have no idea."

"I'll let you know when I hear anything," she said and hung up.

"How often do you two talk? " Kendra asked. Pres hadn't realized she'd been standing behind him the whole time.

"Look, she's helping me. She's the only one helping me, in fact. I have no one else." That did not come out how he intended it, and he almost winced at the sound of his words. "I mean, you help me at home. But, I mean, with the disease."

"I thought Willis wouldn't let you bring anyone else into the lab," Kendra said. He could see she was upset.

"She's not at the lab. She has a clinic," McBride said. "Kendra, I love you! Stop being jealous." He hugged her. Her body was stiff, and she looked down and did not return his gaze. "There's only you."

"Yeah," Kendra whispered in his ear, "just me. And the dog flu. And now her."

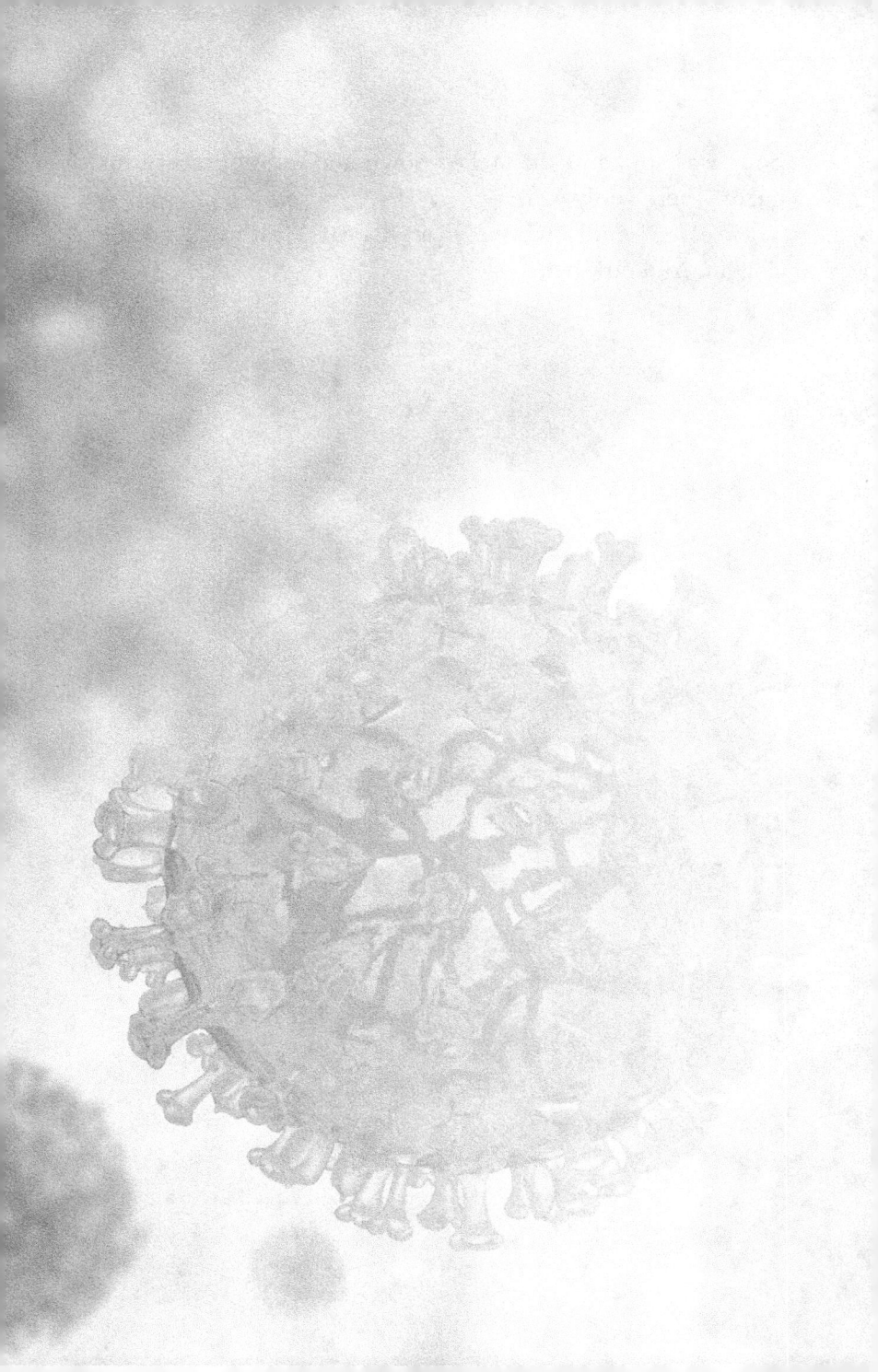

Chapter 12

Seated next to the window on the Alaskan Airlines' Boeing 737, McBride could clearly see the lights of California sparkle across the horizon as the plane ascended. He began to relax, feeling the tension ease as the distance between himself and Pomona increased. The farther he went in any direction away from there, the better.

Kendra was again upset with him, barely talking except for perfunctory comments. She was soured by the hours he had spent away from home on his research, the supposed relationship he had with Maria Santiago, and by the air of gloom that seemed to have settled over the community. Nothing he said or did seemed to help. She was also depressed by the deaths of dogs in the neighborhood, stunned by the many patients at the hospital with mental problems resulting from the loss of their pets, and second-guessing her decision to move from New York with him to California. Couldn't she see that it was chaos everywhere right now? For better and for worse, it wasn't just California.

He could see the way she looked at him, as though weighing what to do. He could feel the coldness in her embrace, the gap between her body and his, even when they were making love. He bought her flowers, and he stayed home whenever he could tear himself away from both the clinic and Novilis. Kendra didn't warm up. He could feel her slowly slipping away, but he could not focus on her completely. He was still trying to figure out how to get what he was learning looking through his electron microscope to the public's attention.

Santiago was too distracted to help much. Overwhelmed by owners bring their dead and dying dogs to the clinic, she rarely had time to talk to him.

As McBride fretted, he became surlier with patients. He tried to be nice, remembering Kendra's comments about his bedside manner, but he was short-tempered. Most patients, mourning the loss of pet dogs, probably needed psychiatric help rather than medical assistance. McBride grew frustrated just trying to understand why they were in the clinic. As a result, Rosen became snippy at work, too. McBride knew she was looking for a replacement, but felt powerless to change his attitude or hers. When Nathan invited him to spend the weekend in San Francisco, he accepted immediately.

When the plane began its descent, he saw sparkling lights across the vast dark plain, almost like fireworks. They were everywhere.

"Dog fires," the man next to him remarked as he peered across McBride's shoulder. He was an advertising account executive named Ernie, who had said hello minutes after boarding and then focused on his laptop for much of the flight. Now, he was flipping through the in-flight magazine.

McBride glanced at him. "They're burning dogs?" he said.

"Dead ones," Ernie replied. "I saw fires like that all over Ohio and Indiana last month."

"They're not doing that in Pomona," McBride said.

Ernie shrugged. "It's to kill the germs," he noted. "If you a traveling salesman like me, you'd have seen it." He went back to doing the crossword puzzle in the in-flight magazine. "Some places, they just toss dogs in the river or the bay."

McBride studied the lights. Now, he could see wisps of smoke slowly drifting skyward as the plane continued its descent toward San Francisco International. There had to be hundreds of fires, small bursts of red and orange in the darkness.

"Air pollution," Ernie noted.

"Don't you like dogs?" McBride asked.

"Sure," Ernie said without looking up. "Someone else's. But that doesn't really matter now, does it?"

It was harsh, but Ernie had a point. McBride had been stunned at the airport to see several cops walking pigs in harnesses on the tarmac alongside lines of luggage. With their bomb and drug sniffing dogs lost to the disease, the government had had to move quickly to find some kind of replacement. As McBride watched, a black potbellied pig rooting around in a flowered valise let loose a rain of black pellets on the fancy luggage. Its handler looked disgusted. McBride knew that pigs had the olfactory sense to perform as well as dogs did, but had they had time to train them properly? If these pigs hadn't even been properly housebroken, how could they accurately detect drugs or worse, a bomb? It was a comical scene, to be sure, but McBride knew it was an ominous sign. Whoever had made the decision to use these poorly trained pigs instead of limiting travel was creating an opportunity for criminals.

Nathan met McBride in the atrium, which featured huge feather designs in the ceiling. The effect was gaudy rather than appealing. McBride was struck by how much older his brother looked. He was a couple of inches shorter and had already begun to get plump. His hair was starting to gray; his face was showing lines. They shook hands. Nathan's grip was weak.

"Everything all right?" McBride asked. What was this world coming to?

Nathan nodded. "I'm just tired," he said.

"I didn't have to come," McBride said.

"I need a break, too," Nathan told him. "Tell some jokes. That'll help."

"A dead dog walks into a bar," McBride responded dryly. Neither of them laughed.

McBride only had a carryon bag, so they were able to leave quickly. He caught a whiff of something burning in the air as soon as they stepped outside San Francisco International. It smelled oily and gamey, like rank flesh and burning hair. He looked at Nathan.

"It's awful," Nathan told him. "The fires burn nonstop. It's illegal, but there's no way to prevent people from starting them."

"You must have a lot of dogs here," McBride said. He could see billowing black clouds in almost all directions.

"Used to," Nathan answered.

They drove in Nathan's Malibu across the Bay Bride toward his home in South Berkeley. Nathan had to slow down occasionally as dense smoke drifted across the road. McBride watched as grief-stricken people emerged from homes, carrying dead animals in their arms. Fires burned in vacant lots, on the streets, and even in driveways, creating a thick, acrid cloud that filled the air. Nathan turned on the air conditioning in the car, but the smell had already permeated the interior.

"It's been getting worse," he noted. They could hear sirens seemingly nonstop. "The police can't do a thing about it," he said.

McBride was struck by the overwhelming sense of gloom that pervaded the city. People were sitting on street corners weeping openly or wandering aimlessly. Brown crepe marked homes. Apparently, brown ribbons symbolized the death of a pet, the same way pink indicated breast cancer or yellow showed support for US troops abroad. Every home seemed to feature a brown ribbon either on the front door or wrapped around a tree. Here and there, front lawns were decorated with small wooden crosses and wreaths.

"The damn disease seemed to spread from Canada to Oakland and up here," Nathan said. He inched by a fire in the street. At least ten people were standing around, holding hands. McBride could see bodies of dogs being incinerated in the flames.

"This must have been what the Black Death was like," he breathed.

"Close enough," Nathan said. "I rarely have many kids in class now. They are so shaken up by the death of their dogs, they just stop coming." He came to a stop by another fire in the road. Someone was tossing a small dog into the flames. McBride was stunned, but people were barely watching, acting as if this were normal behavior. McBride tasted bile in his mouth. The whole spectacle was sickening.

Finally, the left lane cleared, and Nathan could drive around it. "We've been studying disease in biology class," he continued. "That's all the kids who do show up want to talk about."

"What did they decide?" McBride asked, trying to conceal his interest.

"You'll laugh," Nathan said. "They think it's connected to the Rohn flu."

"You've got some smart kids, Nate. That's what I think, too," McBride said.

"No shit?"

"Except everyone else—Surgeon General, Centers for Disease Control, pharmaceuticals and apparently the administration—disagree," McBride said sourly.

"Find any proof?"

McBride told him about his research. "I don't have final results ready to make public but it's definitely related to H1N1, not H3N8," McBride said.

His brother inhaled sharply. "Whoa," he said. "Are you sure?"

"Yes."

"Damn." He turned left. "Have you told anyone?"

"Who? I'm a discredited scientist. Why would anyone listen to me?" McBride said.

"Good point," Nathan said. "No wonder you're depressed."

McBride was no longer listening. His mind was on the carnage raging around him. It was one thing to read reports in the *LA Times* or see them on the news; it was quite another to find himself in the middle of such a disaster. In some ways, he should have known. Still, his life was insular and isolated. Exposed to the enormity of the calamity, McBride was numb. Some people had posted images of their dead pets on trees in front of their homes. Others had placed symbols, like dog bones or dog houses, on their lawns along with brown ribbons. Almost every house had some reminder of a vanished dog. When they stopped at a corner next to a dog park, McBride saw a wall covered with pictures of dead pets. With a chill, he recalled the pictures of missing loved ones posted all over lower Manhattan after 9/11.

"This is a very liberal, family-oriented neighborhood," Nathan continued. "Pretty much everyone had dogs."

A few minutes later, they pulled into a driveway. Nathan's home was a two-story wooden structure with an attached garage. "There's a mother-in-law apartment on top of the garage," Nathan pointed. "That's in case Mom ever needs help. She'd like it here. Most people in Berkley are to the left of the Kennedys."

Smoke drifted around them as they coughed up the front walk. The interior was neat. Nathan had not married—"Do you know what high school teachers get paid?" he told McBride once. "How could I afford a wife?"—but he clearly enjoyed order. Everything was perfectly aligned, from magazines under a coffee table to doilies on lamp stands.

McBride settled on the couch. "You didn't have a dog?" he asked.

Nathan shook his head. "I was never home to take care of one," he said, getting his brother a can of soda. McBride took it gratefully. His throat was raw from inhaling smoke, and he hoped the drink would settle his stomach. "I thought about getting one seriously several times," Nathan continued. "But I never did. Good thing, I guess. I'd be one of the heartbroken masses now."

"Sometimes it seems bizarre to me how people are react-ing," Pres said. "I mean, not to sound callous but, you know, they're dogs, not people."

"You're right that they're not people," Nathan said, "and that's kind of the point. It took me a while to grasp this as well as we didn't have a dog growing up but…well, a dog's love is unconditional. It's totally pure. If you watch a dog interacting with its owner, it allows itself to be totally consumed by love with nothing in the way."

"I would argue that Mom loves us unconditionally," Pres said. Then, before Nathan could raise an eyebrow, "Okay, let me rephrase that: most parents love their children unconditionally."

Nathan chuckled. "Having endured more than my fair share of parent/teacher conferences, I've found that our rela-tionship with Mom is closer to typical than you'd imagine. Pres, a dog never expresses disapproval, doubt, or shame towards its owner. With a good dog, well, it's only ever love."

They sat in silence for a moment, absorbing Nathan's words.

"Any ideas how to get my research to the public?" McBride finally asked, broaching the subject he knew both of them were thinking about. He didn't want to talk or think about their mother any more if it could be avoided.

Nathan shook his head. "I could have you speak at the school and try to get a reporter there," he said.

"Why would anyone believe me? You know everyone is lined up against me," McBride replied. He rubbed his hands. They felt dirty. He could see black soot had seeped into the small lines in his skin. Without waiting for Nathan to answer, he went into the bathroom to wash up. He could see that

Nathan didn't have any suggestions anyway. Maybe there weren't any options.

The doorbell rang. Nathan opened it. A teenage girl was standing there. "Momma asked me to invite you to Cobaka's funeral," she said softly.

"Sure, Lucy," Nathan said. He turned around. "Come on," he called. McBride followed him and Lucy to the neighbor's house. At least eight or nine people were standing around a small hole in the ground in the backyard. They all had their heads bowed, hands folded, staring at the shallow grave. Three were children, including Lucy; the others were adults. One older man seemed to be in charge.

"I don't know if we should say Kaddish," the man said.

"God won't mind, Elliott," a woman next to him said.

"Cobaka was like a member of the family," a boy added.

Elliott nodded and began to recite something in a foreign language. McBride looked down into the grave. He could see a small white and brown short-haired dog lying lifeless on its side. Its head had been covered and its body had been washed but McBride could still see signs of blood in its fur. The man's deep voice somberly rolled across the silent backyard. It seemed so strange there. McBride didn't understand what Elliott was saying, but could hear the mournful tones. He was chanting in a rhythmic way with his eyes closed. He rocked gently back and forth as he intoned the words. Every few lines, everyone would join in with an "amen."

Finally, he finished. One by one, the participants tossed dirt into the grave. McBride and his brother quickly joined in. Apparently, they were only symbolically covering the body, because Elliott shortly produced a shovel and completed the task. Tears dripped down Lucy's face as the body disappeared.

"Your dog?" Nathan asked her gently.

She nodded.

"I'm sorry, honey," he told her. She ran crying to her mother, who looked at Nathan with sad eyes of her own. Nathan gave a weak smile, waved and turned away.

"Day after day," he said. "I don't know how the kids can take it."

"At least they didn't burn the dog," McBride said softly.

Nathan nodded. "It's a religious thing," he said. "Besides it's too much for some kids." He looked toward the family, which was still huddled together. "Backyards all over the area have been turned into cemeteries."

Back in the house, McBride picked up the *San Francisco Examiner*. The front page—and, indeed most of the paper—dealt with what was happening to the dogs. A reporter had called Willis and gotten the same story about the need for more research. A separate story reported that canines in the wild, like wolves and coyotes, were being found dead from the disease. Dingoes in Australia and wild dogs in Africa also had been discovered dying or dead.

"No canine is exempt from this dreadful scourge," Dr. Lauren Jessence from the Centers for Disease Control was quoted in the story. "We're hoping the government will apply the kind of resources needed to defeat it. We are naturally fearful this disease could mutate, like bird flu, and begin to infect food animals or even humans." Representatives of PETA and the SPCA, both of which were demanding action, joined the chorus.

"I never thought I'd ever see anything like this," McBride said.

"With our large gay community, AIDS hit pretty hard out here," Nathan commented, "but, somehow, the death of dogs seems to be an even bigger deal. There's no way to explain to a dog what's happening. People can at least do something to limit AIDS; dogs can't do a thing about the dog flu. And everyone—even bigots, racists, and close-minded people—loves dogs. Jesus, even the Nazis loved their dogs."

"Maybe someone will listen to the truth," McBride said.

Nathan shook his head. "Don't bet on it," he said. "There's too much money involved. Truth isn't part of that equation."

"Now you are getting cynical," McBride told him.

Nathan shook his head. "Realistic," he said.

"Hey," McBride said. There was a small story on the fourth page that Daniel Gunardson, the musher from the Iditarod, would be speaking to city council at a special meeting the next morning. *What great timing*, McBride thought. Maybe Gunardson could have some clues to what was going on. After all, he was at the epicenter when the disease started and had become something of a roving ambassador, sharing his experiences. He hadn't been in California before, as far as McBride knew.

Nathan had no problem making the trip in when McBride suggested it. He knew where the City Center was located, between Van Ness and Turk. It was the home of San Francisco's city hall and government structures. According to the account, legislators wanted to hear more information about the disease.

McBride began to feel better. Maybe something helpful would come out of the trip other than a break from Kendra and the stress at home. For dinner, the two brothers drove to a small bistro perhaps a mile away with an outdoor patio. It was virtually empty. Nathan apologized for the lack of activity, but McBride assured him he preferred the quiet. Smoke surrounded them everywhere, even drifting over their food. McBride kept thinking of homes located near concentration camps housing German Nazi crematoriums where ashes settled on everything. The residents there continually denied they knew anything was happening but here, everyone was aware. There was no hiding from it.

The restaurant had set up a small memorial corner with a table with a black tablecloth, pictures of dogs on the wall, and a single candle. Nathan and McBride briefly chatted about their mother, jobs, what was happening with girlfriends and careers, but, mostly, they ate in silence, glancing occasional at the memorial.

In the morning, Nathan offered to take McBride on a tour of the area. They went back across the Bay. Almost immediately, they could hear multiple sirens. Police cars roared past them with lights flashing and sirens roaring. Ambulances and fire trucks sped across the bridge, too.

Nathan planned to drive down Mission to Van Ness, but a barricade had been set up at Mission and then at Market with policemen waving everyone on. Finally, Nathan simply parked at the Embarcadero Plaza. It was a long walk, he said, but maybe the only way they'd get there. McBride didn't hesitate. Even if he could only ask a question from the audience, maybe he could learn some vital clue.

Mission would have been the direct route, but they had to start down California and then turn left at Kearny. They could hear shouting as they walked and even what sounded like firecrackers as they neared Mission Street.

"Guns," McBride said. He recognized the sound from a shooting range he had been to. The sound was different, though. Rubber bullets? Instead of being repelled, he hurried on. Nathan hung back.

"I don't know," he said.

"It's got to be something local. Maybe someone's trying to rob a bank," McBride said. "We can easily avoid that." He checked his watch. "The presentation starts in an hour," he noted. "I am sure we have time to get past this area and get to the center." Nathan reluctantly continued.

Within minutes, they found themselves on the edge of a full-scale riot. People were running up and down Mission. Police were everywhere. Fireman were turning their hoses on the crowds, which broke away and then reformed. The smoky air was thick with the acrid stench of tear gas. The brothers darted into a small candle store, one of many businesses along the busy street and already crowded with people trying to escape the turmoil. The heavily scented interior aroma mingled with the mixture of gas and burned flesh that filled the air. McBride felt as though he could not breathe. His eyes burned.

Someone quickly gave them water-soaked cloths that helped clear their eyes. Water, they were advised solemnly by a knowledgeable veteran protestor, took care of tear gas. McBride's cloth had an eerie aroma of incense.

"What is going on?" McBride gasped as the pain subsided.

"The asshole who spread the dog flu was supposed to speak today," a wiry young man with a large flowery tattoo on his neck told him angrily. "We're trying to stop him."

"Gunardson?" McBride asked in disbelief.

"I don't know the bastard's name," the young man snarled. "His dogs were the first to die. Then, he went around spreading the damn flu. We don't need his propaganda here."

McBride stared at the youngster, whose face was distorted in pure hate. "No," he tried. "No one spread the disease. Gunardson wasn't in Oakland when the disease got there. The only thing he's spreading is information."

"Who the hell are you?" the teen spat out, "his press agent?"

"I'm a medical researcher, trying..." McBride started. He got no further. Police sirens roared loudly. The thump-thump-thump of guns filled the air. People were running by the store. Looking through the front widow, McBride saw someone fall by the curb.

"Come on," he told Nathan.

"Are you crazy?" Nathan objected.

"Worse," McBride answered. "I'm a doctor."

He cautiously stepped outside. The teen followed. So did others. A young woman, blood running down her face, was lying on her side to the left of the store. Dressed in jeans and a brown blouse, she had apparently slipped and fallen against the brick exterior. McBride knelt over her. Her eyes were closed. She had a pulse, but an ugly bruise was already appearing above her right eye. She would be all right, McBride decided.

He ran back into the store and got a wet cloth. When he came back, she was blinking and moaning. He gave her the cloth. She wiped her face. She couldn't have been more than twenty.

"Pres," his brother called.

McBride whirled. Nathan was leaning over the teenager from the store. He was lying on the sidewalk. Blood was oozing away from his face and seeping along the concrete. It stained the large tattoo on his neck. McBride hurried over and knelt down. He wished he had brought a medical kit. Gently, he turned the young man over. The teen had taken a rubber bullet in the face. Blood was spurting from a gouge in his cheek. McBride tried to stanch the flow of blood with his handkerchief.

"Get some cloths, towels, any clean fabric from the store," he ordered Nathan.

His brother scrambled away. People were running up and down the street. Cops in uniforms were chasing some of them. Screams and cries filled the air, adding to the din from sirens and police loudspeakers. As far as McBride could see looking down Mission, the street was clogged with vehicles and protestors. Fire trucks on one block rained water, making the street slippery. Walls of water knocked people down and sent them rolling into the curbs. Some people were marching, ignoring police barricades set up in front of them. Others were milling around, gawking. Those toward the rear of the throng were breaking away, like a cookie slowly dissolving in water. The core remained solid while the outer fringes dissolved.

McBride could see bodies strewn about. Some appeared to be involved with performance art. They had doused themselves with a red liquid and were lying in the middle of the street. One or two sat up occasionally, then lay back down. Others seemed genuinely hurt with anxious onlookers checking on them.

"What are you doing?" someone asked coldly.

McBride glanced to his left. A chunky cop was standing there with a nightstick. Sweat poured down his face, which was red from running. He was breathing hard. "This man is injured," McBride said. Nathan arrived with some damp paper towels. McBride pressed them onto the wound. They immediately turned crimson.

"This man threw rocks at police officers and broke several windows," the cop said. "He's under arrest."

"He's injured," McBride repeated. "I'm a doctor."

"Well, doc, you'd better move if you don't want to end up in jail, too," the cop blustered angrily. He spoke into his radio attached to his shoulder epaulet. Within seconds, a police car roared up. The driver slammed on his brakes and screeched to a halt by the store. He emerged grim-faced with his hand poised above his holstered gun.

McBride stepped back. The young man was still unconscious, but the wound had stopped bleeding. A cop from the car and his partner grabbed each end of the prostrate teen and flung him into the back seat. In another moment, the car pulled away. The beefy cop continued up the street, billy club at the ready.

"Jesus," McBride breathed. More bullets went whizzing by. He and Nathan fled back to the store.

"We've got to get out of here," Nathan said.

McBride nodded. "People are crazy up here," he said.

"We're fucking serious about our dogs," a man nearby told him.

"If you can tell me how rioting is going to save your dog, I'd be amazed," McBride answered sharply. Nathan pulled him away.

"Don't start a fight now!" he shouted over the steady hum of sirens and shouts.

McBride clenched his fists, but resisted any temptation. Grappling with someone would hardly help the situation. Feeling the angry glare from the man he had been talking to, McBride led Nathan to the door and peered out. The action in the immediate area had slowed.

"Come on," he urged. They stepped gingerly outside and glanced around. The closest police car was several blocks away. A small group of people, all wearing brown t-shirts, were now marching back toward the civic center. McBride and Nathan headed in the other direction.

After sprinting several more blocks, they stopped, doubled over, trying to catch their breaths.

"We're in awful shape," Nathan wheezed.

"I can't remember the last time I ran *anywhere*," McBride agreed.

They finally reached their car. The wails of the police sirens continued. More shots rang out in the distance. He could see people hurrying to park their cars and rush toward the commotion. Many were clad in brown clothing.

They sat in the car, both breathing hard. The rioting receded until it appeared to be just another cool San Francisco day.

"I don't think you'll get to talk to Gunardson," Nathan finally said. He started the car.

McBride's heart was racing. Was this happening all over the country? Pomona may have been the only calmness in the midst of the frenzy. No disease had caused this kind of uproar in the past, except maybe the Black Death in the 1300s. As he recalled from a medical school history class on pandemics, some people took to beating each other with whips to atone for the supposed sin that caused the disease. Communication was limited, and so was knowledge about epidemics back then. People here should have been more sophisticated, more able to cope with such a horrific event, the death of their pets. But somehow, society was still breaking down. McBride gritted his teeth as Nathan steered toward home. He had to find a way to get the truth to the public.

All the way home, they could hear the boom of guns and the roar of sirens like the background to a war movie. It followed them with the tenacity of the smell of burning dogs that never went away.

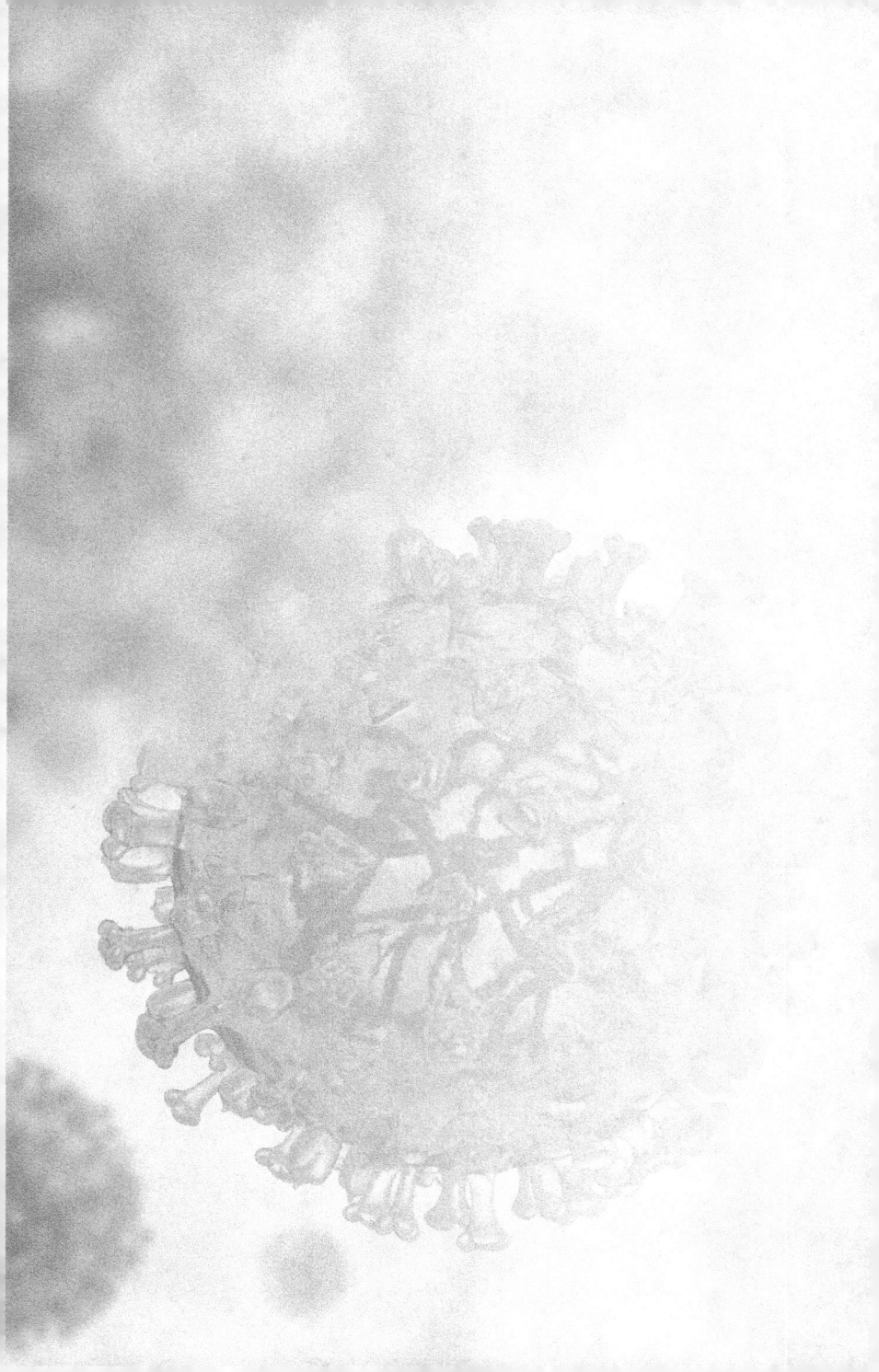

Chapter 13

Rocinha was the largest of the seemingly endless favelas that covered the steep slopes rising above Rio de Janeiro. A vast jumble of asphalt paths and makeshift homes crawled up these mountains with a density troubling to the mind. Thousands upon thousands of improvised shelters were covered with almost anything imaginable: bared insulation, beach furniture, wiring, spun glass, plastic sheeting of all colors. Much of the electronics and hardware had been stolen from the better buildings below in the city, like TV antennae or the odd satellite dish.

The motorbikes were everywhere. Mostly dirt-bikes, they sounded more like rockets as they blasted up the pathways carrying anyone who wanted to buy a ride for a few coins. Once in a while, one might see a small car parked on a platform somewhere—a platform perched on stilts, on air.

Rocinha was one of the poorest places on Earth, not unlike the Kasbah in Algiers. It had a large population of street children, fatherless sons and motherless daughters who by the age of ten or twelve may own a gun or may have sold his or her little body for cash.

The police rarely visited, and when they did, it is usually in full combat gear. Ruled by gangs, Rocinha had its own rules and territories. It was, in many ways, more rigid than the civilized sections of the city below. Up here, there was a way of handling everything quickly. Better not to dally in Rocinha.

For the past few months, the dogs had been dying in droves, as they were in the rest of the world. Unlike the wealthy people below on the beaches of Ipanema and Copacabana, death up here was too common to be seen as a special event requiring special measures of any sort. But a new enterprise had taken shape and was now operating. A new version, that is, of an ancient skill in a very steady market.

Deep inside this barrio, about half way up the mountain-face, an old woman named Maria Ribiero washed dishes in an old plastic washbasin under an open window. Her back hurt, but the labor was familiar and in that, comforting. The water was warm at least—she had heated it on an old hotplate that still worked, at least when the electricity worked—and it soothed the arthritis that had taken hold in her hands in the last couple of years.

The open window let in a little breeze, and through it she could see part of the cement head of Christ on Corcovado. She closed her eyes momentarily and blessed herself, and then listened to the sounds outside: a couple arguing down the street, a small child crying over something lost or broken, someone hammering, the tinny sounds of a cheap stereo pumping samba-reggae. The music annoyed her. She still preferred bossa nova: fingers on nylon strings covering rosewood and a soft voice. She thought the new music reflected the ever-escalating violence of her world.

She took a few steps but then stopped and tilted her head to sense more carefully. There was something else: an indistinct scraping sound like wood or plastic dragging or grinding on the cracked pavement. Her nose wrinkled at the faint smell of untreated sewage, always there but especially strong on hot days like this one. Most of it was familiar: the rotting produce from an open air market, the food smell of beans cooking in lard from a neighbor, the sweeter smell of animal manure mixed with hay in the open sunshine—but there was something else.

She faced the window again and caught the smell this time, the one she was unable to place, and it unsettled her. It reminded her of the slaughterhouse she had worked in briefly as a young unmarried woman, of poverty, desperation, agony, and death.

An unexpected knock on the door made her spin on one foot. It was soft at first, and then harder as if someone knew she was in there, knew she had heard the first knock and was growing impatient with her. She dried her hands on her apron and hurried to the door.

She peered through a small peephole cut in the door and, seeing no one, drew the door wide open. In front of her stood a young boy. His pants were oversized, cut off below the knee and held up with a scrap of cloth for a belt. His shirt had once been white, with Ronaldo's name barely visible on it in faded letters. He looked to be maybe twelve or thirteen, just like any one of the abandoned children roaming the streets looking for food or trouble like stray dogs. Only this boy's face was garish and smeared with blood—two broad stripes on each of his cheeks and a thin vertical line from his forehead down to his chin. His hands were wet to the elbows with blood and it covered his clothes. Maria gasped and put a hand to her mouth. Was he some apparition of revenge?

"Hello Grandmother," he greeted her in Portuguese, as if her were a friend of hers, "how are you this afternoon?"

Maria could only nod a greeting and the boy continued.

"I wish to speak to you about an urgent matter. We have discovered that your dog has died in front of your house and we would like to offer to remove the dog in order that it not draws flies and rot and disease."

"But...but I have no dog."

"Well, Grandma, come and see."

Alarmed but unable to control her curiosity, Maria stepped reluctantly off her rickety stoop so she could see what the boy was gesturing at. When she closed her door, she saw it: a small dog, stunted from malnourishment. It appeared to have exploded in front of her house. Blood everywhere. Its tongue protruded from its mouth, tiny and yet ferocious because it was contorted in agony, lips drawn back, throat constricted as if it had howled its spirit out of its body. The blood had sprayed up onto the front wall of her house and had also pooled around the body of the dog.

"It's unfortunate," said the young boy, scratching behind one ear. "So dirty. What will the neighbors say? Will they wonder if you poisoned it? Maybe they will say you are a witch."

Maria whirled back to the young boy, disgusted by the sight of the dog and enraged by his suggestion. She had lived in her little shack for nearly fifteen years and her neighbors knew her well, knew she was a good Christian woman. Now, she noticed that he wasn't alone. Far from it. Behind him stood a group of eight or ten younger boys, painted with blood like their leader, surrounding a decrepit wooden cart like those that farmers used to haul their produce to market. Only this cart was laden down with the carcasses of dead dogs, many of them still dripping blood. She covered her face and nose with a hand to block the stench. The young boys smiled. When the expression on her face turned to shock, they laughed and then called out to her.

"Good day for hunting, isn't it, Granny?"

"We are dog farmers. Good crop this year!"

"We'll be back next week for the babies!"

The older boy shushed them by simply raising a hand, and turned back to Maria.

"Mother, we offer a service. Just give us a couple of coins and we'll remove the dog, put a blessing on your house and you'll never see us again."

The old woman was utterly horrified. She reached under her apron and rummaged around in a hidden pocket, withdrawing a few tarnished coins and dropping them in the boy's crimson hand, careful not to get close enough to get any of the evil blood on herself. She made the sign of the cross twice.

The boy, shrugged, jingled the coins wetly in his hand and glanced back at his gang, before looking at her again with skeptical look. Maria muttered, reached back into her pocket and carefully dropped more coins into the outstretched hand.

As she retreated backwards into the house, the boys scurried into motion. While two boys held the cart to keep it from slipping away, down the mountain, three others ran to grab the dog. They flung it without ceremony onto the cart, spraying the two boys holding the handles with blood. They giggled and muttered curses.

With the new carcass in place, they quickly proceeded to the next house, which had two corpses splayed in the street in front of it. Whenever they came to a house without a dead dog in front of it, they merely took one down off their cart and propped it up in front of the house to make it look like it had died there.

When their cart was full, they wrestled it to the edge of the favela, where the road ended with only a rickety guardrail blocking a steep ravine that dropped like an abyss, down into the city, maybe a mile below. With much cursing and a few pinched fingers and toes, they backed the cart up to the guardrail and dumped their grim payload into the ravine. The boys then righted their cart and quickly dragged it away to fill it—and their pockets—again.

The corpses of the dogs tumbled and tumbled, head over tail through the underbrush to the bottom of the ravine. Dust and rocks and dirt were kicked up with increasing violence as the bleak payload hurled down, down. Some of the smaller corpses hung up in clots of vines, and larger dogs slid through due to their weight. About halfway down many suddenly took to the air after a lip in the ravine, flipping and spinning ghoulishly. The floor of the ravine looked like a lost canyon inside hell. The scent of blood was thick in the air, like burned metal. It painted the leaves and vines and clotted in the dust.

The dead dogs—hundreds of them, possibly even thousands—lay hooked in trees, dangling from branches and vines. They were piled on top of one other on the canyon floor next to piles of trash and burned out vehicles. Flies, millions of them, screamed with delight. And, if one listened carefully, under their ravenous buzzing could be heard the sounds of beetles and other carnivorous insects gorging themselves on the corpses of the fresh dead. It is said there is more life under the Earth than on its surface. This was where it fed.

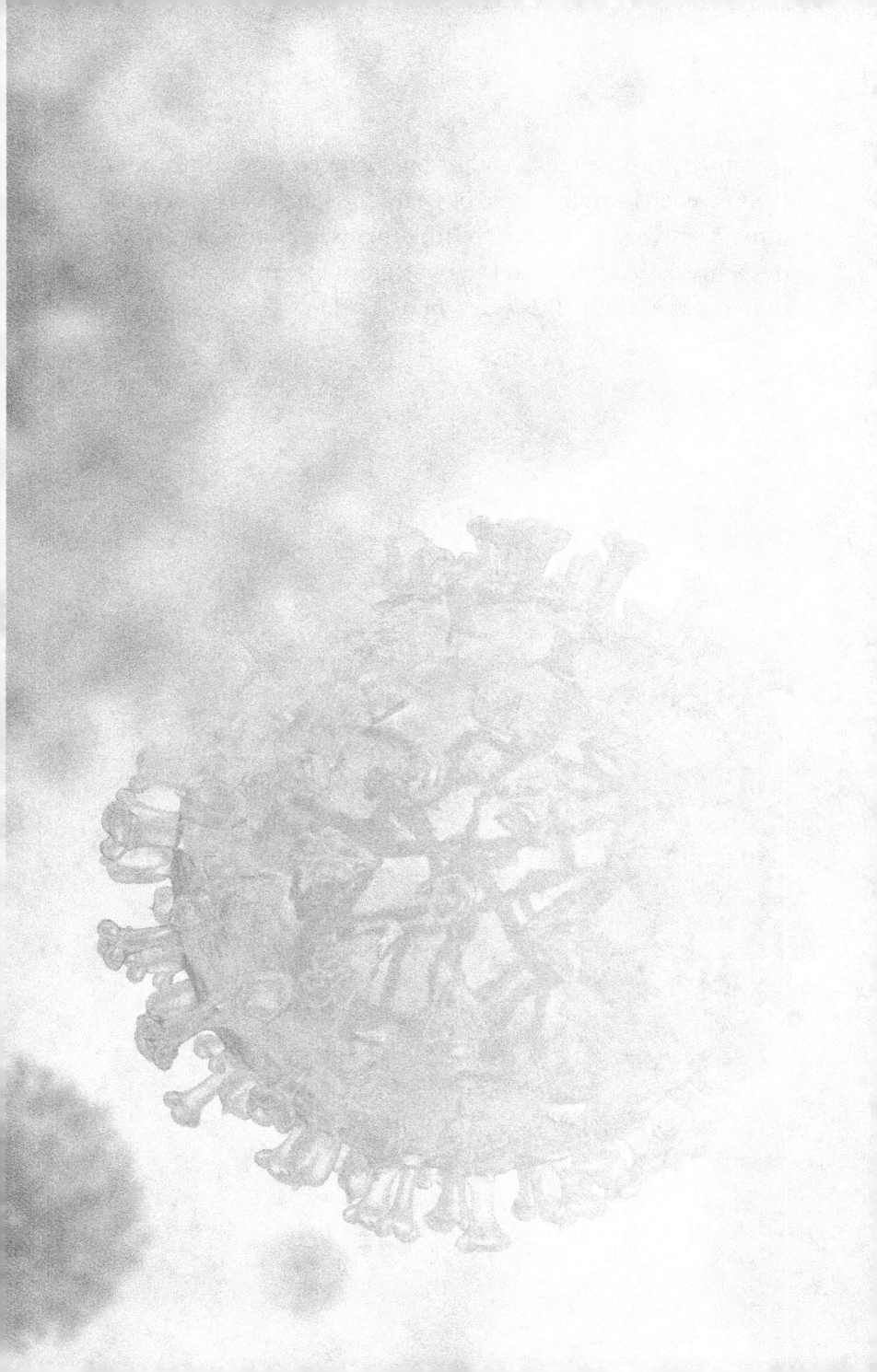

Chapter 14

Mr. cBride stood stunned in the back of the clinic office, staring at his cell phone like it was some alien device from the future. They had only just opened for business. After a moment, he sprung back to life and snapped his cell phone shut so loudly that Rosen was startled. She stopped writing on a file and looked up at him, a shocked, quizzical look on her face.

"Nothing," McBride said, answering the unasked question.

She didn't accept that answer and stared at him, hands on hips. He gazed out the clinic's back window. The familiar sounds of the office at the beginning of the day enveloped him. Mendales was chattering on her wireless earpiece with her family in Mexico while filing. Silverstein was making conversation with a patient who was signing in. It was almost like everything was normal and the world hadn't gone mad. He finally understood why the band on the sinking Titanic had played as the ship sank—playing music was their job, and when presented with a crisis that they had no way of handling, they just did what they knew how to do. Which is what everyone at the clinic was doing, just keeping their heads down and engaging in their daily routines as much as they could, trying not to think about the fact that the ship was going down.

He woke from his escapist reverie to see that Rosen was staring at him with grim expectation. McBride realized there was no point ignoring her. She had endured Crossland's over-the-top petulance; she had no problem countering his.

"No more research," he finally grumbled. "The program has been shut down." He didn't like talking about his new affiliation with Novilis, but he had to provide some explanation.

Everyone in the clinic knew he was doing extra work at night, although they didn't know why. It had become necessary to tell them after his obvious sleepiness became a concern. The regular patient load had fallen off now that Crossland wasn't there, but there were still enough every day to fill the hours and guarantee that McBride had to be wide-awake. McBride had explained that he was involved with research and left it at that. He didn't mention the word "dogs." Silverstein and Mendales had lost pets, but they were still focused on human maladies. They were happy to hear he had returned to research, but encouraged him to get enough rest. That's when he had started taking an alarm clock to Novilis. But apparently that was no longer necessary now.

"Please be informed that your security clearance has been revoked," a prerecorded woman's monotone voice had just told him on the phone. "You are requested to return your security badge at the front gate. All files remain the property of Novilis." That was it: short, direct and crushing. Willis had closed the lab door. He had rubbed in the rejection by using a tape. There was no way for McBride to respond or argue.

"Are you all right?" Rosen asked him.

"I feel like I've been gutshot," he said. "I was close to a breakthrough."

"I'm sure it's a money thing," Silverstein said. "It's always money with research grants."

"You are probably right," McBride agreed. No reason to give voice to his suspicions, already rapidly chattering in his brain. They all nodded.

"There are other grants," Silverstein added.

"I was so close!" McBride told Santiago later in her small animal hospital. The front *OPEN* sign was off; the waiting room was dark with just a small lamp in the corner on. They sat across from each other. The shadows matched his mood. "I really think Willis got scared," he said.

"Why do you think he let you do the research in the first place?" she asked.

"I assume he wanted to see exactly what I was working towards. I'm sure it didn't hurt that he saw dollar signs. When I started to get near to the truth, he shut me down," McBride said. He slumped in the chair, feet extending out across the hard flooring. "God, we really could have done something, helped so many people…maybe even have saved dogs from extinction."

"So, that is it?" Santiago said. "Esta terminado?"

"For me, it is," McBride said. "I can't do anymore. Congress has to do something. Too many Americans have lost dogs and are really upset. There will be Congressional hearings, I'm sure, but I doubt they'll lead anywhere."

They both knew the stories about the riots in Cleveland and Miami. Across the country, people who had lost pets were congregating on the lawns of the homes of their Congressmen to demand action, to say nothing of the more despairing gestures—the beatings, the murders, the suicides. Churches organized prayer meetings, led by the Catholic Church, which provides a regular Blessing of the Pets every October in honor of St. Francis of Assisi. Hope, a little beagle that somehow had endured amid the devastating disease, was now a beacon of light for those touched by the disease. Santiago had a button bearing the dog's blissfully upbeat face on her lapel.

"I can't believe it," Santiago said. "Como se puede detener?" Her voice betrayed her anger and frustration.

McBride felt sick inside. "I even called Pet Research and Animal Health in Connecticut," he told her. "That's the company that developed the approved dog flu vaccine. The research director said all his evidence showed that H1N1 was not related to H3N8."

That had not been the encouraging phone call McBride had envisioned. The director, Dr. Richard Nicols, had been very nice at first, but bristled when McBride suggested that H1N1 was connected to the canine disease.

"Not possible," Nicols snapped. "As a doctor," he continued as if lecturing a schoolboy, "you should know that H1N1 cannot infect an animal."

"Could it be a vector?" McBride pressed.

"Not a chance," Nicols scoffed. "Most vectors are invertebrates anyway. Mosquitoes, ticks, things like that."

"How about rabies?" McBride tried.

"Sure, that's a vector disease," Nicols said. His voice was laced with sarcasm. "I'm not aware of an epidemic of people biting dogs. It's the dogs that are dying, remember?"

"The vaccine isn't working," McBride argued loudly, completely exasperated. "Doesn't that tell you something is wrong?"

"I hardly think shouting will win your argument," Nicols said calmly. "I agree: the vaccine has not achieved the goals we set. However, we are continuing to refine it. The immune response may take longer to activate. Perhaps the viruses are too attenuated."

"Perhaps there's another reason," McBride seethed, quietly. He could almost hear Nicols shrug from across the country.

"If there is, we'll find it by further investigations in the H3N8 virus, using valid data, not emotional claims," he finally said. "Let me know if you uncover any." With that, Nicols hung up.

McBride had only gotten to talk to Nicols in the first place by promising that kind of data. That was when he had access to Novilis's equipment. Now, even his empty promise was gone. And he didn't even have his notes or printouts. The night before, a tightass night security guard had required him to leave his briefcase behind. He had even searched McBride to be sure no papers went with him. A series of thefts in the lab, the guard had said. At the time, McBride had not been concerned—it must have been the guy's first night on the job, he thought to himself, and he was just being over careful.

"You can pick them up tomorrow," the guard had told him. Turns out the guy wasn't a newbie at all, but a higher up, carefully cleaning him out. As a back-up, McBride had also planned to transcribe his notes and e-mail them to himself but he had been too busy. Of course, now that was not a possibility.

"I don't have any empirical data to back any claims I could make," McBride said wearily.

"How about the information I collected?" Santiago asked.

"Anecdotal," McBride said, "you know that won't carry any weight." Her letter sent via the American Veterinarian Medical Association had evoked a steady stream of reports from around the country. They filled her e-mail inbox, which had been hacked, and now they were flooding the Internet. Santiago, as a doctor, knew they were not "hard" evidence like the kind meticulously worked up in a lab. Moreover, who knew how many of the accounts were manufactured by desperate people trying to find an answer? As much as dogs had depended on people for food, water, and shelter, humans appeared to have relied on "man's best friend" for their emotional stability, their very sanity. Normally stable people were now ranting about aliens, government conspiracies, a plague sent by terrorists, a vengeful God, even the Devil.

On the other hand, many of the stories did buttress his belief. Repeatedly, vets around the country found that dogs belonging to such groups as the Amish and Christian Scientists, who refused to get the federally mandated Rohn flu shots, had not initially gotten sick. Only later, after contact with diseased dogs, did they begin to die off. Dogs owned by people who didn't want Rohn flu shots also showed no symptoms and only caught the disease much later. Clearly, the flu was being passed along through body secretions of some kind. Dogs were constantly kissing their owners' hands and faces, eating food and drinking water their owners had touched. It seemed there was no way to stop them from catching it from their owners or to stop the flu that was killing them.

Hope the beagle, one of the few survivors to date, was owned by an Oregon native who lived in a log cabin near the Badger Creek Wilderness. No one came near or bothered the two of them until media caught wind of a thriving dog. So far, Hope had not become ill and there were optimistic reports that they may have found a dog resistant to the disease. As far as

McBride could tell, Hope endured because she had no canine companions nor did any live nearby. However, contact with vectors for the disease was inevitable now that Hope was a celebrity. It was only a matter of time before she, too, sickened and died.

"All of the credible stories support your argument!" Santiago said.

"There are alternative answers," McBride said, shrugging. "Maybe it's an airborne disease that just happened to miss certain pockets of population. Maybe the dog flu vaccine caused the problem. Dogs of owners who didn't get shots died eventually anyway." There was no point disguising the objections: he knew what opponents would say. Without detailed research, the stories were interesting but circumstantial at best.

"So, you are just going to let dogs go extinct?" Santiago said fiercely.

"No one wants dogs to die off," McBride said, raising himself up. "Not me, not anyone."

"Entonces hacer algo!" Santiago burst out. She was crying, the end result of feeling helpless and seeing her one hope seemingly vanish.

McBride wished he could do something. He felt like the more enlightened doctors during the Black Death in the 1300s, who had no idea what was causing that dreadful disease and based it on bad air instead of Jews or other implausible scapegoats. No one guessed that fleas were transmitting the deadly bacilli. The population demanded an answer; the bonesaws provided one. Actually, the "bad air" theory helped a little. To eliminate the supposed miasma, people had to clean up their homes. That, in turn, eliminated living areas for the deadly fleas and the rats that carried them. The toll tapered off in those communities. Nothing that easy was available for the fatal dog disease.

"If I could," he finally said, "I would."

"Can you talk to Dr. Willis?" Santiago continued. "Maybe he doesn't understand what you are doing."

McBride stifled a laugh. "He knows full well," he said. Then, he sat up. Willis? He might provide an avenue to gain access to Novilis. Suppose, McBride considered, that the paranoid Willis thought he somehow had taken a copy of the data home with him. Willis couldn't afford to let the truth out. He could be forced to negotiate. Just maybe, by being threatened, Willis would have to admit the truth. McBride savored the image. It was possible.

Santiago noticed immediately how his manner changed. "You have an idea! I can see it!" she shouted. "Gracias a Dios!"

"Maybe," McBride cautioned. He was beginning to formulate a way to approach Willis when his phone rang.

"Where are you?" Kendra asked.

"At Waverly Clinic," he answered. She was visiting his mother while he talked to Maria.

She paused. "Pres, come get me. The police called."

He scrambled to his feet. "What's happening? Another riot?"

"No, someone broke into our home," Kendra reported.

McBride could only stare helplessly at the ceiling for a moment. Who? Why? He shook off the inertia. "On my way," he said to Kendra and hung up. "Problems at home," he told Santiago and headed for the door.

"I hope everything is all right," she called after him.

"So do I," he yelled back.

"How did the police know where to reach us?" he asked Kendra as they sped home. "We're not in the phonebook."

"I left the number with Jay," she explained. "He doesn't do much anymore other than watch the homes in the neighborhood."

A police car was in their driveway with its flashers on. Neighbors were standing in the yards, watching, whispering to each other under the soft glow of the electric streetlights. It seemed like everyone watched everyone else now. The police radio in the car crackled almost nonstop—Pres marveled that the police even had time to send a car, much less keep a car on the scene till he got there. He never thought he'd feel nostalgic for a time when it took three squad cars, lights flashing, just to give you an unwarranted speeding ticket but now the police were never there when you needed them. The general feeling towards the police now was that you were definitely on your own unless your life was in danger; then you were just *probably* on your own.

McBride parked on the street. Cats pushed aside curtain windows in neighboring living room windows to watch the confusion, but the sound of dogs barking was conspicuously absent. He got out slowly while Kendra ran to the house. She was stopped by the front door by a burly policeman.

"Dr. McBride," a voice said. He turned to see Sgt. Hinebaugh, one of the cops who had saved his neck when he had faced down the senior citizen mob at his mother's apartment complex looking at him.

"This is my house," he told her. "What's going on?"

"Some neighbor saw people inside the house," she reported. "That's not really an offense we can spare manpower for these days, but I recognized your name when they were IDing the tenants of the property. I made it a priority to check up on it and we got here as soon as we could tear ourselves away, but they had already vacated the premises."

"Officer, I…All I can say is thank you. Thank you for remembering me and thank you for coming. Did they take anything?"

"You'll have to tell us," she said. "Come on." They started up the small incline to the front door. "You really pissed off a lot of people at your mom's apartment house the other day," the officer noted, "you think this has anything to do with that?"

"Do you think one of them did this?' McBride asked.

"I'm just throwing it out there," Hinebaugh commented, "but then a lot of people are pissed off right now and just looking for an excuse to vent that anger."

McBride thought for a moment. He couldn't imagine any of the people in his mother's apartment complex driving here from Rancho Cucamonga to break into his home. His mother could have told them where he lived. Maggie wasn't happy he had interfered with the attack on Sonia either. Still, that would have been quite an effort by her neighbors. Unnecessary, too. They knew he'd be back to see his mother. They could have broken his car windows or scratched the car. They didn't have to break into his house. No, he decided, someone else did this.

A different possibility came to mind. The teenager living next to Crossland could not have been happy about being arrested. His mother looked like a real harridan. Either of them wouldn't have hesitated to exact revenge, McBride thought. But, they didn't know where he lived. Since the house was rented, neither he nor Kendra was listed as owner. They could have followed him, he supposed, but doubted they had that kind of initiative.

There was one other person he thought of. Willis might have sent some guards to look for any additional notes stashed in the home. The idea was almost comical. They would have been searching in the wrong place: McBride had his laptop with him. He had planned to do some research or at least retrieve his briefcase today. Would Willis steal the car next? McBride would almost welcome that, he decided.

"Officer, the more I think about it, I seem to have been pissing a lot of people off lately."

The officer grunted amiably and grinned. "Why am I not surprised to hear that?"

Jesus, was he going to spend the next few years of his life feeling constantly threatened or worrying that Kendra was endangered? He reached the front steps. Was there even going to be a next few years for him and Kendra together, or either of them alone? For once in his life, he had no prediction about what the future held. It was quietly terrifying.

It felt strange standing outside the open door and seeing Officer Stickney standing in the doorway. The place was rented, but it was still home. Now, it seemed so alien.

"I don't think they took anything," Kendra reported, emerging from inside the house. Her face was pale.

"There wasn't much to take," McBride noted.

They were still living like squatters, much to Kendra's disdain. She went over to talk to Hinebaugh and report what she saw.

McBride greeted Officer Stickney. The big cop looked to have aged years since McBride had seen him. This dog plague was wearing hard on everyone, but perhaps the hardest on the police.

"We could try to get prints, but they don't seem to have touched anything," Stickney said. "The neighbors said they had gloves on. It's a good thing you have neighbors watching out for each other."

"I'll have to thank them," he said.

"Start with that fellow over there," he nodded in the direction of an old man now standing with Kendra and Hinebaugh.

"I'll go and check with him. How are you doing, Officer? You look fatigued."

Stickney gave a tired smile. "Well, I'm making a killing on overtime, let's put it that way. The kids might get the pool they've been clamoring after this year. It'd be nice to do something nice for them, you know?" Stickney looked right into McBride's eyes, and McBride knew without asking why Stickney was so concerned with his children's happiness right now.

McBride joined Kendra, Hinebaugh and the neighbor. He recalled seeing the man walking with his dog. He was still toothless and decrepit looking. McBride couldn't remember his name.

"Thank you," he said, reaching out a hand. The old man took it. He had a firm grip that belied his sallow appearance.

"Jay was walking along when he saw some people pull into our driveway," Kendra said excitedly. "He's a one-man neighborhood watch."

"Like I told the police," Jay said, "I couldn't see them real good, but there were two men. They walked right to the front door and walked in like they owned the place, but I knew they didn't belong there. I never saw them before."

"How were they dressed?" McBride asked.

"Dark shirts and slacks. Nothing special."

"No masks?'

"Nah. They acted like they lived there. They had a key. I really didn't think nothing about it at first, like maybe they were checking the boiler or something, but then I saw your car wasn't there. I didn't figure you let anyone have your key," Jay continued. He was clearly enjoying being the center of attention.

"Do you have friends or relatives who have a key to the house?" Hinebaugh asked.

"My mother," McBride said. "But Kendra was with her tonight when the police called."

"Could she have given the key to someone else?" Hinebaugh continued.

They considered that option. "I don't think so," Kendra finally answered. "We can check, but she said her dog had hidden it." In fact, Maggie was now blaming the invisible Canada for anything that happened in the house, including when wind blew out a candle or her napkin slipped off her lap during dinner.

"They had a key," Jay said.

"Are you sure?" Hinebaugh asked.

"The man in front walked right up and stuck something in the door," Jay said defensively.

"You did great," Kendra assured him.

"There are skeleton keys," Hinebaugh said. "Or, someone could have made a mold of the lock previously and had a key made."

"It was a key," Jay insisted. "I watched them and called the police."

"That's exactly what you should have done," Hinebaugh said, softening. "Even if they were relatives, you didn't know. Better safe than sorry. You didn't have to get involved, but you called us, and that was the right thing to do."

"If I had Bruno, I'd have sic'd him on them," Jay said. His whole manner changed as soon as he mentioned the dog's name. The elation slipped away and he suddenly looked old and defeated. Kendra patted his arm. He stifled a tear. "Well, I best be going. I guess there's nothing more for me to do here." He slowly shuffled off.

"What do you think they were looking for?" Kendra asked.

"I have no idea," McBride said. He had a pretty clear idea of who it was, but he wasn't going to mention anything in front of the cops.

She hugged him. "This is awful," she whispered. "I feel like I'm living in the inner city somewhere."

"Listen, doc, I wish we could do more for you, but we gotta go," Hinebaugh said. "Follow up with the local precinct if you like. You really should get a security system."

"Great idea," McBride said hoarsely, unable to muster any enthusiasm. He'd talk to the management company that took care of the house about that. This little B & E had brought this little misadventure to a level he wasn't prepared for. He thought longingly back to his long nights alone in New York, before the dog flu, before the Rohn flu, before even Kendra. Life had been much simpler.

"Glad to help," Hinebaugh said, giving a tip to her hat. She headed briskly back down the lawn to the squawking radio.

"You don't think it was random, do you?" Kendra asked. She clutched McBride's arm and stared up at him, wide-eyed.

"I don't know," he admitted, "but I don't think so."

"Do you think this had anything to do with your research?" she continued.

He nodded. "Yes," he said. No way he could hide it from her.

"Why?"

"I don't know," he admitted. "Maybe I stumbled on something the company didn't want me to know."

She looked up at him. "A vector?"

He hugged her. "Maybe."

Kendra tightened her grip on his waist. "That could be very dangerous," she said. "Can you just forget the research?"

He stroked her shoulders and didn't reply. Could he walk away? They didn't own a dog, and Canada was already dead; he could just move on with his life, focus on the clinic and on his relationship with Kendra, which definitely needed some attention by this point. And ignore the chaos that surrounded them, just let the evil continue unabated? No, he told himself, he had to follow this till the end. He knew he had to talk to Willis.

"Are you sure it's related to the research? Do you think it's possible that Nathan came by?" Kendra asked.

"I don't know," McBride said, "that seems pretty farfetched."

He called Nathan soon after. His brother was in San Francisco and hadn't been by the house. He didn't have a key anyway. "Just checking," McBride said without mentioning the break-in.

"Bad dream?" Nathan asked.

"Yes," McBride replied. It felt like the truth.

They slept that night with the lights on and a chair wedged against the front door. The next day, Kendra stayed home from work and had the locks changed. They also decided to move once the lease ran out. "Another few months," McBride assured Kendra. "That's all."

McBride also called Willis's office. Johnson made an appointment for him for the following Wednesday afternoon. He let the nurses know the office would have to close again that afternoon. Rosen was not happy about the schedule change. She came into McBride's office at the end of the day.

"Didn't you stop the research?" she said. "Why do you need the afternoon off? Dr. Crossland never took time off. Our patients know we work every day of the week. Dr. Crossland prided himself on that. Though we've lost some of our regular clientele, these people need us now more than ever, dammit!"

McBride winced. The nurse was not disguising the comparison. Although the comment upset him, he wasn't going to explain. It was none of her business.

"I hope it's the last time," he finally replied.

"I hope so, too," she answered coldly.

He stared at her. "This has been a very trying time what with the house break-in, the collapse of my research project, and Abe's death," he said sharply. "I really don't need the attitude."

"There are concerns greater than your own. I'm thinking about what's good for the clinic," Rosen told him. She started for the door.

"Hey," McBride said, "you're an employee like me."

Rosen stopped. For a moment, she seemed to be surveying the wooden door. Then, she turned.

"You sure?" she said.

Her comment seemed pregnant with a hidden meaning. The office grew very quiet. For a moment, the two of them locked eyes. McBride felt rooted into place. He could see the strange look on the nurse's face. She knew something, he realized.

"Didn't Abe own the clinic?" he asked hesitantly.

"Yes," Rosen said loudly, "he *did*." Her voice cut into him.

"Okay. I understood that it was part of his estate but I'll bite: who owns it now?" He couldn't imagine.

Rosen smiled. "I do. I'm your boss," she said.

McBride gaped. "How...what...?" he managed.

"He signed the papers over to me one day," she said. "He was happy that I brought him flowers."

"Jesus," he gasped, "you took advantage of him."

Rosen tossed her head. "I gave him fifteen years of my life. Lucy was his wife in name only. I deserve something more than a kiss on the cheek and a limp thank-you on my way out the door," she said. "Do you want the clinic to close?"

"No," he admitted.

"So it's going to stay open," Rosen said. She grabbed the door handle. "And this clinic is open on Wednesday afternoons," she said.

McBride shook his head. "I cannot be here," he said.

"I'll find a substitute," Rosen snapped. "I'm starting to think we may need another doctor anyway." She swept out of the room.

McBride felt his strength slip away and sat down. He felt completely overwhelmed. Maybe he should go somewhere else. Kendra kept hinting at that. He didn't want to return to New

York, but Florida might be nice. That was across the country. Or Ohio. There was a state most people ignored. No one would bother him there. He would just need state approval for his medical license. That should not be a problem.

On the other hand, he told himself, there were a lot of things that needed to be resolved. He walked over and looked at the picture of Crossland's dachshund. The little puppy looked so wistful. Could he really forget all this? McBride thought. He knew better. Millions of dogs were dead, and he knew why. He may be the only person in the world who knew. He could not save the dogs that had already died, but he may be able to provide a slightly less bleak future for the humans left behind.

What would happen when the public found out that the Rohn flu shots had led to the dogs' deaths? Would mobs destroy Novilis? He hoped not. The company did good work most of the time. He shuddered to think of the immense research facility in Fontana being trashed. On the other hand, he would be delighted to see Willis hauled off to jail.

He walked firmly from the office. If he lost his job, he'd find another. He had been unemployed before. He simply was not going to give up, not with so many people depending on him. He felt Santiago behind him, encouraging him. He would go to the meeting and confront Willis. He would take his few notes and anything else he could collect to convince Willis that the data was ready for the public. The man would be sweating bullets. McBride liked that image.

He felt almost cocky when Kendra picked him up. He would conquer Willis, make him reveal the truth. All he had to do was take advantage of the situation. A cold chill swept over him. That's what Willis did to create this awful situation. And now Rosen had, too.

"Do you think I'm unethical?" he asked Kendra.

"No," she laughed. "Why would you think anything like that?"

"Just wondering," he said.

Chapter 15

The elevator ride to the third floor of the Novilis research facility went very quickly this time. McBride stepped in and the door to Johnson's office opened instantly. It struck McBride as ironic that the last gate swung open so easily considering how laborious the process to get there had been.

The security guard by the front gate had searched the car. "Weapons," she said. McBride hadn't said anything, but watched her carefully. He kept his computer by his side. She asked him to open the case, but that was all. She fumbled with his new briefcase until he unlatched it for her.

"What's that?' she asked of his papers.

"Nothing important to anyone but me," he told her. "Some of my research findings. I have some reports from veterinarians around the country, the news clippings about the dog flu, and a technical paper filed by two doctors at the University of Indiana who analyzed the composition of the dog flu vaccine on a molecular level, including a partial history of domestic animal vaccination. Fascinating stuff, really."

It worked: the guard's eyes appeared to glass over.

"Can you tell me how to get my old briefcase back?' he asked her.

She had looked at him as if he had posed the stupidest question she had ever heard. "Check lost and found," she said, barely resisting rolling her eyes.

"It wasn't lost. It was confiscated," he told her.

She ignored the comment, walked back into her little guardhouse, and raised the gate. He didn't wave this time as he drove through.

Everything looked so different during the day. At night, long shadows covered huge tracts of the grounds, even with the overhead lights in the parking lot. The place was also quiet then, without the hammering from the construction site or the movement of cars. There were fewer open spots in the visitors' lot, but McBride managed to squeeze in between a Hummer and a giant SUV. Some people, he thought, were apparently unaffected by the rising gasoline prices.

Inside, only the lone guard at the reception desk had greeted him. A variety of well-dressed people passed in and out of the entry, carrying suitcases, computers, and other equipment, with intense, harried looks on their faces. The loud bangs and constant shouting that surrounds all large-scale construction filled the air. Business as usual at Novilis—fiddling as Rome burned.

Inside, the receptionist had been as coolly efficient as ever. This time, he hadn't been asked to wait, but had immediately been directed to the elevator. As he rode up, McBride couldn't help thinking that, under other circumstances, he might have been in what was now Willis's office. He wondered how he would have behaved. Would he have capitulated to arrogance like Willis? He hoped not.

For the second or maybe third time in the past minute, McBride checked to make sure that his new briefcase was secure. McBride had been reluctant to believe his findings at first. After all, in research, a small error could compound quickly. He had to be positive. Novilis had a bank of lawyers ready to pounce. Willis was hardly to going to sit quietly while he was attacked. Despite being prevented from completing his studies, McBride had no doubt of the link between the mandatory vaccination of human beings and the wildfire spread of the dog flu. He had satisfied any and all of his personal doubts.

Johnson was waiting for him. "Nice to see you again," she said casually. She looked tired but happy to see him, and her warm smile required no translation.

He took the proffered coffee this time to calm his nerves. The warm liquid relaxed him, serving as a counterbalance to the air conditioning, which seemed to have been turned extra cold. He wasn't the only one chilled—Johnson was wearing a yellow sweater over her dress. He noticed for the first time gray hairs in her thick brown hair. Everyone was showing signs of stress, Pres thought to himself.

She walked over to take his empty cup and saucer. "He's really pissed," she whispered.

"The coffee was great," he answered lightly, smiling cheerfully. Getting under Willis's skin cheered him. "Where do you get it from?"

"Columbia!" she declared. And then, softer, "He's got something planned for you. Don't let your guard down."

She took the dirty dishes to the small kitchen. "I think I found a bag of the coffee, Dr. McBride," she called. "It's on a top shelf. Could you come in here? I can't reach it."

He got up quickly and joined her.

"There's no camera here," she whispered.

"What's with Hofferman?" he asked quickly.

"Willis has something on him, something really bad," Johnson said. "I have no idea what it is, but Hofferman is his puppet now."

"I got it," McBride said loudly, retrieving the bag of coffee from a cabinet. Johnson was easily tall enough in her heels to reach it. In fact, it was McBride who had to stretch for it.

"It's from a boutique fair trade importer," she reported as if unveiling the greatest secret in the Western World. "He's been called to testify before Congress," she added under her breath.

"How interesting," McBride said. He would love to talk to Congress, too, and tell them exactly what Willis did. Talk about a public forum.

They walked out together. "I've never had such a great cup of coffee before," McBride said.

"It has a heavenly aroma, doesn't it?" Johnson said.

She sat down at her desk just as a buzzer went off. "Vice President Willis will see you now," she reported.

Willis stood up. He smoothed his suit coat. Let Willis wait, he told himself. He had been nervous and unsure of himself, perhaps overawed, on his initial visit. Not this time. After a moment, he picked up his briefcase and stepped into the office. The door slid closed behind him.

Willis was standing behind his desk with an array of papers spread out in front of him. Neither man said anything for a moment. McBride could tell entire scene had been carefully crafted. The sunlight burst through the windows, adding a luster to the furnishings and glancing off the many paintings watching the room. It seemed to encircle Willis, giving him an aura of power, heightened by his carefully coiffed appearance. The somber sense of a hunting lodge gave way to something more celestial.

McBride was momentarily impressed. He took a moment to collect himself and let his pulse ease before launching a long-range attack.

"How long did you think you'd get away with this?" he asked.

Willis gave him a sly smile. "Get away with what?" he asked innocently as he stepped around his desk. The papers on his desk rustled slightly as he moved, creating the only sound in the office. The sunlight seemed to follow him. His arms dangled at his side. Willis did not offer his hand; neither did McBride.

"You know what I'm talking about," McBride said, walking slowly toward Willis. He could see the older man's face. The lines in his forehead were gone. The beginning of jowls under his cheeks had been erased. Plastic surgery? Botox? Or was he just using black magic now? "You know what my tests discovered."

Willis cocked his head. "Are you so sure?" he asked.

"You also know I didn't finish," McBride said. He was no more than two feet away now from Willis. He stopped. "You wouldn't let me finish because you knew what I'd find."

"Really?" Willis said. He seemed totally unfazed by the anger seeping into McBride's words or McBride's proximity to him. He simply perched on the edge of his desk. "You used to be a good researcher. Now, apparently, you simply jump to conclusions."

"You can't dismiss my research that easily," McBride said coldly. His crisp words were designed to grate, but failed. He held his briefcase so Willis could see it. The implied threat lingered in the space between them.

Willis sighed. "What do you think this is? A Wild West shootout? You're the good guy, and I'm the bad guy? Or, maybe, you'll throw a punch at me, and we'll scuffle until security comes in and break things up? What will that accomplish? Don't you already have enough police in your life? I know you're cozy with them, but not cozy enough to dodge an assault charge."

McBride reddened. Willis had been keeping an eye on him, on his girlfriend and maybe even on his mother. McBride stared at Willis. Willis's attack only emboldened him. The man had no shame.

"You stole my research. You got a vaccine approved without concern for the possible consequences of an attenuated vaccine release without proper testing."

"Whoa," Willis said, putting up his hands defensively and smiling at McBride's obvious ire. "I didn't steal anything. I was directed by Charles Crossland to advance the research as quickly as possible. Your team had isolated the viruses. I simply identified the one that was the culprit. Then we expedited the production of the vaccine, which, as you know, was imperative. I should also point out that the vaccine worked. Thousands of lives were saved, if not millions."

"Convenient of you to pin the blame on Crossland," McBride said, "since you now have his job."

"He was old," Willis shrugged. "He felt the need to retire. I doubt he would have been comfortable in such a setting. He had pedestrian tastes."

"And," McBride continued, "you also conveniently overlooked the fact your vaccine is killing dogs."

"Fact?" Willis said. He reached out with his left hand and picked up a sheet of paper from his desk. "The Surgeon General finds no connection between the Rohn flu and the dog flu. Here is that report." He offered it, but McBride did not take it. Willis shrugged, put the report back and retrieved another. "The director of the Centers for Disease Control found no link between the vaccine and the canine deaths." He read from the page: "'Extensive research indicates that the dog flu is a form of H3N8, a known canine influenza.'" He looked up. "Would you like to read this report?"

"No," McBride seethed. "I know what I saw: the virus killing dogs is H1N1. It had to come from your vaccine."

"Let me see if I have this straight," Willis said. "Assuming you are right, you want the country to stop vaccinating people and protecting them from an epidemic because a few dogs are dying." He paused. "Good luck with that," he said, making guns of his index fingers and pointing them both at McBride.

Breathing hard, McBride waited a moment to concentrate. He had done some research too. "The CDC sent a letter to neurologists warning them that the vaccine could increase Guillain-Barre Syndrome," McBride said. "As you know, GBS attacks the lining of the nerves, causing paralysis and inability to breathe. It can be fatal."

"Standard stuff," Willis dismissed the information. "Come on, you of all people know that vaccines don't work on everyone. There will always be collateral damage."

Those words chilled McBride. The eerie silence in the room gripped him like a vise. For a moment, the only sound came from the fake fireplace, which was designed to crackle realistically.

"It's an attenuated virus vaccine," McBride seethed. "You know possible consequences may be irreversible."

"Aspirin can cause your stomach lining to bleed," Willis countered. "Do you want to tell people to stop taking aspirin?" He went back to his desk and sat down, putting his hands behind his head in a superior manner. "Enough of this. The vaccine works. It stopped the flu cold. You wanted to be the little boy with his finger in the dyke, and you blew your chance, so now you're trying to create a new crisis so you can still be a hero. Wait until people find out you are trying to stop the use of a vaccine that's saving thousands of lives every day. China is clamoring for it, India, Africa, the Middle East. You're going to stop the avalanche of desire for this lifesaver? Think again, kid."

McBride took a deep breath. The longer he talked, the more relaxed he was becoming. "New vaccines never behave in the way you expect them to," McBride said. "Maybe the squalene additive in the vaccine is the root problem. It seems to be tied to GBS."

Willis shook his head. "Squalene is a naturally occurring enzyme," he noted. "You might as well blame matrix metalloproteinase 9 for Alzheimer's. That's another naturally occurring enzyme found in the plaque."

"Ethan," McBride said, "we're talking here about a massive guinea pig trial on the American population and now all of humanity. Our research wasn't and isn't finished."

"The government didn't want to wait. Novilis couldn't afford to, and the public wanted results," Willis said. "We delivered. You know, it feels good to be a hero."

"Is that what you'll tell Congress?" McBride said sarcastically.

Willis didn't miss a beat. "Of course," he said grandly. "I will tell the Senators that Novilis has successfully developed a vaccine that stopped the worst human pandemic since the 1918 influenza. With ample funding, Novilis has the expertise and ability to eliminate almost all human maladies."

"I see that the truth doesn't fit into your testimony," McBride said.

"I prefer to tell people what they want to hear. It's worked out so far."

"Have you ever considered politics?"

Willis laughed. "We're all politicians. Except you, McBride. You're just an absent-minded scientist, a Chicken Little crying that the sky is falling."

McBride held up his briefcase. "Then, I guess you don't care what I've found. I might as well talk to my Congressman instead," he said.

Willis's eyes narrowed. McBride was glad to see he had punctured Willis's cheerful demeanor. "Please do," Willis said. "If you'd like, I'll even get you a chance to testify before Congress. Why talk to one Congressman? You can talk to all of them simultaneously. I suspect there will be TV coverage, too. You could be a star. I know some people on the Hill.

I could pull a few strings. Always glad to help out a friend." He smiled. "Maybe I owe you one, huh?"

"You won't like what I have to say," McBride threatened.

"I am not concerned about anything you have to say," Willis told him. "In fact, you are welcome to fly with me to DC for the testimony. I'm sure there's a seat left on the plane."

"No, thanks. I'll figure out a way to get there."

Willis shrugged. "Suit yourself,' he said. "It's a Dassault Falcon X with leather seats, sofas, and a customized entertainment center."

"You may have to walk home," McBride said.

"I have a great deal of faith in Congress and the American people. I'll take my chances."

"I'll leave before you break out with the 'Star Spangled Banner,'" McBride announced.

"As you wish," Willis said. "I actually sing very well. And you should hear me play—I just learned the Jimi Hendrix version. Oh, I forgot—you haven't heard of rock 'n' roll. But your father was a fan of that whole 60s LSD subculture, wasn't he?"

The final indignity. McBride turned and walked away so Willis wouldn't see the flush of rage in his face. He was outgunned.

"One more thing," Willis called. McBride stopped. He turned slowly. Shafts of sunlight encased Willis's thin frame. "Here's some math for you to consider. You were always good with math. About 20 percent of all Americans have a pet. About half of them have dogs. Worst case scenario, maybe 10 percent of Americans have lost a dog. That means a few breeders are out of work. There won't be a Westminster Dog Show this year. On the other hand, 90 percent of Americans have been protected from the Rohn flu."

McBride simply stared at him. He could hear Willis talking, but the mocking tone was beyond irritating. He just wanted to be as far away as possible.

"The ten percent crying over their dogs can get cats. Or ferrets. I'm told they are rather affectionate," Willis continued. "You never had a dog, did you?" With that final jab, he began to collect the reports on his desk, no longer bothering to look up.

McBride peered at Willis. He had never felt such rage and despair at the same time. The door opened silently behind him. McBride hurried out. He stopped for a moment to take a few deep breaths. Willis, he decided, was pure evil. How could he cavalierly dismiss such a tragedy?

McBride clutched tight to his briefcase as though it were a weapon. He had never fought anyone before, but he wanted to take Willis apart. At the same time, he knew both that he was incapable of physically humiliating him and that it wouldn't accomplish anything. Willis had to be brought down intellectually, undermined and toppled, exposed completely.

Johnson smiled at him when he exited the office. McBride nodded and continued quickly to the elevator. His briefcase hung down and bumped reassuringly against his side. It was only a matter of time, McBride told himself. He kept his face rigid. Willis would be watching him on the camera. He hoped Willis would recognize an implacable enemy.

"How did it go?" Kendra asked when McBride picked her up at the hospital.

"I'll tell you when I get home," McBride said. "I didn't want to look in my briefcase until I was sure Willis couldn't have someone spy on me." He heard a siren and tightened. Looking in the rear view mirror, he saw a fire engine rapidly approaching. Its lights were flashing. Where was it heading—to a dog fire that had gotten out of control, a veterinary clinic that had been firebombed? Cars in front of them were slowing and moving to the side. Kendra followed suit.

"I don't think anyone can see in here," Kendra said. "Are you getting paranoid?"

"Maybe," he agreed. He glanced around. Everyone was watching the fire engine. "Go ahead. Look in my briefcase," he said.

She picked it off the back seat and opened it. "It's empty," she reported.

"Perfect," he said and laughed out loud. He stopped as the fire engine roared by.

Kendra looked at him with a puzzled expression. "Right now," McBride said, "Willis is trying to figure out some very strange markings in a special report."

"What did you do?' she demanded.

"I figured he'd try to get the contents of my briefcase, so I made up some interesting reading for him. It's in Yiddish," McBride said.

"You don't know Yiddish," Kendra said.

"I know and neither does Willis, but a nurse at the clinic does," McBride said. Silverstein had carefully translated a treatise that analyzed ancient coprolites. "I hope it was about dog shit," McBride added. "That would be appropriate." He imagined Willis busily looking for an expert to analyze the report, cursing McBride for using some kind of code.

"I was trying to find some paper that would contain a few words appropriate for my research," McBride told Kendra. "Of course, as Willis will find out, the report actually did not relate at all."

"Didn't you take more papers with you this morning?" Kendra asked.

McBride smiled. "After telling the guard what I brought with me, I left them in my car and put the Yiddish report in," he said. "The stuff was still under the car seat when I got back. Most of my real research is in my office at the clinic anyway. I won't risk having it at home or in the car. The office has an alarm system that's pretty good. I don't think Willis would want to deal with that."

He also knew how Willis gained access to the briefcase. When Johnson asked him to look at the coffee container, he had left the briefcase by his chair. There was enough time for anyone to slip out and empty it. He was keenly aware that Willis would stoop to any means to achieve his goals.

"There's a fire," Kendra noted. Down North Garey, they could see two fire engines and police cars converging on some building. Red-yellow flames shot high into the air. A policeman was standing in the middle of the large street, holding up traffic. Barricades were being placed along the sidewalk. A few people were hurrying down the street toward the blaze.

Traffic was soon completely stopped. McBride finally turned off the car's engine. He could see all the action was taking place just two blocks in front of him.

"That's near the clinic," he mused, still relishing his petty victory over Willis.

"Pres," Kendra said in a stricken voice, "it is the clinic."

Pres felt cold, poisonous adrenaline dump into his blood-stream. "Are you sure?" he cried. He opened the car door to see better. There was no question. The clinic was completely engulfed. Flames were bursting through windows and shredding the wood shingles on the roof. He stared at the fire, unsure whether to stay with Kendra or run to the blaze.

"Go ahead," Kendra urged. "I'm all right."

After a second's hesitation, he sprinted through the stopped cars and down the two blocks to the clinic. The sign in front still stood proudly, but heat from the building had melted its east side. The building itself looked gutted. Ash and cinders flew everywhere. What had been a proud old house with wooden sides and a brick base was a blackened shell. The heat had sent some of the bricks flying across the small front yard. The aged structure had not survived long. The fire was already running out of fuel.

Firemen had attached a hose to a nearby hydrant and were still pumping water into the structure. It was a futile gesture—there was nothing to save. Other firemen were dousing the closest buildings on each side of the blaze to keep the fire from spreading.

Rosen was standing in a small cluster of people a few yards away from the ruined clinic. She was crying. Silverstein was holding her. Mendales wasn't there. McBride sped up to her.

"What happened?' he asked, gasping for breath.

Rosen turned dull, brown eyes toward him. Her body shook. "I don't know," she wailed.

"We were in the office," Silverstein started to explain.

"All the patients' records," Rosen sobbed.

"They're backed up," Silverstein soothed her. "I told you. I sent everything to the storage file this morning." She looked at McBride. "I smelled something. I don't know, something chemical. It was strange. Maybe a few minutes later, I saw flames. We just ran."

"Did we have insurance?" Rosen asked.

"Jan, I...I don't know. We'll find out, I guess. Just be grateful no one was hurt," Silverstein said. "Rosa had already gone home, so she's safe."

McBride could feel some of the heat from the charred remains. He glanced at his watch. It was only three thirty. "No patients?" he asked.

"No," Rosen said. She fought back more tears. "We closed the clinic like you wanted."

"Thank goodness," Silverstein said. "We could have had a full waiting room."

"I couldn't find a doctor to fill in," Rosen managed. Her lips were moving, but no words came out. The image of the dying flames played across her face and reflected in her eyes. She grabbed Silverstein's arm and hugged tightly.

"It'll be all right," Silverstein said, lovingly sweeping Rosen's hair away from her eyes.

"Who's the owner?' a gruff voice interrupted. They all turned to see a fireman standing there with a notebook in hand.

Rosen slowly raised her right hand. The fireman asked for her name and identification. "My purse was in there," Rosen said.

"I have mine," Silverstein interjected.

"But you're not the owner," Rosen moaned.

McBride left them to their grieving to study what was left of the building. The fire had clearly started on the north side. The firemen were collected there, studying the charred wood. One of them caught sight of him.

"Sir," he said, standing up. "You'll need to keep back."

McBride moved away. "I worked here," he called. "I was just seeing if maybe something survived." It didn't look like it. His office was on the south side of the building, but falling beams from the upper floor as well as the fire had pretty much obliterated the room. Any files were probably gone, he thought.

"The fire may look like it's out, but can rekindle from hidden smoldering remains," the fireman said.

"There's not much left," McBride noted, his voice cracking. He felt besieged from all sides. He wasn't just outgunned, but also outnumbered. How much more did he have to lose? That thought made him shudder.

The fireman nodded his head. "Total loss," he said.

McBride returned to Rosen. She was feeling better. "I think I can get some space in a building on East Mission," she said. "I'll know by Friday, I'm sure."

"Call me," McBride said.

She nodded. Then, she hugged him tightly. Silverstein patted his arm. For a moment, McBride felt as though he were part of a family.

Traffic was being rerouted with the two northbound lanes being used for all the cars. Kendra had pulled the Civic to the curb and sat behind the wheel, looking worried.

"Do they know what happened?" she asked, looking up through the car window.

McBride didn't answer, but climbed into the passenger side. "No," he said. "But Laura smelled something. It could have been a chemical accelerant of some kind."

Kendra shivered. "Jeez," she said. "This is getting to be too much. Pres, I'm scared."

"It's all right," he said, taking her hand.

She stared at him. "How can it be all right?" she asked softly. "Our house was broken into. Your research was stolen. Your office just got torched. What's next?"

"I don't know," he admitted. Her hand was cold. He rubbed it gently. She didn't say anything. He recognized the look. Something else was bothering her.

"What is it?' he asked gently.

"I called you yesterday, and you were at that woman's animal hospital."

McBride stiffened. "Yes, she's a woman, but she's helping me with my research," he said. "There's nothing between us."

"Honest?' she asked.

"Honest," he answered.

She sniffled. "Okay, I believe you," she said. She used a tissue to wipe her nose.

"Thank you," he said. He pulled her towards him and kissed her. Her lips tasted salty from the tears.

"Hope died," she said quietly as a nice driver let her enter the traffic. "The little dog. Her owner was brought to New York for the Today Show. She got sick there."

McBride didn't know what to say. He stared to his right as they passed the blackened ruins of the Crossland Clinic. What could Willis do next? The man had tentacles everywhere.

He clenched his lips and stared straight ahead, toward the afternoon sun.

Things will get better, he told himself. Willis was not going to win. He must not win. McBride glanced at Kendra, then thought of his brother, his mother. He knew Willis's stance on collateral damage. How much was he going to have to lose to gain victory over such a ruthless opponent?

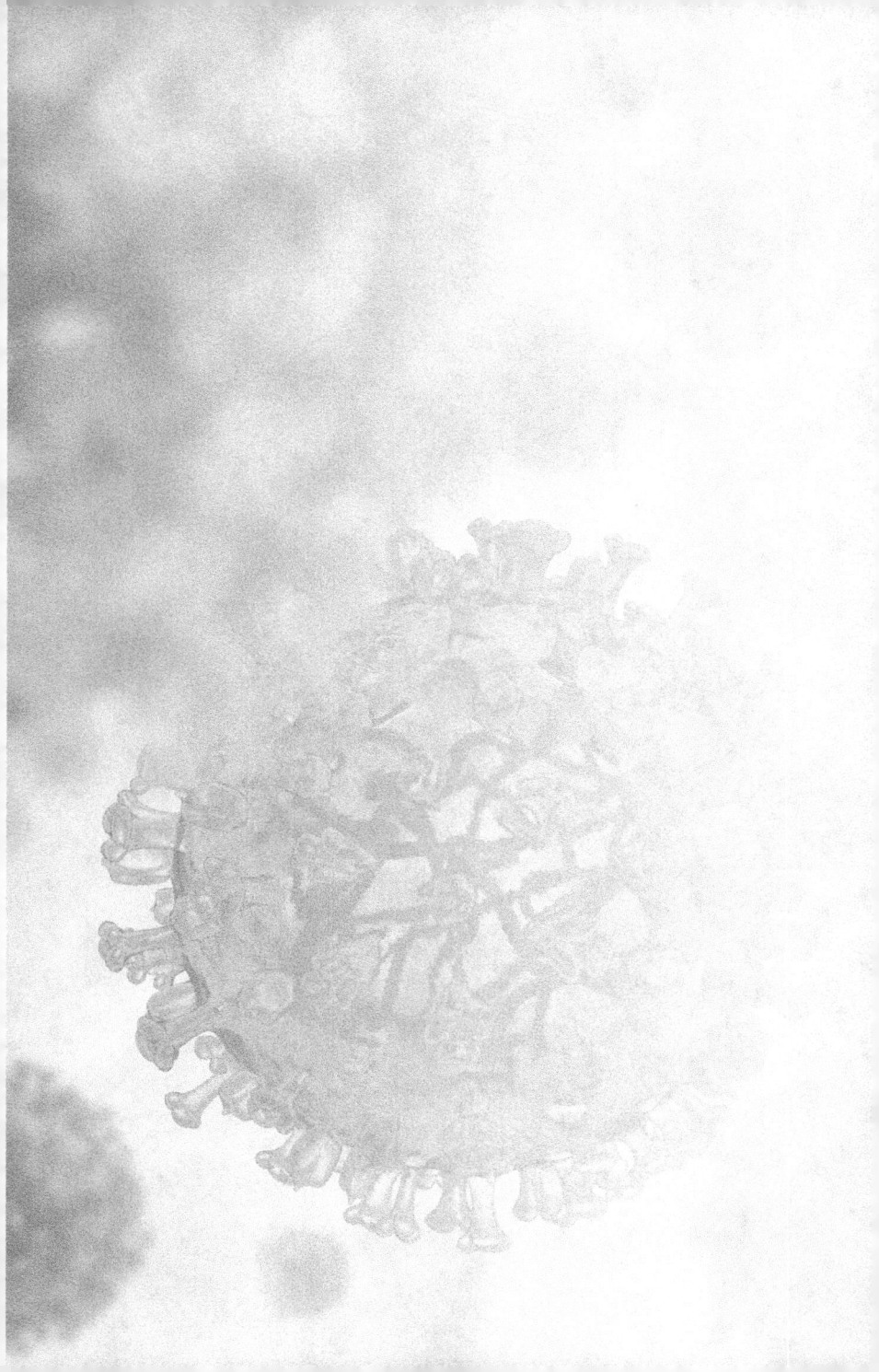

Chapter 16

On the way to meeting his mother, McBride tried to rehearse what he was planning to say. Somehow, he had to cut through her delusional haze to get a point across: she needed to stop upsetting Kendra by mentioning other women. His mother would understand that her jokes had gone too far and were now damaging his relationship, wouldn't she? He hoped so. But it was easy to imagine her looking at him with a quizzical expression and completely misconstruing what he meant. She'd done it a hundred times in the past. Though he found it a despicable habit, sometimes Pres wished he smoked—at a time like now, it would be great to be able to take comfort in a calming habit that provided at least a little mild escape.

He really didn't want to talk to her now, not while preoccupied with Willis and figuring out how to get the truth to the public about the dog flu. However, he could see the pain and a growing sense of betrayal in Kendra's eyes whenever she talked to him. That, at least, he could do something about. She was becoming convinced he was seeing someone other women, grilling him constantly about his relationship with Santiago and asking him at the most inopportune times if he loved her any more. His mother had given Kendra the impression that he was some kind of laboratory lothario—now he had to ask her to dispel it. Once he made sure his mother understood that Kendra was the only woman in his life, at least that distraction would be eliminated. There was only one problem: he would actually have to have a serious conversation with his mother. That would be a first.

The two of them had never enjoyed the traditional closeness between a mother and her child. Pres loved his mother dearly, of course, but very early on in his life they seemed to have reversed roles, with him as the serious parent and her as the capricious child. They rarely communicated now and so rarely argued, but they had often butted heads when he was a child. He and Nathan took after their father: bookish, serious, shy. Mother was the strange, brightly-colored creature issuing outbursts of outlandish, unscientific opinions. He and Nathan, who both loved science and fetishized their absent father, often just exchanged conspiratorial glances before returning to their long-running conversations about evolution, life on other planets, and all kinds of farfetched hypotheticals. Their differences had become more pronounced as time progressed. As soon as they were allowed to buy their own clothes, both Pres and Nate had opted for cardigans, button-down shirts, and ties while Mom flounced around in some garish, ancient tie-dyed outfit she bought at a second-hand store or whipped up herself at some craft retreat. The boys had their noses in science fiction novels or textbooks while she cackled and cursed at the TV or held outlandish rituals with her flaky friends. On the other hand, Pres reminded himself, she was good at teaching them that they were children and occasionally needed to act like them. She was the one who got them outside, dashing around the yard and whooping through the sprinklers and she had taught them her ungraceful but effective underhanded foul shots at the local basketball court.

In-depth emotional conversations, however, were not her strong point. As a result, while living in New York, McBride e-mailed her once a week but rarely called. Nathan's record wasn't even that good.

Maybe, McBride thought aloud, his convoluted relationship with his mother affected how he dealt with Kendra. After all, he hadn't told Kendra where he was going. He simply said he needed to clear his head after the fire.

She had agreed that was a good idea. "It really is burned down, and you need to deal with that," she had said. "Maybe you just need to let it soak in?"

"I just need to confirm to myself that there's nothing to be salvaged," he had replied.

He wasn't sure why he had lied to her. Maybe, he thought, he was worried she would invite herself along to see his mother. He wouldn't have felt comfortable discussing the situation with Kendra there. Talking with her on some sensitive topic was bad enough. Having Kendra watch him would only have made it worse. He refused to let himself think that he hadn't brought her along simply because he preferred to be alone now.

He pulled into Maggie's apartment complex's parking lot and noticed that his mother's decal-covered VW bus was parked in its usual spot amid more pristine cars. She was home. As he got warily out of his car, Pres was relieved at the sense of quiet. While the lot was well-lighted as were entries to the buildings, only an occasional glimmer seeping through the thick drapes in the apartments facing out indicated anyone was moving around. It wasn't even eight p.m. yet, but doors were tightly shut. No light broke through. Here and there, he heard the faint sound of a television set, but that was all. Any festering bad will appeared to have dissipated. Certainly, no one was still angrily marching around on a walker. People seemed to be focusing on their own losses without targeting anyone else now, at least in the sequestered seclusion of suburban California.

Maggie's hallway also showed little signs of life. Pres knocked quietly on her apartment door. He waited impatiently in the silence, drumming his fingers against the freshly painted wall.

"Yes?" a voice finally quavered from within.

"It's me," McBride said.

"Me who?"

"Mom, it's me. Your son. Pres?" McBride rolled his eyes. How could he have been born of such a screwball?

The door inched open. "Oh, Pres," Maggie squealed. "Are you lost?"

"Not sure yet," he said.

The door swung wide. "Down, Canada," Maggie commanded as if the dog were making its usual leaps. Of course, there was nothing there.

"The dog is much better behaved now," McBride commented dryly as he stepped inside. The television was on, and the room smelled of the ever-present incense. His mother had created a small shrine to the dog with two pictures hanging on the wall about knee-high and a red votive candle flickering by the front of the vacant basket.

"Like the candle?' Maggie asked. "I stole it from the Catholic Church around the corner. They have plenty. You want one? Take this one, I can get another one any time I need it."

"It looks beautiful, Mom," McBride said, "but I don't think we're allowed open flames in our building." He worried for a second about his mother lighting her apartment on fire and quickly forced the negative thought out of his head. He kissed his mother on the cheek then leaned back to look at her. Her face was lined with deep ruts, and her lips quivered, but, overall, she seemed as bubbly as ever. Her blue eyes sparkled, and she smiled broadly as if aware of some secret joke.

"Her fantasy is harmless," a psychologist at the hospital had told McBride. "She's still functioning, right? That's more than a lot of people are doing these days."

"It's not the best situation," McBride had argued. "She thinks her dog is in the room with her. She even pets the air and sets out food for him."

"With the mass deaths of dogs, we're only now discovering how strong and how primal the urge to keep and attend to a pet is for human beings. But if you think about it, Dr. McBride, this is something that human beings have been doing for thousands and thousands of years—it's a deep bond that has become part of our collective consciousness. At the very least, it's something we learn from our community at a very early age but evolutionary scientists are positing now that it may actually be hardwired into our DNA. The loss of one's pet is sad, disturbing even. The loss of the pets of the community is proving to be deeply traumatic on a primal level, like losing a limb or having all of one's friends suddenly die. Some people imagine they can still feel an amputated limb. Others talk to imaginary friends. It happens."

"But it's an irrational fantasy!" McBride had tried not to get upset.

"In an ideal world, none of us would have irrational fantasies," the psychologist had said. "This is hardly an ideal world."

McBride couldn't have agreed more.

"If she loses contact with reality to the extent that she can't take care of herself, only then is there really something to worry about. With time, she ought to be able to deal with her loss and make a recovery."

Pres wandered into the living room and sat down on the beanbag. It sagged under his weight and let out a small gasp. Maggie looked around as if the sound had come from elsewhere.

"Canada, go to your room," she ordered. "You're bothering Pres." She pointed a finger and adopted a stern expression. "He doesn't like the candle by his bed," she explained under her breath. After a moment, she relaxed. "I saw the news about the fire at the clinic," she said. "I hope no one was hurt."

Pres marveled at how quickly she could switch back and forth from the stratosphere to planet Earth. "Everyone's fine," he assured her.

"Good."

They sat there quietly for a moment. He took a deep breath. Now was the time. "Mom," he began.

"Don't start," she said abruptly. "You can't move in here."

He stared at her.

"The fire," she said.

"It was at the office, not my home," he said.

"There just isn't room here," she said.

"I know," he said, sighing. And back into the stratosphere again.

"You and Michelle will just have to go somewhere else," Maggie continued. "I'm sorry about that. You are my son."

"Mom, we're fine. And her name is Kendra, not Michelle." He took a deep breath. "That's what I want to talk to you about."

"You're going to yell at me, aren't you?" Maggie quavered. Her lips trembled like a child's. "You look like you always do before you yell at me. Don't yell at me."

McBride took a deep breath. "I'm not yelling. Am I raising my voice?"

"You're about to. I know you have a temper," Maggie replied. "I know you get into a lot of fights."

"Mom," he complained, "that wasn't a fight, I was just trying to prevent you from lynching your neighbor."

"Are you going to hit me, too?"

"Mom, I'd never hit you," he said.

"You never know," she said firmly. "There's a lot of ageism out there. At the Senior Center they said it's not unusual for children to become violent towards their aging parents. I spoke to the Battered Women's Clinic just in case."

"Did you give them my name?" McBride asked nervously. This was all he needed.

"No," his mother said, "I just said 'my son.' Do you know what the woman at the clinic told me?" McBride numbly shook his head. "Sons are often the worst." She glanced at the door. "I bought a double deadbolt lock. Nathan won't be getting in here."

"Oh, Mom." Her paranoia would almost be funny if it didn't have such potentially heavy consequences.

"Cake?" she tried, shifting topics and getting to her feet.

"Aw, Mom, I can't. I'm trying to watch my weight."

"You have your father's build," she said. "You'll never put on weight." With that, she hurried to the kitchen. McBride watched her disappear, recalling how just recently she admonished him that he needed to watch his weight because he had his father's build. Jesus, she was in bad shape.

She came back with two plates. One held a huge slice of chocolate cake; the other was empty.

"This will help you stay on your diet," she said, offering him the empty plate.

He took the plate and put it next to him. For a second, he had the eerie sense the invisible dog would eat his invisible cake.

"Mom, can we talk?" he asked plaintively.

"Now you want to talk?" she asked. She sat down in the closest beanbag and began to eat her cake with a fork. "I mean, when you went to San Francisco, you didn't call. You didn't call when you went to New York."

"I wrote every week," he protested.

"I saw Mr. Rogers and his neighborhood more than you," Maggie said.

"I was three thousand miles away in New York."

"I'm sorry the aviation system wasn't available," Maggie noted with a mouth full of cake. "Weren't there planes between New York and California?"

"Mom, stop it," McBride insisted, "I'm here now."

"I figured it was Michelle's fault," Maggie continued blithely.

McBride shook his head. No wonder, he decided, he avoided talking to his mother. Alice in Wonderland had had more comprehensible discussions with the Mad Hatter.

"What Michelle?" he said.

She shrugged. "I figured you never came by because you had girlfriends. Not that it matters. You run through them faster than Timothy Leary and his LSD stash."

"My girlfriend's name is Kendra," McBride said wearily. "She's the only girlfriend I've had in a long time, and she's staying. I hope."

"What about Maria?" Maggie asked innocently as another forkful followed the previous one into her mouth.

McBride gaped. How did his mother know about her? "How...?" he managed.

"A mother knows these things," Maggie said. "Mother's intuition."

"I don't buy that for a second," he said.

"All right, all right, it was in the e-mail you sent me," she said. Heaving herself to her feet, she led him to the computer in the second bedroom. Cake in hand, she sat down at the chair and opened up her e-mail. Cake crumbs vanished between the letters keys. McBride could see that eating here was a common practice. A researcher could probably figure out his mother's last dozen meals by simply taking samples from her keyboard.

Maggie turned on the computer, an antiquated Mac with a purple exterior. She probably just picked it out by the color, Pres thought to himself. After a moment, she entered her AOL account. She had created a file and saved his e-mails. She moved the cursor and opened one of them. He glanced at the header—it appeared to come from his email address.

Mom:
I found a great gal. Her name is Maria. I really think you'll like her. Don't tell Kendra. I'll try to bring Maria around on Friday."

Pres

McBride read it three times. His eyes grew wider with each reading. "Mom, I didn't send that," he finally said, swallowing hard.

"You didn't bring her over on Friday. Maybe you meant next Friday. You weren't specific," Maggie said.

"Mom," McBride insisted firmly, "I didn't write that. I don't sign my emails like that. I haven't in a long time."

"I noticed that," Maggie agreed. "You usually write 'Doc,' but I figured you were trying to be more grown up for your girlfriends. There are e-mails about a Stephanie and a Michelle, too. I always thought you were good looking. It's nice to know it's not just a mother's idealized impression!"

McBride staggered back. "Have you gotten other e-mails from me?" he asked in a weak, wounded voice. This was awful.

"Sure," Maggie said cheerfully. "You write a lot more now than when you lived in New York. I re-read them all the time. It's like having you in the room with me. Gosh, you are so funny sometimes!"

McBride leaned against the wall. "Mom, I have not written you a single e-mail since I've been back. You know I call now," he said softly.

"Sure you've written," Maggie said cheerfully. "You write a lot. Your memory is really going. You're worse than me. You must be inhaling too much formaldehyde in your lab."

McBride quickly tried to count the emails in the saved file: there had to be at least ten.

She opened another one. It contained a promise to visit.

"You never showed up," she said in a wounded tone. He scanned the emails quickly. Another one talked about a fight at work. "Pres" reported an intern had a sore jaw, but that he himself had escaped harm. "I ducked and threw one good punch," the online impostor reported. "You would have been proud of me. He went down like Nixon against Kennedy." Other e-mails were pure gibberish, as though he had been confused or deranged.

"I love this one," Maggie said after opening one.

Mom:

Gerunds are a very funny animal. They tend to live in thickets, like dormice, but not of trees. Sentence structure is key. On the other hand, when the movie is on, you really don't hear many gerunds. I was thinking about that today and thought you would like to know. Gerundheit. I just sneezed!

Pres

She smiled up at him. "I thought of it as a kind of code. The word 'gerund' could stand for a person, like Gerald. Now, 'strange animal' has the initials S.A. That could mean South America." She smiled at him hopefully. "How am I doing?"

"Great," he mumbled.

"Oh," Maggie squealed. "I liked this one, too. I love it when you tell me about your work."

With a sinking feeling in his stomach, McBride read over her shoulder.

Mom:

My research is going very well. I've just isolated the dog flu virus and determined it's a form of H3N8. I had been afraid it was linked to H1N1, but that's not true. It's very exciting to finally know the truth.

Pres

"That's not true," he exclaimed.

"Pres," she chided him. "You know that researchers find new things all the time. It was true then, but maybe not now."

"It wasn't true then," he protested. He looked at the date. The e-mail was sent while he was using Novilis's lab.

"Are all the ones I sent you here?" he asked.

"Yes," Maggie said proudly. "I was so glad to be communicating with you. For a long time, I only had Canada to talk to. Nathan doesn't write much at all. I think he's plotting something," she said with suspicion.

McBride hastily went to the first e-mail. It was sent little more than two months ago. That was shortly after he began his nightly trips to Novilis. How had the company accessed his personal e-mail? He didn't have to ponder that question for very long. He e-mailed some of his results from the Novilis account they set up for him to his personal account. In order to verify that they had gone through, he had logged into his personal account. They must have been tracking his keystrokes! He knew Willis couldn't be trusted but he had underestimated the lengths that man would go to in order to undermine him. McBride felt like his stomach was trying to turn itself inside out.

He staggered back into the living room and sat down on the beanbag. If he tried to attack Novilis, Willis would simply produce the e-mails. His trustworthiness would be challenged; his integrity had been completely compromised. The bizarre e-mails would undermine his sanity in case any of his results made it beyond the lab. No wonder Willis demonstrated such a cavalier attitude. What did he have to worry about?

"Oh my God," McBride moaned. He rubbed his hands together. He should have punched Willis when he had the chance. He should have done something.

Finally, he stood up. "Mom," McBride said, "I'm going."

"So soon?" she said. "You didn't eat your cake."

"I lost my appetite."

"What a great diet!" she said. She scurried to seize the empty plate. "Good thing Canada didn't eat it," she added.

"Maybe he's on a diet, too," McBride said wearily. He kissed his mother on the forehead. "Please don't believe any e-mail that doesn't have 'Doc' on the bottom, all right?" he asked her.

"Oooh," Maggie said, "it's like playing a game, SDS versus the pigs. I like that."

"Exactly," he said. "And please forget what you read about other women. There's only Kendra."

"Sure, sonny boy," she whispered. "I'll keep it between us." She laughed. "It's our secret." She winked at him. God, had he just made things worse?

He left quickly. The hallway was still quiet. This time, the shadows at the end of the corridor oozed with ominous overtones. He hurried down the stairs, accompanied by an uncomfortable, prickly feeling that someone was watching him. He even checked the dark backseat of his car before getting in. He closed the door gently. The click sounded dangerous. Overwhelmed, he fumbled with his cell phone and called Maria.

"I need to talk to you," he said.

"Is everything all right?"

"Nada de lo que es bueno," McBride replied, instantly feeling foolish. Willis certainly had someone on his staff who understood Spanish. Still, he felt as though he were using a secret code.

"En el oficina?' she asked.

"Si," he replied.

He snapped the phone shut and started the engine. For an instance, he wondered if the car would explode. Had Willis attached a homing device? He had seen enough spy movies to know that could happen. He hurried outside to check the bumpers. Nothing evident except some dirt. He glanced around. No one was visible, but that didn't mean anything. Calm down, he told himself. Willis wanted him alive to support Novilis's claims. His death would only arouse suspicion. At least the logic sounded good, McBride decided. He would have to cling to that as long as possible.

He drove slowly, constantly checking the side view and rear view mirrors. Any car on the road with him could be one of Willis's men, to say nothing of the hordes of folks who were roaming around on edge after losing a beloved dog. Someone might be taping him, recording his words. He turned the radio to a public station. A Mozart symphony was playing. He turned the dial up, as if blasting the music could hide his thoughts from anyone trying to read his mind.

Heading south, McBride peeked into cars driving by, trying to spot someone familiar. Was that Hofferman? Would Willis use someone McBride knew? No, that didn't seem likely. McBride did not see anyone he recognized. Somehow, that seemed worse.

Finally, he steered into the strip mall housing the veterinary hospital. He saw Maria's car to the left of Waverly's front door. Only safety lights by at the end of the parking light offered any illumination. Overhead, clouds had covered the stars and dampened the effects of the moon. Grateful for the cover, McBride parked his car on the right side of the door. When he turned off the engine, the silence was deafening. He checked the mirror, pretending to adjust it. No one was creeping up behind him. Finally, taking a deep breath, he opened his car and sprinted to the office. He rapped quickly on the door. The sound seemed to echo around the empty parking lot. He sure someone was taking his photograph, taping the sounds of his breath, even reading his thoughts.

Maria opened the office door with an expression that was both relief and puzzlement. He moved inside without saying hello, brushing past her and signaling for her to close the door. Only a desk lamp in the corner of the waiting room was on.

"Ques es la problema?" she finally asked. She peered into the darkness. Nothing struck her as suspicious. Slowly and quietly, she closed the door.

Collapsing in a chair, McBride felt all the nervous energy ooze from his body. He was suddenly exhausted. "I've been compromised," he told her.

"Que?"

She sat down across from him. Her hands were clasped between her knees, and she had a frightened look on her face. After a dark moment, McBride felt revived. He was safe here. The tension began to ease. He quickly explained the e-mails. She didn't understand at first.

"If I testify in Congress or say anything to any author-ity, Willis will simply produce the e-mails to show that I was lying, crazy, or gallivanting around with a series of women," McBride said.

"Que lio!" Santiago said.

"Yeah," McBride said. He began to pace around aimlessly, trying to collect his thoughts. There had to be something he could do. He glanced around and flashed back to his first visit to the office, maybe six months ago. He had sat here with his mother's dying dog. He had worked so hard since then and almost nothing had changed. Dogs were still dying, and he had accomplished nothing.

"You can no longer be in front," Santiago said. "We must find someone else who can."

He looked at her. "Who?" He had no idea. However, she had lived here much longer. She might know someone. What other choice was there?

She smiled at him. "Go home," she said. "I will call."

He started to say something, but finally walked uneasily to the front door. She followed. He turned to wave goodbye. Instead, she hugged him.

He stepped back.

"Todo estará bien," she said.

He nodded, but he didn't believe her.

Suddenly, he was alone outside, completely exposed. Once in the car, it felt like a refuge, but even as he began to relax he knew both that the car could be bugged and that even inside of it, he was far from safe. He headed west on Foothill, painfully aware that the car did not hide him. Each headlight that sprayed across his windshield was like a searchlight, emphasizing his presence.

He drove the speed limit so others would quickly go by him. That gave him a chance to take long looks at drivers as they hurried by him. Each one scared him. He was afraid that one of them would be looking back, studying him, threatening him. The young man tapping his steering wheel in time to the music looked natural. He didn't even glance at McBride as he pulled behind and then zoomed by. He didn't look back either. *That could be a cover,* McBride thought. *Someone else might be in a second car.* He recalled that concept from the one or two TV detective shows he had watched regularly. For the first time in his life, he regretted not reading more murder mysteries. He would have picked up some pointers about evading problems and identifying suspects. Eventually, overwhelmed, he resolutely stared straight ahead and headed home.

McBride headed down North Garey: finally, familiar territory. No one exited behind him. He stopped by the burned-out clinic. Police had set up barricades. All that was really left were some bricks and blackened, unrecognizable ashes. The scene was frightening and incredibly dismal. McBride shivered. He had no doubt that Willis was behind it.

"You were gone awhile," Kendra said as McBride returned home. He carefully locked the door behind him before simply shrugging. "Janette called and said there's a meeting tomorrow morning at her house," Kendra continued.

Pres nodded. "Did she say why?"

"Plans for the clinic," Kendra said. "She has a new doctor she wants you to meet."

He stopped. Sure, he thought, why not? Everything was falling apart. His job must be going, too. There was no reason for Rosen to keep him. He had just filled in for Crossland. Rosen didn't know him before that other than by name and his tentative association with Crossland. He only met her when stopping by to talk to his old friend. It was easier for her to let him stay on but obviously there had been tension.

"I can't wait," McBride said laconically.

"She sounded encouraged."

"One of us should be," he said.

Kendra frowned. "What's wrong?"

Thoughts swirled through Mc Bride's head. He didn't want to alarm her, but she had to know. She was studying him. She could feel her eyes probing, as if trying to read his mind. He finally sat on the couch and patted the cushion next to him. She nestled close and put her head on his shoulder. It was the closest they had been in a while.

"It's bad," he said.

"I can handle it," she said. "We can handle it," and reached for his hand.

Slowly, he unfolded the whole scenario. He could feel her body tighten and then relax.

"That's all?" she said. "I was worried you were having an affair."

"Kendra, there's no one else," he said, kissing her. He stopped. "Wait, did you get an e-mail or something?"

"An anonymous one," she said.

"Jesus!"

"One of the neighbors, Jay, said something, too," she continued. "Do you bring someone home when I was away?"

"No," he said angrily. "I was working at the clinic. You know that."

Kendra squirmed out from under his arm and walked into the bedroom. He heard a drawer open. She came back with a picture in hand. It showed Santiago opening a door with

McBride outside. There was no doubt: she was in their house. He stared at it.

"She was never here," he protested. "I have only talked to her at her clinic."

Kendra didn't say anything, but continued to hold out the photo.

"It's been doctored in some way," McBride continued.

"Funny choice of words coming from a doctor," Kendra noted.

McBride took a deep breath, trying to calm his heart. "Kendra, listen to me. This picture has been Photoshopped. I talk to Maria in her office. There are usually clients with their pets there."

"At night?" Kendra finally lowered the picture.

"Most of the time," he insisted. "I've only talked to her a few times anyway."

This time, Kendra sat across from him. "I drove over to the clinic during lunch," she said. "She's very pretty."

"You were checking up on me?"

"Your mother told me about your e-mails," Kendra said.

McBride stood up. "I didn't write those e-mails," he said angrily.

"I want to believe you," Kendra said. Her voice sounded small and weak.

"You'll have to," McBride said. "I'm not dating Maria, and I didn't write my mother."

"Did Nathan?"

McBride buried his head in his hands. He could feel a band of tension cinching up across his forehead.

"No," he said, "Willis did."

"You're sounding paranoid," Kendra told him.

"It's the truth. I sign my letters 'Doc.' It's dorky, I know. It's a holdover from when I was a kid—I started signing letters 'Doc' as soon as I decided I wanted to be a doctor. The e-mails my mother has were signed 'Pres,'" McBride said softly. "You don't have to believe me. It doesn't matter. Very soon, I'll be like my mother, completely nuts and talking to a dead dog. Or who knows, maybe I'll just wind up like the dog."

Kendra studied him. "You know," she said coolly, "you have perfume on you."

"Oh, for Christ's sake," McBride stormed out of the living room. That had to have happened when Maria hugged him. He stood in the bathroom by the sink and stared into the mirror. Bags were forming under his eyes; stress was etching small lines in his face. His hair seemed to have a tinge of gray now instead of just scattered gray hairs here and there.

He heard Kendra walk to the open door. "I don't want to be hurt," she said.

"I don't want to hurt you," he answered.

"Should I just go back to New York?" she said. "There's nothing here for me without you."

He faced her. "No," he said. "Don't leave me. You are the only person keeping me sane." He enveloped her. She was crying hard into his shoulder. He felt for a second like he might lose it, too. What, he thought, would Willis do next?

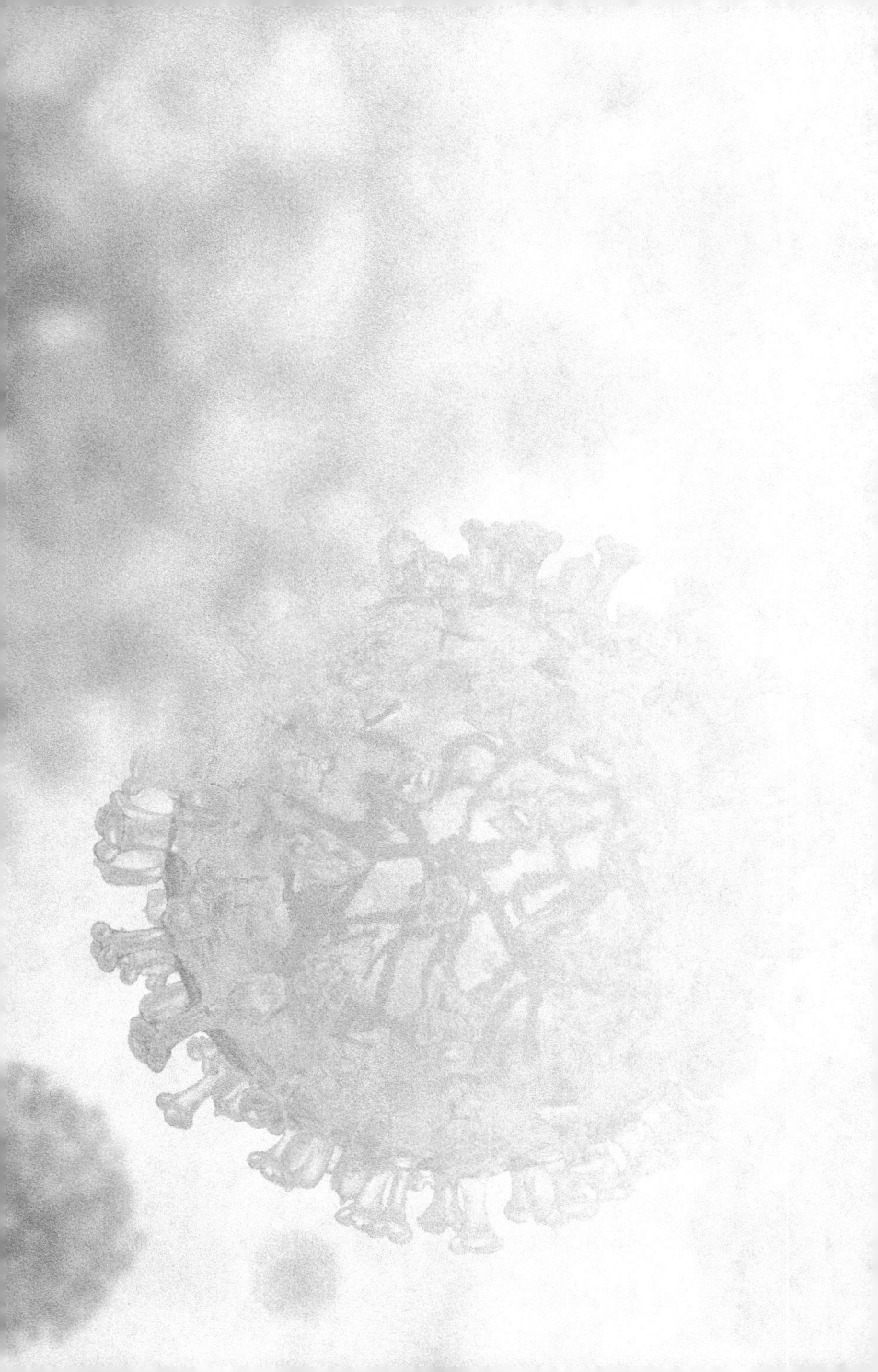

Chapter 17

Dale Hubbard sat up in bed and glanced over at his alarm clock: 1:43 a.m. He had set it to go off at two so they could catch a couple of hours of sleep and still leave town in the darkest hour of the night. Of course, he'd hardly slept, going over the details of their plan again and again and again, trying to think of any detail he'd overlooked. He reached over and switched off the alarm—he wasn't going to get any more sleep now, that much was clear. He glanced over at his wife to see if he had woken her. Rose was already peeling back the covers and getting out of bed. She was a good woman, an excellent partner in every way. He was lucky to have her.

As the coffee brewed, they went over their checklists one final time. The power didn't need to be switched off as their little farmhouse was powered exclusively by a combination of solar and battery power. He would just close the valve for the natural gas they used for cooking when they walked out. The hurricane shutters had been bolted into place as soon as the sun had gone down. Even if someone managed to make it all the way out to the homestead and break in, there wasn't much of value in the house. All the gear they would need for traveling had already been packed into their weather-beaten old VW van, long ago converted to bio-diesel, and the little pop-up

Bluejay trailer they towed behind. As much as moving out to a remote corner of Montana, home-schooling their children and getting off the grid had made their lives challenging, it was now making leaving this ailing country behind that much easier.

Rose loaded Windsong and Sunshine, their twin girls, into the van so quickly that they never fully woke up and were almost instantly softly snoring again. They were good sleepers. Dale figured they probably wouldn't wake up until it was time to cross into the border into Canada. Only one more task remained.

Misty, their pregnant Labrador retriever, lay napping on her cedar bed by the cooling wood stove. She had lifted her head up in surprise at Dale when he descended the stairs in the middle of the night but hadn't found it so alarming that it merited leaving her spot by the stove. Now Dale shook her by the collar.

"Wake up, Misty. We're going on a little drive, girl."

Misty grinned at him—he had always loved that, how some dogs could smile—and rolled on her back to have her tummy rubbed. Now was not the time...but what the hell, she had a long journey ahead of her. He gently scratched her distended tummy, careful of the young lives growing within. As soon as he had gotten wind of the dog flu, he had taken her over to a friend's compound to have her bred with another dog just in case things got worse. And things had gotten worse, far worse than he could have imagined. Still he tried to stay optimistic and visualized a positive outcome: once they smuggled Misty safely into Canada, they would find a safe place to hunker down. Misty would safely deliver her puppies, and when the clueless government had finally found a cure for the dog flu, they could return home with a batch of healthy puppies to be bred with whatever dogs had survived to rebuild the dog population.

"Okay, Misty, time to go." She could lay and have her tummy rubbed all day once they got up to Saskatchewan. He grabbed her collar and gave a tug and she slowly got to her feet and followed him out to the camper.

He opened the small door to the camper, and she got right inside. He got down on his hands and knees and followed her in. As she had been trained, she went right to the open door of the little half-fridge and crawled into the hatch that had been cut in the side. Dale, flashlight in his teeth, watched her tail disappear as she curled up and lay right down. He pushed the hatch closed and it clicked shut. He examined the seam of the trap door once more. He had done a good job of it; glancing at it, no one would be able to tell that a section of the fridge had been cut out so that a dog could hide in the camper's empty water tank, conveniently situated next to the built-in refrigerator.

After extracting himself from the camper and closing and locking the door, he went around to the other side of the camper. He had made sure that Misty's compartment was adequately ventilated but, more to assure himself than anything, he unscrewed the cap that covered the fillhole for the water tank, whistled and stuck a couple of fingers inside. He was rewarded with a warm, wet lick. He replaced the cap. There was plenty of food and water in there for her. Misty was going to be fine.

He walked around the house a final time, checking all the doors and windows, then climbed into the driver's seat, and they were off.

The Canadian border guard was polite but thorough. He inquired where they were headed, how long they intended to stay, the purpose of their visit. Tired as he was, Dale reeled off his story smoothly: they were going to visit friends, Kathy and Rick Robinson, in Saskatoon for a month. The customs guard looked down at the form Dale had filled out, pulled a cell phone out of a holster on his belt and dialed the contact number Dale had written down. After four rings, a woman's voice came on.

"Well, hello there, this is Kathy and Rick. Looks like neither of us is around to pick up the phone, so please leave a message and we'll return your call as soon as we can. Thanks!"

The guard hung up without leaving a message. He wouldn't have been called back even if he had. A month earlier, Dale had purchased a Canadian cell phone plan and Rose had recorded an outgoing message for the phone number as Kathy Robinson.

"You folks have all been inoculated for the Rohn flu?" the guard said, bending down and peering into the van window. The girls had been instructed not to say anything, but that was hardly necessary—they were so infrequently exposed to people other than their parents that they were painfully shy around strangers.

"Yes, sir, you've got all the paperwork for that in your hand," Dale said cheerily. He wasn't going to let the government dictate what he had to put in his body or the bodies of his children, but the papers had been easy to take care of. He was on a message board for people who opposed mandatory vaccination and a couple of well-worded posts had won him a link to a secret site that provided fake inoculation papers. And it hadn't cost him anything—he just input the information for himself, his wife, and the children and then downloaded official looking forms. Best of all, it was free—a public service by a like-minded patriot.

"What about a pet of any kind? A dog? A puppy? Hey girls, do you have a puppy dog?"

Neither of the girls spoke, just stared in awe at the man in the round-brimmed hat.

"No sir," Dale said, smiling, "kids are enough hassle for us."

"You mind if I take a look in the trailer?"

"Go right ahead."

The guard walked back to the trailer, squatted down, and opened the door. He shone his flashlight inside. He glanced at Dale, then climbed halfway inside. Dale watched the guard disappear into the camper and felt his heartbeat thudding in his temples. What was the penalty for trying to smuggle a dog across an international border? Would he go to jail?

A moment later, the guard eased out of the trailer. He walked directly up to Dale's window. Dale felt like he was going to throw up. In his mind, he and his beautiful wife and their beloved daughters were already behind bars.

"Thanks for your cooperation, sir. Enjoy your vacation in Canada."

Dale was stunned. He was so grateful that he stuck his hand out the car window.

"Thank you, sir."

The guard looked down at Dale's proffered hand, shook it quickly and then waved Dale forward and beckoned for the next car to pull in.

As soon as they were out of sight of the border crossing, Dale had to pull over. He was still shaken from the crossing and knew he would have to sleep soon. He walked around to stretch his legs for a moment, then discreetly slid over to the camper, undid the cap on the water fill pipe and whistled, then stuck a couple of fingers in the pipe. Nothing. And then there it was, Misty's familiar wet tongue. When he withdrew his hand, she whined. She couldn't be happy in there, but she was holding on. The worst was over.

When Dale walked back to the van, Rose was already sitting in the driver's seat, smiling up at him and ready to go. Again, Dale was struck by how lucky he was to have her. A beautiful woman, a great wife and mother, and an equal partner in all their pursuits. He climbed into the passenger's seat and was asleep within minutes.

It was dark again by the time they pulled into their spot for the night—a cluster of elm trees on a dirt road off of Highway 11 leading north out of Saskatoon. Everyone piled anxiously out of the car—the girls had been awake and chattering for hours—and grouped excitedly around the door to the camper. Dale knew Misty was a hearty dog, in good health, and that she had probably weathered the ride with minimal distress. It couldn't have been fun for her, but better for her to suffer a little bit to get up here to Canada where it was cleaner and she could bear her puppies in isolation from other dogs and the threat of the dog flu. Still, he couldn't shake a bad feeling. She had been slow to lick his hand at their last food break five hours ago. She had made it and licked him, but he heard her grumbling afterwards. He had meant to get them off the road sooner, but he hadn't mentioned anything about it to Rose as he didn't want to upset her...and then he had fallen asleep. Misty would be fine, he told himself, her mouth and nose had been wet so she couldn't have been dehydrated. She would be fine.

He told the girls to stand back and opened the trailer door and crawled into that stuffy, tight space with a flashlight clamped between his teeth. He wormed his way in and opened the refrigerator door. There was no sound from Misty. She was just sleeping, he told himself. Or waiting patiently, her tail wagging. She had never been a noisy dog. Then he turned the clip that held the false door in side of the fridge in place and pulled the hidden compartment open. Instantly, the floor of the trailer was awash in blood.

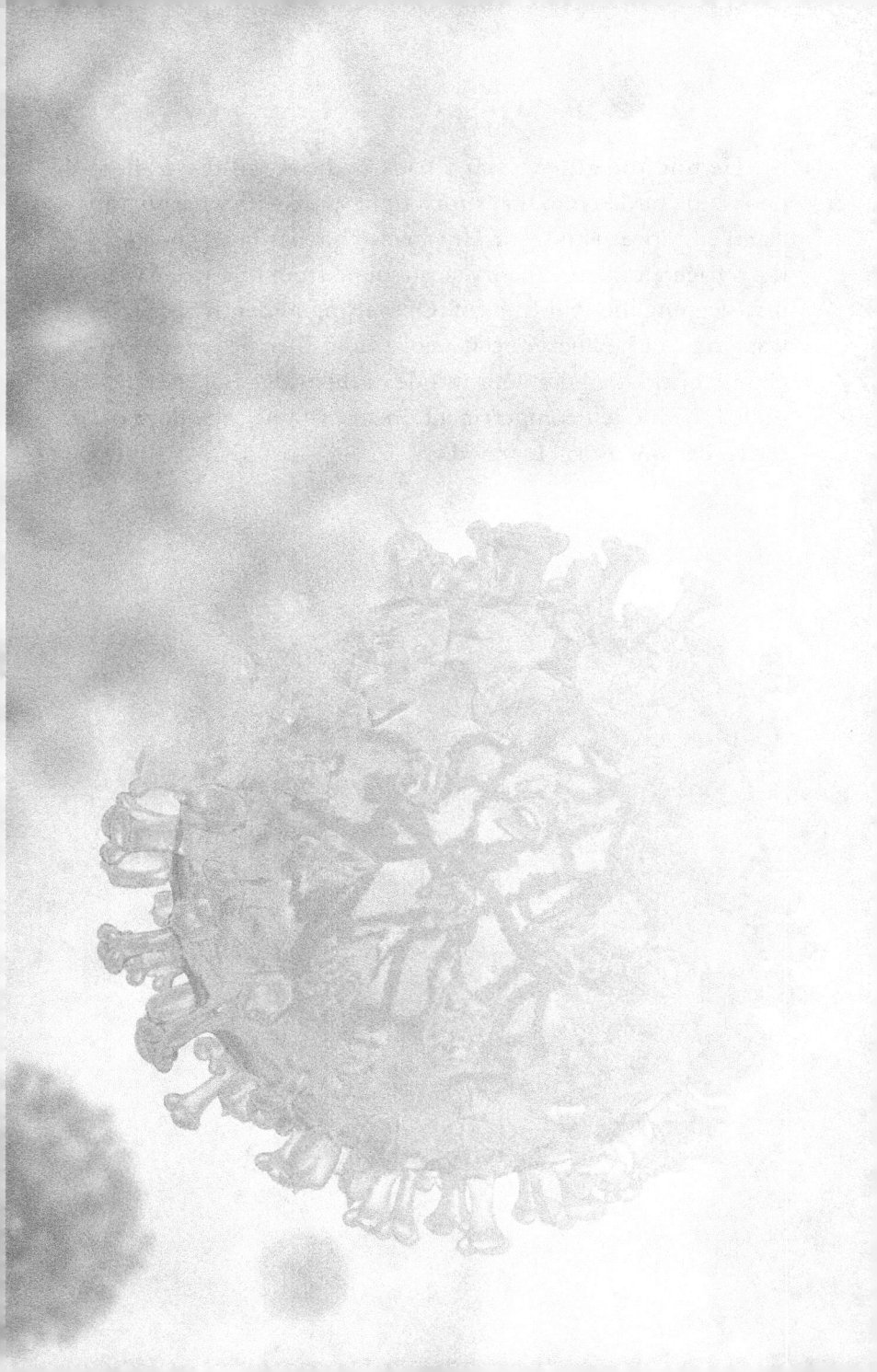

Chapter 18

Branches from a large western sycamore tree bending in the wind outside Rosen's living room scraped across the window as a rainstorm continued Saturday morning. The eerie scratching noise made McBride's skin crawl. He almost jumped each time a gust drove the branches holding the distinctive five-pointed leaves against the glass. Then Rosen's tiger cat, stretching and yawning, caused him to quickly turn sideways to stare at it. The strange young man seated in the corner riveted him for a few moments before clinking tumblers on Rosen's tray grabbed his attention. He looked out of place, wearing a suit while everyone else was more casual. McBride had opted for slacks, sports coat and a striped shirt, but no tie. Years and years of working long late hours had taught him to take shortcuts as far as dress code was concerned whenever they were offered.

A car whizzed down the street, sending water spurting around its tires. It struck him as sinister—what catastrophe was it rushing to meet? Then, a couple with an umbrella came by in close conversation. Were they mourning a shared loss or hashing out the details of some nefarious plot? The world was becoming overwhelming. McBride lay back in his chair, trying just to breathe easily and calm down, all the while listening to his pulse race.

His breaths came rapidly. Of course, there was no way to relax, not as each odd sound crackled around him. All of the trouble areas of his life seemed to be converging: Kendra, Willis, the flu, even Santiago. He felt the pressure building but was unable to do anything to ease it. He gripped the sides of his chair until his knuckles turned white, focusing on the sensation rather than the thoughts cascading through his mind. He was safe here, he reminded himself. No one was spying on him here. No one seemed to be watching him. Still, that eerie sensation of being followed clung to him. A branch brushed the glass, and he almost jumped out of his skin.

His uneasiness contrasted starkly with the neat, orderly living room. Rosen was compulsively organized—no surprise there. Each seat had a small name tag so everyone knew where to sit. White lace doilies graced the backs of both chairs and the long sofa. Any speck of dust that might have mistakenly wandered into the room would have suffered an immediate demise. Despite Rosen's cat weaving contentedly between their legs, he hadn't seen a single cat hair on the furniture. McBride wondered if the living room was more like a museum or a mausoleum.

Rosen waited until each glass had been properly placed on its wooden coaster strategically located by each of the five guests before standing to announce the clinic would reopen in a vacant hobby store located two blocks east of the office. Everyone murmured appreciation and congratulations mixed with relief that their jobs were safe. To toast, everyone carefully clinked glasses together, careful not to slosh ice tea, then

320

politely returned their tumblers to the assigned positions. Rosen's watchful eyes appeared to record every detail.

After a moment, she started to talk about the next item on her invisible agenda. McBride was barely listening, his ears tuned more to eerie noises than to her voice, when his cell phone vibrated. He slid sideways in the chair to shield the screen from view and glanced at the number of the incoming call. Santiago. His heart rate shot up again. What did she want? He was dying to answer the call, but could see from Rosen's quick, stern glance that this was just not possible. He gave her a wan smile and shut off the phone. He slid the phone back into his pocket, where it slept silently but somehow still occupied his feverish brain. What bad news was Santiago calling to deliver now? And why did his heart race so when he saw her name? He had felt a curious combination of dread, fear, and elation.

"Next, I'd like you to meet Dr. Herbert Lester," Rosen continued. She gestured to the strange, hefty man who had been sitting unobtrusively to one side. There was a thin smile on his massive round face, his eyes carefully hidden behind folds of fat as if to not reveal a secret. He ran his pudgy fingers through his thinning reddish hair.

McBride gave Dr. Lester a long look before she continued. From his manner, his corpulence, and his advancing baldness, he could have been in his mid-sixties but he probably wasn't any older than McBride. Rosen described him as having graduated from the University of Indiana Medical School with a specialty in family practice and had been induced to migrate west by friends. California costs defeated their best hopes of opening a clinic, and Lester had been stranded without a position. He had been making the rounds of medical officers in the area and hoped the clinic could use some help. So Rosen had brought him to the meeting for the others to meet.

"We need someone who will be available on a full-time basis," Rosen said, glancing squarely at McBride to make sure he got the message.

"I never miss work. I had perfect attendance all through high school and college," Lester quickly squeaked out.

McBride did not react. The man was like a terrier hidden inside the body of a bear. Though he knew his phone was off, he imagined he felt it pulsing against his leg. Santiago knew he was in this meeting, yet she had called anyway. Something serious had to be unfolding but what? A terrorist attack due to the lack of drug-sniffing dogs? Had the flu jumped to cats now? Had her office burned down now? He needed to get away. A sycamore tree's claws dragged across the glass again, startling him. He had to move just to dispel the panic that was settling on him.

Finally, he stood up and walked across the room to greet Lester. He offered his hand. Rising from his seat with a grunt, Lester responded with a large, sweaty paw like a soft piece of fruit, seeping juice and slowly going bad.

"Welcome to the clinic," McBride managed. His voice echoed inside his head. He felt a roaring in his ears. Lester nodded his thanks. He gave a half-hearted smile. Instantly, McBride felt suspicious. Had Willis sent Lester? McBride disliked the black thoughts welling inside him, but could not dam them. Lester seemed innocuous, but no one was harmless anymore. McBride backed up to his seat as if afraid to turn his back on the new doctor.

Rosen continued to talk, explaining procedures and plans for the coming weeks. McBride did not hear her. He still felt only contempt for her because of the way she had taken advantage of Crossland. True, her manipulation had saved the clinic, but she appeared to have done it for nakedly personal reasons and proceeded to lord over it with an iron hand. If anything, he had tolerated her with a coolness that had radiated through the clinic. McBride knew now he would not be staying but, at the moment, he had no place else to go. Furthermore, there was enough chaos in his life without throwing unemployment into it as well. To avoid looking at her, he stared at Lester, trying to get a read on the man, maybe detect a hint of sinister motivation. Lester simply seemed uneasy, which was a common enough reaction for anyone in a room full of strangers. On the other hand, McBride thought, he could be acting. Lester did not seem to be paying any attention to any of the young women in the room, most notably Sarah Ormond, the newest nurse. She was a very pretty blonde, very much in her prime. Lester, however, seemed drawn more to the painting on the wall over McBride's head. Was he repressed? For a second, McBride wondered if the man might be an android before he caught himself. More sleep, he decided, and less coffee.

Finally, Rosen stopped to open the floor for questions. No one had any. She took that as a compliment to her communication skills and slipped away to bring out small cookies. Each came with its own napkin. Jesus, did she think they were first graders? McBride saw his chance and fled for the hallway and sequestered himself in the bathroom. He quickly dialed Santiago.

"I was in a meeting," he whispered when she answered.

"You have to come here immediately," Santiago responded. Her voice was even softer and more pointed than his.

"As soon as I can," McBride replied.

"Pronto, por favor," Santiago begged with urgency in her voice. Abruptly, she hung up.

McBride stared at the phone a minute before closing it. Paranoia flared in his brain again. Was she in danger? No, she wouldn't have been able to answer the phone. Still, she sounded so short, so harsh. She had always been invariably polite, but that was clearly a command she had just given him. What was going on? He would have to get to her office as quickly as possible.

He flushed the toilet to maintain the illusion and went back to the living room. He would have liked to keep walking to his car, but Lester immediately engaged him in some meaningless discussion about patient protocols. The new doctor seemed to think he could learn office procedures in a conversation, rather than actually seeing where the files, waiting rooms, and nurses' stations were.

McBride studied him carefully while offering some vague, noncommittal pointers. Lester towered over him, yet his shoulders sagged as if he were trying to round himself as much as possible. His chest bulged outward, threatening the seams of his suit coat. From the muscles in his forearm and his rounded stomach, McBride guessed Lester had lifted weights in high school and college then had tapered off while continuing to eat like a power lifter. As a result, his bulk had descended from his shoulders to his middle.

Finally, after having caught sight of some unattached cookies languidly basking on a ceramic plate, Lester loosened his grip on McBride. He moved with surprising agility, deftly sidestepping Rosen's cat and Silverstein to close in on his prey. The plate was empty in seconds.

Taking advantage of the momentary freedom, McBride perfunctorily thanked Rosen for the hospitality and lied about being eager to resume work on Monday. She kept her jaw set, apparently catching the insincerity in his voice. Lamely, he stumbled on, promising to help her keep the clinic a success.

"I am sure you will," she said flatly. Her eyes darted away from him to a glass of ice tea dangerously teetering on the edge of her end table. She hurriedly rescued it, glaring around at everyone as if trying to identify the culprit. Then she hurried for a clean cloth from the kitchen in order to wipe the invisible stain on the table's surface. McBride said a quick goodbye to the other nurses and hurried into the rain.

With the rain still pelting down, he squished into his car and adjusted the mirror. He had to know if someone was following him. To his left, Rosen's front door opened. Lester appeared. McBride floored the gas pedal and hurried away. If Lester were going to follow him, he'd better start running. Lester was still talking to Rosen by the front door as McBride rounded a corner. Maybe there was a tracking device on his car? McBride thought. His phone vibrated on his pocket and he twisted the while for a second, almost careening into someone's front yard before catching himself and correcting.

"Where are you?" Santiago asked.

"On my way."

"Break records," she told him, and maddeningly hung up again.

He didn't. Instead, McBride forced himself to drive slowly and carefully, keeping a careful eye on any car that seemed suspicious. They all did. The steady beat of his wipers added a background beat, weaving in and out of his fluctuating heartbeat. He was sweating heavily by the time he arrived at the Waverly Shopping Center.

He turned in cautiously, edging across the curb and looking around in puzzlement. The small shopping center lot was surprisingly full. Having been to Waverly previously only at night, McBride was momentarily stunned to see so many cars. One looked out of place: a black limousine with a driver standing at attention by its front door. Willis? McBride had thought. No, he would not be so obvious. McBride kept the long black car in his field of vision as he found a parking spot across the lot from the animal hospital.

He got out slowly. It was not raining in Rancho Cucamonga, but the sheen of an earlier shower made everything glisten. McBride felt almost caught in a spotlight and picked up his pace to get into the hospital as quickly as possible and out of view.

The waiting room held a variety of pet owners, waiting patiently with cats, birds and a ferret, but no dogs. He nodded hello as eyes turned expectantly toward him. He awkwardly bobbed his head a moment, then glanced at the receptionist. She recognized him and immediately buzzed him inside.

Santiago was not there to greet him. Instead, she was in the treatment room with a young child along with an older woman and a small, green iguana. She glanced up, saw McBride, and held up a hand to stop him. He waited.

She spoke to the young girl, who was listening intently.

"Honey," Santiago said, "Rocky here has abraded his nose trying to get out of his cage. It looks like he's been ramming his face up against a brick wall!"

"Oh," the girl had moaned. "Can you help him?"

"I'll get some information for you," Santiago said.

She stepped out of the room. "You look awful," she whispered to McBride.

"I've been ramming my head into a brick wall, too," he replied.

She ran a hand through his hair and straightened the collar of his dress shirt. "Wipe your face," she said. He complied with a handkerchief. "I wish you had stood closer to the razor when you shaved." He didn't say anything, but tried to straighten his shoulders. "Well," Santiago finally said with a twinkling smile, "just like Rocky, we'll get you a big feast of some mealworms and some vitamin supplements and you should be on the road to recovery!"

"Are you going to tell me what's going on?" he asked. The smile quickly disappeared from her face.

"Go to my office," she responded. "There's someone there to see you."

With that, she spun away to a rack of pamphlets, grabbed one, and hurried by him. "Here you go, Amanda," she said, offering one to the little girl.

McBride didn't wait for the child's response. Instead, he started toward Santiago's office. His shoes left wet imprints on the linoleum. The office door was closed. He tried to turn the knob, but it was locked. He stepped back. Then, he knocked. In a moment, he heard a click from the inside. The door slowly opened a few inches onto a dark interior.

"Dr. McBride?" a low voice asked. No one was visible.

"Yes," McBride had answered before he could think. His back stiffened—should he have identified himself? He hadn't expected a confrontation, but quickly steeled himself. The door was opened to allow him inside. For a moment, the hall light revealed the silhouette of a man well over six feet tall with shoulders broad enough to hang curtains from. McBride stepped inside. The man closed the door, sending the room into almost complete darkness. Only a small stream of light managed to wiggle through the closed window blinds and the lace curtains. That was enough for McBride to see the tall man move to a chair turned to face across the room.

"Sit here," the man commanded.

McBride complied. His eyes slowly adjusted to the dim light. He suddenly realized a third entity was sitting across from him. The man had a lit cigarette in his hand and took a puff. The light from the glowing cigarette briefly illuminated his face. Then, just as quickly, the image vanished. No one said anything. McBride tightened his hold on the chair. He was puzzled but not yet frightened. He trusted Santiago and was sure the smoking man was not Willis or one of his cronies. Santiago wouldn't have set him up. Still, he had no idea who his hosts were and why they were in Santiago's office. He took several deep breaths, feeling his pulse rate taper off a little. His head cleared.

The room was deathly quiet. McBride could even hear someone's shoes clicking down the hallway. They sounded enormous in the weighty silence. The big man across from McBride blew more smoke for a second or two.

"I…" McBride started. A hand fell on his right shoulder. He stopped talking.

"Un momento. I waited for you, Senor Doctor," a deep voice with a Latino accent said. "You can wait for me."

McBride did not reply. He could smell the acrid scent of tobacco mixing with the light perfume that marked Santiago's presence anywhere. It lingered in her office while she saw patients and was refreshed upon her return. Ordinarily, the scent was comforting, alluring even, but complicated by the stink of tobacco, it seemed foreboding. It smelled like treason.

Something about the man across from McBride was menacing but his face remained hooded by the darkness in Santiago's office. Heavy-set with a large frame, thick limbs, and a massive neck and head, he filled the small visitor's chair completely, overwhelming it. For a few moments, McBride heard only the sound of the man breathing. He coughed once or twice. The tall man beside McBride seemed to have vanished into nothingness. McBride could no longer feel his presence.

The cigarette was stubbed into an ashtray on Santiago's desk. Then, the man sat up. The man's tall companion sprang to life from some dark shadow, hurried across the room and lit another cigarette. The original flash of light was concealed by the tall man's body and quickly faded away. Only the red tip of the cigarette was clearly visible. Whenever the man raised it to his lips, McBride was rewarded with the quick image of thick jowls, a dark mustache and sullen dark eyes. He also had a brief sense that the man was wearing a very expensive suit.

"I am not here," the man in the dark office growled. He face was wreathed in shadows, and his big hands, clearly visible, hugged the sides of the chair. "I must protect myself."

McBride swallowed and leaned forward in his chair. He did not speak. When the man spoke, he used abrupt sentences as if used to being obeyed and unused or unwilling to listen to anyone else's point of view.

"Que comprende? Do you understand?" the man said.

McBride nodded at first, then realized the man probably could not see the gesture. "Si," he answered slowly.

The man stubbed out the second cigarette. They were now in almost complete darkness. "Maria has asked me to help you," the man said. "Qué quieres?"

McBride took another deep breath. That was not an easy question. What could this man do? Create a cure for the dog flu? Force Novilis to admit the truth and stop the government from mandating vaccinations? He was obviously a bigwig in the Latino community, someone with the raw muscle to accomplish something requiring a direct approach. That left only one likely possibility.

"Someone needs to reach a trusted Congressman or Senator, to let them know why the dogs are dying," McBride said.

The proposal hung in the air, floating along with the tobacco smoke and the somber hint of danger.

"I am told that it is a flu that is deadly to dogs," the man responded coolly.

"The flu exists," McBride said, "but that's not what is killing them."

The man shifted, suddenly showing interest. "Hablar conmigo," he demanded.

McBride did. He described his research and how the virus had jumped from humans to their pets. He did not try to detail the evidence. The man probably would not understand. Instead, McBride talked as if speaking to a student at office hours or a new colleague joining a research team.

"Why do you think Novilis is not telling the truth?" the man asked. He gave a low chuckle. "No, do not answer. I understand. The company does not want blame and will lose a lot of money if the truth is known. No es así?"

"Si," McBride replied.

"Bueno," the man said, slowly coming into view as McBride strained to see him. "You will meet with Rep. Gary Stubbs. Me debe favores."

McBride caught the ominous tone in the comment. Stubbs probably owed more than a favor to this man. McBride could imagine why: Stubbs was a Republican in a strongly Democratic Hispanic area. He couldn't have taken office without some powerful assistance in the district.

"Thank you," McBride said, "but I cannot talk to Rep. Stubbs."

The man looked at him. "Maria told me about the e-mails," he said. "Ese es su problema."

McBride arched an eyebrow. "Es un gran problema," he noted.

"Senor Willis has his own weaknesses," the man said. "Everyone does. You are smart man. Find one."

He stood up. McBride was surprise to realize the man was relatively short, but broad. His deep voice made him seem immense. McBride sprang to his feet and extended a hand. The thin man stepped forward, as if to block any contact. The heavy-set man ignored the hand anyway.

"Do not attempt to contact me," he said. "A alguien le llamará."

"Adonde?" McBride asked. He got no answer. The thin man brushed by him to open the door. Then the room was empty.

McBride sat quietly, collecting himself. It took a few moments. He felt clammy, still damp from both the earlier rain and the sweat. Where was this quest to overcome the dog flu taking him? Now, he was getting mired in politics. He shuddered. Still, he felt he had no choice. He would need his research, his notes, his files, anything and everything to show Stubbs. He had some material e-mailed from Novilis to his home computer, but not all the data. It would have to do. Willis certainly wasn't going to volunteer to send him the rest.

He would also have to learn about Stubbs. Not particularly politically oriented, McBride knew nothing about the man other than that he represented this area in Congress. Maybe Stubbs had pets. That would be a good way to break the ice. Maybe his mother could help with this. She lived for a good political debate and, as McBride recalled, didn't have many kind words for Stubbs. Then again, Stubbs was conservative. McBride's mother was sure every conservative was a Satanic figure sent to inflict unjust punishment on kindly, good-hearted incense burning citizens.

"Esta bien?" Santiago asked, poking her head into the office. She flicked on the light.

The sudden brightness made McBride blink. He smiled at her.

"I felt like I was meeting with Deep Throat," he admitted.

"Quien?" she asked.

"Never mind," McBride said. Only a person whose mother loathed Richard Nixon would catch the reference. He told her what happened in the brief meeting.

"He will do what he says," Santiago said. "El es un hombre de honor."

McBride nodded. "He thinks I can neutralize Willis. I don't know how. I'm not sure I can talk to Stubbs under the circumstances."

She thought for a moment. "I will go with you to see Mr. Stubbs," Santiago said and turned away.

McBride started to argue, but realized she wasn't able to hear him and wasn't likely to listen anyway. Boy, Kendra was not going to be happy about this turn of events.

Sitting in his living room soon after, McBride told Kendra about the meeting. No more secrets, he had promised her. So, he filled her in on what he had done that day.

"She insisted on going with you?' Kendra asked.

"You can come, too, if you like," he said sheepishly.

"Sure," Kendra snapped. "I'll leave my job to go talk to some government official."

He tried again to explain how the e-mails forced this situation, but Kendra was not appeased.

"There has to be someone other than her who can go with you," she insisted.

"All right," he conceded. "Who?"

She had no reply but barreled on anyway. "What happens after you talk to Shubbs?" she asked.

"Stubbs," McBride corrected. "I hope he brings it up at the Congressional hearings or goes to the media or does something to get the news out. We have got to stop people from getting these shots."

Kendra sighed. "It's back to that, isn't it? You didn't get credit, so now you want to get even. No more vaccines!" She shook her head. "I bet if your name was on the vaccine, you'd be out there promoting the hell out of it."

McBride stared at the floor. "Kendra," he tried, "it's not about the vaccine. We are talking about the death of millions of dogs. What's going to happen after that? What other animals are going to die? That's what I am raising hell about."

"Nothing has happened so far," Kendra noted.

"Kendra, have you turned on the news lately? Hundreds of thousands, maybe millions of dogs have died. The few that remain are hidden. The President's dog is in quarantine, for God's sake, and the world seems to have lost its mind with grief! What do you mean, nothing?"

"Listen," she said, "I am really upset with what is happening to dogs. Who isn't? We have people in the hospital with all sorts of mental problems because their dogs died. I had a blind man yesterday so used to using a guide dog that he blindly stepped into traffic when he wasn't thinking. It's horrible. But the Rohn flu is worse. You are suggesting stopping a vaccination that, despite its side effects, has been remarkably effective. Millions of people would have gotten Rohn flu and how many would have died? That's just not acceptable."

McBride nodded again. "I agree. I just think the Rohn vaccine should undergo the kind of testing it should have had in the first place, Novilis should be censured for releasing that vaccine and a replacement should be made a top priority. Is that too much to ask considering all that humanity has lost?"

"The genie is out of the bottle," Kendra replied.

"I can't give up," McBride said, "not when I know something is wrong."

"It's Willis, isn't it?" Kendra sniffed and stalked back to the bedroom. "By the way," she called, "take a shower before you get in my bed. You reek of perfume."

In the bathroom, McBride began to question himself about Kendra's comments. Was this personal? Was he trying to attack Willis simply because of what happened back in New York? He hoped not. Wasn't he trying to do something good? His entire life seemed focused around this dog flu that was decimating the canine population. Every day the media was filled with terrible stories about dead dogs and how people were unhinged by the loss of their pets. After the initial traumatic impact, the ripples moved slower, but their impact affected life on earth in broad, far-reaching ways. Wolves, foxes, and coyotes were dying; so were dingoes and every stripe of canine around the globe. Canine Armageddon, the media was calling it. Families had been devastated, and public services had been stretched to the breaking point, but now the long-term ramifications were manifesting. The cost of mutton and wool had gone through the roof as sheepdogs had perished. Thousands of jobs in the dog care and dog food industry had disappeared virtually overnight. Thousands of blind people who had been fairly self-reliant with the assistance of their guide dogs were now burdening public assistance. Farmers were predicting record crop losses to deer now that both their guard dogs and deer's natural predators were gone. Global security had been compromised due to the dearth of drug and bomb sniffing dogs, and there had been a series of terrifying near misses. One trigger-happy aspiring terrorist detonated his device before the plane had taken off. The government classified it as a "minor breach" but it was anything but minor to the families of the four people killed by the blast. And what if the plane had taken off?

With all the drama surrounding the hold left by dogs' global disappearance, the Rohn flu was hardly mentioned anymore. Millions of dollars were being poured into research to find a cure with no success, just enough false promise and auspicious dead ends to keep hopes high and keep the money coming. Should McBride just ignore the truth and let the search continue? Someone would eventually stumble over the same facts linking the dog flu to the Rohn flu. Wouldn't they?

McBride savored the cool water of the shower flowing across his tired body. It would be easier to give up this effort. Kendra would be happy; Willis would not bother him, and would turn his sights on someone else. His job at the clinic would no longer be threatened by his unavoidable absences. He ran a wash cloth across his face. The perfume went down the drain, but not his inner drive to help.

While toweling off, he glanced at himself in the mirror. He had begun doing pushups, as many as he could in the morning and then again, pushing himself till failure in the evening. He told himself it was to relieve stress, but in his heart, he knew it wasn't true. As beleaguered as he was, McBride finally felt alive. He was no longer just a chubby researcher with a chubby girlfriend grinding away in the lab. He was the lonely voice of reason in an insensate world. He was hunted, he was persecuted, but he also finally had a cause and a purpose. He had discovered information that could benefit humanity, and he was charged with getting the truth out there.

He knew couldn't stop. Research was designed to reach a conclusion. He knew no other way than to follow his work to its end.

Maybe Kendra would never understand. McBride didn't know. Their lives had changed, the world had changed, and he had changed. At the moment, Kendra seemed a relic from some distant, more innocent past.

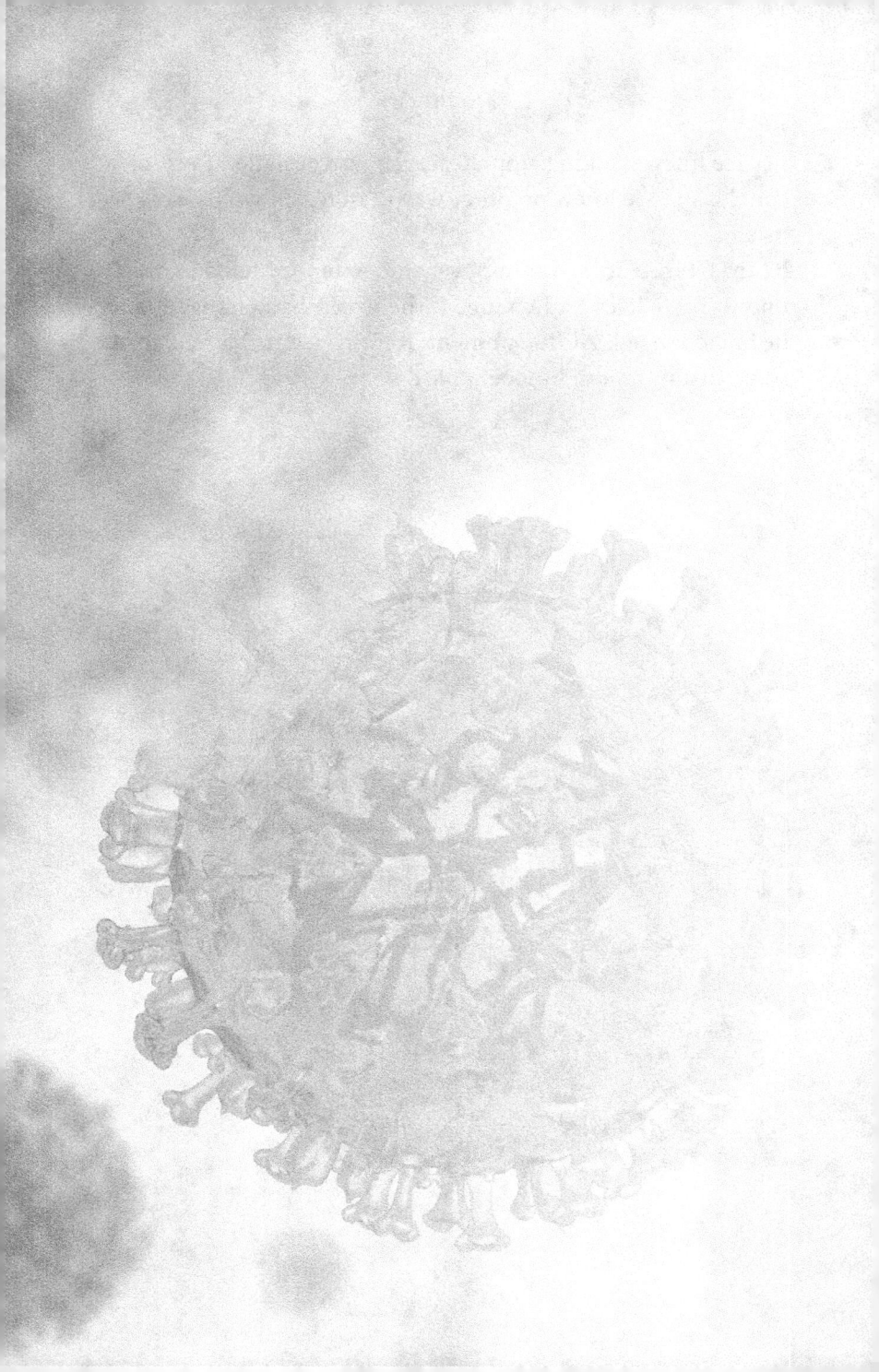

Chapter 19

U pon entering Rep. Stubbs's building in Santa Fe Springs, McBride could feel sweat start to drop down his forehead and prickle under his suit coat. The air conditioning was cranked inside the small headquarters, but he felt strangely hot. He had remained calm during the thirty-minute ride here, relieved that he would finally have a chance to talk to someone in government. Of course, once he found the office on Clark Street and stepped inside, the perspiration started to flow. He could feel it running down his legs, almost pooling in his socks. He was sure it was soaking the folder containing what little research he'd been able to gather.

McBride thought he had e-mailed most of the findings to his home computer, but a frantic search turned up only some preliminary research that had been filed with a misspelled tag. McBride had finally given up his search around three a.m. Staring at the computer, he wondered if Willis had somehow tapped into his computer and removed the data. The line between paranoia and rational suspicion became blurrier every day.

He shifted uneasily in his small plastic chair, feeling as though someone were watching him. In a way, someone was: Rep. Stubbs's clean-shaven, semi-friendly face graced every beige wall. Some of the images were huge, giving a close-up view of his elongated nose and his stolid, thin-lipped mouth. Others were smaller, the kind that usually appeared on placards and signs. He seemed far more benevolent pint-sized, McBride decided.

He glanced at Santiago, who sat beside him, hands folded on her purse in her lap. She appeared so relaxed, composed, and pert with a half smile on her face. She had arrived several minutes after he did. McBride had insisted they drive separately, fearing that Willis might have him followed. If Willis was unaware she was joining him, he wanted to keep it that way. Of course, Willis wasn't the only one tracking McBride's every move.

"Separate targets," he had explained to Kendra.

"Transference," Kendra had scoffed. She had been thoroughly disgusted with him. "You are still angry about getting fired, so you blame Willis. Or you're upset about Rosen or even at poor Dr. Crossland. So now you see bogeymen everywhere. What's next? Aliens?"

"Why not?" McBride replied casually. "After what I've seen, I'm not ruling anything out."

She had thrown her hands up in the air and walked away. He had watched her leave and was surprised to realize that he felt nothing. Should she support him? He had asked himself this on the ride to Rep. Stubbs's office. Why should she believe him? He tried to focus on more positive times, the bliss of their first lovemaking in her apartment, of her obvious excitement at seeing him every day in the lab and the hope and excitement they felt the moment they moved in together into their Pomona home. Now, he felt empty. The blissful memories had been corroded. If he closed his eyes and imagined Kendra, her face was always upset: sour, sullen, disappointed, angry. He found himself apologizing to empty air every time he was about to see her, preparing for yet another in a series of seemingly endless confrontations with her.

Still, Kendra's obvious disappointment had been nothing compared to Rosen's reaction when he told her of his need to leave for the meeting with Stubbs.

"Good thing Lester can cover for you," she had snapped with anger burning in her eyes. Her lips were taut, her fists clenched. It was clear that McBride's time at the clinic was limited. What wasn't falling apart now?

"We're all relieved," McBride had answered sarcastically. He hadn't added that, given his size, Lester could cover most everything, including, apparently, a supper that could easily feed a family of four each night. He was gentle with patients, as far as McBride could tell, but he also lacked the experience to diagnose illnesses efficiently and correctly. The dummy hadn't even seen that a woman with congestion that morning had been simply having an allergic reaction to the ever-present smog.

After quietly enjoying Lester's struggles to help the patient and waiting to be asked for assistance, McBride had finally provided the obvious answer. Lester's eyes narrowed as if he resented the help; then he hurried off to tell the patient the news. McBride watched him go, wondering aloud to Silverstein if the floor of the new office would be able to survive the constant elephantine tread of such a heavyweight. She just winked at him, expressing her agreement without actually saying anything.

Silverstein's camaraderie could not soothe McBride now. His anxiety had become like heavy shackles he dragged with him everywhere he went. His body was wracked with the tension caused by the fire, his deteriorating relationship with Kendra, the fight to get the truth about the dog flu to the public, Rosen's obvious distaste for him, and the constant threat of Willis's evil machinations. He closed his eyes, trying to count backwards slowly to himself, anything to ease his jangled nerves. The sweat continued to flow. His shirt was soaked.

He opened his eyes, searching for a distraction. The office featured only the large room with four desks with a dark corridor leading to a restroom and more offices in the back. McBride could see family portraits on two of the desks; a third had cartoons taped along its side. The fourth contained a young woman and only a couple sheets of paper. Stubbs's campaign motto served as wallpaper, appearing like Daniel's handwriting in the Bible: "Stubbs—That's the Ticket." The message was unrelenting, like the hum of the air conditioning and the McBride's omnipresent uneasiness. The familiar scent of Santiago's perfume was the only thing that brought him even a modicum of comfort.

In a corner of the office, a young woman sat staring at a computer. Because of her light-brown dress, she almost blended into the walls. Each time the phone rang, she would remove her earbuds, answer it briskly, take a note, restore her earbuds, and then resume her staring at the computer. Her name was Gaia, according to her nametag, and she had met McBride cheerily at the door. Rep. Stubbs would be there shortly, she had informed him. He was never late. Minutes later, Santiago had received exactly the same message, word for word, with the same half-laugh at the end.

"It's four thirty," McBride noted under his breath. Santiago looked at the wall clock for confirmation. Their appointment had been scheduled for four.

"Do you think he's actually coming?"

"He will," she said firmly. "El Capataz arranged this." McBride stared at her.

"When El Capataz says he will do something, he does."

"El Capataz?"

She shrugged. "He tells people what to do," she said.

"Maybe Stubbs wasn't listening," McBride countered. "The Man Who Is Never Late is now thirty minutes late. When is he getting here?"

"He will be here," Santiago answered serenely. She was clearly unaffected by the passing time, like someone blithely waiting for a prophet or a promised miracle.

McBride continued surveying the room, trying to soothe his nerves and distract himself from watching the clock. In the corner was a brown bookcase with campaign literature on it. He thought a moment and then decided to pick up a brochure. At least, he would have something to do. He gestured to Santiago. She shrugged.

"Who knows?" McBride whispered. "Maybe we'll get an idea or two from something there."

He got up, placed his file on his chair. Gaia did not react, but occasionally tapped on her keyboard. McBride strolled across the room.

"Is it okay if I take a brochure?" he asked.

Gaia glanced at him. He pointed. She nodded.

"Sure," she said happily. "I have more boxes in the back. Help yourself."

He looked down at the multiple flyers, all festooned with American flags and splashed with red. The same picture of Rep. Stubbs stared back with a winsome expression as though bemused by the attention. One showed him with a woman and two children, presumably his family. A third depicted him speaking behind a podium; in another, he was standing next to former Vice President Dick Cheney.

Idly picking through them, McBride saw something almost hidden to the left of the bookcase under the corner of one of Stubbs's massive signs. A shadow from the bookcase and the angle hid it from clear view: a wicker frame with a rumpled blanket inside. The tiny nest looked familiar but it took him a moment to place it. A dog bed. He stared at it. It was like an artifact from a distant past. For a moment, he thought his mother had transported Canada's bed here. However, there were no candles or empty dog bowl nearby. Still, there was no question of the affection with which it had been arranged: the blanket had been tucked carefully into the edges of the basket, and the area around it was spotless.

Was it a prop, something Stubbs kept here to demonstrate his tie to the suffering dog owners? McBride decided that wasn't logical. The basket was hidden away, almost completely out of sight. Few visitors were likely to see it. Maybe, McBride wondered, Stubbs had owned a dog? He hoped so. That would be a strong way to reach him. There was one way to find out.

"Do you have a dog?" McBride called to Gaia. His voice almost echoed in the otherwise quiet room.

Gaia glanced at him, clearly distracted. "No," she said after a moment's hesitation.

"There's a dog bed over here," he noted.

Gaia did not answer. Instead, she fumbled with the papers on her desk until she found a sheet. Even from his distance, McBride could see it was a list. She read down it, marking each one item with a finger until reaching the bottom. At that point, she checked the list a second time and then simply looked puzzled.

"No," Gaia finally answered. "There is no dog." From her open, smooth features, McBride decided, she must be in high school. She returned to her typing. McBride glanced down at the bed, then at Gaia. He shook his head.

"It looks like a dog bed," he said.

Gaia frowned. She again picked up a piece of paper next to her and read it to herself. "I don't know if I am allowed talk to you," she said nicely, but plainly worried. "I'm not allowed to talk to media." She held up the paper as if they could inspect it at a distance. "I have a list of people I can talk to."

"Oh, no," McBride said. "We're not reporters. I'm a doctor. We both are. Are doctors on your no-talk list?"

Gaia quickly scanned her sheet and seemed to relax. "No," she said. "I guess you're okay." Then, another thought creased her mind. She stared at them. "Rep. Stubbs is all right, isn't he? He isn't sick, is he?" she gushed.

McBride quickly reassured her. "We're not here to examine him," he said. "Besides, Dr. Santiago is a vet."

"Whew," Gaia said. She wiped her forehead. "I was so worried. He's such a good person. I can't imagine him getting sick. Why, the people need him!" She smiled at Santiago. "A vet?"

She read down a different list. "Rep. Stubbs has voted for every veterans' appropriation bill since taking office."

"Has he voted on any issues about dogs?" McBride pressed, not bothering to correct the girl about Santiago's profession as a veterinarian.

"Rep. Stubbs loves dogs," she said firmly.

"Is that why there's a dog bed here?" McBride asked.

"There is no dog here," Gaia replied with strained dignity.

McBride sighed and wandered back to his chair. He picked up his folder and sat down. Apparently he wasn't going to get anything out of this timid girl.

"Miss," McBride called. Gaia looked up with an exasperated expression. "Are you allowed to tell me when Rep. Stubbs is arriving?"

"He will be here shortly. He is never late for an appointment," Gaia repeated the mantra from her earlier greetings.

"We had a four o'clock appointment," McBride noted.

Gaia glanced at the clock. "He will be here shortly. He is never late for an appointment," she said again despite the fact that Stubbs was now clearly over half an hour late.

"Are you a volunteer, dear?" Santiago asked.

"Or a replicant," McBride muttered under his breath.

Gaia shook her head. "I am a full-time employee. I have a degree in political science from UCLA," she announced proudly. "This is my first job. I'm hoping someday to manage a big campaign. Ms. Geller isn't here right now. She normally runs the office. She left me directions about what to do." She seemed very proud of herself.

If anything, her whimsical attitude helped McBride calm down. Maybe, he thought, Gaia might provide some insight into Stubbs before the meeting. At least, they were talking to each other.

"I voted for Rep. Stubbs in the last election," McBride lied easily. He had been living in New York when that election took place, but Gaia didn't know that. Deceit had gotten much easier for him over the last six months.

"That's great," Gaia said. "A lot of people did."

"I liked his position on gun control," he continued. What Republican didn't have a position on that topic?

"Yes," Gaia continued. "Many people do. He is a proud member of the NRA." She found another sheet of paper. "The right to bear arms remains an inviolate Constitutional right," she recited, stumbling over "inviolate" so that it sounded like the Second Amendment took place in a small purple flower.

"Do you have a list of his positions?" McBride asked.

"Yes, sir," Gaia said. "I'm putting them on line right now. You can read them if you want." She walked over with the sheet, then paused. "I think," she added.

"You are putting them online, right?" McBride coaxed. Gaia nodded.

"Then, he must want everyone to be able to see them."

His logic convinced her. She handed him a neatly typed paper. Each of maybe a dozen headings was followed by a sentence or two explaining Stubbs's position on each topic.

"Thanks," McBride said. He scanned it quickly. Nothing on H1N1 or the dog flu. "I don't see any mention of the Rohn Flu vaccine," he noted.

"I think he's in favor of it," Gaia said, "but don't quote me on that!" She checked her sheet and bit her lip. "Of course, he may have voted against it. I can check with him when he gets here." She looked up with bewilderment in her eyes. "Maybe he didn't take a position on that topic."

"It doesn't matter," McBride assured her. She smiled appreciatively. From this distance, he could see she was older than he originally thought, but not by much. Wearing a big Stubbs's button on her lapel, she had added dark mascara and extended her eyelashes to make herself appear older, but the smooth cheeks and unlined forehead gave stronger evidence of her youth.

"How about what is happening to dogs?' he asked.

"I don't think he's in favor of that," Gaia said seriously. "He was very upset when Pookie died." She leaned over and, in a conspiratorial whisper, said, "That's whose bed is over there. It's not on my list of approved topics, so I can't talk about him."

Santiago straightened. "Pookie?" she whispered back.

"His pug," Gaia explained in a soft voice. She glanced around as if someone might overhear her. "Rep. Stubbs used to bring Pookie to the office before he got sick." She lowered her voice even more. "I didn't like Pookie. He got really upset when strangers came in and used to mess the floor. He bit people, too. Don't tell Rep. Stubbs I said that."

"That will be our secret," Santiago assured her. Gaia giggled.

The phone buzzed. "Oh," Gaia squealed and ran back to answer it. "Yes, sir." She looked up. "Rep. Stubbs will see you now." She smiled triumphantly. "I told you he would be here."

McBride glanced at the clock: four forty-five. For politicians, "punctuality" must fall into the same subjective category as "truth," McBride decided.

Gaia led them down a short hallway in the back. The rear door was sealed, but Stubbs must have entered unseen from that direction. Beyond the bathroom were offices on each side, both with doors closed. She knocked on the door to the right and went in. A moment later, she re-emerged.

"This way, please," Gaia intoned in what presumably was her attempt at a professional manner. She stepped aside so they could enter.

McBride suddenly felt cold. The sweating stopped abruptly. He took several short breaths, the way he had before meeting with Willis. That was the wrong memory to conjure right now. This was different, he told himself. Stubbs was his first real chance to do something. The flu was continuing to devastate the diminishing canine populations worldwide. No one knew what to do. He had felt so helpless, up until now. He straightened his shoulders and took a firm grip on his file. He had stood up to Willis. He could do the same with Stubbs.

Stubbs was standing behind his large wooden desk. The room was bright with overhead neon lights augmented by a floor lamp stationed behind Stubbs. The light seemed to create an aura around the representative, projecting his image forward. The desk was covered with paperwork in neat, organized piles. The in-basket was stuffed; the out-basket had even more. A large picture of Stubbs stared at his guests from one wall. The rest of the office was thickly varnished wood paneling, garishly reflecting the glaring light.

Blinking, McBride extended a hand across the desk. Stubbs shook it artfully, avoiding crushing McBride's hand while giving the impression of strength. Standing this close, McBride realized the representative was definitely older than his pictures made him seem, with thinning brown hair and deep lines etched around his hazel eyes. He was about medium height, a few inches shorter than McBride was, with a paunch that gave the impression of wealth, power, and a soft life. Although his navy blue suit was clearly expensive and perfectly tailored, it could not disguise his rounded shoulders and less-than-robust appearance. An ashtray on his desk was almost full, and the stale scent of tobacco lingered in the still air. He clearly had been there awhile and had not allowed the meeting to start on time. Had Stubbs expected them to leave in frustration?

He also noticed something else: Stubbs was not relaxed. Tension had spread across his face. He kept his shoulders straight and seemed somehow to be backing away even as he shook hands.

"Please," Stubbs said with a thin, nasally voice, "make yourselves comfortable. I had expected only Dr. McBride." He sat down.

McBride quickly introduced Santiago as his colleague. They shook hands, too. Stubbs clearly felt outnumbered and already had his hackles up. Well, fine. McBride and Santiago sat down.

"So how can I help you?" he asked with his hands pressed together in front of him. The question was directed to McBride, though McBride couldn't dismiss the feeling that Stubbs wasn't actually seeing him.

"As you know, sir," McBride began calmly enough, "many dogs are dying. All of us are very concerned. Since you had a dog, I am sure you are, too."

"Of course." Stubbs was direct, almost abrupt. His face stayed rigid, like a card player disguising any tells. However, McBride was puzzled– Stubbs was showing no indication of interest. This meeting clearly was just an obligation to him. El Capataz may have unlocked the door, but Stubbs obviously felt forced to be here. He was going through a familiar ritual; that was all.

"As you also know, the vaccine for the dog flu has not been working," McBride continued. He smiled, trying to get some flicker of response. He could feel the sweat starting to slide greasily down the sides of his chest.

"That's why we are holding Congressional hearings," Stubbs interjected, as if talking to a child. "You may not be aware that I'm on the House committee that will be working on legislation to protect dogs."

"Actually, I am," McBride said quickly. Stubbs stiffened even more as if stung by the response. "I have been studying this disease and have brought some of my research. I have information that I believe is vital for your committee and the public to know." He held out the file. His hand trembled.

"Thank you," Stubbs said. "Leave it here. I will be very pleased to take it with me to Washington." He took the file and, without even glancing at it, placed it on the top of the "Out" file on his desk.

McBride watched Stubbs's nicotine-stained fingers retreat back behind his desk. He felt his stomach sink. "Don't you want me to go over it with you?" he finally gasped. He could tell they were being dismissed; his carefully prepared folder of research was going nowhere but Stubbs's circular file.

"He is an incredibly talented researcher who has some compelling discoveries," Santiago added.

"We have excellent researchers working on this," Stubbs said coolly. "I am sure they will be glad to review Dr. McBride's studies."

There was a long stretch of silence. Finally, McBride burst out, "You are really don't care, do you?"

Santiago brushed his left leg with her hand, signaling him. She was too late.

"I am always interested in my constituents and their concerns," Stubbs said smoothly in practiced tones. "I take all concerns brought to my attention with enormous interest. I also care about dogs. I was saddened by the loss of my dog. I join with the Americans around this country who mourn the loss of their dogs and look to the government for an answer. However, as you must be aware, I must rely on expert evidence to reach the best conclusion." He smiled through gritted teeth. "I have been in regular contact with Surgeon General Dr. Charles Witherspoon and Dr. Lauren Jessence from CDC, and I have great faith in their expertise. Perhaps you should contact them to share your data." He gave a quick nod and stood up. "Thank you for coming in. I am sorry, but I have another appointment," he said, extending a hand. "I try very hard not to keep my appointments waiting."

"Sir," McBride said, startled by the abrupt ending, "I don't think you are taking us seriously."

Stubbs's faced hardened. "Dr. McBride, I'm afraid I must ask you to leave or I'll have to call security."

"What, your padded brassiere at the front desk has a gun?" McBride snapped.

Stubbs put his hands on his hips. "Please, don't make this a safety issue," he said.

McBride stood up. Santiago grabbed his arm. He looked down at her. She was shaking her head. He stopped.

"Please wait outside for me," she said.

"But…" McBride tried.

She shook her head. "Esta bien," she said.

McBride buttoned his suit coat. "I'll be right outside," he said. He shot one look at Stubbs and headed into the main office. Gaia was still there, but ignored him. Looking through the front window, he could see a police car parked in front. The officer was on the radio inside the vehicle. McBride stepped into the dwindling sunlight. He stared at that car. What was going on? Why had Stubbs, after having granted the interview, refused to give them a chance? He tried to make sense of what had happened, but could not. How had the meeting deteriorated so fast? What could Santiago do?

The policeman was clearly watching him. McBride stood in front of the headquarters' brick exterior. He wished he had something to do to look like he belonged there. He felt scruffy, exposed, like some street person who knew how society looked down on him.

The cruiser door opened, and the policeman emerged. A burly man in a short-sleeved uniform with powerful arms clearly visible, he straightened his belt and walked around the back of the car to approach McBride.

"Can I see some identification, sir?" he asked in an authoritative tone.

Still outraged by Stubbs and the meeting, McBride started to retort something about a police state, but resisted his impulse. Glaring fiercely, he retrieved his wallet and gave the cop both his driver's license and his ID from the clinic. The cop took them back to his car and called them in as McBride watched. In a few moments, the officer came back and returned the cards.

"You might want to move on, sir," the cop said.

"My colleague is inside meeting with Rep. Stubbs," McBride said through clenched teeth. "I'm waiting for her."

"Rep. Stubbs is the person who contacted us," the cop said. He widened his stance and placed his hands on his waist above the gun on one side and a Mace holder on the other. The leather straps holding both items in his belt had already been unsnapped.

"My God," McBride replied, feeling anger surge within. "He called you before we even met!"

"Please move on," the cop replied. "Don't make this any harder than it has to be."

"Can I sit in my car?" McBride asked.

"You can't stand here," the cop said firmly.

"Fine," McBride said. "I don't want to be associated with Stubbs anyway." He walked up the street to where his car was parked. There were still thirty minutes left on the meter. He leaned against the car, arms folded. Well, shit, maybe his mother was right. She never trusted Republicans and couldn't say anything nice about a single one of them. As far as she was concerned, they were the devil's spawn, undermining the country with their hypocrisy and lies. The son of a bitch had called the cops on him before he even set foot in the office? McBride seethed. What could be more disingenuous than that? The man was definitely evil.

He was still fuming when Santiago appeared. She stepped outside the office and looked in both directions before spotting McBride. The cop simply watched her. As she walked away, he said something into the radio attached to his shoulder epaulet.

"What the hell were you…" McBride started as soon she reached him, stopping short when she held up a small hand. She had beautiful fingers, delicately tapered but strong.

"Luego," she said calmly. She climbed into the car and sat there, purse and hands on her lap, with the same serenity she showed waiting in Stubbs's office.

McBride pulled away from the curb. He drove down Clark past the cop, who ostentatiously turned to watch them.

"Slow down," Santiago told McBride. He complied. There was no reason to add a speeding ticket to the evening's problems. He saw the entrance to I-605 and merged into the traffic heading northwest.

"Qué sucedió?" he asked quietly, speaking over the wind now cooling the car as it seeped through the partially opened driver's window.

"Nada mas," she replied. "He was afraid of you."

McBride did not look at her, but was stunned. "Me?" he muttered. "What did I ever do that would make him afraid."

"You have two police reports on file."

"Police reports? That's ridiculous! No one has made a report against me."

Santiago took a deep breath. "He showed me," she said sweetly. "Wasn't there some kind of riot at your mother's apartment? Didn't the police have to come to your house?" She glanced at him. "No?"

"Yes," McBride almost shouted in frustration, "but I wasn't arrested. I was…" He stopped. What was the point? He took the next turnoff, Washington, and stopped at a gas station just off the exit. He rolled into a corner, away from the pumps, and pried his hands off the steering wheel. They were shaking with anger, frustration and the cold fury of disappointment. After a moment, he looked at her.

"This would be funny if it weren't so awful," he said.

"Dígame," she said calmly.

He did, slowly and completely. She listened. He found himself staring at the soft curl of her lips, the gentle slope of her chin. She was so pretty. He continued talking, but his mind started to drift.

"Suena possible," Santiago murmured when he finished. "Who would do such a thing?"

He felt drawn into her brown eyes, which suddenly seemed so deep and pure. He leaned towards her, inhaling her soft perfume and feeling irresistibly drawn toward her.

"No se," he told her. She gave him an encouraging glance, coyly turning her head away and then looking back.

"Realmente?"

"No," he admitted. "I am sure Willis is doing this. He has the ability to access any records and change them, or to bribe people to do it for him." He leaned back and stared at the ceiling. "You probably think I'm paranoid, too."

"No," Santiago answered. She patted his hand. "I believe you."

He turned to face her. "Thank you," he said. His voice cracked. "No one else seems to."

"I have no choice," she said. "You seem to be the only one who knows the truth."

He forced himself to concentrate on the problem, although Santiago remained a delightful distraction. "What did Stubbs say?" he asked.

"He suggested I watch the committee hearing on CNN or C-Span," Santiago reported. "Then, he came around the desk and wondered aloud if I had time for dinner."

"He's married," McBride burst, surprising himself by his response.

Santiago did not react. "I doubt that has been a concern for a man like him," she said.

"Can El Capataz get us into that hearing?" McBride asked.

Santiago shook her head. "He has many friends, but only here in California. He has no influence in Washington," she said.

McBride slumped back in his seat. "Now what?" he asked no one in particular.

"Perhaps, we can go to Washington anyway," Santiago teased. "I told Senor Stubbs that I would love to see him in action. Then, maybe, I might be available for dinner," she said lightly. "He told me that he would be sure I got a seat at the hearing." She pulled out an envelope. She had scrawled "Rayburn Congressional Office Building, directly across the street from the Capitol" along with a date and time.

McBride stared at her. "Santiago! I could kiss you," he said hoarsely.

She turned to face him. "Por qué no?" she asked.

McBride couldn't think of a reason; he couldn't think. And so, finally, he gave in and her lips yielded softly under his.

Chapter 20

M cBride stood helplessly on the corner of Independence Avenue and First Street S.E. with the US Capitol Building to his right. Despite the early morning darkness, he could still clearly see the Rayburn Building, a large, classical structure covered in white marble with an array of thick concrete columns in front. It towered above the throng collected around it. However, there was no way to get anywhere close to it for the hearings. A sweaty, boisterous, shoving mass of people clogged the wide street, flowing over the concrete stairs in a massive clamoring tide of humanity. They clung to the statues on either side of the wide main entry, smothered the sidewalks and crammed into every available space, singing, screaming, shouting, holding up signs decrying the death of dogs.

One large group wore red t-shirts labeled "Canine Defense League." They were interspersed through the crowd. Red seemed to be the chosen color of the cause, creating from a distance the impression that the crowd was rapidly bleeding out. Others in the huge crowd had T-shirts with images of specific dogs on their shirts or carried signs emblazoned with disturbing pictures of mounds of dead dogs emblazoned with inflammatory words like "holocaust" and "murder." One man even carried a huge, heavy cross with a Scooby Doo stuffed animal drenched in red paint nailed to it like Jesus Christ. Had the world gone mad?

Here and there, television reporters had set up with their mobile transmitters, talking into cameras, interviewing people and fending off attention-seekers as well as a few eager to interfere. The tall antennae on top the vans stretched about the crowd like the feelers of giant insects. McBride passed by one reporter who had not been able to get any closer to the hearing either.

"This is," she was saying, "the largest group of protestors to hit Washington since the Vietnam War." She looked around. "They are often somber, mostly orderly, here to rally Congress to do something about the death of their beloved pets." Then, she stuck her microphone in the face of the closest upset person for a sound bite.

McBride quickly shied away before being targeted, inching on, finding small cracks in the throng, leading Santiago forward. He realized Independence was too packed for much progress, but there was also no point trying to find a side entrance to the Rayburn Building, the site of the hearings. McBride could see that side streets, South Capitol and First Street S.W., were equally packed. People there were simple not moving, packed together by the limited space almost to the point of embracing.

All around him, he could hear fragments of loud conversations as people shouted to be heard above the noise. They were one-upping each other with tragic stories about their pets or devising elaborate schemes to solve the problem. Each was sure exactly what must be said to the officials conducting the hearing and positive of their facts. Their bravado was undiminished by the fact that none would actually get a chance to speak to anyone with the power to effect change. As everyone was well aware, only a handful would even get inside the hearing room. However, most thought their presence would add pressure on lawmakers to respond.

Some enterprising vendor with a large, decorated truck had set up shop in the rear, dispensing food to new people steadily arriving to add to their presence and their voices to the throng. People hurried in on foot, departing cabs and even chartered buses. Their concerned faces disappeared into the spreading mass, their voices adding incrementally to the roar of the crowd.

The cab that brought McBride and Santiago had gotten no closer than a mile away. The two of them had walked a few hundred yards until completely blocked by the growing mob. Now, in complete frustration, McBride stopped trying to wedge his way forward. He could see no opening anywhere as people pressed together, bound in their mutual sadness and anger. The close quarters and shared grief appeared comforting to many who were crying openly. A few had broken down completely amid the massive crowd, heads down, weeping.

"It would be nice to see the statues in front of the office building," Santiago said in McBride's ear. "I have been hearing about them for years."

"That may have to wait for our next sightseeing trip. I can't imagine that we're going to get close enough to see them this time around," McBride countered bitterly.

Santiago remained so unaffected by what was happening. He was tied in knots, and her placidity baffled him, occasionally winding him up even more. Throughout the long flight across the country, the day in a hotel planning and preparing, the anxiety over the eventual confrontation and the carefully thought-out timing so they would arrive early enough to obtain two of the available two hundred seats in the hearing room, McBride had imagined final vindication for everything he had endured. Instead, it had all been a complete waste of time, just more insult on top of injury on top of insult. The citizen army in front of him would have to represent his concerns. Of course, none of its foot soldiers had done an ounce of any research on the dog flu but, fueled by sadness and frustration, they were determined simply to get within a half mile of the well-publicized hearings on the terrible disease, thereby keeping the one person with the information needed to unravel the crisis far away.

"They are ten-foot marble statues by C. Paul Jennewein. One is called the Spirit of Justice. The other represents the Majesty of Law," Santiago read from her guide book, nearly crushed to her chest. "Inside, there's a six-foot bronze statue of Sam Rayburn, an oil portrait, and a marble relief."

"Must you?" McBride snapped. He rubbed his forehead. He was getting a fierce headache from the endless noise. A gray dawn began to break across the dark skies, adding to his sense of doom. The hearing was due to start at ten a.m. By then, McBride figured, they might have forced their way only a few yards closer. That would not be good enough.

"Perhaps we can find a policia," Santiago said.

"Sure," he said sarcastically. "With my 'police reports,' maybe we can get an escort into the hearing."

"Algo es possible," Santiago answered.

She began to edge through small openings between people to her right, slowly worming toward the sidewalk. There was less resistance in that direction, and McBride reluctantly followed. He was glad she was calm, but she had no substantial worries. Her job was secure; she was part owner of the veterinarian clinic. Her partners would cover for her while she was away. Her only real concern was the devastating effect of the dog flu.

His situation was far more complicated. McBride had lost his job. He knew that would happen the moment he told Rosen of his plans. He had waited until the end of the day after the last patient had left. Rosen went into what was now her office. He followed her in. She had been sitting behind the desk. Unlike Crossland's old office, she had eliminated any sign of a human touch save one picture of her cat placed on the desk. Otherwise, the walls were bare. Her chair was small and simple, far removed from the overstuffed leather seat Crossland had preferred.

McBride cleared his throat. She glanced up at him and then continued typing on her computer. "Yes?" she finally said.

Her simple one-word query had elicited a long response from McBride. For a long moment, she had not said anything after he had informed her of his plans to fly to Washington, DC in two days and why. She had simply stared at him.

"A hearing on dog flu," she finally mumbled.

He nodded. He had no illusions what her response would be. However, Rosen had a surprise for him. Slowly, she opened a desk drawer and found a file. She shuffled through the folder until she located a piece of paper. After reading it, she had silently passed it along to McBride. It was a copy of an email she had printed out. "Be aware: Dr. Preston McBride quits jobs abruptly. He left his research position with Novilis without even the standard two-week notice."

Open-mouthed, he had read the note three times. "Where did you get this?" he finally gasped.

"I received an e-mail from their Human Resources Department along with the personnel notice confirming your hasty departure. Quite a scene, from their account," Rosen replied. "Fortunately, Dr. Lester is certainly an adequate replacement in the clinic." She put the paper back in the file. "I have lots of material on you, Dr. McBride. There will be no need for you to return here after your little trip," Rosen had intoned ominously. She then tapped the closed file on the desk as if it were a gavel. The dull thud had sounded to McBride like a heavy door closing forever.

"Any chance I can get a look at that file?" McBride asked.

"In court, if it comes to that," Rosen said, adding icily, "Just close the door behind you." With that, she returned to her typing as if he was already gone.

McBride had felt light-headed as he had walked away. The other nurses glanced over at him, but no one said anything, not even Silverstein. Maybe Rosen had planned this, he thought. He had known something like this would happen someday, but, somehow, was unprepared when it did. He had been unemployed before, and he had survived. Besides, he still had Kendra to rely on. Together, the two of them would find a way to make ends meet until he got back on his feet.

When he arrived home, Kendra had been sitting in the living room, tense and nervous, ostensibly reading the newspaper.

Mostly she was just turning it over and over, flipping pages and folding them back, knowing that she wouldn't find what she was looking for yet still unable to cease looking. She was obviously brimming with nervous energy and every instinct told him it was best to wait to drop this latest piece of bad news but somehow, he couldn't help himself—it was too much for him to bear alone. Sitting beside her on the couch, he told her that he was leaving the clinic, but would be going to Washington DC before looking for a job.

"Washington? Sure, why not? What the hell difference does it make?" she had muttered.

"I don't understand," he said, his stomach already plummeting. Her response had been one of resignation, as if he had given the wrong answer, but one she had anticipated.

She folded up the paper once more, placed it on the floor and stood up. "I'm leaving," she had said. "My mother told me I was an idiot to follow you out to California. She was wrong...but I was wrong, too. I mean, there are so many ways for relationships to fail, for things to not work out. Never in a million years would I have been able to guess that this was how it would happen," Kendra told him, her eyes brimming with tears. "The same plague that has claimed all those dogs has claimed you, too."

No explanation, apology or desperate promise helped, search as McBride did for one that might make an impact. Kendra had made up her mind. "I'm not interested," she had said coldly. "Don't tell me I don't understand. You are putting dogs above our relationship, above your job, above everything," she insisted.

"Kendra, that's just not true," he claimed, reaching for her. She shrank back. "It's not just dogs," he continued. "This disease could spread. It could hurt other animals and maybe even people."

Tears gracing her cheeks, Kendra smiled at him. "Pres, listen to yourself. In the same breath, you tell me that you're not prioritizing this disease over our relationship and then go on to say how dangerous it is. There's not one shred of evidence that this could spread to people. You know better than all the researchers. You know better than the government. You know better than all the studies. You, the great Preston McBride, have all the answers." She had drawn herself up. "I can tell you that you overlooked one thing in your research, oh, brilliant one. You failed to recognize that the relationship between a man and a woman is like a living organism. You neglect it for long enough and it dies. It's dead now, Pres. You can't bring it back to life now. It's already begun to decay."

With that, she stalked into the bedroom and started to pack. McBride heard a suitcase unzipped, drawers yanked open, clothes pulled from the closet. Hangers clanged onto the floor.

He started to follow her into the bedroom, but then caught himself. That was just a reflex—he didn't feel anything. Well, sure, he felt a trace of sadness for the good times they had had together, but if there was a dominant feeling in the anxious void that his mind had become, it was relief. This was the end—no more worrying about it. Even watching her tears and obvious distress had not really moved him. He waited a few moments, then left. He took the car; it was registered in his name, anyway. He had not looked back.

Santiago had already purchased the airline tickets and met him at the clinic. He approached her tentatively, no longer confident and assured. He was beyond overwhelmed. Crisis after crisis kept happening, each successive one before he'd had a chance to deal with the transformation brought on by the last. Everything was happening too fast. His life was no longer something he recognized. He had turned into a ball in a pinball machine, eternally disoriented, bouncing at high velocity from one clanging bumper to another.

Maria had been sitting in her office where the faint smell of perfume pleasantly hid the scents of animals and antiseptics. In the past, seeing her had invariably lifted his spirits. This time, he had simply collapsed in a chair, the same one he had occupied when meeting with El Capataz. Looking at her face as she cheerily told him about the tickets, McBride had not felt close to her either. His emotions needed a rest. He needed to not feel anything about anyone for a while. Like ten years. Most urgently, though, he felt the need for a buffer between himself and any other woman: Kendra, his mother, even Maria.

Of course, that was impossible. A day later, the pinball clanged off another noisy bumper, reversing direction yet again, and he and Maria drove to LAX together, beginning their trip to DC. McBride no longer cared what Willis might do. What could happen that was worse than what had already taken place?

Santiago had chattered about the weather, an occasional bird flying by, the dissipation of the smog, the daft and deft drivers that accompanied them, and some of her more recent patients. She seemed to be trying to fill the empty air as McBride concentrated on the road and his troubled thoughts. Still, McBride had a hard time stringing together a single sentence. Like an engine that is run too hot and too hard for too long, he felt like his mind had just seized up.

They sat side-by-side on the plane, but oceans apart in psychic space. He deliberately rented separate rooms in the hotel. She had not shown any reaction, positive or negative. They had talked into the night but kept their conversation limited to the subject at hand, and their goodnight kiss had been chaste and quick. His feelings for humanity in general and Santiago in specific were not warmed by the experience of becoming hopelessly entwined in a human quagmire after undertaking an exhausting and pointless task.

As McBride followed Santiago, who was delicately inching through the thick crowd, he wondered what would happen to the two of them when this was over. She did not discuss her thoughts. Her focus was exclusively on rescuing dogs from this disease. Even their brief, passionate interlude in the car had seemed strange, almost manipulative in order to keep him helping her rather than because of her feelings. Maybe, he thought, he was simply a means to the end. When this was over, she would simply walk away as she was doing now. She didn't appear to be concerned if he were still in tow; she wasn't bothering to check behind her. He felt his spirits sag even more. Perhaps he needed to stop wondering about what was going to happen to them and start wondering what was going to happen to *him*. For once in his life, Pres had absolutely no projection about what the future might hold. Anything was possible. At this point, Pres would not be surprised if the earth opened up and swallowed him.

Santiago had found a uniformed cop. McBride felt rooted in place, bewildered by the crush.

"Senor," Santiago said to the cop, who was simply watching everyone pass by. Ostensibly, he was guarding the Madison Building of the Library of Congress, but was simply flattened against an empty kiosk in front of the massive structure. The stairway and front portico overflowed with more people.

The policeman gave her a blank expression. His eyes were wide, and he seemed to be staring into the distance.

"Where does a witness go?" she asked.

The cop stared at her. "What?' he mumbled.

"For the hearing," Santiago said patiently. She fumbled in her purse and produced a legal-looking form. McBride leaned over her shoulder to see it.

SUBPOENA
BY THE AUTHORITY OF THE HOUSE OF
REPRESENTATIVES OF THE CONGRESS OF THE
UNITED STATES OF AMERICA
TO: Dr. Preston McBride

You are hereby commanded to appear before the Committee on Natural Resources

Of the House of Representatives of the United States at the place, date and time specified below.

To testify touching matters of inquiry committed to said committee or subcommittee, and you are not to depart without leave of said committee or subcommittee.

The legalese continued. At the bottom of the page was the bold signature of L. Hubert LaCrosse, chairman of the committee.

McBride was now the one stunned. He felt himself pushed into Santiago by people behind him. She stood rock solid and held him up.

"Where did you get that?" he whispered.

"El Capataz," she replied. "Acabo de llenar en."

"Oh, my God," he murmured. He was becoming more impressed with her by the second. There was definitely a lot more happening in that tiny dynamo of a woman than he had estimated. A quick thought crossed his mind. "Does the committee have my name?" he asked.

She shrugged. "Eso no importa. Una vez que usted es adentro, usted tendrá un asiento."

"Won't you be there?"

"Yo sólo tengo uno. Si ellos permiten que mí permanecer, hago."

McBride started to protest. He was discredited. Willis had seen to that. That's why Santiago was here. Still, she didn't have the knowledge he had, nor could she answer the technical research questions. He would have to face the committee and Willis alone and largely unprepared. There was no choice. He hoped she could join him, but if not, he would have to fly solo. That realization gave him new energy. He would get his opportunity, provided that he actually got to the hearing room. Amazing as Santiago's revelation had been, he still could not see how a lone cop could accomplish that miracle.

The officer handed back the subpoena.

"I'm his representative," Santiago said blithely. McBride noticed immediately that she did not lie and claim she was his attorney.

"Yes, ma'am," the cop said. "Please follow me."

He turned. Santiago hooked her arm onto McBride's, and they plowed through the crowd up the Madison Building stairs. A small smile played about her lips, and as she squeezed his arm, McBride's spirits soared. The uniform encouraged people to move aside, even when it seemed that the law of conservation of mass prevented it. Fewer people had gathered at the front of the Madison Building, so there was a little room to maneuver. The cop led them through the building and out the back. They walked onto Constitution Avenue and headed toward the Capitol. Even fewer people had gathered there at that hour, although some CDL protesters were poised by the steps, handing out pamphlets and raising signs. McBride took a proffered flyer and stuck it in his suit pocket.

From there, they took the subway that connected to the Rayburn Building. There were only three cars, each carrying only a couple of people. No one was talking. Once inside the Rayburn, they were led through a security checkpoint to the hearing room. The large brown doors there were closed, and uniformed guards stood in each side.

"Witness," the policeman said.

Like magic, the doors opened before them. All three walked inside. The huge room featured massive ceilings and light ecru-colored walls. A camera was set up on a tripod on one side; a massive flat-screen television was attached to the wall. It had a blank screen. A large-two-tiered dais covered the back wall with empty chairs and microphones. Behind the dais, the wall was covered with rich, brown wood paneling and gold-rimmed purple velvet curtains, creating a dramatic backdrop and focusing gallery members' attention there.

Young men and women in immaculate navy blazers were placing packets of information by each chair on the dais. A large table with more microphones sat facing the dais not more than four or five feet away, leaving ample room for photographers to squeeze into. It had eight empty chairs. Behind the table were five or six rows of gleaming wooden pews, room for two hundred people, provided none had concerns about personal space. A few people were already seated, but the quiet inside the room contrasted strangely with the hubbub outside the building.

McBride felt his breath swept away. Despite the many conversations, he never really expected to be in such a situation, yet here he was. He hoped desperately that he wouldn't make an ass of himself.

A clerk was seated to the far right with various sheets of paper on her desk and a computer. The cop approached her with McBride and Santiago in tow. An older woman with gray hair and a no-nonsense expression, she took the subpoena and typed something into her computer.

"I am sorry," she said, handing back the subpoena. "Dr. McBride is not on the list of approved witnesses for this hearing." She spoke in a stolid, authoritative voice that created a roadblock to any discussion.

"But ..." McBride started, feeling like a child. So close yet somehow always just out of reach. Santiago stepped around him.

"Ma'am," she said with emphasis. "I am Dr. McBride's representative. We have come from California at great expense in response to what we believed was a valid subpoena."

"You may file a request for reimbursement," the clerk responded laconically.

"Could we at least attend the hearing?" Santiago continued. Her accent seemed to have disappeared. "This is of vital importance. Dr. McBride initially helped developed the vaccine for the Rohn Flu. His expertise may be needed."

The clerk looked up at him. "I am not responsible for allotting seats," she said. She turned back to her computer.

"It would be awful if your name was called, and you were not here," Santiago said to McBride, talking loudly so the clerk, cop, and everyone else could overhear. "I cannot believe there has been a problem."

"I am so disappointed," McBride echoed, following her lead.

"Happens all the time," the cop said. "I once brought some bigwig from Sudan. I think it was Sudan. Maybe Surinam. One of those African places. And he wasn't on the list either." The cop laughed. "He just turned around and hightailed it home."

Santiago didn't take the hint. "I think we will stick around, if that is all right, with you, Officer," she said, her eyes glowing warmly up at him.

"I'm not the one in charge of seating," the cop said. "I never figured out how anyone gets a seat in here."

"Maybe they just sit down," Santiago offered.

The cop shrugged. "No skin off my nose," he said.

They found a spot behind the table and sat down. The cop hung around for a few minutes, as if unsure what to do, then departed. Several times, security people came over to check on them, but when Santiago produced the subpoena, they would nod and leave. One ran a metal detector over them in a quick check and allowed them to stay.

McBride felt a surge of panic each time one of the security men drew near, but slowly began to relax. Santiago had done it. Somehow, she had gotten them into the hearing. He was amazed and proud of her. As his depression fled, his warm feelings toward her surged back. He inched closer, making sure his hip was in contact with hers. She patted his hand.

"Feel better?" she asked with a coy smile.

He nodded. "I'm just afraid one of those guys will take a close look at the subpoena, and we'll get bounced out of here."

"Eso no es un problema," she said softly. "It's real."

"How?" McBride began, then answered his question himself. "El Capataz is quite a friend."

"Es mi tio," Santiago replied.

McBride felt relief sweep through him. He was not going to have to confront El Capataz to maintain a relationship with Santiago. He may have to seek the uncle's approval, but that was a lot better than facing a rival suitor.

Once again, she resumed her usual position: purse on her laps, hands folded on it, looking straight ahead.

"I don't know how you can be so calm," he said.

She glanced at him. "Have you ever sat in an immigration office? You sit there for hours. You cannot leave, even to go to the bathroom, because that's when they will call your name. I am very good at sitting."

"I never developed that kind of patience," he said.

"Really," she answered dryly, "I hadn't noticed."

He shook his head and took a deep breath. "Maria...I know I've been impossible lately. I'm trying...I've got a lot on my plate right now. But I will try to be a better person."

She looked at him with both kindness and curiosity. "Lo siento," she said softly.

He had no reply. Somehow, she seemed to understand. There was nothing more to add.

"It doesn't look like we're going anywhere soon," he murmured. "Why don't you tell me how you got here? We've been... involved together for a long time, but, you know, we only ever talk about the dog flu. I trust you completely, but I realize that I hardly know a thing about you."

She knew what he meant and looked at him as if gauging how many details to offer and which ones. "I like your eyes," she finally said. "You have a softness in them. You care. You must have grown up in a loving home."

McBride shrugged, but did not reply. It was a strange environment, with his mother bouncing around from one cause to another. She even marched in a campaign to bring pay toilets to the UCLA campus. No issue escaped her view. His father, of course, was almost entirely out of the picture, even after he had been released. But his shadow had loomed huge over all of them. Neither he nor Nathan turned into axe murderers at least. Maybe that was proof enough that they had come from a "loving home"?

"I guess," he said.

"I did not have such a home," Santiago said. For the first time, he saw pain whisk across her face, but as soon as it had manifested, it was gone. She spoke in a low voice. When she was six, her father had snuck across the border from Mexico. She and her three brothers had cowered in the back of the family truck, fearful of the border patrol. Her father picked artichokes and grapes; her brothers joined him in the hot, dusty fields. She was left alone and began to care for the pets and livestock in and around the migrant camps. In time, people brought her animals. She had found her calling.

Later, when she wanted to become an American citizen, she learned first-hand how dangerous her father's actions had been. She knew long hours of work at low pay, and the constant fear of immigration raids. Yet she had succeeded. In her late teens, she became an American citizen with her parents and two surviving brothers. Then she had attended the Western University of Health Sciences in Pomona and was one of its first graduates of the College of Veterinary Medicine.

"El Capataz protected me," Santiago said.

McBride didn't say anything, but wondered about the relationship. Was El Capataz really an uncle, or someone interested in Santiago for other reasons? Her face disguised her feelings. Instead, she talked laconically, almost reciting. Was she hiding something? She was a beautiful young woman. McBride found it hard to believe she had not been involved in some disastrous relationship as a young woman. Mexican immigrant women, in his experience, married young. He saw enough of them in the practice: twenty-two or twenty-three years old, pregnant, with several children in tow. Maybe she had been married before. El Capataz? That was possible. Or, maybe, she had been his girlfriend, in thrall to an older man who had rescued her from poverty. He wanted to know, but felt the moment was not appropriate. They would need a quiet place, away from this aggravation, to talk and learn about each other.

People were starting to arrive. The doors swung open again and again, allowing brief views of the corridor. Someone sat down next to Santiago. McBride glanced around. The room was filling. One by one, people were going through the security check and being scanned for weapons. Then, they hurriedly took seats, cramming together as if imitating the situation outside. McBride saw many with the CDL t-shirts. No one could carry a sign into the hearing room, but some produced headbands or armbands to express their messages. Faces were grim, lips set. There wasn't a lot of conversation, only a quiet undertone infused with angst.

"What can they do?" a tanned elderly man to McBride's right said to the woman on his other side, "Pass a law to make dog flu illegal?"

"They're talking about quarantine," she replied.

"They've waited too long," someone in the row behind chimed in.

"They have to do *something*," the woman said.

"It's all over the world," someone else said. "If we quarantine dogs here, we won't stop the disease somewhere else."

"Maybe someone else has a solution," another man added.

"Shhh!" several voices urged together.

The room stilled, and a gray-haired man in a suit slowly walked onto the dais from a side door. He sat down behind a sign identifying him as Waycross Brimfield, a representative from Tennessee. Ignoring the crowd, he began to read over his packet of materials. One by one, other representatives followed him.

McBride felt his pulse pick up. The hearing would be starting soon. His opportunity was coming. He closed his eyes and tried to think calm thoughts. Only a few more moments, he told himself.

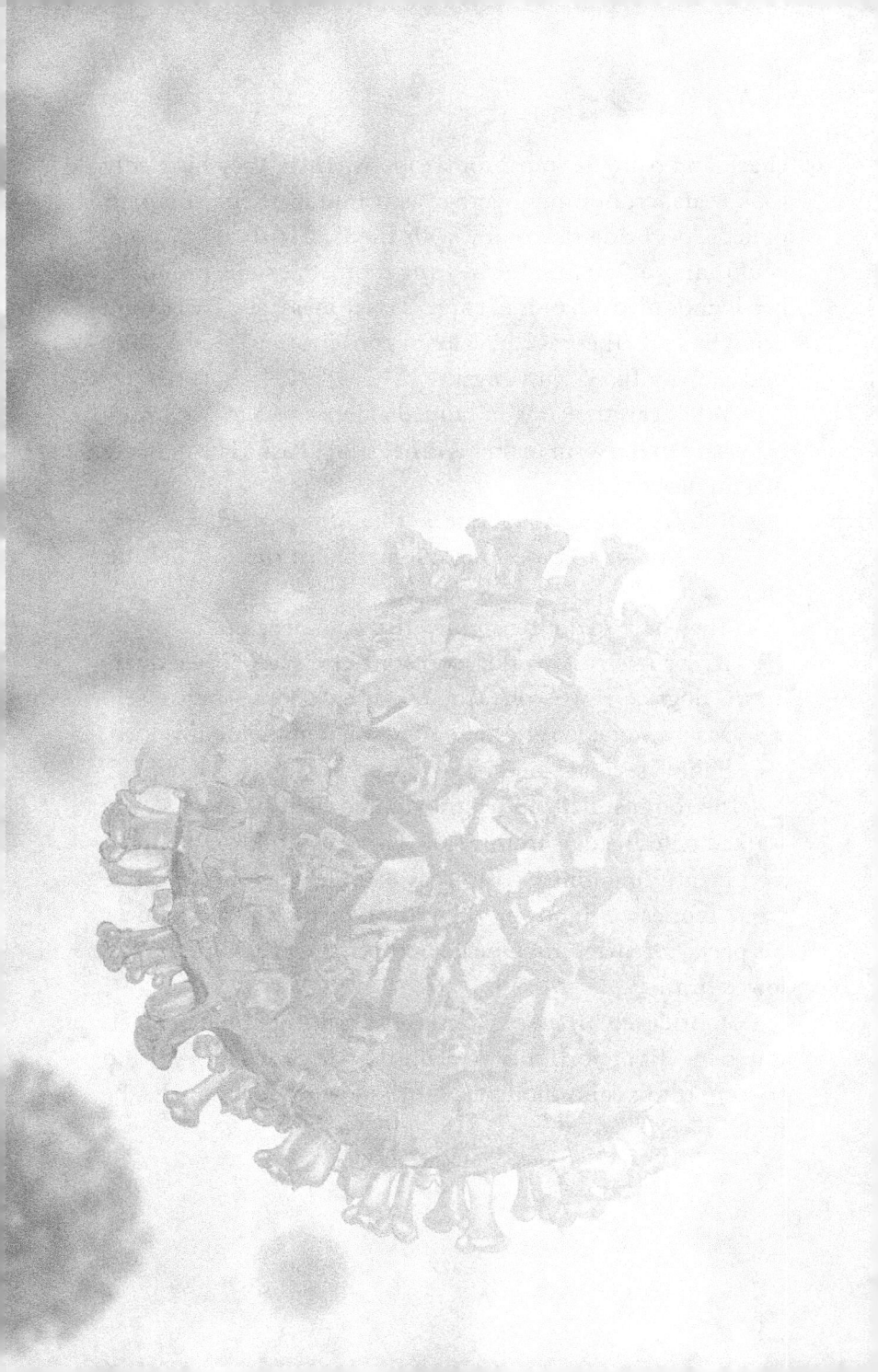

Chapter 21

Slowly, the dais began to fill up. One by one, representatives found their seats. They seemed to know where to go; none checked their metallic nameplates set in front of them. McBride watched their unhurried arrival with great interest. The committee was a mixed bag of young and old elected officials, male and female, black, white, and Latino. The old, tanned man next to him explained that this committee had not been considered prestigious so membership had been reserved for newcomers and those being punished by the leadership. Now, with attention focused on the dog flu, the committee members had been thrust into the spotlight. Most were unknown nationally; many were barely recognized in their own districts. Great, McBride thought, a concentration of inexperienced and resentful legislators under extreme scrutiny and pressure, just another wildly unpredictable variable.

He studied the nameplates set up in front of each seat. None of the people represented there had any kind of positive reputation, starting with the chairman, L. Hubert LaCrosse, who was seated front and center. He was a portly, white-haired man with an ill-fitting suit and a rumpled expression. McBride had never heard of him, but the woman behind him had and cheerlessly brayed her information to anyone who cared to listen. An eight-term congressman from Montana, the woman said, LaCrosse was given to long-winded speeches exceedingly short on useful content. His seniority had earned him a committee chair; his tendency to be a gasbag had relegated him to this one.

"Anyone want earplugs?" the woman asked factitiously.

Just what they needed, McBride thought, yet another politician enamored with the sound of his own voice both for its own sake and as a means of forestalling actually doing something to help his constituency. McBride did recognize Samuel Frissen, a representative from Utah, but only by name. His mother hated him, he recalled, which may or may not be a bad thing. A thin, wizened creature with a bald head and gleaming, beady eyes, Frissen was an anti-abortion advocate with a long history of opposing nearly every cause Maggie had favored. She placed Frissen right next Sen. Jonas Lavermore, the ultraconservative Republican from South Carolina whose support of the tobacco industry, the National Rifle Association, anti-abortion activists, and the death penalty won him a seat in her specific, but well populated, hall of infamy. His mother never mentioned either politician without the same grimace she wore when caught in a particularly noxious smog bank.

Actually, McBride decided, from a distance, Frissen looked fairly innocuous, more like an old man who had accidentally wandered into something simultaneously important and incomprehensible. A frown was etched into his thin face, and he kept looking around as if wondering how he could quickly get out of this predicament. Whether malign or just ineffective, he wasn't going to contribute much to solving the problem.

Rep. Stubbs was among the last to arrive. Looking dapper, he sat down on the far right of the dais and, unlike the others, did not pick up his packet. Instead, he scanned the crowd. He saw Santiago, and his face lit up. As if suddenly realizing his position, he straightened his shoulders and began to read. Stubbs kept up this ruse for only a few seconds before he began peering at Santiago surreptitiously. McBride watched him with rising disgust. He was tempted to put his arm around Santiago, but desisted. This was no time for a display of jealous insecurity.

A moment later, a troop of eight well-dressed men and women came marching into the room and sat at the table. McBride held his breath. There was Willis, dressed in a dark suit and bearing a serious expression that spoke of both sincerity and power. He busily directed people to seats behind the table. He sat in the middle, looking scrubbed and in control. His face was set; his graying hair trimmed. Most of the black was gone, but the resulting shade seemed to reflect more wisdom than age. McBride stared at him. He wanted to look away, but could not. Something in Willis's appearance drew him in. His heart sinking, he realized that it was Willis who looked like a leader, more so than any of the committee did.

A small notebook was slid in front of Willis. He did not so much as glance at it. A young woman McBride hadn't seen before sat to Willis's right. Their chairs were very close, imply-ing intimacy, although McBride saw no real contact. Still, it made a lot of sense considering what he knew of Willis—it would be desirable for him to have both a romantic partner he could exert pressure on through his position at work and a subordinate he could exert pressure on through their personal relationship. She opened her briefcase and produced a stack of papers, which she placed at the end of the table. Though he did not know her or her agenda, McBride already pitied this young woman.

McBride recognized only two of the other people at the table from their television appearances: US Surgeon General Dr. Charles Witherspoon, and the director of the Center for Disease Control, Dr. Lauren Jessence. Jessence, never robust, looked particularly wan, as though the stress of the session was pressing down on her. She also appeared older now under the bright media lights than she had on TV, with lines clearly visible around her eyes and mouth. Her neck was creased and saggy. Witherspoon, on the other hand, had a steady smile and radiated confidence. A tall, thin, wiry man, he actually towered over the others even when seated.

Exactly at ten a.m., even though several chairs were still empty around him, LaCrosse gaveled the meeting to order. The crowd hushed. The only sound was the steady click of cameras by photographers gathered in the well between the table and the dais. The witnesses stood, raised their right hands, and swore to tell the truth. Willis actually stretched out his left hand as if he were resting it on a Bible.

"Where are the others?" McBride whispered to the man to his right.

"Other committee meetings," the man answered softly. "They have several simultaneously." He wrote down their names on a small pad. "We'll target them in the next election. They ought be here, damn it!" McBride could see the heading on the man's notebook—CDL. He should have taken one when they were being distributed outside. It would have come in handy.

LaCrosse cleared his throat. "I want to begin by acknowledging how important this committee meeting is," he said. "The thousands, if not millions, who have traveled to Washington, DC for this session know it. The committee members know it. The witnesses know it. Our nation's leaders know it. We are embarking on an effort to rescue our beloved animals, man's best friend, from possible extinction."

Several people applauded. LaCrosse rapped his gavel. "We will have no interruptions," he said. "Our work is too important for that." He smiled quickly, as if relishing his control as well as the obvious advantage that no one could interrupt him.

LaCrosse then began to recite statistics: 46 million families in the United States have at least one dog. Americans spend at least $40 billion a year on pets, a total increasing on average by about 5 percent a year. "To most owners, a dog is part of the family," the representative continued.

LaCrosse launched into a long story about his own dog, a schnauzer he'd had while growing up. Though the audience was composed almost exclusively of dog lovers, there still wasn't a wide eye in the place when he finished his tedious tale and resumed his rote statistical recital.

"Two years ago, there were an estimated 78 million dogs in this country, either in homes or shelters or feral," LaCrosse continued. "At last count, the total was down to less than 5 million with the numbers dropping rapidly." He nodded at the witnesses. "That is why we have invited the foremost experts in the country to come here to discuss the issue and help Congress to select the best solution possible to this awful situation. No reasonable proposal will be ignored."

McBride checked the clock. LaCrosse had been talking for more than twenty minutes. Maybe he should have accepted that offer of earplugs. The heavily tanned man to McBride's right was already breathing heavily, a prelude to falling asleep. He hadn't taken a single note. Santiago remained upright and facing forward, although even she stifled a yawn. Witherspoon wasn't as polite; he was yawning openly. Jessence was busily reading something. Only Willis seemed completely alert, staring intently at LaCrosse as though having been invited to the Sermon on the Mount.

After a moment, McBride retrieved the CDL pamphlet from his pocket. It gave him something to focus on rather than LaCrosse's voice, which flowed in a somnambulistic rhythm that any hypnotist would have envied. CDL claimed to be a national movement with millions of dollars already invested in research. McBride was stunned to find out that the group was sponsored by Ralston Purina, Central Garden and Pet, Petco, and several other related companies. He had assumed it was a bunch of radicals like those he had encountered during his trip to San Francisco—he had no idea that they had corporate backing, and from such huge companies. It was just further proof that the situation was dire.

When LaCrosse finally ceased talking—although there was no indication he had exhausted his supply of words—members of the panel then engaged in a lengthy discussion. Each one preceded their on-topic comments by some long personal statement about his or her own dog as if it were a mandatory requirement. Not everyone spoke, including Stubbs, who continued to stare at Santiago to McBride's consternation. The guy was just out-and-out creepy.

Finally, Witherspoon was invited to speak. He took a drink of water to refresh himself and read from a prepared statement, thanking the committee for this opportunity and stressing the event's importance.

"Each of you has been thrust into the spotlight as a desperate nation looks to you for answers," he intoned dryly.

He then described the government's efforts to date, including the research done on the flu and the efforts to find a suitable cure. He labeled the results to date as "spotty, but encouraging." So far, he said, only complete isolation seemed a plausible solution until a vaccine could be developed. "Owners may be able to visit after decontamination," he added.

McBride shook his head. That approach wouldn't work, he whispered to Santiago, since the Rohn flu vaccine was actually the vector of the disease. Any visitors who had received a vaccination would simply spread the disease to any dog they petted. She nodded and held a finger to her lips. He stopped talking.

LaCrosse then invited Dr. Ethan Willis, president of Novilis Pharmaceuticals, to testify. Willis took out his own paper, shifted the microphone in front of him, adjusted its height, and took several moments to ready himself as photographers fell all over each other taking pictures of a rock star of the pharmaceutical world.

McBride watched the almost-comical scene with undisguised interest. He felt his pulse quicken. Willis was sitting almost directly in front of him. He had not acknowledged McBride, but had to know he was there. McBride wondered what Willis thought. Was he worried that McBride was there? Surprised? Or was he so confident that no one could shake him? There was no sign of uneasiness, not even a hint of red in his face. McBride knew that Willis needed to be exposed but at that moment, he really just wished he would die in the same horrible manner that so many millions of dogs had perished.

Willis identified himself, stressing his years as a research virologist, thanked the committee and agreed that no more serious issue faced the country than the death of so many dogs. Then, still reading from his notes, he talked about the millions of dollars being poured into the research. Since Novilis had perfected the Rohn flu vaccine so quickly and expertly, the company had been asked to help with the dog flu after previous companies had failed. His voice was calm, confident, and reassuring.

Finally, Willis requested that slides he had brought be projected onto the screen previously placed to the left side of the dais. Everyone turned to see the slides.

"This picture," Willis said, "shows the H1N1 virus, commonly known as the Rohn flu."

McBride saw the familiar image on the screen. How long he had labored over that bug, testing ways to defeat it?

"This is an image of the H3N8 virus, commonly known as dog flu," Willis continued.

McBride sat up. *No*, he thought fiercely. He even felt Santiago tighten next to him. Willis was deliberately trying to confuse the issue. The H3N8 was *a* dog flu, but one that started in Florida and not the one killing animals around the world. McBride waited. Maybe Willis had a third slide, one which showed the H1N1 was the same virus causing the deadly canine disease.

Instead, the next slide showed both viruses side by side. "As you can see," Willis continued, "these are unrelated viruses."

McBride began to tremble. Willis was willfully lying under oath to the crowd, to citizens, Senators and Congressmen. McBride felt an urge to stand up, to shout, to interrupt him in some way, any way. The committee was listening so intently. The crowd was completely rapt. Willis oozed credibility. Everyone believed him. They didn't know any better. He felt Santiago's hand on his leg.

"Sea callado. No diga nada," she whispered.

McBride swallowed hard and tried to control himself. He looked at Witherspoon. That man had to know what was going on. Anyone who worked in the field who looked at the Rohn flu and the dog flu viruses had to see they were nearly identical. He looked tense; his lips were held tightly together as though afraid something would slip out. Why wasn't he saying something? McBride wondered. He glanced as Jessence. She seemed even paler. Her eyes were fixed on some point in front of her, and she showed no emotion of any kind. What was her problem? McBride thought.

Willis left the slides on and faced the committee. "However, despite the obvious differences," he continued, "Novilis Pharmaceuticals were concerned that there could be a link between the Rohn flu vaccine and the dog flu. We are not immune to the rumors about that. Indeed, we considered such an eventuality. As a result, we devoted thousands of man-hours to this research. We wanted to eliminate any possible cause, even to the expense of our shareholders."

The crowd murmured its appreciation. McBride felt like his head was going to cave in.

"Dr. Willis," LaCrosse chimed in, "the committee and the nation are grateful for the diligent efforts made by you and your company. This nation remains strong because of those ideals represented by Novilis. I am sure I speak for the committee and for Americans everywhere when I stress the valued service and great sacrifice made by your company. We are proud to have you..." He continued for several more mind-numbing minutes of flattery before allowing Willis to resume.

"I am happy to report that we were able to completely absolve the vaccine from any complicity in this dreadful disease," Willis said. He extended a hand. The young woman at the table provided him with a sheet of paper.

"After months of work, I received a report from one of our researchers"—the sheets of paper previously placed on the table were then given to the sergeant at arms for distribution to committee members—"demonstrating the clear differences between the two viruses. This should resolve rumored fears that the Rohn flu vaccine somehow was connected to the dog flu and allow us to focus our attention on this dread killer without side issues."

McBride felt ready to explode. He shivered, barely able to stay seated. Only Santiago's hand on his arm, gripping it tightly, held him in place. Violent thoughts surged through him. They were all in this: the health officials, Willis, maybe even some of the Congressmen. What could they possible gain by letting Willis lie to everyone?

"Have you any recommendations?" asked J.C. McGivern, a representative seated to the left of LaCrosse.

"This will be a lengthy investigation," Willis said. "I imagine we're facing a disease as insidious and hard to pinpoint as the AIDS virus. As you know, that disease mutates rapidly, making it difficult to create a vaccine. That may be why some people thought H3N8 resembled the Rohn flu. Billions have been poured into AIDS research to date, and I fear the same may be needed for this dog flu. I can assure you that Novilis stands ready and willing to take on this burden, no matter how long we have to work on it and without concern for cost."

Several people applauded, leading to another rap of LaCrosse's gavel. "All of us are extremely grateful to Novilis," he said.

"Sure," the old man next to McBride murmured. "That company has lined the pockets of politicians across the country." McBride looked at him. "The pharmaceutical industry has a giant lobby," he explained softly. He gestured toward Stubbs. "That man has a plant in his district in California. He gets a big chunk of cash." He nodded toward Wanda Zelaski, an elderly, stocky woman in the back row of the dais. "She's from upstate New York where Novilis is based. Money is no object."

"How do you know?" McBride stammered under his breath.

The man smiled. "Research," he said, "all this information is out there, but no one seems to care enough to track it down."

Willis was still talking. "I would now like to have my associate, Dr. Lorraine Wagner, discuss the actual research. She is the new director of laboratory research at Novilis," he said.

He sat down, and the young woman to his right took the microphone. Petite with short brown hair, she read a brief statement about how the work that the company was doing was so integral to the "canine crisis" and how grateful she was to be part of it. Her voice was high-pitched, probably reflecting her nervousness. Sitting behind her, he could also see that her body was trembling. Willis had been rock solid; she was having trouble sitting still.

"When did you start the research?" LaCrosse asked.

"Research started in May of this year," she said.

"Were you hands-on or supervising?" Frissen asked.

She hesitated and glanced over at Willis. He nodded. "Actually," Wagner answered, "I did not conduct the actual research."

"Who did?" Stubbs asked.

"Highly skilled biological researchers at Novilis," Wagner replied.

Her voice shook and McBride felt her tremor echoed in the rage rising in his chest. They were talking about him.

Frissen interrupted. "Is it true that some of this research involved testing on fetuses?" he asked in a high-pitched nasal voice. "Mr. Chairman," he continued, "I want to put on record my opposition to any research involving unborn children."

"Sir," Willis took the microphone and replied calmly, "we don't use fetuses in any of our research. We use chicken eggs. They are available at the supermarket."

Frissen blinked once or twice at Willis's response and then clamped his mouth shut. "I had understood..." he finally whimpered.

"I doubt he understands anything," the man sitting next to McBride whispered.

Stubbs pressed on. "Is there any chance that one of the researchers could be brought here to provide first-hand information?" he asked.

"Ms. Wagner," Zelaski chimed in. She had not said anything previously. "All of us are proud of your company's accomplishments, but I want to support Rep. Stubbs's request." She sat back, smugly content to have contributed something.

Willis gave a happy smile. "This was a team project, of course," he reported, "and the leader of the laboratory at that time has chosen to pursue other interests."

"Still," Stubbs said, "I would like his name. I would think the nation owes him a special debt of gratitude."

Wagner sighed and looked down at Willis, who was turned to face her. In that position, he stared almost directly at McBride. Their eyes met.

Willis turned around to face Stubbs. "The man who led the research was Dr. Preston McBride," he announced.

McBride was stunned. He gaped. Santiago grabbed him tightly. He looked at Stubbs. The man knew. He had to. Stubbs was trying to separate him from Santiago, McBride decided, trying to publicly embarrass him. He felt the anger boiling inside but fought to control his emotion.

"Dr. McBride provided detailed reports of his research," Wagner continued. The screen lit up with a page of extensive data, all too small to read. McBride recognized the report. That was information garnered while he was working at the Novilis facilities in California, not while he was employed by the company. He could not tell if it had been doctored.

"You'll have to explain, Dr. Wagner," LaCrosse suggested.

"The findings clearly show that two separate viruses are involved," Wagner continued. More slides followed. "Each of the tests that were conducted show the separation H1N1 from H3N8. These tests used dog tissue to isolate the virus and are conclusive proof that the vaccine has no connection to the dog flu."

McBride now had no doubt. Willis had altered the data. He also could no longer control himself. He stood up.

"That's not true," he yelled. "You are lying." His voice exploded in the quiet room. Wide-eyed, Wagner twisted her body to stare at him. Willis stood, putting himself between Preston and the table.

McBride would have punched him had he been in reach. He felt Santiago tug at him and knew that he should defer to her, but rage finally overwhelmed reason.

"Your entire testimony is a carefully constructed lie," he snarled. "You are all lying. These two," he pointed at Witherspoon and Jessence, "you," Wagner's turn, "and most of all, you," he pointed at Willis. The words gushed out of him. He could see only Willis's face, serenely calm and unconcerned.

"Sergeant at arms," LaCrosse yelled, hammering with his gavel. "Remove that man."

"Be quiet," Willis told McBride quietly, unfazed by the commotion. He gave a wry smile. "No one is listening to you."

McBride heard the commotion around him. He saw Santiago's stricken face, the open-mouth stares of others in the audience. The tanned man next to him was furiously taking notes. McBride didn't care.

"I'm Preston McBride," he shouted. "This man is not telling you the truth. None of them are."

"Sergeant at arms!" LaCrosse bellowed. His face was bright red. "We must have decorum." He stood up and pointed his gavel at McBride. "Young man," he thundered, "you will not disrupt a congressional hearing."

"He's lying! The virus is being spread by—" McBride screamed but was unable to finish his thought as both arms were suddenly pinioned by two burly uniformed men. They dragged him down the aisle. He stumbled over feet and legs. "He's lying! Ask him; he knows the truth," McBride continued as loudly as possible. He felt himself propelled down the side of the room, past the television, and by dozens of people pointing and whispering about him. "The virus, the Rohn vaccine, he…" he stuttered, unable to get out a coherent thought. In another moment, he was being pushed out the brown doors. Cameras were clicking all around him.

"Please," he begged the guards, who did not let go. Instead, they dragged him silently and relentlessly past the security area, where dozens of people stared at him, down the stairs to the subway, and back across to the Capitol. There, he was given a stern warning to stay away. The next time, they said, he would be arrested.

McBride watched the guards leave him. He felt lost. He tried to smooth his coat. He had really gone too far. He knew it. The yelling, the claims. Santiago must be furious with him. Now what? Did El Capataz have some answers up his sleeve? Not likely. Willis was going to get away with it. The dogs would continue to die as Novilis grew richer. Everything inside him collapsed. He sat down on a bench, completely overcome. He had no job, no career, no place to stay. Santiago would not stay by him. Even his mother seemed to have abandoned him for the phantasm of her dead dog. Where was he going to go? What could he do?

Willis no longer had to manufacture evidence against him. The blowup in the hearing would be sufficient proof. He should never have come. He knew his temper would get the best of him. Finally, he stood up. He decided to go back to the hotel and wait for Santiago. Separate rooms were a blessing now.

In the atrium, he passed a burly man in a gray suit surrounded by reporters. He was standing by the long staircase with the red carpeting. McBride stopped. He thought he recognized the man and paused. He sought any distraction so he didn't have to focus on the din in his head.

"Sir," one reporter asked, thrusting a microphone toward the man, "do you really think the feminist movement is somehow connected to the deaths of so many dogs?"

"Son," the man replied in a deep baritone that rolled through the building, "don't twist my words. You have a way of grabbing ahold and making them squeal like a possum in a bear trap." The reporters closed in with all the subtlety of biplanes attacking King Kong. "I was simply saying that if womenfolk stayed at home, then they could care for dogs. I have two tick hounds that are just fine because my Bessie feeds them, washes them, and takes good care of them. I just think too many women have lost sight of their God-given responsibilities of being home. Instead, they're busy finding jobs and forgetting why God made them."

"Senator Lavermore," another reporter asked quickly, "are there other problems that you think women are responsible for?"

The name stunned him. That was Lavermore? He stared at the Senator, who was tall, round with a few black and white strands of hair carefully combed across a bald top.

Lavermore glanced at the reporter, clearly picking up on his attempt to entrap the Senator. "You must think I just fell off the turnip truck," he said genially. "I'm particularly fond of women. Married one, you know. I would never say anything against women. I only think that if they stayed home more…"

"Barefoot and pregnant?" a reporter interrupted. Lavermore shrugged off the snide comment and continued, "And return to the ways God intended for them, why, this world would be a happier place." He held up his hands. "Gentlemen, I'm so sorry. I've got a meeting to go to." With that, he simply pushed through the clot of reporters.

"Interesting guy," a voice said in McBride's ear. He looked over: the tanned man from the hearing was standing beside him. McBride shuddered. He did not need to be reminded of what happened, but there was no escape.

"I'm sorry," he started to say, fumbling with the words.

"The name is George Asher," the man said crisply. "No apology necessary."

"Thanks," McBride managed.

"Let's go outside," Asher suggested.

Puzzled, McBride followed. The day had gotten sunnier, but dark clouds still lingered. Occasionally, they would block the sun, creating deep shadows. The two men walked down the concrete steps and across the street to a park with benches along a long walkway.

"I like to feed squirrels occasionally," Asher said. He pulled some peanuts from his pocket. "When you're doing something like that, you can get away from the day-to-day grind and forget things for a moment."

Glumly, McBride stared at the concrete. "I don't think that'll work for me," he said, "I don't think anything will ever make me forget today, even for an instant."

"What will?" Asher asked.

"I don't know. Maybe finally just getting someone to listen," McBride said.

"I'll listen," Asher said, casually tossing a peanut to a gray squirrel that ventured toward them.

"What good will that do?" McBride said. "Who are you?"

"Still got that CDL brochure in your pocket?" Asher asked. McBride nodded and took it out. "Turn to the inside panel," Asher directed. McBride complied. He read a list of names of CDL officers. Asher was the president and founder. McBride glanced at his companion.

"That's you?' he asked. Asher nodded. "Wonderful," McBride said sarcastically. "Now what?"

"Do you know what CDL really is?" Asher asked. McBride shook his head. "We're a lobbying group," Asher continued. "Registered and legitimate. We now represent about ten million people. That gives us a lot of access."

"To whom?"

Asher tossed out another peanut. "I can see you don't know much about politics," he said. "Instead of people, think of votes." He glanced at McBride, who was trying to concentrate on whatever Asher was saying. At the moment, however, his mind was spinning. He watched a gray squirrel grab a peanut, open the shell and begin to nibble on the nut inside.

"Votes," McBride repeated absently.

Asher shook his head. "I was hoping you could help us," he said. He took McBride's palm and poured a handful of peanuts in it. "Maybe this is the best you can do—help out a few squirrels."

"What?" McBride gaped, staring at the peanuts, then up at Asher.

"Never mind," Asher said. "I thought you knew something about why dogs were dying. I guess not." He started to walk away.

"I do," McBride called angrily. He tossed away the nuts and hurried after Asher. The old man stopped. "I really do," McBride said.

"Then tell me," Asher demanded. Standing in the walkway, a breeze rippling through his hair and passersby walking around them, McBride did: all about the research, the different viruses, the lies that Willis told. Asher listened. Not once did he look away.

McBride finally stopped, feeling exhausted. He had no idea if Asher had even understood what he had said.

"Do you have any proof?" Asher finally asked.

McBride's head fell. "No," he admitted. He explained about the computers and how Willis changed the data.

Asher shrugged. "You won't convince anyone," he said firmly, "not without something more than your word. Lots of people can make claims." He held out a card. "Son, if you can get some real data, I can get you to someone who will tear this wide open." McBride took the card. "Call me when you do," Asher finished. He walked off slowly, a thin man barely creating a shadow on the sidewalk.

McBride glanced at the card. How could he get into Novilis's computer? Who had the data? It was all in Willis's control. He wasn't going to give McBride access. McBride stumbled back to a bench. He had put himself in the spotlight and now was easily identified as a crackpot and a threat to Novilis; he had made it ever harder now to get the information he needed. If only he could be small and easily overlooked, like a busy squirrel, forever working at completing some task people found meaningless. Never bothering anyone, always around yet never really noticed.

Someone like Susan Johnson, he thought. He picked up his cell phone. He dialed Willis's office, almost holding his breath waiting for someone to answer.

"Office of President Ethan Willis. May I help you?" a familiar voice said.

"Susan," McBride gasped. Suddenly, the sun seemed so bright. "This is Preston. Are you free to talk?"

"One moment, sir." Susan's voice became unusually bright and cheery and he was placed on hold. After a moment of muzak, she returned. "Where are you?" she asked. Her voice was hushed and intense.

"Washington."

"That's where Ethan is," she exclaimed.

"That's why I'm calling," McBride said. "He's here, and you are there."

There was a long silence.

"What do you want?" she finally asked.

"Can you access his computer?" He was suddenly aware that his hands were shaking.

"Sure," she said. "Either I or Hofferman have to do that regularly. He's always calling for us to send him something."

"Then," McBride said, feeling good for the first time all day, "take down my e-mail address." He gave it to her. "I need you to go into his files."

"He'll kill me if he finds out," she said.

"Oh, I don't think you'll have to worry about that," McBride said. "You help me, and I don't think you'll ever have to see him again."

"Tell me exactly what you want," she said without hesitation.

"In a minute," McBride continued. "Can you reach Connolly?"

"Back in New York?"

"Yeah," McBride said.

"I have a company directory," Johnson said.

"Do you think he'll help?"

Johnson laughed lightly. "I don't know anyone who wouldn't help cut Willis down," she said.

"Got a pad?" McBride asked. "Here's everything we need to start the process."

Chapter 22

In the quiet of his hotel room, with nothing but the distant rumble of cars rolling by ten stories below to break the silence, McBride waited anxiously for some sign that Santiago had returned. Finding out what happened at the hearing after he had been ungraciously booted had been relatively easy. Coping with Santiago's response to the incident was not going to be that simple. Now, with their relationship in doubt, McBride was beginning to realize that he depended on her for more than just camaraderie in his battle to unearth the truth about the dog flu.

Most news networks had broadcast ample coverage of the hearing on line and on television. CNN rarely touched on any other subjects all day. Reporter Sunittra Bammi had been particularly active, appearing in multiple interviews from various parts of the world. McBride had watched the reports with one ear cocked toward the hallway for Santiago's light footsteps, her key in the lock, anything. The House committee had principally discussed quarantine, although some members seemed to be leaning toward doubling the dosage of the existing dog flu vaccine. Frissen stood defiantly alone: he didn't want to do anything, preferring to let God decide the fate of dogs. He had his say and then thankfully shut up. The committee politely ignored him until he roused himself to propose a congressional commendation for Ethan Willis and Novilis. With enthusiastic support from Stubbs and Zelaski, the idea gained quick committee approval. Frissen settled back into his seat and never said another word.

Other discussions had delayed the committee, but with the demand for action pressing on members—there was no way to ignore the thousands outside the building or the steady flow of commentary on the internet—a vote was expected within a couple of days on a bill of some kind. House leaders had already signaled they were prepared for a quick floor vote on whatever the committee approved, while the Senate was anxious to abate public pressure with prompt acceptance of virtually anything its counterparts agreed to. Suggestions for either a Senate committee taking up the issue or a joint committee were scuttled to avoid delaying the process.

To McBride's great relief, his outburst received minimal attention, mostly treated as a spectator overcome by the loss of his dog reacting too strongly to innocuous comments by pharmaceutical executives. He hadn't even been identified until a late story finally mentioned his name and called him "a disgruntled former employee who left the company under controversial circumstances." The reporter sounded sympathetic, at least to McBride.

Not everyone had the same attitude. Around mid-afternoon, during a break in his presentation, Willis looked straight into the camera and said that he was sorry such a "gifted researcher had allowed himself to get carried away by emotion." McBride almost threw his shoe at the TV, but stopped himself after taking aim: one emotional outburst a day was proving to be more than sufficient. Earlier, he had been particularly appalled by the array of statistics posted in front of the committee. Virtually all of them were purported to have come from his data but none of the conclusions matched his recollection. His findings had been distorted, if not completely reversed.

McBride did receive three calls on his cell phone. One, from his mother, erroneously congratulated him for taking on Frissen. She called on him to be more forceful next time. "I didn't know you had it in you, Pres," Maggie told him, "but my psychic was sure you'd do something important. I should have sent my bat with you, if only I could find it! Florence must be so proud of you."

"Who?"

"Your latest," his mother had answered happily. "You are so popular. Who knew a balding, saggy old man like my son could attract so many young women?"

Nathan also rang. He had been surprised to see his brother on television. "Couldn't you find some other way to get attention?" he had kidded.

The third call had come from a correspondent with the Washington Star. When McBride declined comment, the young man had asked if he'd be interested in learning more about the Unification Church. It seemed like everyone had a misguided way to save the world. McBride had turned down that offer, too.

Mostly, he spent the day thinking about Santiago, even while collecting and collating the information Johnson and Connelly sent him. That had taken most of the afternoon. He had spent it in the James Madison Library. There, using a public computer, he had been able to comb through the data and prepare it for presentation at his next meeting with Asher.

While waiting for the computer to sort through the pages of research, he tabbed over to CNN to see what was happening at the Rayburn Building. He often found himself looking to see if Santiago had come for him even though he knew where she was. When someone testified, he was usually able to catch a glimpse of her in the background, sitting quietly, listening intently.

He made sure to be back at the hotel before evening began to settle across Washington, DC, as he had expected her to return to her room after the hearing. He was disappointed to discover she still had not arrived. Finally, he heard the door to the next room quietly open, then close. He sat up. Santiago was walking around in her room. Her steps were light on the carpet, just barely audible. She must have stayed at the hearing until it ended. Maybe she was hungry afterwards and stopped to get something to eat then?

He had tried to think of something to say to her, something plausible: He was a passionate person? He had planned everything, thinking his outburst would force the committee to listen to him? He had been overcome with thoughts about dead and dying dogs? None of it convinced him, and if he couldn't convince himself, there was no way he would be able to convince her. He had simply not controlled his temper.

His pulse shot up. This was worse than when he had to talk to Kendra or Rosen about his plans to go to Washington, DC. At that time, he hadn't really been talking about himself, but about his plans. Now he was going to have to reveal some of his inner thoughts. The very idea terrified him.

Finally gathering himself, McBride walked outside and stood in front of her door. The hallway was empty. He could hear a quiet buzz of an ice machine a few doors down. Somewhere, someone laughed out loud, and then the hallway returned to near-silence.

He knocked on her door. For a long time, nothing happened. Then, finally, he heard the latch turn. The door opened just an inch or two. He saw Santiago's face; her dark eyes surveyed him without expression. The chain was still in place.

"May I come in?" he asked.

She hesitated and then unhooked the chain. It clanked against the door. Without a word, she pulled the door open. He stepped inside. The curtains were closed; only a small light by the bed illuminated the room. Santiago retreated to the other side of the room. She peered outside, pulling the curtain aside and ignoring him. McBride stopped only a few feet inside the room.

"Lo siento mucho," he began contritely. He stared at the floor. "I embarrassed you. I embarrassed myself."

Santiago did not respond. Silence filled the room. McBride heard a roaring in his ears. This was going so wrong; everything was going so wrong. Finally, Santiago finally sat down on the bed and looked away.

"I do not care about being embarrassed," she said softly. "I want to stop the deaths of dogs. That is all."

"I agree," McBride said in the same mournful tone. He hoped she realized he really was contrite. He also did not try to approach her, although she obviously was in need of comfort. The strain of the past months weighed heavy on her eyes and radiated from her face.

"I know you care, that you are muy apasionado. I like that about you," she said. "However, there are times for calm reasoning. Politicians are used to people yelling at them. Sucede todo el tiempo. So, they do not listen anymore. They get defensive instead. I hope your outburst has not delayed our efforts for action."

"I hope not, too," he echoed. After letting the words settle into the carpeting, he took a step toward her. She did not react. "I may have found a way to get the facts into the open," he told her, eager to change the subject.

"With or without a rabieta?" she asked quickly.

He shrugged off the comment, hoping to emphasize his progress and de-emphasize the setback he had caused. "We can do it quietly this time," he said. He sat on the bed beside her and told her about Asher. Her eyes brightened.

"Bueno," she breathed.

"Muy bueno," he agreed.

"How did you get the files?" she asked. McBride told her how Johnson had eagerly downloaded everything from Willis's computer, while Connolly had found and sent data from the first rounds of tests more than a year before. "I have made several copies on jump drives." He retrieved one from his pocket and gave to Santiago. She took it as though it were a piece of jewelry and promptly placed it in the safe in her room.

"Willis won't know what hit him," McBride said happily as she returned to the bed.

"When do you talk to Senor Asher?" Santiago asked, unmoved by his warm reaction.

McBride checked his watch. "He'll be here in thirty minutes," he reported.

Santiago surveyed him, as if seeking some answer in his face. He waited.

"You are on your own," she finally said.

He hesitated. "Porque?"

She pursed her lips. "This is politics," she said slowly, looking down as if afraid to see his reaction. "You know how to treat a patient. That is good, but it is not politics. I am here because of my uncle. Rep. Stubbs knows I am traveling with you, but if he—or anyone connected to Novilis—thought I was working against him, my uncle would be the one who would lose influence. He has done too much for la gente pobre. I cannot interfere. That is why I did not follow you from the hearing. I must seem independent."

She reached over and took his hands. "Whatever happens," she said, "you are on your own."

McBride gazed into her eyes. She was very serious. He finally nodded. With his temper tantrum, Willis no longer needed to discredit him. He had done a fine job of that on his own. Santiago had done all she could. She had gotten him this far. She wasn't deserting him; she had just reached the limit of how far she could go. It wasn't what he had hoped for, but he felt much better than he had all day and pulled her hands to his lips. His eyes fastened on hers.

"Muchas gracias," he said.

"Ir. Prepárate."

He nodded. She pulled her hands away. He was grateful for that, since he couldn't force himself to let go. He headed for the door.

"Mi querido, no tratar de nota a este momento," she called after him.

"Nada mas," he replied and went back to his room. His cell phone rang about fifteen minutes later.

"Meet me in the restaurant on the first floor," a voice said, then hung up abruptly.

McBride recognized Asher's voice, but why hadn't he identified himself? McBride placed his printouts in a folder and stared out the window while he waited to leave. For once, he was totally prepared. The sun was setting to the west, casting an eerie gray glow over the city. Already, lights were going on everywhere, as if trying to beat back the darkness. There was a sense of calmness with relatively few cars on the roads and even fewer people. What an illusion, McBride thought. In the dark offices and shady corridors, numerous cabals were rehearsing their plans for some secret move. Why should he be any different?

The elevator seemed so slow. He kept one disk and the printed files in his black leather briefcase, holding the handle tightly. After exiting the elevator, he surreptitiously checked the contents just to ensure that the research was still there. Willis had gotten his hands on it before; that could not happen now. Besides, he had a backup jump drive in his room, as did Santiago.

Asher was seated at a table on the far side where he had a sweeping view of the entrance and a wall behind him. He reminded McBride of an old-time gambler fearful of being shot in the back. There had to be at least fifteen other people scattered around the room but Asher had chosen a table isolated from other diners. A steady hum of conversation surrounded McBride as he walked slowly toward Asher. He half-expected someone to rush out and try to take the briefcase but nothing happened. He jerked impulsively when a waitress stumbled for an instant while walking past him, but that was the only hitch. No one stopped talking as he passed by an occupied table. No one looked up. He listened intently for any hint of trouble, but heard nothing to alert him. Asher did not look up as McBride reached him.

"Don't sit down," he said under his breath. "Do you have everything?"

"Yes," McBride said in a matching low voice. He shivered. This felt as sketchy as exchanging a brick of heroin for a stack of cash. Asher was sipping soup, appearing intent on his bowl and spoon. McBride glanced at his watch and looked around, as if he were waiting for someone else.

"Ten a.m., Capitol Rotunda," Asher said. He continued eating.

McBride waited, expecting more details.

"*Leave*," Asher hissed.

McBride hesitated, then complied. He did not look back. He did wonder what was going on. He wasn't doing anything illegal. What could Asher be worried about? Why the cloak-and-dagger?

Santiago had little insight to offer when McBride filled her in. They sat on the balcony to her room, feeling the cool evening air wash over them. He told her about seeing Lavermore after being removed from the hearing. Santiago groaned at the mention of his name. The Senator had vehemently opposed immigration reform, she said bitterly. He called for a militia to be set up along the Mexican-US border to shoot anyone trying to enter the country illegally. He had demanded the country pass a Constitutional amendment making English the official language of the country. She hated Lavermore maybe as much as his mother did. Maggie had simply had more time to amass her venom.

Quickly moving on, McBride talked about where he ate lunch and dinner—fast food sandwiches while he worked—and the information he had finally collected.

"What do you think will happen tomorrow?" he asked.

She smiled at him and put her hand on top of his. "Yo no sé de mañana. Tu habla demasiado," she whispered. He felt the warmth seep through him. "Sólo me interesa en este momento en lo que va a pasar esta noche." She pulled him toward her.

There was no reason for further conversation.

At ten the following morning, McBride walked up the long concrete steps to the Capitol. The briefcase brushed against his leg with every step, reassuring him. Here, too, multiple demonstrators had gathered with their signs and slogans. They were not packed as densely as at the Rayburn Building, but they took up most of the steps, leaving only two paths for those entering and exiting. Many were drowsy from the long day before; a few were still sleeping despite the hubbub.

He tiptoed carefully up the long concrete stairway. Still wary, he kept looking for anyone or anything suspicious, but was greeted only by tired glances and an occasional snore. In a few moments, he reached the front door and stepped inside. Few demonstrators were there. Maybe, McBride wondered, the many uniformed guards had discouraged them. Two guards stood beside the entry, but McBride barely noticed them as he passed through security like an automaton. He simply stared in awe.

With the light bursting through the windows in the dome, murals on every available surface and the green marble in the walls, entering the rotunda was like walking into a cathedral. It seemed at once both ancient and new. Yesterday, he had been too distracted by the emotional aftermath of his outburst to notice. Then, too, Lavermore had been busily diverting attention with his impromptu media conference. Today, one of many among gawkers, lawyers and congressional aides, McBride could soak in the atmosphere.

For several minutes, he allowed himself to enjoy the sensation. He could feel people brush past him, but barely realized they were there. He had traveled across the country because of Willis, and now back again. After a few moments, he saw Asher across the marble flooring, looking at his watch. That broke his reverie. He started walking across the floor. The old man didn't change expression as McBride neared. Instead of a greeting, he simply nodded, stood up, and headed out. McBride followed.

Once outside, Asher produced business cards for people in the crowd and began distributing them. "Less than a year ago," he explained to McBride, "I was selling dog food in a pet store. Now, I'm head of one of the largest lobbying groups in the country." He put a hand to his lapel. "I get to wear expensive clothes, eat in expensive restaurants, and talk to important people. Next year, I could be back in the retail business. I'm going to enjoy this while I can."

"What about dogs?" McBride asked, a bit stunned by Asher's cold, self-serving speech.

"Of course, dogs," Asher said with irritation. "That's why I'm here."

People read the cards, sprang up to shake his hand or pat him on the back. Asher eagerly embraced them, welcoming the adulation. The cards vanished. He produced more from his other coat pocket. They, too, were quickly handed out. No one asked about McBride, who followed awkwardly in his wake.

"They probably think you're my attorney," Asher told him.

"Not your bodyguard?" McBride teased.

"Try to look intimidating. Maybe that would help," Asher suggested.

After a few minutes, they extracted themselves and headed across the street. Asher waved at passersby like an experienced politician. "I haven't kissed any babies yet," he noted as an aside to McBride.

"Who are we going to see?" McBride asked when the crowd finally thinned.

"Be quiet," Asher said, suddenly talking very low. "Everything you say can be heard by anyone," he said.

"Who's listening?" McBride wondered, glancing around. He was abruptly aware why Asher was prattling about himself. However, no one seemed the least bit interested in the conversation whatever the topic.

"You'd be surprised," Asher said. "This is Washington, DC, the capitol of the most powerful country in the world. We are being watched; everyone is. Not everyone who came up to say hello back there was a friend."

McBride felt a chill sweep through him, the same sensation that filled him while driving away from Crossland's house. The hair on the back of his neck bristled. He glanced around, trying not to be obvious. Anger began to fill his mind. He closed his eyes and took a deep breath. This was no time to be upset. He had to focus. Slowly, he began to calm down. Still, he could not help looking carefully at everyone he could see. Everyone looked suspicious. But clenching his briefcase in a firm grip, he felt ready. As long as he had the data, he thought, Willis could not touch him.

They walked down Constitution Avenue toward the Hart Senate Office Building, an eight-story white concrete structure.

Crowds of people had also gathered outside there. Someone had built a doghouse from cartons on the stairway and was lying inside. He wore a Goofy hat from Disney with floppy ears and was dozing peacefully next to an empty bowl. Once again, McBride had to pick his way through the crowd, stepping carefully to avoid mashing someone's extended fingers or toes. Asher was shaking hands, patting backs, encouraging people. McBride didn't say a word, only smiled as curious eyes surveyed him.

"Hi," Asher continually repeated, "I'm head of the CDL." That always drew a warm response.

McBride wanted to say, "Hi, I'm almost completely SOL," but refrained despite the temptation.

"Nice people," Asher said as they finally entered the building and passed through security.

A guard inside asked for McBride's briefcase to be opened. Unlike in the Capitol, when he had been distracted, McBride hesitated for a moment and then complied. The guard ruffled the pages, picked up the drive, replaced it, and then handed back the briefcase. McBride had watched him very carefully, but there seemed to be no substitution or removal of anything. He grabbed the briefcase and held it against his body. The guard eyed him before focusing on the man behind them.

Not many others were inside, just a few uniformed guards anxiously watching them. The lobby consisted of rows of glass windows overlooking a central area with small trees in white planters and some kind of dark sculpture. Black aluminum clouds slowly revolved above black steel mountains. The image, McBride decided, was decidedly ominous, but even it failed to shake his confidence.

Asher stopped by the elevator. "Your outburst yesterday limited the number of people who will talk to you," he said softly. McBride put both hands on his briefcase and nodded sadly. "This may be your last chance."

The door opened. At least five people, all in formal suits, piled out. One middle-aged man with white hair glanced at McBride with a wild expression and then hurried on. McBride watched him. The man looked familiar.

"Senator Haberstaad," Asher said casually. "Late for another meeting."

McBride nodded as if he knew about the Senator's constant tardiness. "He's shorter in real life," he noted.

"They all are. In more ways than one," Asher said. "Small people in big jobs. Don't confuse persona with reality."

They rode up as people got off and on at each floor. Typically, no one even acknowledged the other passengers.

McBride focused on which Senator might be willing to listen to him. His mother always spoke highly of Senator Coonis from Maine and Senator Williams of Minnesota. Both, she reported, had good hearts. In her mind, that meant they voted they way she would have. McBride hoped Asher had made contact with one of them. He wanted to ask, but kept silent while Asher made innocuous comments about the weather as long as others were within earshot. Of course, McBride told himself, any Senator would do. All of them had to be eager to save dogs and please their voters simultaneously.

On the seventh floor, Asher indicated it was time to exit. "Listen to me," he said in a low voice as he drew McBride to one side. "This guy is very pleasant. Everyone likes him. You wouldn't know it from the media, but he's a really nice guy."

McBride was glad to hear that. "He's also probably the only guy who will talk to you. The only other Senator who said he would was Haberstaad, and you just saw him getting out of dodge."

"I understand," McBride nodded. Few Senators would want their picture taken standing next to a man who had been unceremoniously removed from a committee meeting. Whoever met with him would definitely want to do so in private. He hoped it was Coonis—at the very least, his mother would be impressed.

"Don't bury him in facts," Asher cautioned. "No Senator wants that. He's looking for a decisive victory on a hot issue, and this one has the media on it like flies on shit."

McBride thought about all the data in his briefcase. Was he supposed to ignore it? That was the basis of his claims. The Senator had to want to get familiar with at least some of it. Who went into an argument unarmed? He smiled at Asher, mentioning none of his doubts. This was no different that walking into a treatment room to see a patient, he reminded himself. He typically followed the cues, letting the patient talk. He could do the same thing now.

"Good," Asher said. He turned and walked down the hallway. McBride hustled to keep up with him. The old man walked quickly.

"Nice tan," McBride said, filling the emptiness.

"Side benefit of heading the CDL," Asher said. "I have to look healthy. No one wants a wheezing old man as their president."

"How old are you?" McBride asked.

"Old enough to know better than to answer that," Asher said with a dry smile.

McBride looked at the nameplates on doors. He recognized a few names, all from news reports. His pulse picked up. Seeing someone famous on television did not move him, but he felt strangely affected by seeing a door with a familiar name on it. His mother would have welcomed the opportunity to interact with any of them, treating them like old friends or implacable enemies. He could not be that sanguine. He was still trying to control his emotions as Asher stopped by a door.

A reflection glared off the nameplate from the overhead light. McBride blinked and could not read it for a moment. Then he felt his energy suddenly drop. The name was all too clearly visible: Senator Jonas Lavermore.

McBride shuddered. "I can't," he mumbled.

Asher whirled to look at him. "What do you mean 'I can't'?" he asked coldly.

McBride pointed at the name. "I hate everything that man stands for."

Shaking his head, Asher said, "So? Who the hell cares what he thinks? He is willing to listen to you. Don't be an ass. You've alienated every other possible ally."

McBride felt sweat begin to flow under his suit. "There's no one else?" he asked.

"Some guy in the House," Asher said. "I didn't think that would be a worthwhile idea."

"Who?" McBride asked desperately.

"Gary Stubbs."

"No, no," McBride mumbled. He could parse why Stubbs might want to talk to him. Asher didn't know the history, and he wouldn't have thought twice about it, except that Stubbs was on the committee and had witnessed McBride's angry tirade.

"It's up to you," Asher said with his hand on the door knob. "We can walk away. That'll be it. Whatever you know will be your little secret. But you've come a long way to go home empty-handed now." He stared at McBride. "It's your call, McBride. Our future is in your hands."

McBride tried to think. It didn't matter that his mother would be appalled—that never took much—but what about Santiago? He knew what she thought about Lavermore. His insides churned. If he went in, would he lose her? But, if he walked away, his efforts and his sacrifices would have been for nothing. Willis would win. Dogs would finally go extinct, and human suffering over their loss would increase exponentially. The conflicting thoughts raced through his mind, colliding, breaking into shards that felt like they were tearing at his brain. He could feel every facet of the issue tugging at him.

He needed to ratchet up his courage and decide now.

He stared at the nameplate. Why go on? Everything behind him was gone—Kendra, his job, even his home. He could not live there anymore, not without any income. Nothing lay ahead, except possibly Santiago. And, he admitted, she still could walk away once this was over. Still, he did have one burning motivation. Kendra had accused him of being propelled by ego. She was wrong. He was driven to get Willis not for what he had done to McBride, but for what he had done to world, to dogs and to the people who had cared for them. He had broken a special trust, and he must not get away with what he was doing. He must be exposed, and the people he had harmed must decided his punishment.

He turned to Asher. "I'm ready," he said calmly. He tightened his grip on his briefcase as the door clicked open and they walked inside.

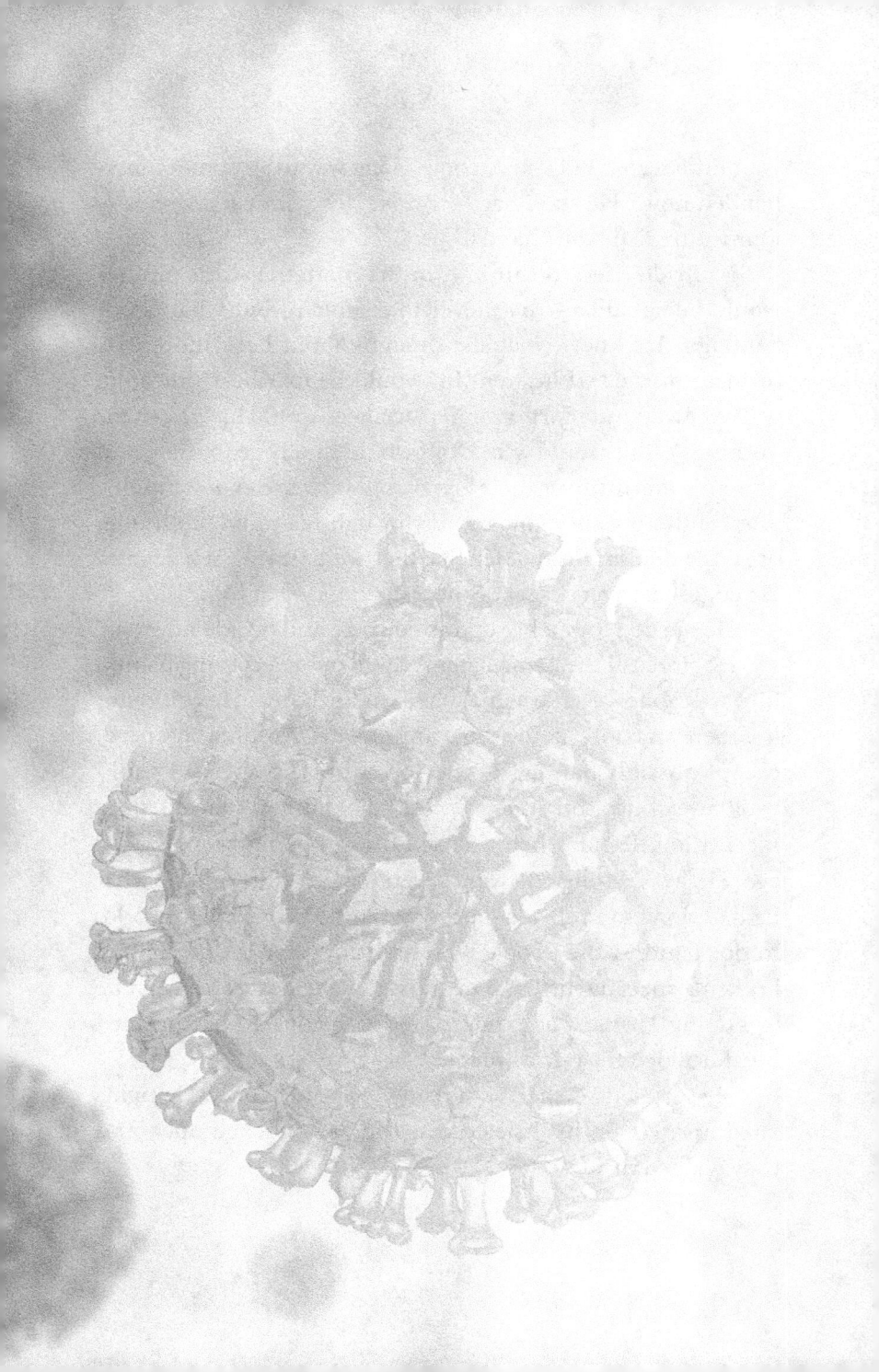

Chapter 23

Asher entered the office first; McBride followed tentatively behind. He felt sweat blossom anew. He wanted to be relaxed, even suave, a convincing presence amid the resounding confusion that a Senator must face daily. Instead, he felt weak and nervous, as though attempting to confront some vicious beast armed with a knife of cardboard painted silver. Come on, he encouraged himself. He straightened his shoulders. What could Lavermore do? Tell him to leave? Treat him like road kill? That had happened before, McBride reassured himself. This time, at least, he had the hard data, the data he had worked so hard on, data that had been rudely stripped from him, distorted and used against him. He clenched his briefcase as though it were a cross being held before a vampire and stepped into the light.

Lavermore's office was large and airy with a black stuffed couch against one wall and rich brown wooden paneling all around. It was divided into two parts, and the entrance to the inner office was closed. A large desk with a secretary anchored the outer room. Behind her, plaques and both black and white and colored photos covered the rear wall: Lavermore with presidents Richard Nixon, Ronald Reagan, George H.W. Bush, and George W. Bush; Lavermore with Sen.

Sam Irvin, with David Duke, with James Watt. Some of the people McBride recognized. Others he did not. There were awards from the National Rifle Association, the Moral Majority and Conservative Caucus. The National Review had apparently named Lavermore its "Man of the Year" in 1988. McBride carefully stifled the sneer that was creeping onto his face.

Standing there, reading the plaques awarded to Lavermore by so many organizations he detested, McBride immediately saw there were no images of dogs. He glanced around. Nothing in the room seemed related to Lavermore's personal life: no knickknacks, souvenirs, or family pictures. Instead, he could only see names and faces he detested. He felt a chill as though he had wandered into some ghastly other world where his worst nightmares were a reality. A small voice in his head kept urging him to leave, but he remained firm. He could not abandon his lone opportunity. Facing Santiago after his tirade during the hearing had been a cakewalk compared to her likely response if he retreated now. Lavermore was their best hope—and their last.

Amid the laudatory awards and official photographs, McBride also spotted copies of front pages from Newsweek and Time that labeled Lavermore "Mr. Reactionary" and "The Man from Bunk." Included was a caricature of the Senator with his ears oversized standing next to an elephant with the caption "Dumb and Dumbo." Although the images were not meant as compliments, Lavermore clearly was not offended. In fact, he seemed to have prized them, giving them prominent and obvious positions. No visitor could miss them. Their presence somewhat reassured McBride. At least the man had a sense of humor. He also was well aware what people thought about him and didn't care.

Beside the back wall, flags of the United States and the state of South Carolina stood across from each other, limp in the slight breeze from the air conditioning while a Confederate battle flag graced the wall above the couch. The air stank of old nicotine, perspiration, and cheap carpet.

Asher introduced himself and McBride to the secretary, who was an older woman with gray curly hair and a round form developed from long years behind a desk. She spoke in a take-no-prisoners smoker's rasp that chilled McBride. The Senator would be with them shortly, Asher was informed curtly. The woman returned to her computer. Her demeanor made it abundantly clear that she had no time to chit-chat.

McBride settled into the couch. It gasped under him while the Confederate flag rippled briefly above him. To his left, an end table contained a package of cigarettes. The ashtray held two stubs, one with lipstick on it. McBride shuddered. His mother had inculcated him with a dread of tobacco in any form. Just sitting this close to an ashtray appalled him; it smelled like they were inside one.

"Yes, ma'am," a polite Southern voice said from the back. A woman in classy red business suit appeared in the doorway, glancing back over her shoulder into the office. Elegantly attired with her hair neatly coiffed, she could have been another Senator for all McBride could tell. "Don't you worry, ma'am," Lavermore continued. His dark shadow appeared next to the woman. "I'll give your proposal my complete and thorough consideration."

"Right," the woman muttered as she marched by McBride and out the door. Her lips were pinched close together in obvious anger, and her eyes were dancing with fire.

"You enjoy this right fine day," Lavermore called after her. The door slammed in response.

"Well, now," he said with a low chuckle, rubbing his hands together as if with delight, "that filly could curdle grits." He glanced around. McBride could see he was shorter than he seemed in front of the microphones the day before, yet still just as imposing. His hair had been carefully combed. His suit must have been brushed and ironed by a crew of devoted servants. The creases in the pants were sharp and straight. He looked at Asher with a broad smile on his wide face. The grin seemed to crack the skin, spreading up his cheeks and around his eyes and back to his ears, which were overtly large. The cartoonists hadn't gotten him wrong.

"Mr. Asher," he boomed. The Senator glanced down. "And this must be Dr. McBride," he said. McBride stood up as Lavermore extended his right hand. McBride felt a strong, powerful hand squeeze enthusiastically. They shook.

"Come, come," Lavermore said, guiding them into his office. McBride felt like if he stepped into that office, he would never come out but still felt powerless to refuse the invitation. Both men remained mute—the Senator's presence simply overpowered them. The cologne he had apparently bathed in enveloped all three of them.

Wealth and power radiated in all directions inside his private office. One large picture of Lavermore controlled the back wall, while an array of honorary degrees ran across the left wall. On the other side, Lavermore had posted another flurry of photographs documenting his powerful connections. He seemed to have shaken hands with every single world leader during his tenure. The presidents and prime ministers often appeared in their native dress, but Lavermore invariably wore the same implacable suit. His facial expression never varied, always that overly genial grin of a Southern Bible salesman. The back wall was covered with framed and laminated newspaper stories marking his four victories in senatorial elections. In addition, several of the reports told of his political efforts: "Lavermore Blocks Global Warming Agreement," read one. "Lavermore: No Government Funds For Abortions Under Any Circumstances," another reported. The man was evil, and proudly so.

Once again, McBride noted, Lavermore avoided anything personal or relating to his private life. Even his broad desk, stacked high with stapled packets and loose piles of paper, did not hold one single family photograph that McBride could see. There was no computer either. A bookcase ran along the back wall. It held law books and technical journals but, of course, no novels or anything that hinted at the Senator's reading interests.

The man apparently had no personal life. There was nothing on display that indicated his life had consisted of anything except his political achievements.

"Have a seat, gentlemen," Lavermore said, indicating two high-backed wooden chairs. His voice rarely seemed to lose its volume or enthusiasm and was tinged with a rich Southern accent. It spread across them like syrup. He appeared perpetually in good spirits, with a jovial smirk and a sparkle in his dark eyes. If anything, McBride decided, he was the jolly uncle everyone shunned at family gatherings, the one who drank too much and cheerily said whatever came to mind no matter whom he offended. McBride imagined him smiling under a white KKK hood and shuddered.

"Cigar?" Lavermore offered. "Made of fine South Carolina tobacco." He held out an ornate box with an array of cigars clearly lined up inside.

McBride declined, but Asher took one and tucked it inside his suit coat. Lavermore did not light up either, but bit off the end of the cigar, spat the piece into a nearby wastebasket and then placed the cigar on the empty ashtray on his massive desk. "I'd offer you gentlemen some liquid refreshment," he continued, "but my doctor ordered me to cut back to a gallon a day, and I fear I've already hit my limit this morning." He laughed loudly. Asher forced a grin. McBride was too focused on what he needed to say to respond.

"Young man," Lavermore teased him. "You feel right free to laugh whenever I tell a joke, you hear?"

"Yes, sir," McBride stammered. "I guess I'm preoccupied with how serious the situation has gotten."

"Aren't we all?" Lavermore agreed insincerely. He settled back into his chair with a sigh. "You know, since I turned sixty, I've been having more trouble with my back. You'll forgive me if I fidget just a bit. These chairs look nice, but they're not designed for prolonged occupancy."

"We'll try to be brief," Asher assured him. "Senator, we know you are very busy and are grateful you're willing to take a minute to talk to us about an issue of great concern to everyone."

"My pleasure, sir," Lavermore replied courtly. "I hear about this issue every day from my constituents and am eager to develop some solution."

McBride noted that response would work with any topic. Did Lavermore even know why they were there?

"Thank you, Senator," Asher continued. "This dog flu has been terrible, as you know."

"Dog flu?" Lavermore mused. His face brightened. "Yes, dog flu." He scrambled through paperwork on his desk. "One constituent in Columbia wrote me about that very topic." He gave up searching after a moment. McBride's spirits plummeted. Was Asher just wasting his time?

Asher ignored Lavermore's interruption and continued. "I thought you might like to listen to Dr. McBride for a moment. He's done extensive and groundbreaking research on this disease, which I know is of great interest to you," he said.

"I'm all ears," Lavermore said, "as you can probably tell. Cartoonists have great fun with them." He swiveled to face McBride. "I believe the floor is all yours, sir," he said.

McBride retrieved his files from his briefcase and placed them on the desk. Lavermore took the folder and flipped through while McBride slowly and carefully explained the situation: the manipulation of information, the outright lies, the real source of the disease, Willis's deceit, Novilis's complicity, and more. He didn't know how long he talked, but just let the words flow. Though he did his best to remain calm, there was no way to disguise his emotions.

"I believe he burned down the medical clinic where I worked, sent people to search my home for research, and even doctored e-mails to be ready to counter any claims I made," McBride continued.

Lavermore sat up. "Doctored e-mails? That man is devilishly clever, don't you think?" he exclaimed. "Isn't it amazing what a fellow can do with modern technology? I've heard about mass mailings of e-mails, but this is a new twist. I would have never thought of it. Would you, George? Good thing I have Sylvia to handle it for me."

"It's not a positive thing, sir," McBride offered. As clever as Lavermore obviously was, he was also still just a simple country boy in many respects.

Lavermore shook his head. "My boy, you don't know how hard it is to come up with new ideas in this business. I feel like a pig who just found a new mud bath," he said.

McBride pressed on. The data was spread across Lavermore's desk with changes highlighted, pictures, and long pages of research statistics. He ran through what it showed. Lavermore appeared to listen. He glanced at the various graphs and numerical files, but much like Hofferman more than a year before, his eyes quickly glazed over.

Finally, Asher intervened. "Thank you, Dr. McBride," he said. "What a fascinating account." He laid a hand on McBride's to stop him.

Lavermore roused himself. "I'd say the barn is full," he noted thoughtfully. He pawed the paperwork. McBride almost cringed to see those meaty hands grabbing at his research.

"Are you sure about this?" the Senator finally asked. "We don't want to be accusing a fine company without real evidence."

"Yes, sir, positive," McBride said. He leaned forward and waited for a response. Lavermore was relaxing, rubbing his eyes and gazing off into the distance. At that angle, his stomach jutted out. It resembled a pillow that had been plumped to its extreme. He suddenly seemed to realize that McBride had stopped talking.

"This is very interesting," Lavermore said. He leaned back in his chair and surveyed the ceiling. "I can see the possibilities." He closed his eyes and pushed his fingers together. "You know," he mused, "this could carry a fellow pretty far."

McBride glanced at Asher. What did that mean? Asher put a finger to his lips.

"We're just trying to solve this crisis," McBride said.

"Of course you are," Lavermore soothed. "Why, that's what we all want. I am very fond of dogs. Had two blue-tick hounds at one time." He shook his head at the memory and launched into a convoluted tale about hunting deer, his tick-hound's inability to scent a skunk and other mishaps. He chuckled heartily throughout the telling.

"Great story," Asher said. He grimaced at McBride.

Silence filled the room while Lavermore further pondered the situation. He finally nodded as if reaching a decision and sat up.

"Gentlemen," he said, "I suggest we begin an immediate probe into the dog flu. I am sure many voters would appreciate their Senator taking a direct interest in such a serious problem."

"Excellent!" Asher enthused. "Without presuming to offer advice, I would think a hearing would be the perfect way to approach this."

"There is a hearing right now," McBride said with obvious puzzlement. Asher ignored him.

"A hearing?" Lavermore thought aloud.

Asher jumped in, "I would never have thought of that. A hearing! Senator, that's a great idea."

Lavermore beamed.

"Maybe we could carry that one step further and actually discuss the situation with Dr. Willis first. As president of Novilis, I am sure he can bring great insight to the situation."

Lavermore couldn't stop smiling. "How soon do you think we can get Dr. Willis here?" he asked. "I'm sure you gentlemen will want to ask him some questions…on my behalf, of course."

"He must have known you'd want to talk to him," Asher said. "After all, he's in Washington right now."

McBride slumped in his chair. Who were these people getting elected to office? Stubbs was more interested in seducing Santiago than doing his job. Lavermore was a charismatic moron. The Senator had never even questioned why he, as a man, opposed abortion. This was the person they had to rely on to end the dog flu charade? He groaned inwardly. Meanwhile, Asher continued to slather on the praise.

"I must admit," he said, "I didn't think anyone could grasp this issue so quickly. It must be all that experience you have in the Senate, sir."

Lavermore heaved himself from his chair. "It's twenty-seven years and counting," he said. He strode over to the side-wall with the various plaques. "You can see how hard I work," he said. "I was in Egypt, China, Tahiti, and Argentina alone last year. They got something in Buenos Aires called milansea. It's just old chicken-fried steak with a different name. They just like it tougher. This year, I'm going to Mexico, France, the Canary Islands, and Italy. Come back this time next year and you'll see a whole new wall of pictures. And," he added hastily, "a great chance to introduce the world to the views and products of South Carolina. My constituents want to know I'm looking out for them." He wandered back to his desk. "Did I offer you a cigar?"

"Yes, sir," Asher and McBride spoke in unison.

"Gentlemen," Lavermore said, "I think we're onto something here." He plopped back into his chair with the grace of a harpooned whale.

"So you'll want to get Dr. Willis here for a discussion?" Asher prompted. "Maybe introduce him to the media? That would put you right out front on this really important issue."

Lavermore stirred, about to slip into another stupor. "Sylvia," he called to the secretary. She appeared in the doorway. "Find Dr. Willis for me," he ordered.

She gave a puzzled glance at Asher.

"He's president of Novilis," he told her. That didn't change her expression. Asher had to supply several more clues before the information struck a chord. She wrote something on her steno pad and retreated.

"She's the aunt of an old friend," Lavermore confided to them. "Sometimes, politics can be such a dirty business." He broke into another smile. "So, Georgie, how are things these days?"

"Oh, I'm busy, like you," Asher replied.

"Plenty of time to work on that tan, though, right?"

Asher nodded, smiling. "I have to look good, like you," he said.

"And, you, Dr....McBride?" Lavermore asked.

"Just working on the dog flu these days," McBride said through gritted teeth. He was stunned and appalled that these two appeared to be catching up like two old poker buddies. "I'm unemployed..." He stopped. Lavermore wasn't paying the slightest attention. Maybe, McBride thought, Lavermore's mind was already back on the Buenos Aires beaches.

"Senator," Sylvia said from the doorway, "Dr. Willis is on his way to the airport."

McBride sat up. "He's getting away," he muttered. He felt overcome and sagged back into his chair. There had to be some way to stop him. Lavermore needed a moment to digest the information.

"Well," he finally said, "we could try for later in the year. We don't want to hold the good doctor up in his travels."

McBride leaned forward. There was no time to wait. Dogs could be extinct if something was not done. Moreover, if Willis were leaving, that meant the House committee was ready to vote for a useless quarantine. The Senate wouldn't do anything different. Willis's attempt at smothering the facts would succeed. Anger surged through him. He struggled to contain himself.

"Sir," he tried, "maybe you could invite him back? It will be so hard to get him to return from California if he leaves."

"Hmm," Lavermore said. "California?"

"Think of your national constituency, sir," Asher added.

The exercise of thinking caused lines to appear on Lavermore's forehead. Then, suddenly, he made a decision. "Sylvia," Lavermore barked. "Let Dr. Willis know that's he due in my office as soon as possible." He leaned over to McBride. "What shall I tell him?" he whispered.

"He's getting a Congressional Medal of Honor," McBride suggested, unable to believe that what he was saying.

Lavermore's eyes lit up. He repeated the idea to Sylvia, who quickly exited.

"He'll be here for sure," he said.

"Why not host him downstairs in the rotunda?" Asher suggested. "You know how reporters love that. Think of the coverage."

Lavermore did. The thought spread joy across his face. "You have nailed this one, gentlemen," the Senator exclaimed. "I feel like a raccoon with his head nose deep in a jar of Grandma's preserves."

"Yes, sir," Asher said. "We'll see you tomorrow morning in the rotunda."

Sylvia was back. "He can be here by nine a.m. tomorrow, but has to catch an afternoon flight," she reported. "Should I alert the media?"

Lavermore nodded. "Let FOX know. Call Glen and Bill. I want to get the most mileage out of this one," he said. "Don't forget the New York Times. Last time, that reporter—what's her name?—threw a hissy fit when we didn't invite her." He calmly rattled off a long list of officials to invite, including Novilis Chairman of the Board Alvin DiAngelo. For a moment, McBride was impressed with Lavermore. He had set up an entire media strategy in seconds, talking about the positioning of the rostrum, lights and placement of various reporters. At least the old coot knew his way around the press, if nothing else.

McBride breathed a sigh of relief. With the media conference in place, maybe he and Asher could work out how to attack Willis. Lavermore would be pretty useless when the time came.

Lavermore leaned over and collected McBride's file. "You won't mind if'n I spend some time going over this material, do you?" he asked.

"No, sir," McBride told him. He had other copies. Besides, Lavermore was just going to be wasting time, given the highly technical data in there, the photographs and the rest. Then again, Lavermore couldn't wind up more befuddled than he was right now. He was just an old man who had been handed a live grenade and wasn't sure what it was.

"Well, then," Lavermore said with the good cheer he seemed unable to turn off, "let's see if we can fuck up the works again. What do you think?"

"Yes, sir," Asher said.

"Boys," Lavermore said, standing up with the apparent intention of launching into an oration. "I just tell myself: what would Sam do? And then I try to do the same. That ole hound dog turned himself into a national idol with Watergate. Someday, I'll find my Holy Grain."

"Grail," McBride muttered to himself.

"Tomorrow just might be where the chicken fat hits the fan," Lavermore continued.

"We can't wait, sir," Asher said. He reached over and offered his hand, clearly eager to depart. The Senator clasped it enthusiastically. He almost hugged McBride and guided them to the door, as though shooing little children home.

"Don't you worry about a thing," he boomed. "Sylvia, cut off my calls. I've got some heavy reading to do."

McBride could still see his harried image reflecting off the frame photos as he followed Asher from the office. To his amazement, they had only been in there for forty-five minutes. It had felt like an eternity.

"I'm glad he's not worried," McBride told Asher once they got outside into the sunlight. "I am."

"Don't underestimate him," Asher warned. "He'll be ready." He paused. "He has to be."

McBride stopped. "Why?" he asked. "The man's got the brains of a pair of ice skates."

Asher shook his head. "He smells an issue that will make him relevant again. He'll be ready. The old issues like the feminist movement and abortion have lost their wow factor. He knows that dog flu will get him back in the spotlight. Why the hell do you think he was willing to talk to you? He got the same e-mails everyone else did, but he doesn't give a fuck. He has other priorities."

McBride felt sick to his stomach. The distant blare of car traffic, the murmur of conversations, the heavy tread of ponderous men in thick wool suits, the click-clack of women's high heels all blended into a single sound, then faded away. He felt surround by silence as a sudden realization smashed into him: this disease that had killed millions of dogs and had the potential to wipe out the entire canine genus was just another opportunity for all kinds of hustlers, money-grubbers, megalomaniacs, and of course, politicians.

"Lavermore doesn't give a damn about dogs," he muttered bitterly. Asher shrugged. "And neither do you," McBride spat out. He heard a roaring in his ears.

Asher smiled. "It's a means to an end," he said.

"Not to me. Not to millions of people," McBride said grimly.

Asher was nonplussed. "Come off it," he snorted. "What happens if you show that the Rohn flu vaccines have caused dogs to die?" McBride stared at him. "Nothing," Asher continued. "That's what. You can't stop the dogs from getting the disease. You can't save a single dog. You know that. So what's left? Ego. You versus Willis. What the hell does that mean to the rest of us?" His voice was hard, like a nail driving into McBride. "So, Lavermore gets something out of it. I get something out of it. The poor shmucks who lost dogs get nothing. You get nothing."

"Didn't you ever care?" McBride said in a hushed voice. He was appalled.

"Sure," Asher said, "when I started. I cried when my dog died. I did. Then the bucks started rolling in. My priorities changed. I figure this lobbying group has about a year to run. Then I'll need a new issue. Until then, ride 'em, cowboy." He turned on his heel and walked away. "See you tomorrow," he called back over his shoulder.

"I don't know whether to laugh or cry," McBride told Santiago back in the hotel.

"Well, don't cry," she said. "It's a start. It doesn't matter what the issue is—dog flu, illegal immigration, or global warming—we have to begin somewhere." Her eyes searched his. "We have made a good first step. Tomorrow, we will take the next step."

McBride told himself she was right. "I can't let Lavermore blow it," he said. "El Stupido can't stand up to Willis."

She took his hand. "Then it's up to you," she said.

He nodded. Tomorrow would be his last chance. The thought chilled him. "I feel like there is a black cloud hovering over me and a deep abyss below me, both of them just waiting to swallow me," he said softly.

"That's because you never sat in the back of an old truck, pushing through a dark night without its lights on," Santiago told him. "You're scared to death, thinking each jolt will be the last before everything ends. I survived. You will, too. We do what we have to do."

He hugged her. He would need her strength, he thought. Thank God she had so much.

"Let's go to bed," she said.

Chapter 24

Morning crept slowly across the horizon. McBride brushed aside the curtain and blinked as the rim of the sun blossomed into view. The sun may have heralded a bright day, but McBride was anything but chipper. All he could see was Willis escaping. He had slept little, mentally running through every possible scenario for the upcoming news conference with Lavermore and Willis. In the most dramatic, he abruptly stepped up to the microphone, shunted aside the doddering Lavermore and directly accused a smug, shocked Willis. Even as that approach played out in his head, with strobes flashing and reporters clamoring for more information, he realized there was no difference between that and his outburst in the hearing. Why would anyone listen now?

On the other hand, he had no faith in Lavermore to handle this confrontation for a positive outcome. How could he? Willis was a rattlesnake, and Lavermore was like a senile groundhog. The geriatric Senator had less than a day to examine the vast array of research McBride had supplied him with. Didn't aides handle that sort of thing? Everyone knew that elected officials couldn't read everything that passed across their desk. They'd never leave the office and still fall reams behind in their reading. Willis's superior knowledge would almost certainly short circuit anything the aging white-haired reactionary might try to spring on him. If the topic wasn't alcohol, tobacco, or guns, Lavermore was out of his league.

As the second hand continued to roll around the dial, McBride became increasingly apprehensive. Santiago didn't say anything, but she dressed calmly and quietly with little apparent concern. Occasionally, she smiled at him, perhaps trying to reassure him. Each time, he smiled back, unable to muster much conviction.

"Just be patient," she told him, "and have faith."

He nodded in assent, but didn't mean it. How would he restrain himself this time? One look at Willis, and he was bound to erupt. The man had cost him so much, to say nothing of the plague he had unleashed on the world.

She looked hard at him. "Promise?"

He took a deep breath. "I promise," he said.

"No mas colera," she insisted.

"No mas," he repeated.

Shaving was a lengthy, cumbersome affair, partly because he had inherited his mother's tender skin and his father's heavy beard and partly because he didn't want to cut himself. Having a bandage on his face today didn't seem like the best idea. Imagine confronting Willis and facing reporters with blood dripping down his chin. On the other hand, that might make him seem tougher, battle-hardened. In the end, he opted for the clean image. Still, he had to pause several times to stop his hand from shaking.

With nerves churning his stomach, he limited breakfast to a bowl of cereal and one cup of coffee in the hotel restaurant. Nothing else on the menu seemed appealing anyway. Santiago enjoyed her Spanish omelet with apparently no limit to her appetite. As McBride munched, he eyed the small St. Jude medal that Santiago slid across the table to him. It featured an old man in a robe holding a staff. He recalled from childhood that Jude is the patron saint of lost causes. Appropriate in this case, he decided.

"Maybe we should bury him upside down in the Capital lawn," McBride suggested.

"That's St. Joseph," Santiago frowned. "I think it would only give St. Jude a headache."

They arrived early at the Capitol, mounting the white concrete steps around eight thirty as the visitor center was just opening. The Rotunda was nearly empty. Every footstep created an echo that ricocheted off the various presidential busts and historic paintings. The sound rolled up the sandstone walls and swirled around the dome that hovered high overhead. A podium had been set up to one side of the large entry with maybe fifteen chairs in front of it. Trumbull's painting of the Surrender of Lord Cornwallis at Yorktown loomed behind it.

Security was perfunctory and efficient—few protesters had gotten wind of Lavermore's hastily scheduled press conference and were otherwise occupied protesting other events around Capitol Hill. Santiago busied herself looking at the various carvings and oil paintings. McBride found himself glancing toward her. How could she be so calm?

"I have faith," she told him when he asked.

"That makes one of us," he murmured.

Around eight forty-five, two official-looking men with earpieces attached to black cords running beneath their collars came in to carefully arrange the chairs. They had looked straight before, but the men spent more time adjusting them than a seamstress does aligning a hem on a new dress. Then they took up positions on either side of the podium.

Seconds after they finished, men and women holding notebooks, microphones, and cameras began to arrive. They chatted with each other and settled into the seats. Several burly men set up cameras or plopped down onto the floor with cameras at the ready. They took pictures of the empty rostrum and the two officials standing like London Beefeaters with stern, long faces. Strobes flashed, bouncing light around the Rotunda.

Two well-dressed women hurried in with crews in tow. Both had microphones with TV call letters attached. McBride figured they were from local stations. The women took up positions near the front. Bathed in light from the cameras, they each recorded brief segments amid the hubbub.

There were radio news people, too, identifiable by their recording devices. The chairs filled quickly with late arrivers milling around. Conversation increased. The sounds filled the Rotunda.

McBride was not surprised that everyone seemed relaxed, even jovial. He wished he felt that way. But they were just audience members for this circus: he was the one putting his head in the lion's jaws. He settled against a wall across from the podium, trying to be inconspicuous. He didn't want any of the reporters to recognize him. Santiago took a position on the same wall, far enough away that a stranger wouldn't recognize any connection between them but close enough for McBride to draw comfort from her. He was amazed by how placid she seemed, apparently immune from the rising excitement that engulfed him.

From his vantage point, McBride could survey the crowd. He recognized one small woman. She was a CNN reporter he had seen on television. So it wasn't just the local news who would be covering the hearing. Nearby was Asher, wearing a fresh CDL shirt. He was scowling, arms folded across his chest. Every now and then, he would shake a reporter's hand and distribute a card. Then, far to the left of Asher, McBride caught a glimpse of Dr. Alvin DiAngelo, Novilis's chairman. McBride didn't know him, but had seen his portrait enough to recognize him. When Willis became president, DiAngelo had been moved to the board of directors. He seemed shrunken and agitated, with deep lines in his cheeks and forehead. He had taken a seat on the end of a row of chairs.

McBride was wondering why DiAngelo was there when he felt someone move close. "What's going on?" a soft voice asked him, startling him.

A young woman stood next to him. He had not heard her approach. She was smiling and holding a microphone that read "Fox Five." He did not recognize her. She introduced herself as Dolly Madison, a reporter sent to cover the program. For a moment, McBride thought she knew who he was and did not reply. "You look like Secret Service," she said without a hint of irony. "You must know what's happening. Something about a Congressional Medal of Honor?"

Trying to sound authoritative, McBride filled her in, explaining that Senator Lavermore invited the media here to recognize Dr. Ethan Willis's efforts to preserve the health of the public. Madison took some notes.

"That's all?" she said when he stopped.

"It could get interesting," he told her, not wanting her to lose interest in the proceedings. "Dr. Willis may have to answer some serious questions."

"About what?"

McBride swallowed hard. "The connection between dog flu and the Rohn flu vaccine."

She looked at him blankly, and then something appeared to click on behind her eyes; she had smelled a story.

"Ooh," Madison said, "I'll bite. What does dog flu have to do with Lavermore?"

"We'll just have to wait and find out," McBride said with a weak smile.

She stepped back and signaled her camera crew. Immediately, she was awash in bright light.

"Intrigue is building today," Madison began, and proceeded to repeat virtually word for word what McBride had told her, concluding with "this could get interesting."

McBride listened in astonishment. At least he had told her the truth. Imagine, he thought, if he had been in a more playful mood. He watched as Madison concluded her report and wandered toward the gathered reporters. She stood on one side and chattered with her cameraman.

At 9:05, a young man came in and adjusted the microphone. McBride kept checking his watch but no one seemed particularly concerned about the time. Tourists now were filing into the Rotunda, and they joined the crowd, creating a large half-circle facing the podium. McBride mused that they knew as little about the planned event as Madison. Somehow that made him feel better. Everyone was there for a show, and he suspected that they would get one.

Finally, at nine fifteen, Lavermore strode into the Rotunda with several assistants, including Sylvia, caught in his tailwind. He happily kissed cheeks, shook hands, and played to the crowd, waving at cameras. Finally, he took his place behind the microphone.

"I thank you ladies and gentlemen for joining me this fine morning. I tell you, an offer of some warm grits and even warmer spirits can really get a turnout," he said cheerily. The reporters laughed lightly. "I am not one to waste time," the Senator continued. "I know how busy you all are, what with the deadlines for your gossipmongering and whatnot." Another laugh rose from the crowd. "No reason, as my mother used to say, not to slop the hogs first and get that chore done as quickly as possible."

He made a slight nod and glanced to his right with an expectant look on his craggy face. McBride felt a chill creep across his body: Willis and two other men marched into view. Willis was smiling, but his companions were grim faced and stolid as though heading into a courtroom. McBride decided they must be attorneys. Each carried a black briefcase.

"Ladies and gentlemen," Lavermore said, "I am as proud as two peacocks to introduce Dr. Ethan Willis. As you all know, since you've been covering the hearings going on in the House of Representatives on the dog flu, his company has been leading the fight against that deadly scourge."

Willis came up to the podium. Lavermore gravely shook his hand, smiling quickly as cameras went off. McBride wondered how long it would take for one of those pictures to appear on Lavermore's office wall.

"All of us are so grateful to you for your efforts," he continued with his arm around Willis's shoulder. "I am right tickled to call you my friend."

McBride blanched. What was Lavermore doing? This wasn't supposed to be a coronation. He took a few steps closer to the podium, suddenly feeling exposed. His worst fears were coming true. Lavermore wasn't going to do anything with the information he had worked so hard to get to him. What was next: announce the Congressional Medal of Honor so they could all go home happy? He started to feel anger surge from his taut stomach. He clenched his fist. Be patient, he told himself. He could see Santiago staring at him. Her look stopped him. He had promised; he would be patient. He walked slowly closer, readying himself, anyway.

"Dr. Willis," Lavermore said, "the nation is mighty proud of you and everything you've accomplished."

"Thank you, Senator Lavermore," Willis answered, leaning into the microphone. "You have always stood up for what is right. I'm pleased to be on that side."

God, how that oily voice grated on McBride. He could see that Willis had darkened his hair. If anything, it was now almost jet black. From a distance, he seemed young. The effect was chilling. He was like some modern day vampire, growing young from the blood of millions of innocent dogs.

"Now, being an old farm boy from South Carolina," Lavermore continued, "I was wondering if you'd help explain some of this very complex information. I am sure our friends from the media would appreciate a little assistance, too. Right, boys?"

There was an uneasy chuckle from the crowd, but no one answered.

"I'd be glad to, Senator," Willis said right away, smiling cordially.

McBride was only ten or fifteen feet away now. Once Lavermore's comment sunk in, he slowed and then stopped moving. There was some trace of danger in it, as though the Senator was laying a trap. His face did not give a hint of anything wrong. He was still grinning that broad grin which took up his entire face. Willis paused for a second, appearing to catch the scent of a predator. The lines in his neck stiffened.

Sylvia stepped forward with some pictures, handed them to Lavermore, and then retreated. Willis glanced at the images and then obviously relaxed. As Willis's calm returned, so did McBride's tension: the gasbag Senator was going to throw Willis a softball after all.

"Now, Dr. Willis," Lavermore said, showing the color photo to Willis and the crowd. "What's this? It looks like something a schoolboy might have drawn in second grade." McBride could see the picture was of a virus, the same picture that had been flashed on the screen at the hearing.

Willis smiled. "No, sir," he said. "That's a picture of H1N1, the virus causing Rohn flu. Novilis developed the vaccine that's stopped that disease cold. That," he added, "wasn't child's play."

Lavermore grinned. "I don't suppose it was," he said. "And this photo?" He showed another one both to Willis and to the reporters.

"Oh, Senator, that's H3N8," Willis said. "That's the flu virus that's tragically killing so many dogs."

"They're not the same?" Lavermore asked. "I mean, I'm no scientist but they look pretty much the same to this old country boy."

"No, sir," Willis said, smiling, going along with the show. He pointed to some of the variant features. "They're both viruses, but under an electron microscope, they are vastly different."

"These are the photos you showed to the House committee, I believe?" Lavermore said.

"Yes, that's right." Willis now was almost gleeful.

"Now, this is where I'm puzzled," Lavermore said.

Willis cocked an eye at him. "You?" he said. "As the reporters know, you are always on the forefront of progress." His light sarcasm drew a muffled laugh from the media.

Lavermore laughed, too. "Oh, I keep my ear to the ground, Mr. Willis, " he noted. "In my line of work, I have no choice. Good thing I've got the right tools for the job."

That drew more laughter. The Senator then produced a third photo. "What's this?" he asked innocently.

Willis looked. "Why, Senator, that's another image of an H1N1 virus," he said with the look of a man in complete control.

"Really? Now, I am as lost as a raccoon in a Hilton Head sauna," Lavermore said. "See, this was retrieved from a dog. A poodle mix, I believe." He looked on the back of the image. "Yes. The dog's name was Amante. She lived in Pomona, California." He smiled at Willis, who leaned back. "Died there, too, in a fountain of blood. Now how do you suppose the Rohn flu bug got into that little dog?"

Willis swallowed; his smile turned cold. "I'm sure that's a mistake. The Rohn flu only affects humans. The dog flu only affects canines," he said with authority.

Cameramen moved in closer, sensing a drama playing out. Willis edged further away from Lavermore, tilting his head to accent the way his body tried to increase the distance between them. A stillness swept over the crowd. McBride noticed with alarm that while he had been rapt by the performance onstage, the crowd had doubled in size, mostly with men and women in red CDL shirts. He looked for Asher—had Asher leaked information? Asher had unfolded his arms. He was staring intently. For a moment, even the cameras stopped clicking. McBride held his breath, too. My God, he thought was Lavermore really attacking Willis? Had the old bear lured Willis in only to turn on him, teeth and claws bared?

"No, no," Lavermore said casually, "I can read it right here on the back." He showed the crowd. "It looks pretty official. Just to be sure, I made up some copies here for the members of the press assembled so they can verify it."

Sylvia now moved in from the side of the podium, where she had waited patiently for her cue, and began distributing packets to reporters, now clamoring for the information. The CDL protesters remained attentive, but ominously quiet.

"Sir," Willis said, his face slightly red. "I don't know who wrote that caption, but I can assure you that no dog has died from H1N1. I have reports from both the Centers for Disease Control and the Surgeon General."

"Of course, Dr. Willis," Lavermore went on. "There must be a mistake." Willis nodded. He obviously didn't trust the Senator now and continued inching further away. He had the whole podium between himself and Lavermore now. "Maybe we could ask some expert to help us," the Senator continued.

"I don't doubt your word, but that darn tag on the back of the photo keeps gnawing at me like a badger at an anthill."

"You have to understand," Willis said, "the sample may have been contaminated, or maybe someone just plain misidentified the virus. Things like that happen in a lab."

"You are so right," Lavermore enthused. His grin broadened perceptibly. "I recall you mentioned in the hearing yesterday about someone at your company who did a lot of research on the Rohn flu. Am I right?"

Willis nodded.

"Now what was that fellow's name?"

"I believe you're thinking of Dr. Lorraine Wagner, our director of research," Willis offered nervously.

Lavermore pretended to think about that name. "No, sir, I don't believe that's right," he finally said. "No, not a woman. I sure would have remembered that." The reporters laughed lightly. "I recall now. McBride. Wasn't that the fellow? Dr. McBride?"

"He's no longer with the company, Senator," Willis said.

"It happens that he's here," Lavermore said grandly. "Perhaps we can ask him to sort out this question."

McBride felt his pulse hammering in his chest. Was he actually going to be able to face off against Willis? He took a short step toward Lavermore and then stopped. Patience, he told himself. Lavermore didn't ask him to speak; the Senator merely noted his presence.

Willis gestured at one of his companions carrying a black briefcase. The man stepped forward. Willis opened it with an ominous, deep click. "That won't be necessary," Willis said coldly. He reached inside the briefcase and pulled out several sheets of paper. "I have copies of e-mails Dr. McBride sent that confirm the fact the H1N1 flu didn't cause the deaths." He looked around. "I should have made copies. However, I didn't expect…"

"Dr. Willis, please," Lavermore said, "I am sure our friends in the media can get copies. I wouldn't be surprised if they hadn't tapped into your company files already. I couldn't do that. I'm just as likely to use a typewriter as a computer. But I heard how e-mails can be tampered with. Why, the other day, my cousin over in Spartanburg wanted to break up with his sweetheart and, wouldn't you know it, somehow that email didn't go through and now he's walking down the aisle this Sunday. Don't that beat all?" He gestured at Sylvia, who brought over some more papers. "Besides, I have some e-mails of my own."

Willis stared at him. His face went from red to pale. He had developed a slight tremor, and was clenching and unclenching his hands in frustration.

"Like there's this one," Lavermore held up a sheet of paper and read. "You sent this about eight months ago to a man named Charles Crossland. I believe he had your job at one time. It's so hard to keep things like that straight. Folks seem to come and go in jobs in your industry as though there were some kind of revolving door. Anyway, let me read it."

"I don't think that will be necessary, Senator," Willis tried.

"Oh, I don't mind," Lavermore said. "I used to read a lot to my little girls and have had a lot of practice." He cleared his throat. "I don't think it will do the public much good to learn of the connection between the Rohn flu and the dog flu," he intoned.

"I didn't write that," Willis interrupted loudly. The strain was getting to him quickly, highlighting the deep furrows around his eyes. He seemed to have shed his formerly youthful appearance in seconds.

"That's odd," Lavermore said. "It came right off your computer. I had one of those computer guys that we have access to here on Capitol Hill verify it. I can't explain how he knows it's real, but I'm sure he could."

Willis glared. His eyes fell on McBride, seeing him for the first time. Rage filled his face. McBride shrugged innocently, which seemed to infuriate Willis even more.

Lavermore continued to read, repeating the first line: "I don't think it will do the public much good to learn of the connection between the Rohn flu and the dog flu. As a result, I suggest we meet on this. I understand you have recommended public disclosure, but that will hurt the company. I have taken the liberty of forwarding my comments to Dr. DiAngelo. I am sure he will realize I am right." He looked up. "This is where I get confused again. Right about what, Dr. Willis?"

"Where did you get that? It's a private document," Willis seethed. His jaw jutted forward. One of his companions waved his hand to get Willis's attention, but was quickly surrounded by large men in CDL shirts who quickly forced his hand down. Willis did not stop. "Give me that!" He grabbed the sheet out of Lavermore's hand. Cameras clicked as rapidly as automatic weapons.

"I believe this was written about a week before Crossland took his own life," Lavermore said. "What a shame. And quite a coincidence, don't you think so, Mr. Willis?" He took another sheet from Sylvia. "You can hang on to that paper, I had Sylvia here make up a whole bunch of extras in case anyone wanted one." Sylvia again moved swiftly around the room, distributing the memo.

Willis watched the flurry of activity that followed Sylvia's movements. The sheet he held slipped from his hand and drifted to the marble floor. He drew himself up. He had been trapped and he knew it and now was trying to find a way—any way out. McBride moved closer as if to block his exit.

"Senator," Willis began, "the Surgeon General of these United States…" he began.

"A fine gentleman," Lavermore interrupted. "I have known Dr. Witherspoon for years. He used to work at Novilis, didn't he? It's so hard for an old man like me to keep the details straight but that's one I properly recall. I think it's a matter of public record, ain't it?"

"And the Centers for Disease Control…" Willis pressed on. The other man who had entered with Willis was now waving at him, too.

"Ah, Dr. Lauren Jessence," Lavermore said. "I didn't approve of her getting that position, as you know."

"Both of them agree with our findings," Willis continued. "A human disease cannot jump to an animal."

Sylvia brought another sheet of paper to Lavermore, who took it gratefully. "Now, Dr. Willis," he said, "I don't want you getting upset. You're all shaking and pale, like a revenuer who just caught sight of a fine, upstanding South Carolina backwoodsmen holding a shotgun and standing next to a still." He put the paper on the podium. "I just got a couple more things that have me as puzzled as a rooster when clouds block the sunrise. I have here a list of donations your fine company made in the last few years to us political folks."

"You got money from Novilis," Willis snapped.

"So I did. Why look, there's my name," Lavermore said, pointing to the sheet and reading: "Senator Jonah Lavermore, five thousand dollars." He looked up. "That was in 2008. And I'm mighty grateful for the help in my re-election campaign." He smiled. "Of course, there are other names here: Dr. Charles Witherspoon, a hundred thousand dollars in 2008, a hundred and twenty-five thousand dollars in 2009, a hundred and fifty thousand dollars in 2010, and five hundred thousand dollars this year." He paused. "Dr. Jessence didn't get anything until last year. Look at that fifty thousand dollars in 2009 and four hundred thousand dollars in 2010. Dr. Willis, your company should do better than to give less to a woman. I thought you supported equal rights."

Both of the men who came in with Willis were now gesturing feverishly for him to be quiet. One approached him and whispered something to him. Willis started to close his mouth, but outrage broke the seal, just as it had done to McBride the day before. McBride smiled to himself. Willis should have learned patience.

"Senator," Willis reverted to threatening, "I don't need to remind you that Novilis is a private company."

"And I'm mighty grateful for that reminder, sir," Lavermore noted. "Oh, here's another interesting thing, Rep. Wanda Zelaski and Rep. Gary Stubbs both seem to have done right well by you."

"Our two largest plants are in their districts," Willis countered quickly.

"No doubt, no doubt," Lavermore said. "I'd be the last person to say anything disparaging about a political donation, but I find it might peculiar that in the election year in 2010, neither of them got more than two hundred thousand dollars, but this year, both were given one million." He left the question unspoken.

By now, the cameras were going off nonstop. Asher was staring hard at Willis; so was DiAngelo. The tourists in the back, many of whom had been chatting with each other, had gone silent.

"Senator," Madison waved her hand.

"In a minute, young lady," Lavermore said. "I am sure Dr. Willis has a solid explanation for all this."

"I have no intention of answering your question or any question in a forum like this," Willis snarled. "I was lured here under false pretenses and have no chance to defend myself."

"Sir," Lavermore held up a hand. "Let me extend a hand of Southern hospitality. I invited you here to tell you about being nominated for the Congressional Medal of Honor and to ask a few innocent questions. Us country boys have a time plowing through this kind of data. That is for a wiser man than me. I just muddle along and try not to get too confused."

"Exactly," Willis said.

"Still," Lavermore said, "let me lay the scene for you, so's you don't get as lost as I've been. In the last eighteen months, this country, in fact, this whole good earth has been ravaged by a strange plague, Biblical both in proportion and its capacity to cause pain, suffering, and death. Doctor, we've seen police dogs die in their harnesses, we've seen lil' puppies dyin' in the arms of lil' girls, we've seen seein' eye dogs die in the middle of the road, leaving their blind owners to walk into traffic. When a man loses a friend, he goes into grieving. When a man loses his best friend, well, sometimes he goes right insane. And that is what we've seen—humankind, Doctor, gone collectively insane with grief and suffering.

"An alienated teenaged girl kills herself when her one true confidante dies. A man kills his neighbor out of anger that his neighbor has caused his dogs to die. A woman blows herself up in front of a veterinary clinic...and takes six other innocent people with her. A man, his dogs are dead, so he gets drunk and straps his four boys into his dogsled and all five of 'em freeze to death. And that's just in our country.

"That plane that crashed in India? They would have caught those terrorists if they'd had bomb-sniffing dogs. That's over six hundred died right there. Shepherds dying trying to save their flocks in Scotland. Every man woman and child in a poor neighborhood has their handgun cocked and loaded with their finger on the trigger because their early warning system, their security guard, their protector...is dead, drowned in its own blood before their eyes.

"Oftentimes, when a man loses his best friend, if he doesn't go insane, he goes into deep depression. And that's what's happened, the world over. Millions of people out of work because their job depended on a dog in some way." They didn't seem so important, you know, just at the bottom of the pyramid, far below horses and cattle and, of course, far, far below us. But you know, Doctor, what happens when you pull out the bottom bottle in a pyramid of milk bottles? Well, I don't have to tell you that, you rightly know! Everybody's hurting right now, the world over. Well, almost everyone. Seems like you've done quite alright. Big promotion, big raise, I bet you drive a nice car. Novilis is the hero of the country, and you, the hero of Novilis.

"Now, if we go way way back to before this whole mess started, well, it seems to these old eyes that, somehow, I don't know how, that ole' Rohn flu somehow jumped into dogs. Right around the same time you started sending out your 'mandatory' inoculation for Rohn flu. Is that what it looks like to you?"

"How?" Willis thundered. "That's impossible!"

The two lawyers waving at him gave up. They both looked completely dejected.

McBride almost blurted out the answer: a vector. He had had a hard time swallowing it when Kendra had first proposed the idea. But once again, she had been right. The attenuated virus used in the Rohn flu vaccine jumped into dogs and killed them. That's why the only dogs that initially survived were living in isolation or belonged to owners who didn't get the vaccine. Only later, did many of the dogs contract the flu by being exposed to body secretions from vaccinated humans or infected dogs. With a twinge, McBride recalled again just how much he had gotten from Kendra and how little she had gotten from him.

"Dr. Willis, I'm afraid that is something you'll have to answer," DiAngelo said. He stood up. "I never saw the memo you sent Charlie. You told me that he was interfering with the research!"

"The vaccine worked," Willis cried. "It stopped the flu."

"It also killed nearly every dog in America and is on its way to wiping them out globally," Asher said coldly. He stepped forward, waiting until camera lights swept over him. "You knew it, and you did nothing."

Willis looked helpless. "What could I do?" he asked plaintively. "Our mandate was to halt the spread of Rohn flu. We did that. We have saved millions of lives around the world."

McBride could almost hear his real explanation imbedded in that excuse: deaths of the dogs were just collateral damage, nothing more. He knew that's what Willis thought. He wanted to confront Willis with that, but still did not move. Patience, he reminded himself.

"Is that what you want?" Willis addressed the crowd. Mr. Cool finally appeared to be on the edge of melting down. "Do you want the Rohn flu to kill everyone? Or do you want a vaccine that protects you? We had no way of knowing it would kill dogs."

Again, McBride almost shouted a response, pointing out that he had warned Willis, but held himself back. It really didn't matter now. Willis had known full well about the dangers of an attenuated virus being used in the vaccine. The truth would come out. Lavermore, Asher, and now even DiAngelo had punched so many holes in Willis's defenses that he couldn't keep the whole story from coming out much longer.

"It's not acceptable for my company to produce medicine that causes such deaths," DiAngelo said.

"We're talking about dogs compared to people," Willis said, his voice rising in both pitch and volume. His face was red and shiny with sweat. "As you know, Dr. DiAngelo, our goal is to make a profit. We did that. This vaccine and the subsequent research has earned us billions. This is a *business*."

A horrified gasp went up from the assembled crowd as reporters wrote furiously in their notebooks. Still, Willis continued berating them.

"We met a public need and the needs of our investors. If you are insisting we shouldn't have produced this vaccine in a timely manner to confront a deadly disease and made a profit while doing so, then you are attacking the basic tenets of the capitalist system which you have profited from. DiAngelo, you made tons of money from this vaccine! Thousands, hundreds of thousands of people have profited, not just from our vaccine—from my vaccine—but from the dog flu as well!" He pointed a shaking finger at Asher. "You! What did you do before my vaccine? What did you drive, a ten-speed? He probably drives a Lexus now! You wouldn't just be broke without my vaccine, you would be dead!"

The bustling room, now packed with protesters, reporters, gawkers, and an increasing number of policemen and security, grew quiet for a moment. Willis was indicting not just his boss, but every single person who had made money from both the Rohn flu vaccine and the resulting dog flu. The man was coming undone, but the accusation stuck: "man's best friend" had been sacrificed for the profit and safety of mankind. It was the harshest of betrayals, and even if not everyone in the room had been complicit in the evil act, they had all benefited from it.

"You don't think a company has a moral obligation to provide products that don't cause such devastation?" Madison finally asked.

Willis turned to face her. "Tobacco," he said. "Alcohol. Remember them? Both are legal products produced to earn profits. Our vaccine saved lives. Tobacco has killed billions of people over the years, and alcohol has been a scourge of mankind for millennia. Many of you here have lost dogs, but who in this room hasn't lost a loved one to illness caused by smoking or an alcohol related accident, to say nothing of the millions of lives destroyed by alcoholism, the millions of lives degraded by addiction to tobacco?"

"Please," Lavermore interjected, his smile finally leaving his face, "I think there will be plenty of time for questions on such serious topics. After all, Dr. Willis will have to explain his previous testimony to Congress."

"There's nothing to explain," Willis said. He glared around the room like a wounded bull facing a pack of wolves. His eyes flared as he gazed from face to face. Then, he turned and charged away from the podium, brushing aside questioning reporters. Several followed, then gave up, stymied by the phalanx of lawyers and private security officers that immediately surrounded Willis. They were quickly surrounded by red-shirted CDL members who stood stone-faced in front of Willis's entourage, effectively preventing his escape. Willis's eyes danced around the room in panic, finally alighting on McBride's face.

"Pres," he gasped.

As if Pres were an old friend who time had estranged from him. The name came out short and clipped. He caught his breath as McBride waited. They looked at each other for a moment. "You know," Willis said, his voice barely under control, "there's a real opportunity with the dog flu. You should come back and work at Novilis. I could make you director of research. Lorraine can go back to the steno pool."

McBride blinked. Was Willis really offering him a job? He could picture Hofferman, that walking eunuch, and Johnson, suicidal and depressed. "No," he said quietly, patiently. "I think it may be time for me to move on to something else."

Willis sniffed.

"Ethan," a thin voice called.

Willis whirled around. DiAngelo was wading through the bristling crowd towards him. His face was set. "My father built this company up from nothing with long hours, hard work, patience, and perseverance," he said. "I'll be damned if I'll let you kill it."

"Remember the warnings on radiation gel?" Willis taunted him. He towered over the company chairman.

"I was in open court," DiAngelo replied. "It may worth recalling that I can't be fired. That's not something that every Novilis employee enjoys, Ethan." The implication was clear.

DiAnglelo's eyes fell on McBride. For a moment, McBride saw only anger, then recognition.

"Preston McBride?" DiAngelo asked. McBride nodded. DiAngelo pressed a card into his hand. "Call me," he said. He then spun on his heel and strode out.

Willis stood there gaping. Finally, glaring, he stormed out, surrounded by lawyers quietly grilling him over the debacle.

McBride watched his turbulent exit. He thought he would feel triumphant. Instead, there was just emptiness inside. What did he get for his victory? Lots of dead dogs and still no way to end the epidemic. The true definition of a pyrrhic victory, he thought.

McBride walked over to Santiago, who was still leaning against the wall, a small smile on her face.

"You won," she said.

"I guess," he said. He took her hand, and they started toward the exit.

Asher was standing by the door.

"Looks like you'll need a new issue," McBride told him.

"I'll find one," Asher told him. "Lavermore thinks he can ride this to the Presidency." He nodded at the Senator, who remained the center of a dozen or so reporters, all throwing questions. He was shaking hands with tourists, smiling at the cameras and insuring plenty of coverage for himself and his new cause. "He'll be looking for a few trusted advisers," Asher said.

"Do you support his stance on any single important issue?" McBride asked.

"No," Asher admitted, "but I suspect I can be convinced. Good luck, McBride." He gave a quick wave and then made a beeline for Lavermore.

McBride and Santiago moved outside. The sun was still shining.

"Everyone will know now," McBride said, "but it's too late."

"Maybe dogs can be saved in remote places where people didn't receive the vaccine," Santiago said.

"Yeah, the backwoods of Mongolia or Tibet," McBride told her. "That is, if the virus is done mutating."

She looked at him. "What do you mean?" she asked.

"Other animals could be in danger, too," he said. "The virus doesn't know the difference between one animal and another."

Santiago stared at him. "Are you serious? Could the same disease kill housecats, for example?" she said.

He nodded. "Why not? It all depends on the virus and how it mutates. Housecats, wildcats…sheep, goats, pigs, cattle…even whales and dolphins. The entire ecosystem could be affected," McBride admitted. "As much as our world has changed, there could be a lot more surprises on the horizon."

Santiago took out her St. Jude medal and kissed it. "Pray," she said.

McBride felt the little piece of metal in his pocket. "I wonder," he thought aloud, "how many miracles it has left?"

Chapter 25

McBride rang the doorbell to his mother's apartment. God, it felt good to be home. The story about the link between the dog flu and the vaccine was all over the newspapers, TV and the Internet. He felt both vindicated and slightly sad. There was no happy ending, just the shock and horror as the American public became aware of the horrible crime that had been committed. Santiago had headed to her clinic immediately after the plane landed; she was in high demand after having been gone for several days. What would he do now that he had brought the cause that had overtaken his life to the fullest conclusion that he could? He was exhausted and was just now realizing that he had let his life fall into a shambles. He was broke and had no place to stay but was reluctant to call DiAngelo for a job, lucrative as it may be. Wasn't it a money hungry scientist who had kicked off this disaster in the first place? He wanted to go and live in a cave. His mother's apartment was the next best thing.

She did not answer the door right away. He waited, his concern rising as the seconds ticked by. Finally, he heard a noise.

"Who is it?" his mother called in a weak, tremulous voice.

"Pres," he replied, "Mom, are you okay?"

One by one, a series of deadbolts were undone. Then, before opening the door, Maggie asked, "Are you alone?"

"Yes."

"Are you sure?"

"Mom, yes."

The last lock was release, and the door opened. His mother peered out, looking around and opened the door. "Come in, come in," she told him. "Hurry." She ushered him in without so much as a hug or a kiss. The locks were swiftly restored as soon as he stepped inside.

Maggie looked wan and scared. Her hair was uncombed, and there was a wild expression in her eyes. McBride kissed her cheek, saddened by the further degradation in her appearance.

"What's the matter, Ma?" he asked. He could hear the television blaring in the living room. "Canada acting up?" he teased.

"Didn't you hear?" she exclaimed. "God, I can't believe I raised sons who don't read the newspaper! That dirtbag Lavermore"—she grimaced violently—"is being touted for president. Lock up the women and children. The country is going to hell in a handbasket. I may have to move to Costa Rica."

"Mom," McBride said, trying to calm her down, "the next election is years away, anything could happen." He looked around. The house was a mess with newspapers on the floor amid paper plates. The shrine to Canada was in disarray. One candle was burning, but others were dark and lying on their sides, wax melted into the carpet. The cushions on the couch had been shoved in different directions—had she been living on the couch? Maggie was as disheveled as the apartment: as his eyes adjusted to the dim interior lighting, Pres noticed food stains on her dress, sleep in the corners of her eyes, and what looked like spaghetti sauce in the corner of her mouth.

"Where's what's her name?" Maggie asked.

"Kendra has gone back to New York," McBride told her. Despite his growing affection for Santiago, he still felt pain at the mention of her name. He had treated her badly. Another walking casualty of the dog flu. At least the deaths seemed to be slowing—not many more dogs left to die.

"Lost another one, huh? Oh, Pres, you are so bad with women, I don't know how you get so many of them!" Maggie said. "Was she mad you were arrested?"

"I wasn't arrested," he told her.

"Oh, well. You're still a young man, plenty of time for that." She tottered into the living room. She plopped down on a beanbag and seemed to stare into the lone candle.

McBride watched her and shook his head. Something was really upsetting her, something far beyond anything that had affected her before. "Mom," McBride said crisply. "What's wrong?"

Maggie gazed up at him with tears in her eyes. "Who said anything is wrong?' she asked.

"Mom, look at this place. Look at you," McBride said. "You always kept things clean."

She sighed. "I never could hide anything from you," she said. She sighed and struggled to her feet. Slowly, she walked into the dining room, rummaged through a mound of dirty paper plates and produced a letter. She gave it to McBride.

"Oh, Captain," she moaned. "What am I going to do?"

He read the letter. It was from a collection agency requesting payment for services rendered. Maggie owed. McBride gaped at the amount—$21,111.18.

"Twenty thousand dollars! What's this for?" he asked.

"A dog whisperer," Maggie said, hanging her head. "It was the only way I could communicate with Canada."

"A dog whisperer?"

Maggie nodded. She plopped back down in a beanbag and stared at the floor. "It's like a ghost whisperer or horse whisperer," she said softly, as if that made sense of the egregious collection notice. "I would call this number, and the woman at the end of the line would tell me what Canada was thinking. She knew all about him." She smiled up at McBride. Her eyes were clouded and unsure. "It was as if she knew him."

"Mom!"

She closed her eyes. "Sit. Speak. No. Heel. Stop. Come. Supper. Walk," she recited.

McBride watched her. Damn it! He had no idea she had gotten this bad. How was he going to raise the money to pay the bill? Was she going to lose her apartment? She could not stay alone. Maybe Santiago would have an idea. There had to be a nursing home or someplace he could take her so she would have regular supervision. But how would he pay for that?

He felt so hopeless, so lost. The dog flu had claimed yet another victim. He sat down next to his mother and wrapped his arms around her.

"Sit. Speak. No. Heel. Stop. Come. Supper. Walk," she said hopefully. She smiled sweetly, but tears dribbled down her cheeks.

He glanced at the television as she leaned against him. "Police are investigating what looks like a cult that is killing cattle," the announcer said. "For the third straight day, police in Yolo County have found dead cattle. California ranks fifth in the nation with about five million head, according to the California Highland Cattle Association."

"This problem is not restricted to just Yolo," man in a cowboy hat, plaid shirt and jeans said into the camera. "We're hearing reports all over the country about dead cattle. These Satanic freaks must be nationwide."

A cold chill raced down McBride's back. He sat up and struggled to concentrate on the news. He could feel his mother's shoulder bone pushing against him. God, she was so thin. She continued to repeat her mantra, over and over: "Sit. Speak. No. Heel. Stop. Come. Supper. Walk." An image of a dead cow appeared on the screen. It was lying on its side, its lips pulled back as if in horror, its bloody nose resting in a small lake of clotted blood.

"We're not sure what cult is involved or how they are killing cows, but we are organizing a twenty-four-hour armed citizen's groups to stop them," a sheriff's deputy said.

"New reports are now indicating sheep and pigs may also have been targeted by this cult," the newscaster continued.

McBride scrabbled for his phone with shaking hands. He was able to dial one handed. Santiago answered after several rings.

"Pres," she said in an agonized voice, "two patients are here with dead cats. At least fifteen more died while we were in Washington."

"Oh, my God," he whispered. "It's starting."

"Sit. Speak. No. Heel. Stop. Come. Supper. Walk," Maggie chanted her hopeless entreaty over and over.

McBride let the phone slip from his hand into his lap. He held his mother as tight as possible and stared across the room at the blank wall. He thought of the St. Jude medal still in his pocket and tried to detect its presence against the flesh of his leg. He felt nothing.

"What can we do?" Santiago's voice pled from the phone in his lap. She sounded so small, like all her faith and all her personal strength had left her.

McBride couldn't think of an answer. Everything seemed gray in front of him. Finally, he slowly reached for the phone and pressed it to his ear.

"Pray," he said.

END